Praise for *An U*

M000303743

"A very powerful story . . . it made me feel a little more human when reading it."

—Amazon Top Reviewer

"From the first breath this epic journey seizes the mind and the soul in an intelligent and passionate web of brokenness and hope....Caron's story captivates because it's our story...of innocence lost and redemption unexpectedly found. You will undoubtedly find yourself in these delightful pages!"

—Jerome Daley, Life coach, speaker, & author of *Soul Space* and *The New Rebellion Handbook*

"Caron Guillo weaves a rich tapestry with *An Uncommon Crusade*, ushering you into another time and place with characters you can't help but love. Her unique writing style blends three journeys into a powerful story of understanding, forgiveness, and transformation."

—Jodi Thomas, New York Times Bestselling Author & Writer in Residence, West Texas A&M University

"Although this novel uses the Children's Crusade of 1212 as its background, it is not a historical chronicle, but a very personal story, with few of the actual political players of the period appearing in a major role. Instead, the story traces the lives of several of the young followers of Nicholas of Cologne as they travel to Jerusalem, and over the years after the Crusade disperses. Each of the characters . . . comes across as bold, rich, and easy to relate to rather than overworked. The author does a good job weaving the divergent stories together, both in terms of the pacing and in the way they come together at the end of the tale . . . an enjoyable story with believable characters and an exciting plot."

—Publishers Weekly

An Uncommon Crusade

Caron Guillo

Love,
Enjoy!
~Caron

WRITTEN WORLD
COMMUNICATIONS

AN UNCOMMON CRUSADE
Copyright c. 2011 by Caron Guillo
Published by Harpstring Books,
an Imprint of Written World Communications
PO Box 26677
Colorado Springs, CO 80916
Writtenworldcommunications.com

All Rights Reserved. No part of this publication may be reproduced in any form, stored in a retrieval system, or transmitted in any form by any means—electronic, mechanical, photocopy, recording, or otherwise—without prior written permission of the publisher, except as provided by the United States of America copyright law.

This is a work of fiction. Names, characters, and incidents are products of the author's imagination or are used for fictional purposes. Any mentioned brand names, places, and trademarks remain the property of their respective owners, bear no association with the author or the publisher, and are used for fictional purposes only.

Some Scripture quotations taken from the HOLY BIBLE INTERNATIONAL VERSION r. NIVr. Copyright c 1973, 1978, 1984 by International Bible Society. Used by permission of Zondervan Publishing House. All rights reserved.

A Scripture quotation is taken from the *Holy Bible, New Living Translation*, copyright c. 1996. Used by permission of Tyndale House Publishers, Inc., Wheaton IL 60189, USA. All rights reserved.

A Scripture quotation is taken from the *New King James Version*. Copyright c. 1979, 1980, 1982 by Thomas Nelson, Inc. Used by permission. All rights reserved.

Brought to you by the creative team at WrittenWorldCommunications.com: Kristine Pratt, Dale Hansen, Rowena G. Kuo, Rachel H. Davis, and Corinne Benes

Library of Congress Cataloging-in-Publication Data
An Application to register this book for cataloging has been filed with the Library of Congress.
International Standard Book Number: 978-0982937716

Cover art by Carrie L. Lewis
Printed in the United States of America

Acknowledgments

Though writing is largely a solitary venture, being a writer is not, which is why I have so many good people to thank. Far more, in fact, than I've included here.

Nicole. You're my cheerleader and inspiration. Without your encouragement, I'm not sure I would have kept at it.

Bob, Christopher and Caleb. You've put up with me, prayed for me, rooted for me and had to fix too many of your own dinners because of me. Thank you.

Pam. Big sister extraordinaire. Thanks for believing in me.

My early readers. Harry Haines, Alice Armstrong and Bev Harris—thank you for walking through every word of my first draft. Thanks to my ABNA pals Leslie Curnow, Rebecca Kyle, Susan Petrone and Adriana Renescu for reading and offering great feedback. Teri Morgan, you always believed this story would find its way to print; thank you. Val Conrad, Travis Erwin and Lisa Pawlowski—you each had a hand in breathing life and authenticity into the manuscript; I owe you.

Terry Burns of Hartline Literary. Thanks for reading this story through in one sitting and then signing on to be my agent.

Rachel Heston Davis. I'm still singing your praises as an editor. Thanks for your patience even when I used up my quota of hearts doing things.

Rowena Kuo. Thanks for the late night laughs as we hammered out the final details together.

Kristine Pratt and the Written World Communications team. Thank you for loving this story as much as I do.

Split

aples

terranean Sea

Damascus

Acre

Bet She'an

'Atlit

Mount Tabor

Jerusalem

Holy

Lands

Alexandria

Damietta

Egypt

Cairo

Part I

Chapter 1

Mid-March AD 1212, the Black Forest, Holy Roman Empire
Sixteen-year-old Elisabeth's lying-in began at dusk, her water spilling in a warm and sudden rush.

Mama's husband, Ort, cursed and trudged out the warped wooden doorway of their single-room hut beside the cooper's workshop. Off to the village tavern, more than likely. Elisabeth's older sister protested before running for the midwife as Mama ordered. Elisabeth hadn't a clue what she should do other than swallow back the fear that accompanied the birth pangs.

"The midwife won't come," Methild said an hour later.

Mama's head snapped up. "Why not?"

Methild crossed her arms. She didn't bother to spare Elisabeth's feelings with a whisper. "The priest has forbidden the old woman to help."

Mama's eyes shifted to Elisabeth. "Very well. Get fresh hay from the shed," she told Methild. "And we'll need a knife. Bring one of Ort's sharpest."

The blood drained from Elisabeth's head, leaving her dizzy. "Mama?"

"The knife is only to cut the cord." Mama's eyes softened. "I've given birth to six children, daughter. I know what to do."

Of course. Elisabeth watched her mother bustle about the cottage, loosening knots and unlatching the chest in the corner to encourage Elisabeth's womb to open. So many times in childbirth, and no more than two of Mama's babes had survived. Three died in infancy, but not poor James. Elisabeth remembered him as a gentle and kindly big brother before fever took him a dozen years ago.

Despite the shame Elisabeth's pregnancy had brought, she knew Mama hoped for another boy in the family. And not only because of Ort's threat to turn out Elisabeth and the child unless she delivered a son. Mama wanted a grandson. She'd never said so plainly, but Elisabeth guessed she wanted to see James in the child's eyes. Or *Vati*— Elisabeth's papa.

Another spasm gripped Elisabeth's abdomen. She groaned through it, freckled hands gripping the tattered blanket beneath her. Wisps of ginger hair matted on her forehead, and smoke from the central fire pit made her choke and gasp.

She normally loved the smell of the cooking fire. Found comfort there, stirring a pot of soup, making something delicious from the very little they had. But tonight, the fire's wispy gray fingers wrapped themselves around her throat like death itself.

A person couldn't die cursed by the church, could they? Or by God? Where would their soul go?

"Push," Mama said much later. The moon shone bright beyond the single unshuttered window.

Pain rippled Elisabeth's torso. "I can't," she gasped. "Not again."

"Now, with the tightening. The child's head is nearly out."

Sweat ran into her eyes and stung like fire, but Elisabeth bore down twice more until she felt the child slip from her womb. She fell back to the soiled blanket and scattered hay on the earthen floor, the

2

stink of blood and sweat heavy in the air.

"A boy," Mama said before her joyful face faltered. "Oh, Blessed Mother."

Methild, who'd been useless all evening, stepped close, brows knotted. She raised a hand to her mouth.

Elisabeth lifted her head. "What? What is it?"

Mama did not look up but instead busied herself with the child. "How long since you felt him stir?"

Elisabeth avoided Methild's somber gaze. "The movement stopped a week ago. Ten days, perhaps." Wasn't that the way of things when the babe's time came?

Mama's shoulders sagged. She ceased her efforts and lifted an expressionless face. Methild turned away.

Elisabeth's chin trembled, and tears filled her eyes.

"Serves you right," Ort said to Elisabeth when he returned some time after midnight. "God killin' the brat while he was still in your belly. That's proof aplenty of your sin if you're asking me."

She did not look in his direction. "Mama, let me hold the baby." Though she hated the man who fathered the child even more than she despised Ort, the babe was part of her. A part she'd sworn to love and protect.

"But he's dead, Elisabeth."

"Let me hold him. For just a little while."

"You're going daft, now, are you?" Ort challenged. "After all the suffering you've caused your mother?"

Elisabeth refused to release Mama's gaze. *"Bitte."*

By the glow of dying firelight and faint candles, Mama's face twisted in anguish at the plea. At last, she yielded.

Elisabeth took the boy in her arms, grateful that at least Mama had wiped him clean. She laid her cheek on his blond head—so blond it was almost white—and felt the delicate strands of his fine hair against her face. There was no warmth, just cold, velvet skin.

3

It was because of her own foolishness that he didn't live to be baptized. That no priest would have done the job even if he had. Now he'd never see heaven.

She'd make it right, she would.

At first light, she buried the child under a dark fragrant fir where at least his body could rest in the shadow of something beautiful.

Chapter 2

Late May AD 1212, German Provinces, Holy Roman Empire
Simon watched the ragged sea of children part and leave the road to curl like waves beneath the shrubbery, each child pulling close a blanket or frayed cloak against the cool breeze that swept away the heat of the day.

How long had they traveled from Saint-Denis to Cologne to this remote location? A month, perhaps? A month of begging for their supper, sleeping in barns or alongside brooks that sang them to sleep with the hum of water over stones.

Simon separated himself from the hundreds that traveled with him. He needed a moment of solitude after the day's noisy march. The sun had not yet set, nor the fires been lit, though the raucous sounds of children squabbling over firewood drifted down the road.

"I found it first!"

"*Nein*, my hand is already upon it. Find your own."

Simon sighed. Wasn't there plenty for everyone here in this region near the Rhine? He drew some distance away, found a secluded spot on the far side of a scanty bush, dropped his pack, and situated himself on a decaying willow.

He ran his fingers back and forth through his hair. Oh, but the scratching felt good, which probably meant he was as lice-eaten as everyone else. Probably stank like the others, too.

Cher Dieu, what had he gotten himself into?

Was this crusade truly the reason God led him away from Villebonne? Everything inside of Simon balked at the idea, and yet—

There was something to this movement. Something born of innocence. Bigger than all of them put together.

The orange globe of the sun faltered, giving up its lofty position above the hills. Only another half hour of good light. With a quick glance over his shoulder, Simon drew a miniature book from his bag, pages bound on one edge by a simple leather thong sewn into the parchment. He opened the volume, releasing the aroma of damp lime mortar and the bitter scent of iron gall ink. Meticulous script marched across each page.

For the briefest of moments, he sat again in a high-backed chair beneath the scriptorium window, parchment steadied by the tip of a knife. He dipped a quill into the inkhorn at the top of his steeply sloped desk and scratched out a few words from the exemplary placed alongside his copy, careful to keep the nib at a right angle to the page.

In a twinkling the image was gone, replaced by the trees around him—and the sharp, salty odor of his sweat.

A gentle voice called from the shrubbery. "Simon?"

He stood, hastening to stuff the book back into the pouch with the others, careful lest he damage the precious thing. His heart pounded against his ribs at the near discovery. Moisture beaded across his brow.

"There you are," Kateline said. "I've been looking for—are you ill?"

Simon strained to relax his features, which increased the alarm on her pretty face.

"Is your stomach troubling you, too?" she asked. "It seems the blackberries were not yet ripe—"

"*Mir geht es gut*," Simon said, speaking Kateline's native

language even as he felt himself redden. "You caught me unaware, that's all."

Her eyes brightened with amusement, and her pink lips parted in a smile to reveal a full set of teeth. The golden hair around her shoulders absorbed what daylight remained and reflected it back in a celestial glow. She stood tall, the top of her head reaching his shoulder. Far taller than many a man. "You thought yourself alone then?" she said and chuckled at the absurdity of it.

Simon forced a smile and eased the pack behind him. "Well, I'm glad you've found me."

"Found you? Or found you out?"

He swallowed. "What can you mean by that?"

She placed her hands at the small of her back and began a slow circle around him. "You're up to something, *mein freund*. Mischief, is it?" Her warm smile belied the tenor of her accusation.

He hitched the pack onto his shoulder. "I've come away only to pray."

She paused, eyes narrowed, a corner of her mouth lifting with humor. "Well, I don't believe that, though the Lord in heaven knows we need your prayers."

"I should help with the fires," he said. "You know Conon is more likely to rub his fingers raw than manage a spark." He moved to step past, but she stopped him, hand on his arm.

"What's wrong, Simon?"

"Nothing." Only a small lie, that.

Kateline shook her head. "You are distressed. It's not like you."

Simon could feel his face heating again. "You startled me."

"No," she said with a soft tone that failed to hide the concern in her gaze. "It's something else entirely. What troubles you?"

He took a deep breath. Scratched his neck. "You won't say anything to the others?"

"Of course not."

7

Restless, Simon began to walk. Kateline fell in beside him, moving with a graceful stride that made his plodding gait seem more awkward than usual. In his opinion, Kateline's beauty of spirit and form made even her rough woolen kirtle seem as elegant as a noblewoman's. The hem of her long tunic, frayed and mud-stained, moved with the gentle rhythm of her feet. Though Simon tried to smooth his step to match hers, his own feet were much too long and his knees far too big for his skinny frame.

Up the road, away from the unruly crowd of young commoners he went, gathering the courage to confess. He'd not entrusted himself to anyone since leaving Villebonne. But this was Kateline. He took a breath to speak. Once. Twice. Then finally, "I've Scripture in my pack."

Kateline froze, and her lovely mouth dropped open. Simon glanced at the hundreds of young men, women, and children swarming the roadside behind them. She followed his gaze and resumed their walk at a faster pace with one hand tight upon his arm.

"You can read?" she whispered, though without cause. Their conversation fused itself into the ruckus of young travelers making camp.

Simon nodded.

Her eyes grew round and sparkled green, like sunlight off water. "And you carry Scripture?"

"I do."

"Such a thing is worth a life's wages. Ten lives. How — ?"

"I took it."

She walked without a word for several moments, clearly worrying over the news. "Tell me more," she said.

"You might disapprove."

"I already disapprove, but I'll hear you out."

That didn't make him feel any better. "I grew up in the abbey at Villebonne."

"Villebonne?" Kateline looked at him with wide eyes. "I've

heard of it."

Simon nodded. "There were too many mouths to feed at home. I was presented as an oblate to the church when I was but nine years old."

A sideways glance showed him that Kateline's lower lip stuck out.

"The monks educated me, and I learned quickly." To what end, he still wondered. "When I read the Holy Word with my own eyes, something changed in me." He dared to look in Kateline's direction. "I realized true men of God are bold and courageous, and I wanted that kind of faith. My passion for Christ grew until I ran out of patience for—" He hesitated to go on, but the expression on her face compelled him. "The monks did nothing but say their prayers," he said in exasperation. "I could bear it no longer."

"You broke the vows of your parents?"

In retrospect it seemed the least of his sins, but he wouldn't tell her that.

Kateline frowned, and her eyes shifted toward the bag at his shoulder. "May I see?"

They'd rounded a bend in the road, shielded from view of the masses, but Simon hesitated. Anyone could meet them coming from the other direction. He led her into the trees where the shadows grew thick, then removed one of the small books and carefully opened it.

Kateline expelled a deep breath.

"Touch it if you like," he said.

She wiped her hands on her tunic and then traced the edge of the page with a delicate finger, dainty nail embedded with the grime of travel. A smile lit her face, but she caught it and cast a wary eye toward him. "You stole this?"

He put the book away. "I made them."

"Them?"

He nodded. "Three altogether."

By unspoken agreement they headed back toward camp, walking in silence for several steps before he began again. "I was a scribe. A good one. I worked so far ahead of the others that I found time to study the Scriptures on my own." He glanced down at her. "I never neglected my duties."

She nodded, and he could tell she wanted to believe him.

"I began to transcribe portions of the gospels and some of the epistles for my own use. Don't think poorly of me—I repented of that sin."

"But you took the parchments anyway."

His eyes searched hers. "I repented *afterward.*"

A laugh burst from Kateline's mouth before she straightened her face.

"Do you despise me now?" he asked.

"I could never despise you, my friend and brother."

Relief eased the tightness in his gut.

"You are contrite, Simon," she said. "And *Gott* is merciful. I believe he will bring good from your misdeeds." She paused. "You know you must tell Nicholas that you can read. And that there is such a treasure in our midst."

Of course, she spoke the truth. For good reason he'd carefully guarded his abilities and the contents of the pack, but surely he had no right to keep such secrets from the child-leader of their movement. He could trust Nicholas.

His stomach churned at the thought, though, and he tossed upon the ground all night. Kateline's words still sounded in his ears when he awoke the next morning. Perhaps it was time to entrust his secrets to someone else.

The bright morning sun shone through the green canopy above him, warming the air. Color splashed across the land and sky, so different from half a lifetime within the confines of granite and marble—lifeless and gray, silent and unyielding.

The heavy sweetness of flowers in bloom tickled his nose. He wiped a hand across his face, then stretched his long arms and stood, hitching up the ill-fitted leggings beneath his purloined tunic before heading to the brook.

Several small figures still slept beneath cloaks or threadbare blankets—Georg, short hair sticking out in all directions, Artur, misshapen arm flung out upon the grass, Benno and Claus, snuggled together like kittens in a basket. Twins, they were, and Simon hadn't a clue which was whom. He stepped over and around them.

A few were already at the stream, sipping handfuls of cold water. A curly-headed boy no bigger than a *fae*—and just as full of mischief—captured Simon's attention. The child's cheek dimpled with glee while he flung icy droplets upon his groggy and increasingly irritated neighbors.

"Watch out," Simon said to Conon, "or someone much bigger than you might decide to give swimming lessons today."

The boy looked up, and a wide grin broke across his face. "They might try," he said, raising tiny fists, "but they'll have to fight me first."

Simon tipped his head back and laughed, ruffling Conon's dark curls. "I wager they'd lose."

Within the hour the line of march formed again. Nicholas donned a long gray coat. Simon had to admit the coat lent authority to the young fellow's leadership, giving him the look of a soldier of the cross and providing breadth to his otherwise narrow shoulders. He could be no more than twelve years of age, but possessed a vigor and charm that set him apart from the shepherd boy, Stephan, whose holy vision spawned their movement.

If Simon were not so tall, he would have had a hard time spotting the lad amongst the press of commoners. A couple of young men hoisted the child to their shoulders, and Nicholas lifted a carved wooden cross someone had given him three days ago, signaling the crusaders and setting the column in motion. With the songs and shouts of a thousand children ringing in Simon's ears, another day began.

By mid-morning, the jubilance of the crowd tapered off to stories of knightly deeds or the miracles of the saints. Tales that united the hearts of the children and fueled their enthusiasm so that the rigors of the journey seemed but a small test of their faith.

Simon's stomach squeezed. Whether from lack of nourishment or the thought of sharing his secret with Nicholas, he couldn't say. He'd put off talking to Nicholas all morning, but the multitude that normally hovered close to the boy had thinned. Best to take advantage of the rare opportunity to speak privately.

Simon caught up with him and walked only a few paces before addressing the child. "I've important things to speak of," he said with more boldness than he felt. If he wasted time with pleasantries, Nicholas would grow restless or someone would come within earshot.

The boy picked a crumb of bread from his tunic and popped it into his mouth—a morsel left from the small loaf Georg offered him an hour ago—then craned his neck to look at Simon, squinting against the glare of the sun. "Go on."

Simon swallowed. "You will want to know that I can read."

"Read? Well, now, that *is* news. And how do you come by that ability?"

"The monks taught me."

Nicholas considered this then smiled. "So we have an educated man among us, eh? This pleases me."

"That's not all."

The boy's eyebrows arched.

Simon peered over his shoulder. Nicholas led the marchers. Nicholas always led. But others were drawing close. "I carry three small manuscripts. Portions of Scripture worth a lot of coin."

A bright spot formed on each of Nicholas's smooth cheeks. He glanced at Simon's satchel, eyes glistening with interest. "You must give them to me."

"What?"

"Simply for safe keeping, of course."

A sniggle of uncertainty tickled Simon's throat. "It's too much to concern yourself with."

Irritation swept across Nicholas's face, but only for an instant. "You're right. I don't want to trouble myself with it. But you must read to me now and then so that I might better lead my—er, the crusaders."

Simon smiled, glad that Nicholas so quickly abandoned his impulsive request. He was a child, after all. "Certainly. Nothing would give me greater pleasure."

"Good." Nicholas nodded. "Very good. But you mustn't tell anyone else. It will be our secret."

"Agreed."

Three boys drew up just behind them, waiting to gain the attention of their leader.

"That's important, you know," Nicholas said, whispering. "Tell no one else."

Simon dipped his chin and let a young man with a gift for Nicholas take his place beside the boy. The gifts came often—hats to shield his head from the intensity of the noonday sun, a handful of strawberries found in the woods, a blanket to soften the ground at night. Simon had ceased to think much of them. Nicholas certainly never asked for anything.

Simon exhaled deeply. He needn't have worried about his little confession after all. Nicholas recognized the importance of keeping the presence of Scripture confidential.

"Walk with me," Kateline said from behind Simon, Conon at her side. She clapped her hands at a small girl who skipped ahead. "Stay close, Giselle."

The child made a wide circle and came running back to the boisterous horde that followed.

Kateline said nothing about the manuscripts, of course, but

gave Simon a smile and a knowing look. Instead, she asked. "Do you think we'll reach the Black Forest soon?"

"We're still a fortnight away." Simon swung Conon to his shoulders.

Kateline wrinkled her nose, upon which budded a few brown freckles. "Not many villages there, I suppose."

"Not in its heart, I wouldn't think, but we'll be—*Autsch!*" Simon winced and angled his neck to look at Conon, who clutched his hair for balance. "You're going to pull it out by the roots, you know."

"Sorry, Simon," Conon said, not sounding remorseful at all. "We'll get a taste of crusading then, won't we?"

Simon chuckled. "In the forest? Against whom?"

"Dragons," Conon whispered, his bravado disappearing like a vapor.

Simon shared a look with Kateline then spoke to the boy. "There are no dragons, you know. And even if there were, you have no reason to fear those who can take your life. Only the one who can destroy the soul."

They arrived in the village of Offenstadt late in the afternoon, weary, hungry. Nicholas lifted the carved crucifix and advanced to the village green. People gathered in curiosity as children and young commoners surged into the humble community. Erich and Reto located a barrel and helped Nicholas onto it. Simon watched the poverty-stained crowd grow quiet.

"Good brothers," Nicholas began, "may the God of our Lord and Savior Christ Jesus bless you as you listen to my urgent message today. Christ is in chains even as I speak, oppressed by Muslim tyranny."

"Hear, hear," someone said.

The throng shifted forward, straining to catch the boy's fervent words.

Nicholas continued. "What would you do if someone took your master's lands as the infidels have done? Would you not challenge them, defend your rights as his people? So we—poor, pure, and the youngest of God's children—claim his lands as our inheritance, the Holy City for his glory alone." He held the cross high in the air with one hand, as the other hand swept toward those still entering the village.

Simon shared in the ripple of excitement that spread through those gathered. Some cheered, raising fists into the air, and he marveled again that Nicholas could so quickly stir a crowd. Even Stephan had not possessed the power of the boy from Cologne.

"The Lord appointed me, Nicholas, to take up this cross and stand before you today. For more than a hundred years, armies have failed to secure Jerusalem, but I will lead these pure ones to Palestine. There, in righteous glory before our Heavenly Father, we will find victory alongside your own offspring."

At his words, mothers grabbed the hands of their children and hurried for home.

"Do not fear, O family of God," Nicholas assured those who wavered. "Lend us your children, your young men and maidens. We march to honor, to reward, to everlasting peace."

In the end, Offenstadt rejected the message. It had happened before, though rarely. And the few loaves the small community provided as a guilt offering did little to ease the hunger pangs of the youngest crusaders.

Neither did any souls join their movement, as far as Simon could tell.

Several villagers crept out of their homes at dawn the next day to see them off—or perhaps to guarantee their departure.

Simon scanned the tiny hamlet where it sat adjacent to the manor, the lord's main hall and outbuildings surrounded by a stone wall in sore need of repair. Smoke, bluish-black in the dawning light, rose from the vent on the tile-roofed bake house and from the central smokehood of the manor house. Outside the walls, wisps of dark gray seeped from the ridges of nearby homes and hovels to join the purple, pink, and silver-white streaks spreading across the heavens.

"Hugo," a buxom maid called, gaining Simon's attention as well as that of a thick-muscled young man striding toward the milling crowd. She stood outside a thatched, leaning wattle-and-daub cottage, timber posts likely weak with rot where they'd been sunk into the ground for stability. "You're not going with them, are you, *mein liebling?*"

"Don't let the hayward get wind of it," *mein liebling* said.

She pressed a hand to her hip and tilted her head, pouting. "But I'll be lost without you. Who will make me smile of a day?"

He gave her a wink and continued on. "You'll have to ask your husband, Brigitta. Surely the old grump will be in a better temper once I'm out of the way."

Her laughter bubbled on the morning breeze, a breeze that carried the woody scent of hearth fires stirred to life. The thought of a satisfying pottage made Simon's stomach rumble, though he'd be happy enough to sit down to a watery gruel.

"*Hallo,*" the young man said when he drew near. "Shouldn't we be going now?"

Simon took in the fellow's worn tunic and castoff footwear. The shabby blanket wrapped around his meager bundle. A cottager, no doubt—like Simon's own father had been—hiring himself out to the local lord and landholding *villeins.* "Nicholas leads us."

That should have been the end of the matter, but the sturdy young man tipped his head to one side as though he didn't understand. "Well, there's no reason to stand about. The sun will grow hot soon enough."

"We've managed to get this far without your opinion on the matter." Simon hadn't meant to say it. Not really. Why should he care if this Hugo wanted to assert himself?

Hugo simply smiled. "Are you always such a feisty little hen so early in the morning?"

The insult lodged beneath Simon's ribs. "We don't need

16

troublemakers, so if—"

Another voice called Hugo's name, and the young man turned toward a scraggly-haired fellow who joined them, leaving Simon to clench his teeth at the interruption.

The newcomer spoke again. "What are you still doing here with the sun shining bright as a new *pfennig?*"

"Shining?" Hugo looked to the bank of clouds glowing red on the horizon. "I can barely see your ugly face, praise the saints."

A crooked grin broke across the young ploughman's narrow jaw, but faded quickly enough. "You're really going then?"

"You know I am," Hugo said.

Simon stepped away, trying to gain control of his annoyance. It wasn't like him to rise so quickly to an offense.

He pretended he couldn't hear Hugo's conversation above the clamor of the gathering crowd.

"By winter I'll have a new life, Eginolf," Hugo was saying. "You know treasure awaits soldiers of the cross in Jerusalem. I can buy my family's freedom. Take the miller's daughter to wife. No one will own me anymore."

"Someone will always own us," Eginolf said. "Be it the crown, the church, or the devil himself."

Hugo chuckled. "Then I'd rather trust myself to Lucifer before giving that dog-hearted hayward a hand over me again."

Irritation swirled afresh in Simon's gut at the blasphemous words.

Nicholas arrived, lifting his cross to the cheers of the crowd, and the irregular column began to move.

Simon walked past Hugo and Eginolf, who stood with an old dagger in hand, hilt extended. Hugo took the knife and tucked it into his belt. Each wrapped the other in a brief embrace.

"Take your time," Simon couldn't help saying. "There's a place for you farther down the line."

Chapter 3

Early June AD 1212, south of Offenstadt, Holy Roman Empire
Hugo wiped moisture from his brow with a calloused hand and inhaled the pungent scent of sun-warmed grass. *Ja*, and wasn't it a fine day to be hiking the road behind the prettiest young maiden he'd ever seen?

Kateline walked just ahead of him, her head tipped toward tall, scrawny Simon who seemed to prickle whenever Hugo came near. She and Simon often talked. If Hugo were a wagering man, he'd bet they shared some secret about the contents of that pack Simon carried. And Hugo *was* a wagering man.

The gawky young fellow must think Hugo the devil himself, the way he hovered near Kateline whenever Hugo came near. But how could Hugo resist her chaste smiles, those delicate features, the way her fair face turned pink when she laughed?

True, these scant impressions of her were all he had so far, but perhaps he could find occasion to gain more. If he could ever get past Simon. An interesting challenge, that.

The thought didn't bother him for he liked a challenge. And what else was there to do on the road to Jerusalem?

Jerusalem.

Hugo sighed.

He'd argued with Eginolf the night before he left.

"Come with me," Hugo said. "We've always wanted this, to be soldiers of the cross."

"That was childish play."

"But this is real." He put a hand to his friend's thin shoulder. "We can make something of ourselves. What is there for us here?"

"Life."

"Life? Every man and woman in this village toils in the field all their days, and for what? A poverty so deep it threatens to drown them." He scowled at Eginolf. "We were born for more than this."

Eginolf shook his head. "That group will march to their deaths."

Hugo had recognized the familiar sound of fear in his friend's voice, and his anger drifted away like steam from a pot. Eginolf always borrowed from Hugo's courage. Perhaps in this endeavor there wouldn't be enough for both of them.

And maybe Eginolf was right about the risks, but today the sun shone in a cloudless sky, damselflies danced among the wildflowers, and life pulsed through the chanting multitude that swarmed the roadway.

Late that afternoon, Hugo smiled when Nicholas loudly complained he'd traveled far enough in such miserable heat. Sure, and why didn't he remove his woolen coat, then? The boy's face flushed red as a ripe apple, hair sticking to his head in damp curls, and he smelled like a wet puppy.

"We should break camp before dawn," Hugo mellowed his voice so that the child wouldn't take offense. "Let the little ones rest during the hottest part of the day then continue on in the cool of the evening."

Nicholas took a cup of water proffered by a helpful crusader and squinted at him. "Who are you?"

"I am Hugo. And your friend."

The boy looked him up and down, measuring him for several

seconds. "Well, Hugo," he said between sips, "I've been thinking the same thing of late."

Hugo knew that he had not, but at least the child could see reason. Or, at the very least, found Hugo's size intimidating. "Then I needn't have mentioned it. Clearly, you are wise beyond your years. And a great leader, mindful of his followers."

Several of those followers had gathered round by now, clamoring for the boy's attention.

Nicholas flashed a winsome smile. "I think we're going to get along well," he said before accepting a small bit of cheese from one of them. He used a ragged fingernail to scrape the mold away.

Hugo dipped his head then turned to scavenge for his own supper.

He didn't get far.

A band of small raiders dropped down from the trees above. Hugo abandoned his search and defended himself against the mock attack. It was a daily occurrence since joining the crusade a week ago.

Hugo spun the boy clinging to his broad back around and down to the ground. "Ha!" he said, hand gripping an imaginary sword, the tip of the non-existent blade positioned over the child's chest. "I have you now, you ungodly invader."

"We're not Mohammedans, Hugo" another boy protested.

"Oh, but you are," he said, turning and moving with exaggerated steps toward a child creeping up from behind. "And you've no hope against a crusader of the—"

Just then, a lad dove for Hugo's legs. Hugo tripped and sprawled to the ground. Two little ones scampered out of the way. Small fists flew at him, landing wild but soft punches. Hugo tucked his head and laughed, until one fist crashed into his temple. His vision sputtered like a torch then went dark. A headache flared to life. Enough.

Hugo rose, shedding children like a water Nyx rising from the deep. He growled, holding aloft his thickly muscled arms.

21

The boys yelped and scattered, making a reckless retreat through the trees, squealing as they went.

A tinkling laugh sounded nearby. Hugo turned to see Kateline, eyes alight.

She spoke, mirth in her voice. "One of these days they're going to defeat you, you know."

Hugo closed one eye against the throbbing in his temple, ignoring the way his heart raced beneath his ribs. "Aye. Perhaps I should travel with reinforcements."

She grinned and stepped on a slim fallen branch, bending to grasp hold and snap it into a good-sized log for the fire.

Hugo closed the distance between them. He broke the rotting bough into four more sections and gathered the pieces.

Kateline, hands clasped in front of her, smiled her thanks and began to walk.

"You joined us at Offenstadt, I believe," she said.

"Yes . . . milady."

Her eyes darted to his before she looked down. "I am neither high-born nor accustomed to honeyed words."

He adored the way her lips formed the prim response. "Really?" He gazed at the outline of her perfect profile and the golden tresses that cascaded over her shoulders. Most young women wore their hair in thick braids, but the free-flowing waves suited her. "That knowledge astounds me. Yet I must confess, so does your loveliness."

She blushed and kept her eyes downward, but her lips curved into a modest smile.

Hugo was about to press his advantage when Kateline spoke. "What's this?"

He followed her gaze to see Simon on the road speaking with merchants traveling the opposite direction, Nicholas nearby.

Hugo growled inwardly. One way or another, it was always Simon interrupting his moments with Kateline.

"Perhaps he gains information," she said, changing her course toward them.

Hugo lengthened his stride to avoid looking like a puppy following its master. "Let's find out."

Foreign words coursed from Simon's mouth in a fluid stream. Not French—it hadn't taken Hugo long to figure out that Simon came from lands west of the empire. Not German, either, though the young man spoke Hugo's tongue like a native. Italian, perhaps?

Hugo put down the logs and planted his legs in a wide stance, arms crossed in front of his chest. Simon jabbered on, and Kateline watched him with a great deal of pride on her face. Hugo would have minded more, had she not spoken to him in the woods. Given him that lovely smile. Nicholas watched Hugo, studying him while Simon's conversation continued. Twice, the boy leader lifted a hand to deter interruptions from parties of admirers. Why call them anything else?

"Well?" Nicholas asked Simon when the men departed.

"We're little more than a week from Heidelberg," Simon said. "After that, we should head to Geneva and cross the Alps by way of the Mont Cenis Pass. It will be hard travel, but there are some villages along the way and a monastery in the mountains where we can find rest and provisions."

"We're so many," Hugo said. Agitation at the lack of planning flamed to life in his chest. "What are a few villages and one monastery to supply thousands?"

Nicholas narrowed his eyes.

"God supplies us," Kateline said.

He would not argue with her, though he'd seen little evidence of God's provision. "You're right. But we're to be wise, are we not? We need to make plans. Divide into companies and establish leaders over them." He looked around the small circle.

Nicholas's brow furrowed. "Go on."

"Form a forward party of two hundred or so—large enough to

23

convince those you meet that we're a sizable movement."

Simon spoke up. "And what will happen to the children that lag behind?"

"We'll choose able leaders to look after them. The advance group can spread the message of our crusade and prepare the villages for those headed their way." He looked at Simon, Nicholas, and Kateline in turn. "It will be like cultivating a field for harvest."

Understanding dawned on Kateline's face. "Each hamlet will supply only a company or two. In that way we will not deplete the resources for those behind."

Hugo nodded. "If every section knows in which village it is to request aid, then we'll gain the good will of the empire rather than its annoyance."

"I like your ideas," Nicholas said.

Simon protested. "But if we separate, the—"

Nicholas interrupted. "This fellow knows what he's talking about, can't you see?" He smiled at Hugo. "I will set you over it. Take as many days in Heidelberg as you need to organize your leaders. I want each of us in the forward party. What can we do to help?"

Hugo's heart sped up with the familiar thrill of good strategy. "We'll stagger our departure from the city." He spoke to Nicholas. "Lead as you've been doing, but formulate your words to encourage the crusaders for the difficult journey and to inspire support for our campaign among the citizens along our route."

He turned to Simon, disregarding the fact that the young man looked more inclined to argue than follow his instructions. "When we arrive in Heidelberg, gather the most charming of our group to graciously plunder the city for whatever the people will contribute. We'll need food, blankets, shoes, and as many wagons as they might grant us."

Hugo saw admiration in Kateline's eyes. "You must pray for us, milady. Pray with all the purity of your gentle heart."

Her smile sent the blood coursing through his veins.

That night, Hugo stretched out in the shadows just beyond the glow of one of the numerous low fires and watched Kateline where she sat surrounded by a dozen children, a small girl on her lap.

Simon appeared, dropping his satchel to the ground beside Hugo before folding his bony limbs and plopping down. He spoke not a word, and Hugo wondered if he sat close only to keep an eye on him. To make sure Hugo didn't approach Kateline without his knowing about it. Did Simon have his own intentions on the lovely girl?

In the distance one child called to another and a clear, high voice sang a languid tune, but most of the camp had settled for the night, and there were few sounds save the crackling of sap heated in the fires, the hum of quiet conversation, the gentle chirp of courting crickets.

And Kateline's sweet voice. Hugo was close enough to hear that.

"So," she said to the children perched round her, "Jesus performed a miracle on the mountain that day. He fed all those people with only two fish and five small loaves."

A young boy spoke up. "I'll wager they ate every bite."

"They didn't," she said, the light flickering against the golden strands of her hair. "The holy apostles took up twelve baskets of fragments not eaten."

"*Twelve* baskets?" another asked.

"Big baskets," she said with a nod and a grin.

"Why didn't they eat it all?" the girl on her lap asked. "I wouldn't have left a crumb."

"I'm hungry," someone complained.

Kateline gave a tender smile to the little ones. "So am I, but our Lord reminds us to seek food that does not spoil. That's why we make this noble pilgrimage."

"If he fed them, why doesn't he feed us?"

"He does," Kateline said. "He's caused many generous souls to provide for us along the way." She bit her lower lip and looked at them.

Hugo wondered what he'd ever seen in the miller's daughter.

"Why don't we pray to our Lord now?" Kateline continued. "He will not forsake us." She crossed herself and bowed her head, and the children did likewise.

Hugo turned to Simon. "We should find some."

Simon's own gaze had lingered on Kateline, but now swiveled back to Hugo. "What?"

"Food." Hugo sat up and jerked his chin toward the children. "Something to fill their bellies."

"We're almost to Heidelberg."

"We've more than a week to go. How many do you think will last that long?"

"God has called us, and he will—"

Hugo interrupted. "The forests are full of game *tonight*."

Simon's eyes narrowed. "Poach from some lord's demesne?"

Hugo picked a tall blade of foxtail and twirled it between his fingers. "The forests belong to God, do they not?"

"Yes, well, I'd rather trust God's provision than pillage the countryside and bring the wrath of the empire upon us." He glanced back to Kateline. "You're willing to endanger our movement simply to impress Kateline, but Nicholas won't tolerate thievery."

That Hugo very much wanted to gain Kateline's favor was none of Simon's business. Besides, Hugo had in mind the welfare of the crusaders nearly as much as anything. "You think the gifts for our young leader come from the abundance of the children?"

Simon's brows wrinkled at that. Sure, and hadn't the knobby-kneed colt realized it before?

Hugo rose and tossed the foxtail to the ground. Simon might have words to impress Kateline, but he would take action. "If God won't feed the children, then I will, for I'm not content to sit by and watch them starve."

Hugo paused. Nothing stirred in the moonlit meadow a mile down the road from the crusader camp. Nothing but a few cattle lowing at passing clouds. He slipped the noose around an aged cow's neck and pulled.

The short length of twine intended to bind up his worn out shoes made no impression on the beast. She stood looking at him with mournful eyes, her breath warm upon his forearms and sweet with the scent of rotting grass.

"You are God's answer to prayer tonight, old girl. Though your flesh may be tough, you'll fill many a young belly." Hugo yanked on the thin rope. "Come on, you stupid creature."

She didn't budge. He tugged at the twine until it snapped.

A low growl escaped his throat. He wasn't trying to impress Kateline, but care for her? Yes.

He eyed the bovine, then took his blanket from where he'd wrapped it round his waist and used it to circle the stubborn creature's neck. She resisted, shaking her head from side to side before settling.

"Easy. That's it," Hugo crooned, moving along her flank.

He slapped her rump. "Hie," he whispered, loud as he dared, wary of watchmen who might be tending the stock in the field.

Her tail swished lazily, and she bent her head to the ground to nibble at the churlock. He jerked on the blanket and pounded her shoulder twice with his fist. She took one step toward another mouthful.

"Move, you Jezebel." He tugged at the makeshift lead.

"Idiot."

"Lazy wretch."

He raised his eyes to the heavens. "*Please*."

The animal's head lifted at once. She looked at him, bellowed, and then charged forward like she'd seen a night demon, knocking Hugo to the ground on her way toward the road. He sprang to his feet and pounded after her.

The old cow reached the rough flagstone surface, ran along it for some distance, then sagged to her knees and toppled sideways. Hugo made way to her as she wheezed a heavy sigh.

He watched her for a wary moment. Nudged her with his foot. She didn't move. He put his ear behind her front leg, down low. Nothing.

The sky glowed pale pink the next morning by the time Nicholas lifted his cross to set them in motion. Hugo felt a twinge of guilt knowing that for all their effort they wouldn't travel far this day.

They hadn't yet gone a quarter mile when a scout returned to them. The boy drew Nicholas aside and spoke to him in an excited whisper.

Nicholas turned, smiling. "A cow up ahead. Dead on the road."

Kateline glanced to Hugo, who'd managed to place himself between her and a scowling Simon. "Praise be to God," she said, face radiant.

Nicholas gave orders for the masses to remain behind while the four of them hurried forward. They reached the animal within minutes.

"Do you think it diseased?" Kateline asked.

"It looks healthy enough," Nicholas said. "Just dead."

Simon's eyes moved from the knot bulging at Hugo's brow to the fresh stains upon his leggings, and his face grew even more stern. "It's a wonder she died right here upon the road."

Hugo cleared his throat. "A mighty wonder, to be sure. But enough talk. We should feed the children, don't you agree, Nicholas?"

The boy's face glowed, and he licked his lips. "Right away."

They camped where they were for a full day. To Hugo's surprise, Simon directed the butchering, temporarily confiscating Hugo's dagger and issuing instructions to half a dozen young men wielding an assortment of knives and one small hatchet.

Kateline and a bevy of maidens took over the sausage making, washing out the stomach and intestines in a nearby stream and sending the younger children to forage for wild onions and garlic, berries and nuts—anything edible to mix with the blood and scraps that would fill the casings.

Hugo oversaw the distribution and roasting of beef, and by afternoon the air was awaft with a stomach-rumbling combination of wood smoke, roasting meat, and boiled black pudding.

"Keep turning it like this." He rotated the makeshift spit formed from the trunk of a young green tree while two boys of about fourteen looked on. "That's the way. I'll come round again soon."

He headed to the next cooking fire thinking it a pity they had no bread.

Simon stepped into his path, muck from the butchering still on his tunic. "We're not bandits, Hugo. The cow wasn't yours to kill."

Hugo's scalp bristled. "The children are starving. Can't you see that?"

"Nicholas says God has promised to provide for us."

"Then I guess he did." The thorny bramble of a boy had no right to cudgel him. "You're one to cast stones."

"Because I butchered the beast? You'd already done your thieving."

"Because I know what you have in your pack." He hadn't known for sure, but Simon's fluent conversation with the merchants yesterday, coupled with the look of slight panic on the young man's face now, confirmed his suspicions. "That's right. I've seen you slink away to do your reading. Brought along a few stolen manuscripts when you left the monastery, did you?"

Simon's lips thinned, and the fists at the end of his gangly arms tightened until the knuckles grew white through the stain of cow's blood.

The skinny fellow wouldn't dare throw a punch, much as Hugo knew he might be tempted. Without a word, Hugo moved on toward the next fire pit, leaving Simon to stew in his own hypocrisy.

Chapter 4

June AD 1212, Lord Tancred's lands, Holy Roman Empire
Elisabeth sat at the trestle table cutting cabbage for the evening meal
while Methild pretended to rake the rushes that covered the floor.

Her sister looked toward the open doorway several times before
she spoke. "I fancy the blacksmith will call on me today."

"No, he won't," Elisabeth said. "He's too busy with his work."

"I mean tonight. You know that."

"Then why are you watching for him now?"

"That's how love is."

Elisabeth might have said the same thing nearly a year ago.
Instead she hacked at the cabbage, knife slashing through to the wood
beneath with a loud *thwack*.

Methild lifted her eyes to the thatched roof and heaved a sigh.
"Just because you can't have—"

"Don't even utter his name," Elisabeth said through clenched
teeth.

"You're always so cross. It's been months since you lost the
baby, yet you're still making us all miserable. Why don't you just
confess your sin to the priest and be done with it?"

"Because I'm innocent."

"So you say."

Elisabeth's hands shook as she threw the vegetables into the stew.

That night, as was his custom after a day of delivering the barrels he made, Ort shared the local gossip. Elisabeth ignored his droning until, for once, he said something out of the ordinary. "They say that rabble horde of children from Cologne is camped not two days from here."

She glanced up. Methild sat oblivious, picking at a loose thread on her tunic.

"Children?" Mama asked.

Ort nodded. "And young people."

"The rumors are true, then." Mama glanced at Elisabeth. "They're on a crusade to Palestine."

"They're not crusaders," Ort said, wiping his chin with the back of one hand.

"But the potter's wife says there's been a vision. If God has called them, then they have a holy mission to fulfill."

"Probably no more than a bunch of ruffians out to loot the countryside."

Mama gave Elisabeth a peculiar look that made a chill seep down her spine then turned to face Ort. "But what if God favors them? They could find success in the Holy Lands. And forgiveness."

Ort grunted. "They won't find success."

§ § §

"Ortwinus!" Elisabeth heard a yell two afternoons later.

Ort responded with a call from the cooper's workshop behind the cottage. The men spoke low to one another, but Elisabeth cared nothing for what they had to say.

Mama looked out the door while Elisabeth continued to mend

the split seam of the mattress cover.

"What is it, Mama?" Methild asked, sidling up next to her.

Mama shushed her eldest daughter, listening from the threshold.

"Elisabeth," her mother said at last. "Tie off the thread and come along."

Elisabeth looked up to see Mama's face flushed red. She complied. When she reached the door, Mama grabbed her wrist and hurried her down the path toward the village.

"Can't I come?" Methild called.

Mama didn't answer, but Elisabeth turned to see her sister pick up her skirts to hurry after them.

The crusaders had arrived. A multitude of children and young people congregated on the modest bit of grass beside the communal ovens. One boy stood atop a tall stump, a carved cross lifted above his head. He spoke, but Elisabeth couldn't hear him for the taunts of the crowd. Ort was already there and among the loudest. Mama did not push her way to his side. Methild caught up to them then began to inch her way toward the blacksmith.

Elisabeth rose up on tiptoe to see over the shoulder of that dolt, Hesso, who blocked her view. Mama noticed. She led Elisabeth out of the throng, looked this way and that, then marched her to a nearby hut. A ladder leaned against it, and Mama motioned her up.

From such a vantage point, Elisabeth saw over the heads of the crowd, though she still couldn't hear the speaker while the villagers jeered. The boy on the stump kept talking. Beside him stood a muscular young man glowering at the raucous assembly, lips drawn. A wavy-haired maiden knelt close in prayer, seemingly oblivious to the tumult.

Despite the contempt of the crowd, something stirred within Elisabeth—the first bit of life she'd felt since the baby died in her womb. Could this group be destined for glory in Palestine? There were three hundred at most. She thought from the gossip that there would be more, and wondered what it was that so alarmed the villagers, for their reaction held obvious fear.

Elisabeth's mouth twisted as she examined the faces of the townspeople. For all their gossip and judgments and pride, they were fools, the lot of them. Her eyes moved back to the boy who labored to make himself heard above the insults. Despite his youth, his countenance held the air of a grand leader. Likewise, she studied the young woman who knelt in prayer. How could she be so peaceful in this turmoil?

The crowd began to shift and quiet. When Elisabeth saw why, her stomach turned.

Six riders broke through the assembly. The first of them walked his horse right up to the young speaker, who seemed not a bit intimidated.

"Why do you disturb my people?" Lord Tancred asked.

The boy bowed his head in respect then raised vibrant eyes. "Forgive me, my lord, but I bring good news today."

One of Tancred's eyebrows lifted, but otherwise his sweaty face remained rigid. "I do not want you riffraff stealing from my forests and fields or robbing my people."

The crowd shouted agreement. Tancred's eyes roved over them, smugness tugging at his lips. At length, he raised a hand to still them. "Off with you," he said to the crusaders. "Peaceably," he added, though Elisabeth could tell he preferred a chance to display his power.

A fire flamed on the boy's cheeks. "But you have not heard our message from the Lord."

"The church has not sanctioned this movement."

The child lifted the cross high. "God has."

Elisabeth's heart roused at his bravery, but she stayed motionless where she stood on the ladder.

"Insolent child!" Tancred said, even as Ort and other villagers booed the crusaders.

The boy spoke, and the hecklers quieted to hear how he would respond. "I am Nicholas of Cologne, and I tell you, the Lord Almighty has called these children to march to Jerusalem in order to set him free from the tyranny of the Saracens."

Tancred surveyed the crowd of children and laughed. "With a paltry few?"

"There are ten thousand more behind us."

A hush spread over the people.

"We ask nothing of you today," Nicholas continued, "and will not put a great burden on you, but request that you ready provisions for several hundred."

Tancred's face turned red. "Get off my lands, you arrogant peasant."

"We're asking with the greatest humility, milord." Nicholas motioned to the children on the green. "Let us stay the night, and we will depart at first light."

Elisabeth shrank against the ladder when Tancred's third son, Wilhelm, goaded his horse toward the young woman on the ground.

"My father commands you to go," Wilhelm said with a sneer, reaching down to lift her by the hair.

Shock registered on the blonde's beautiful face, and her hands flew to where his fist seized her. She floundered, tried to find her feet.

The brawny young man Elisabeth noticed earlier rushed forward, fury on his face. Another rider positioned his horse between them, training his sword on the heart of the would-be rescuer.

Every breath held.

"We'll go," Nicholas said calmly, as though it was his idea in the first place. "Call off your men and let us withdraw in peace."

After a moment's hesitation, Tancred dismissed the horsemen with a nod.

The champion ran to the young woman's side, steadying her in his arms. Someone helped Nicholas from the stump, and then the children moved forward as one, their attention on the carved crucifix, chins held high. Even the girl walked on her own strength, face composed and dignified.

Only one set of eyes scanned the dividing crowd—those of a gangly young man standing taller than anyone Elisabeth had ever seen. He returned her stare. A gust of ill wind tossed a loose strand of hair across her face to catch in her lashes, but still she did not move or look away until his somber eyes blinked and turned aside.

Tancred and his men rode in the opposite direction. So confident were they that their will had triumphed, they never once looked back.

Elisabeth descended the ladder, trembling. It was the first time she'd seen Wilhelm since the rape.

§ § §

Elisabeth said nothing through supper.

Neither did Mama.

But Methild did. " . . . and Gerta says the new blacksmith is looking for a wife. She says he's set his heart on winning the tanner's sister, but I told her he couldn't possibly be interested in her. She's too old. Besides, Gerta knows full well he's spoken to me twice. I think she's just jealous because he hasn't paid the least bit of attention to her and—"

"Shut up, girl," Ort snarled.

Methild's mouth hung open in mid-sentence for a moment before she clamped her jaw closed and tore a piece of bread from the trencher she used as a bowl. She dipped it into the thin pottage and chewed sullenly, giving Ort scornful glances when he wasn't looking.

He soon pushed himself up. "I'm going to the village."

Mama clutched the table, the sudden loss of his girth tipping off balance the rough bench on which she sat. The act succeeded in rousing her from her thoughts as his words had failed to do. "To the village again?"

"I need to confirm an order for barrels."

Elisabeth's eyes shifted toward him. No doubt he would instead make way to the ale house—a reeking, dark place where the local men gathered to drink stale beer from dirty cups, pretending they sat in a tavern equal to those she heard Heidelberg possessed.

"Take Methild," Mama said. "She wants to see her cousins."

Methild's lips parted, and she began to shake her head.

"And stop in to see the blacksmith," Mama added. "I may soon need a new pot."

Methild froze, and then a smile broke across her face. "Oh, yes. Our pot is in terrible condition."

Ort grumbled, but Methild followed him out the doorway. Mama stood looking after them for several moments, then came to Elisabeth. She took her hand and sat down with her on the bench beside the table.

Mama leaned close. "You must go with them."

Elisabeth's forehead crinkled. "You don't want me to clear the dinner things?"

"I'm not speaking of your father and Methild."

He'll never be my father, Elisabeth silently corrected.

"The crusaders," Mama said.

Elisabeth's mouth went dry. "Go with them?"

"It's the only way, daughter. You cannot find pardon for your many sins unless you do this."

"But, I—I don't *want* to go."

"You have to."

No. Even when Ort threatened to turn her out, Elisabeth always knew Mama would protect her, keep her close. "You can't mean it." She searched her mother's face. "Mama?"

Mama's eyes brimmed. "You will perish under the weight of your trespasses."

"I'm innocent. Why won't you believe me?"

Mama shook her head and looked down at their clasped hands. "The priest has refused you penance, my child. There is no hope for you here." She shrugged her shoulders. "In Jerusalem, maybe."

Elisabeth couldn't breathe. It felt like someone held her down, pressed her to the ground, crushed her with bruising strength. A square-jawed face, once adored, came to mind, and she pushed the agonizing memory away. She'd lost so much that midsummer's night. Was paying, still, for her foolishness.

"Dry your eyes," Mama said, standing and walking toward the door.

Yes, her cheeks were wet with tears. She rubbed them with the edge of her apron, fighting down the panic that threatened to surface. "Don't make me go."

Mama ignored her plea. "Take nothing with you," she said, voice little more than a whisper, "except what's left of the loaf."

Elisabeth stared at the dying fire, its amber coals blurred by the moisture in her eyes. A log hissed and cracked, falling to the ashes, sending up a small shower of sparks that glowed bright in the darkening hut.

"And a blanket," Mama continued, looking out at the dusky sky. "Take a blanket. It will be a chill night."

Elisabeth's heart thumped painfully. "You want me to go *now*?"

"Later, when Ort sleeps."

Resentment burned in her chest. "He'll be glad enough to see me gone."

Mama turned. "Not without a profit, he won't."

Ah. Of course. He'd never meant to simply turn her out had she delivered a girl, but to sell her services as a chambermaid or laundress or spinster. The look of remorse on Mama's face suggested that he had such designs for her even now. Yes, best for Mama's sake that it seemed Elisabeth ran away of her own accord.

She didn't want to go, couldn't bear to leave. And yet—

The truth was that she could no longer stay. Could no longer endure the mistrust and suffering that plagued her in this place. Elisabeth drew a ragged breath. "All right, then."

Her mother closed the short distance between them, pulled Elisabeth to her, and wept.

By the time Ort and Methild arrived home, Elisabeth and Mama had taken down the trestle table, laid out the thick straw mattress, smothered the fire so that it would not smoke or go out before morning, and said their farewells.

Ort fell to sleep quickly, his breath sour with drink and heavy in the close confines of the hut. Mama lay beside him, though Elisabeth knew she did not slumber. Methild had found little success fanning the blacksmith's interest, and so she tossed at the foot of the mattress for nearly an hour before settling.

Elisabeth let another quarter hour pass before she timed her movement to Ort's deep snore and dared to lift herself from the earthen floor where she lay. Even the soft crunch of the rushes that covered the dirt sounded frightfully loud.

Her eyes were accustomed to the dark, but still she moved slowly in the blackness, stepping silently toward the doorway. Surely they could hear the pounding of her heart, but no one roused. She pressed a hand to the outside of a pocket stitched into the seam of her kirtle, and felt the comforting shape of a small smooth stone from the Rhine.

Elisabeth lifted the latch carefully, quietly, pushing against the wood no more than necessary and maneuvering sideways through the gap. The door eased shut behind her.

Cocking her head to one side, she listened, but heard nothing worrisome.

The moon rose high above the trees, illuminating the clearing where their cottage sat. A slight breeze rustled the air, carrying with it the tangy aroma of sap and the sweet scent of summer clover.

Elisabeth adjusted a thin blanket about her shoulders, glanced back once, and then fled through the night, looking neither to the left nor the right, afraid she might see the demons that chased her from home.

Elisabeth heard only her labored breathing and the sound of her feet slapping the ground. A pain shot through her side, and she slowed to catch her breath. She'd been running off and on for more than an hour.

She feared the travelers would be too far ahead by now. That she'd come to a crossroads and not know which way to go. That she'd meet with a bear or bandits. That she'd find the crusaders.

She wasn't even sure she'd followed the right road. Her pace slowed until she finally stopped.

The trees held close to the path, surrounding her with hidden dangers. Had the night been filled with the muffled sounds of nocturnal animals, she would have felt at ease. This eerie spot, however, remained deathly quiet. She sensed a presence, though, and knew she was not alone.

Ghosts were said to inhabit the Black Forest, and while she lived her entire sixteen years along its northern edge, she'd never traveled into its heart. If phantoms silenced the animals in this place, perhaps they also aimed their wicked intentions on her. Goosebumps scuttled across her skin.

Though God did not favor her, she knew he reigned over the spirit world. She could at least bluff with a threat to call down the heavenly host.

"I know you're there," she announced. "Forces are at the ready, and I am prepared to alert them to your presence."

She never had a chance to warn them to leave her alone or else she'd carry out her threat, for in that moment two of them hurtled out of the shadows to pounce on her. They tackled her with surprising speed. Too terrified even to scream, she rolled onto her back to claw and slap at her assailants.

"Grab her arms," one said.

"I can't. She's moving too fast."

"Just do it you—*oomph*."

She got the first one full in the groin with her foot. He dropped to all fours. She kicked him twice more, three times, then scrambled to her feet.

"Stop her," he gasped.

In one clumsy movement, the other threw himself at Elisabeth and knocked her once more to the ground. She rolled with the force of the hit and landed face up. The attacker sat backwards on her chest. He pinned her arms with his legs, rump in her face. She jerked one knee up to make solid contact.

"Ow!" he cried, wobbling atop her. "I think she broke my nose."

Elisabeth could see only the injured party's hind end, but felt the other press his weight on her ankles.

No fiendish spirits, these. For a long moment the three of them lay panting.

"I can't breathe," she wheezed.

"We won't fall for that trick."

"Cover her mouth before she screams," the boy at her ankles said.

And who would hear me? Elisabeth wondered before a hand clamped over her lips. His sweaty palm blocked her nostrils, and his seat still crushed her chest. She panicked.

"Hold tight now," one of them said as she struggled.

"I'm not lettin' go."

The moon wavered, and the shadows pressed close until everything grew black as death.

Chapter 5

June AD 1212, Black Forest, Holy Roman Empire
Worrisome thoughts harassed Simon. He could feel them wriggling through his mind, trying to disturb his prayers. And pray he did.

"Why were those men in the village so mean?" Conon said.

"I don't know." Simon wrapped the boy's small hand in his large one. Tancred's aggression disturbed him deeply, but he didn't want to let on, so he changed the subject. "I'll wager there will still be berries on the vine for us tonight."

Conon's eyes grew round. "That big man will chop off our hands if we pick even one."

"You may be right."

So much for easing the child's fears.

Nicholas walked just ahead with Kateline beside him, leading his forward party southward, each crusader subdued, tromping the road with a heavy step. Hugo was somewhere behind, a foul mood stifling his bravado this evening. Simon rather preferred him stifled.

"Hugo!" Nicholas's call echoed over the heads of those in front. "Where's Hugo?"

Simon turned to see the young man moving up the line.

"*Ja,*" Hugo said when he drew close. "What is it?"

"Choose a suitable encampment," the boy said, "then instruct the others. I'm still too vexed to speak."

Hugo surveyed the countryside. "We're not in safe territory yet. Tancred may very well carry out his threat to use force against us."

"I'm not going any farther."

Simon spoke up. "Hugo's right, Nicholas. We've not crossed the tributary that borders the manor lord's lands. Remember? I showed it to you on our map."

Securing a map in Heidelberg had been an enormous achievement. Even Hugo had been pleased by Simon's success. The citizens of that city were generous, also providing for each group a wagon and a beast to pull it.

"I'm tired," Nicholas said. "We're stopping."

Hugo's jaw clenched, and it seemed he bit back a surly response. Pivoting, he lifted his voice to the children. "Into the woods over that hill, out of view from the road. No fires tonight."

Did Kateline notice that Hugo avoided her gaze? Simon thought so, for her smile faded when Hugo turned and walked away.

The crusaders made their way beyond the rise to the trees below, blending into the forest like raindrops in a river.

Simon settled Conon and went to find Nicholas, passing by Hugo as he did so. The older fellow had gathered a group of broad-shouldered boys to serve as sentries and was instructing them to take shifts through the night. Not a bad idea, considering Tancred's threat.

"Nicholas," Simon said when he came upon their leader huddled alone against a fir. "Have you eaten?"

Nicholas didn't look up. "I don't want anything."

"You must keep your strength."

The boy raised eyes that glittered in the moonlight. "How dare the man speak to me as if I am nothing but a peasant?"

Simon's brows lifted. That Nicholas was a peasant in little more

44

than rags might have influenced the lord's words, but Simon understood the boy's meaning. "God will deal with him."

"I should take that dagger of Hugo's and slit his throat."

"The offense is not against you, Nicholas, but against the children that follow and the God that sends us on this journey."

Nicholas turned his back and hunched up the shoulders of his small frame. "Of course."

Simon lifted his face to the limbs above and sighed. It was a night for sour moods. Maybe sleep would help them all.

A voice called out, strained and urgent. Simon's eyes flew open in time to see Hugo bolt upright. Simon rolled over to follow the young man's gaze.

Two sentries lurched toward them. A maiden struggled and ranted between them, small but feisty as a cat in a rain barrel.

"Get Kateline," Simon said to Conon, who'd also awoken.

The child gawked at the wild young woman for a moment before scrambling to do Simon's bidding.

Hugo grimaced. "What's going on?"

"She's a spy," one boy gasped.

Even Hugo's bad temper couldn't prevent a corner of his mouth from turning up at the spectacle. "I see."

Simon rose to stand beside Hugo. The moon shone like torchlight through the trees.

The young woman stilled and looked up through long hair pulled loose from her braid. "I'm not a spy," she spat out. "Let me go."

"I would," Hugo drawled, "but you seem dangerous."

Indeed, Simon thought. He couldn't help grinning. The lookouts had fared poorly. One boy's nose looked swollen, and a dark swath stained his face. Blood, no doubt.

The maiden glared at Hugo through her locks, then shook her head to toss them aside. "I came to join the crusade." She tried to jerk away from the boys, one of whom nearly lost his footing.

"She followed us, Hugo," the other boy said. Sweat glistened on his face. "Tracked us to this spot. Threatened to call forces down upon us, but we subdued her."

Hugo's voice turned serious. "Where are you from?" he asked her.

"She's from the village that turned us away," Simon said. "I saw her there." He'd noted the fire in her hair and the intelligence in her eyes as she stood on a ladder watching their departure.

Hugo turned to him, one eyebrow raised. "You're sure?"

Simon nodded.

Hugo rushed the young woman, put his dagger to her face. Her eyes narrowed after the first moment of shock, and she stood her ground.

"Hugo, what are you—"

"Quiet, Simon," he said, elbow up, knife at her cheek. "How many men follow us?"

The girl looked from the blade to Hugo. Her lips thinned. "There are no men."

"Hugo, that's enough," Simon said. Hugo wouldn't harm her, but Simon couldn't just stand there and watch him bully the girl. "Put the knife away. She's trustworthy." Of course, he had no way of knowing whether she could be trusted, but he felt it to be true. "Let her go."

Hugo stood for several seconds and then lowered the blade. Conon ran up, followed by Kateline. She went straight to the young woman, untied her makeshift bonds, and handed the cloth belt to the boy whose tunic hung freely. The redhead rubbed her wrists and scowled at Hugo.

"Go wash your faces," Kateline said to the boys before turning to their captive. "Are you hurt?"

"They attacked without cause."

"It looks like you defended yourself admirably," Kateline said with humor in her voice.

A glimmer of a smile touched the young woman's lips. "I always do."

"Let's go." Kateline put an arm around the maid's shoulders. "You need rest."

"I lost my blanket on the road."

"Hugo will find it for you," Kateline said as they walked past him. Their voices faded into the trees like shadows.

Simon focused his attention on the ground. So did Conon.

"What are you standing there for?" Hugo snarled.

Simon looked up to see irritation nettling the young man's eyes. Hugo's gaze shifted. "Locate the blanket," he said to Conon.

The boy moved to do as he was told, but Simon put a hand to his shoulder. Hugo's brow furrowed.

"Kateline bids you do it," Simon said.

Hugo's lips tightened, then he exhaled loudly. "Fine." He stomped off in the direction of the road.

When they could no longer see him, Conon's face tipped up to Simon. "Is he in trouble with Kateline?"

Simon's smile returned. "I think he is."

§ § §

It took a quarter hour for Hugo to track down the blanket. He snatched it from the road and turned to make his way back to the encampment. How dare the scrawny newcomer turn Kateline against him? He'd done nothing but defend the camp, defend Kateline. But now Kateline had even more reason to think poorly of him. And it was the girl's fault.

He found the two young women seated, speaking softly so as not to disturb the others who slept nearby.

"Kateline," he whispered from a short distance away.

She said something to the young woman, then stood and walked to meet him.

"Here." He held out the rough-woven cover.

Her countenance softened, and a wide smile caressed her face. "Thank you, Hugo," she said, taking it. "Won't you come apologize to her?"

"Apologize?" He'd do no such thing.

"She did us no wrong," Kateline said. "Her only motive was to join our company. Through no fault of her own, she's been attacked, bound, and threatened."

"I was trying to protect you," he said. "To protect the children. What if the manor lord sent her as a decoy in order to ambush our small band? It's my duty to look out for all of you."

Kateline placed a delicate hand on his chest. "I know, Hugo, and I am grateful that we have you to do so."

Her look made his knees sway and weakened his resolve. "All right. I'll speak to her."

Kateline smiled and led him to the redhead, kneeling down beside her. "Elisabeth," she said, "Hugo has found your blanket."

Elisabeth looked at him, eyes narrowing.

He cleared his throat. "I'm sorry I threatened you. I only meant to safeguard the children."

She said nothing in reply.

"Elisabeth?" Kateline said. She shot Hugo a look that begged his patience.

The young woman crossed her arms over her chest and stared straight ahead. "Apology accepted."

He walked away, taking pains not to growl within earshot of Kateline.

"Hugo."

He turned to see Kateline lift her tunic and step over a fallen log to follow him.

"Thank you for helping Elisabeth," she said, smiling at him.

His heart ached with shame to see such kindness upon her face.

She glanced over her shoulder at the newcomer, then placed a hand on his arm and began to walk. "You've been far too quiet tonight," she said at last.

"I have dishonored myself."

She stopped and looked up at him. "How?"

"I failed you today, Kateline. In the village. I allowed the tip of a sword to pierce my courage."

"You're no coward. Didn't I thank you while we were still on the green? In fact, my heart swelled with respect for you the moment you moved to defend me."

"But I let a mere weapon stop me."

"As well you should have."

Her lips were full and her expression warm. Hugo wanted to kiss her, but didn't dare.

"The situation was tense," she said, "but not dangerous. Had you pressed my rescue, we would all have been at risk. You were wise to wait." She lifted tender eyes to his. "I don't know what I would have done had you been harmed."

The blood seemed to drain from Hugo's limbs, only to come crashing back in like a river flooded. He couldn't find words to respond.

Her eyes faltered at his silence. "Rest well." She turned to go.

Hugo caught her hand, and she stopped. He dropped to one knee, swallowing hard. "I wanted to die when that swine assaulted you today."

Her face softened, and she took a step toward him.

He closed his eyes and brought her fingers to his lips. They smelled of pine and smoke. "I will never let harm come to you again."

Chapter 6

June AD 1212, German Provinces, Holy Roman Empire

A firm hand shook Elisabeth. At first she thought it was Mama, but then she rolled over and opened her eyes to see Kateline in the faint light of dawn.

"Awake, friend," Kateline said. "We must get an early start to make sure we clear the manor lord's reach."

Elisabeth felt hollow, like one of Mama's gourds with the insides scraped out. Just a husk. She missed Mama. "How long 'til we reach Jerusalem?"

Kateline smiled. "Impatient, are you?"

Desperate, she might have said had she been inclined to speak the truth, but she wasn't. Besides, Kateline turned aside without waiting for her response.

Elisabeth sat up and pulled the blanket close against the morning chill. It did nothing to warm the aching coldness in her heart.

Little girls and young maidens moved about, stealing glances at her, giggling behind their hands. Washing their faces at the stream.

"Come on, then," a horse-faced girl said, arms linked with two others who stared unabashedly at Elisabeth.

She stood and followed.

The trio pestered her with questions—what was her name? Did she really break Eckart's nose? Had she been this way before?

Even Methild's prattling was better than this.

They joined the line that etched toward a rickety wagon where twin boys handed out pieces of bread for breakfast. The younger children grew louder despite the hushing of the older ones.

A group of boys at play scampered through their midst. That tall, ungainly fellow from yesterday stood nearby in conversation with Kateline. He was the same one who held her gaze in the village. And who smiled like a buffoon when those sniveling boys dragged her into camp. One of the smallest lads hugged the young man's leg for an instant before rejoining the others in their game.

She shrank from the commotion, wrapped her arms around her waist as line inched forward. Stared at the ground. Shut them out.

"Elisabeth, is it?"

That young man.

She nodded.

"I'm Simon," he said, pronouncing it "See-mon." He hitched up a leather pack on his bony shoulder. "Come see me after you get your breakfast. I need to make sure your feet are shod."

He clomped off without waiting for an answer.

Elisabeth stepped forward and accepted a portion of bread without comment, then sought a place to sit out of the flow of jabbering crusaders. She'd always felt less lonely in solitude than in the company of others. She tore off the moldy bits of crust and bit into the remainder without appetite.

How she missed home. If she were there right now she'd be uncovering the coals and rekindling the fire with fresh tinder. Making a porridge out of the grain Ort brought home yesterday.

Elisabeth's heart squeezed. If there were any way to return

home, she'd do so this very minute. But she couldn't yet, could she? God needed pleasing.

If she could please him. Was it truly possible to save her soul? Tears prickled her eyes, but she wouldn't let the crusaders see her cry, so she dug her nails into her palms and blinked back the moisture.

At length, she spied Hugo through the trees. Her mouth twisted into a scowl. Yesterday, she'd thought him of noble character when he tried to defend Kateline in the village. Now she knew differently. Hugo was a beastly, vicious man.

He issued an order to a couple of lads. Square jaw, strong chin, light eyes. Tunic pulled tight against the muscles of his chest.

Now that she considered it, he looked—

—like Wilhelm.

Elisabeth exhaled, and wondered if she would ever be free from thoughts of him. He'd stripped her of more than her chastity in the forest a year ago. Grief and guilt were all she had left now. And fear. So many fears. She'd lied last night when she told Kateline that she always defended herself admirably.

Elisabeth swallowed the bread that stuck in her throat.

Would she feel guilty if she were truly innocent? Mama thought her at fault. Perhaps that's why the babe died after all.

Simon's voice interrupted her thoughts. "You didn't come for shoes as you were instructed."

She glanced up. "I don't need any."

"Hugo says you do."

She hoped her look made it clear she didn't care what Hugo thought.

"Just bind your feet," he said, holding out rags to her.

"I've never worn shoes, and I don't need those."

His jaw tightened, but he knelt in front of her, lifting her right foot to do the job himself.

She jerked it away. "Don't touch me."

Simon froze then tossed the leather strips on the ground next to her. "Fine. Do it yourself. No one will be carrying you when your feet are too bloody to walk."

"I don't need to be taken care of."

He sat back on his heels and sighed. "I'm not your enemy, Elisabeth. I'm only hoping to help you safely to our goal."

When she said nothing, he rose and galumphed away.

Within minutes the chaos of the morning seemed to sort itself out, and all at once the crusaders were on the move. Elisabeth picked up the scraps—just in case—and joined the ragtag band. More quickly than she hoped, they tired of attempting conversation with her, and she walked alone while the others clustered together in small groups.

Well. What a poor start. She'd come off as disagreeable and ill tempered, but no wonder. Most of the adventurers acted as if the whole affair were a feast day—gossiping and giggling, flirting and romping. Didn't they realize how much was at stake?

But maybe her isolation was for the best. It wouldn't do them any good to get close to her—they'd only risk sharing her curse.

Until last summer, she wouldn't have thought herself cursed. But looking back on her life, she could see a horrible pattern. *Vati.* James. Mama's other babes. Had their deaths all been because of her? Certainly she, herself, had suffered. And the poor child she buried, never to see heaven.

Unless she made it to Jerusalem. Then, perhaps, God might show mercy. At least to the babe.

"Do you intend to lead us to Palestine yourself?" a voice behind her asked.

Elisabeth turned to see Nicholas, a smirk upon his face. Some two hundred children followed him. Confused, she looked ahead. No one. She'd out-paced them all.

Nicholas passed as a blush heated her face. Behind him came Hugo and then Simon, laughter in their eyes.

Only Kateline had a kind smile for her. She looped an arm through Elisabeth's. "Come on," she said. "You can share your energy with me."

"What have you there?" Kateline asked later that afternoon when they stopped to rest beneath the trees, sun hot enough to wilt the hawkweed.

Elisabeth followed Kateline's gaze to the object she turned round and round with her fingers. Her hands stilled. "Only a stone."

Kateline sat down beside her. "It's pretty. Did you find it here?"

"No."

Elisabeth remembered the day *Vati* held her hand while they walked beside the Rhine.

"It's so wide," she'd said of the river.

Her father replied with a rich, gentle voice. "Yes, and deep enough that you must not let go of my hand."

She wouldn't let go. Ever. She liked the way it felt when his long fingers wrapped around hers. "Can we put our feet in?"

"It's too cool today. Your mother wouldn't want you to get wet."

"I won't tell," Elisabeth pledged.

So they sat on the bank and dangled their feet in the frigid water until she could no longer feel her toes. *Vati* rubbed them between his hands, and they warmed again. She giggled when he tickled her.

"Look," he said, reaching into the water along the shore to fish out the pale pink stone.

It sat smooth as glass in her palm. She'd seen a glass window once in the manor house when she accompanied Mama to deliver some needlework. Elisabeth wrapped the stone in her small hand and smiled up at *Vati*. "I'll keep it until I die."

He chuckled, stroking her hair. "Always so earnest, my little 'Lisbeth."

She'd wanted that moment to last forever.

Kateline startled her out of her thoughts. "The stone must be special to you then, to bring it with you." She offered a gentle and understanding smile.

"Not really."

Kateline shifted the neck of her tunic and pulled out a small medallion dangling from a finely woven chain. A simple cross adorned its surface. "My mother's," she said. "It's the most precious thing I've ever owned."

Elisabeth looked from the pendant to her pink stone and back. She closed her fist over the stone and stood. "I'm thirsty," she said, and headed for the brook that gurgled nearby.

Kateline hastened to stand. "I didn't intend to pry." Her brows crinkled with concern. "I only meant to be friendly."

Elisabeth assessed Kateline's kind face. Had she ever truly had a friend? But it would do neither of them any good. "We're not friends."

Kateline's lips parted in surprise at the words, but she said no more as Elisabeth walked away.

§ § §

Elisabeth woke herself crying out.

"Are you all right?" Kateline's voice was husky with sleep and tight with alarm.

Elisabeth sat up, heart pounding, sweat on her forehead. The blanket restrained her. She struggled out of it and rose, fleeing the horror of her dreams.

She sought escape along the stream's edge, but the river grasses hemmed her in.

"Elisabeth," Kateline said, following. "What is it? What's troubling you?"

"It was only a nightmare," she said. "Please go away."

"I'm concerned for you."

"I'll be fine." But she wouldn't. How could she be?

Kateline persisted. "No dream, however unpleasant, should cause such misery."

Elisabeth didn't answer.

Kateline laid a tender hand upon Elisabeth's shoulder. "I would be your friend."

She shrugged out from under the touch, but could not reply.

"I would share your sorrow."

Elisabeth sank to her knees at the edge of the stream. Bitter longing flamed in her breast. Oh, that someone could lift the burden of her sorrow. The words barely came, so tight was her throat. "You cannot."

A toad splashed into the water.

Kateline hesitated for a moment, and then quietly retreated.

Elisabeth wiped a hand across her forehead, loosening the strands of hair that had gone stiff with perspiration. Smelled the sour odor of her panic.

The warmth of the summer night and the earthy scent of mud and wet stones made it far too easy to relive the trauma of Wilhelm's violence against her. A wave of nausea rolled her stomach.

He'd led her to a stream like this one, and she savored his kisses until he sought the flesh beneath her tunic.

"*Nein*," she'd said. "Leave me be."

Elisabeth rubbed her wrists, not wanting to remember his painful grip. She heard again the sound of his hand against her cheek, like a whip against the ox. Saw the humorless laugh that contorted his once-lovely face.

She'd twisted against his grasp. "Go rut with the pigs."

"Like this, you stinking sow?"

She covered her ears now, trying to block the memory of his grunts and curses. Of the screams that gave out with her voice.

Tears had stung her eyes that night, but she'd refused to cry, biting into her tongue until she tasted blood.

"You wicked girl," Ort said later, "throwing yourself at a nobleman. And you of no more importance than a fly on the rump of his horse."

"You are a fornicator of the worst sort," the manor lord's priest had declared. "What do you expect when you act the whore? You'll find no penance here."

The chirrup of locusts and the sudden *whoo, whoo* of an owl brought Elisabeth back to the desolate present. She looked at the stream, black in the moonlight, wriggling like a serpent. Maybe Ort and the priest were right. Maybe she could have prevented the attack. She'd been a foolish girl, indeed. And paid dearly for it.

But no more.

She stood, her skirt damp from the sodden ground, and clasped her hands to her chest, pressing them tight against the unbearable pain there.

"Holy Father," she said aloud. "I am a fornicator and a murderess."

Did anyone hear her confession save the nodding heads of the river grasses?

"My own child rots in the grave because of my foolishness. Though the devil himself stole my virtue, I deserve no mercy . . . but hope for it. Lift your curse from my despised soul.

"I beg you."

Chapter 7

Early July AD 1212, German Provinces, Holy Roman Empire
Hugo put his hands to his hips and surveyed the camp, heart lighter than it had been in a week.

Nicholas's advance party had set out from Heidelberg a full two days ahead of the first company. Their small number—just over two hundred—contrasted with the five-to-eight-hundred-member units behind them. Fifteen companies in all. Runners communicated between them every four days. Hugo put the least determined groups in the rear, explaining privately to Simon and Kateline that their ranks were more likely to dwindle along with the food supplies, but at least they might disperse before meeting the hazards of the Alps.

And now they'd encountered a friendly village the day before. The manor lord leapt at the chance to supply the companies that followed, simply because Lord Tancred had not. As was the case for most of the Holy Roman Empire in the German provinces, bitter factions tore at the unity of the region.

Hugo made way to where Nicholas sat eating fresh cheese and bread still warm from the communal ovens. A pack of children sat round the boy, laughing at something he'd said. Nicholas took the adoration well.

"We are amply supplied, Nicholas," Hugo said. "The lord's representative rode off this morning to rally those in outlying areas to prepare for the children who follow."

Nicholas spoke with his mouth full. "Good. Did you request a mount for me?"

"He's been generous, Nicholas. I didn't think it wise."

The boy wiped his mouth with the back of one hand. "I'm the leader, Hugo. I shouldn't have to walk like everyone else."

The children expressed their agreement.

Hugo's jaw tightened. "Perhaps next time."

Nicholas scowled.

"Another runner arrived last night," Hugo continued, changing the subject. "He brought word that all those behind us fare well. We sent him back a few minutes ago with an extra portion of food for his trip."

The boy only nodded and bit into his bread, then turned his attention back to his attendants.

The march got underway after breakfast, the crusaders singing with renewed zeal after the boon to their rations.

Hugo hung back to walk beside Kateline. Her eyes looked strained. "Are you well, milady?"

She smiled at the title. "Yes. I'm troubled, 'tis all." She let go the hand of a young girl. "Go find Heida, *liebes mädchen*." The child pivoted then skipped away.

Hugo wanted to take Kateline's hand himself. "I suffer to think that anything disturbs your beautiful heart."

"Do not suffer on my account. It is Elisabeth I worry over."

Perhaps he could offer his arm? "I can understand how she vexes you."

No need to offer, for Kateline slid her hand into the crook of his elbow. It didn't matter whether she did it knowingly. Her touch— intentional or instinctive—was a gift.

"She bristles whenever I try to be friendly." Kateline shook her lovely head. "I'm ashamed to say I hardly want to make the effort any longer. But, the truth is, something distresses her deeply, and I feel sorry for her."

"I simply bemoan the fact she joined us. It's a miracle she hasn't shooed me away from your side already."

Kateline smiled at that. "She is strangely protective, for all her rebuffs. Whatever disturbs her also drove her to us. Otherwise, I'm certain she wouldn't be here."

"Ah," Hugo said. "Then I shall hope she finds contentment quickly."

Kateline's laugh sounded soft and sweet in his ear.

"Hugo," she said after a moment. "What brings you to this place?"

A corner of his mouth turned up at the obvious inquiry. His mind worked to come up with an answer for the question beneath, where he knew her thoughts spun. He'd left Offenstadt for the promise of fortune, and, in some measure, for the adventure of crusading. Much had changed in the weeks since.

The crusader song ended with a cheer. Hugo looked over his shoulder at the children behind then shared a smile with Kateline. He had to admit that his feelings for the young ones had altered. Grown, somehow. And by no means only for the children.

Another song began.

Hugo answered Kateline, hardly knowing where the words came from. "I believe God made me for this journey. That he trained me in my youth to lead, to fight for what is right, to carry out a noble task." He took a measured breath. "To care for you."

Her hand tightened on his arm, and her eyes searched his. "Do you know him, Hugo?"

"God, you mean?"

She nodded, and he sensed everything hinged on his answer.

He was as decent a Christian as the next and started to say so, but her guilelessness demanded his honesty. Even as he spoke, his heart stirred in anticipation. "No, Kateline, but I would have you teach me."

Her face lit. "It is a journey like no other. A journey you will never regret."

That night he tried voicing his own thoughts to God instead of the prayers his mother taught him. *God, I am Hugo.* A scraggly blanket covered his shoulders as he lay on the ground. *I don't know why you'd want to hear from one such as me, but Kateline said I should pray in my own words.* He paused. *Bless us. And . . . and give us this day our daily bread.* He turned to look at the moon glowing through the trees. What kind of sorry effort was that? He wanted to try again, but no more words came. He sighed. *Never mind.*

The morning sun had just broken over the treetops when Hugo heard a commotion.

Five or six children fluttered around Kateline, voices chirping like hatchlings in the nest. She cast a glance his direction, worry flooding her features.

Hugo dropped the twine used to bind up his castoff shoes and headed toward her, Simon right behind him. "What is it?"

"Benno and Claus."

"The twins?"

A tow-headed boy spoke up. "They've gone missing."

"You're sure?" Simon asked.

Hugo rubbed a hand through his hair, smoothing the prickles of anxiety that scuttled across his scalp. "Probably hunting for strawberries."

"*Nein,*" said another child. "Their blanket is still on the ground where they slept. They'd never leave it behind."

"Not even for strawberries," Artur said, twisted arm hanging limp at his side.

"Have you looked for them?" Kateline asked the little ones.

They all spoke at once. "Yes." "Everywhere." "We've called their names." "I've been through the camp twice."

Hugo raised his hands to quiet them. "Don't worry. We'll look again. You two go that direction and circle round the camp to the west." A couple of barefoot boys sprinted off to follow his orders. "You three, go through the center of the—"

"What's wrong?" Nicholas interrupted. "Why isn't someone handing out breakfast?"

"It's the twins," Simon said. "They're missing."

Nicholas looked especially young—sleepy eyes muting his features, a crease on his cheek. "Bruno and Claus?"

"Benno," Hugo corrected. "We're looking for them now."

"They'll turn up soon enough." Their leader yawned and scratched his chest. "And if they don't, they'll have to join one of the other groups behind."

The children exchanged glances, unsure whether to be concerned for the missing boys.

"No," Kateline said. "I think the children are right. Something's amiss."

"They've likely abandoned our movement," Nicholas said, "so why trouble yourselves?" He looked toward the food cart. "Who's in charge of our rations?"

Hugo swallowed his irritation and forced himself to speak with calm resolve. "Simon can appoint someone to distribute the bread. But we're going to look for the twins."

Nicholas frowned. "I want to get going. It's already warm."

"Give us an hour," Simon reasoned. "In the meantime, perhaps you can inspire us with the parable of the lost sheep. I'll make sure everyone has eaten and is ready to march at your command."

Nicholas straightened his back, enlivened by the prospect of preaching. "All right then. One hour."

Hugo had to admit Simon handled the boy with shrewdness.

He, for one, felt tempted to thump their leader's forehead to knock a bit of sense into him. Better, though, to have distracted him into doing what he did best—talking—and let Hugo and the others take care of the issue at hand.

Nicholas's most devout followers gathered round him to hear the story of the shepherd who left his sheep safely in the fold and went looking for one lost lamb.

Hugo instructed the rest. "Start at the center of the camp and move outward, like spokes on a wheel. Go the distance of one furlong then wait for my word. Call out if you find them."

Kateline reached for his hand and gave it a gentle squeeze that warmed the blood in his veins. "Thank you," she whispered.

"We'll find them."

And they did, not fifteen minutes later.

Elisabeth found them, in fact, her shrill keening alerting the searchers who followed the noise. Hugo reached her first, Kateline behind him, others scrambling to catch up.

"They're dead," Elisabeth cried, eyes wild with panic. "I'm so sorry. They're dead, they're dead."

Kateline wrapped her arms around the girl while Hugo looked down to a wide ledge some forty or fifty feet below the ridge where they stood.

The fall had been enough to break Claus's neck. Benno lay beside him, eyes closed, blood upon his leggings. Hugo scrambled down the precipice, careful of the unstable earth that had given way beneath the boys. Babies, they were. Babies who would otherwise be home with their mothers.

He reached Benno, who moaned when Hugo called his name. So. He lived.

It might not be a good thing.

Benno's left thighbone pushed through the tear in his leggings, but the bleeding seemed to have slowed. Hugo cast his eyes toward

Kateline, who stood at the edge of the small cliff, hands to her sweet breast, tears streaking her cheeks. Elisabeth had collapsed nearby and rocked back and forth on her knees, hands to her face. Several children pressed close, varying degrees of grief and shock marring their expressions.

"Move back," Hugo called. "It's not safe."

He watched long enough to see that Kateline ushered the young ones away from danger. Two or three of them clung to her, their cries reaching his ears.

Benno began to tremble.

"Are you cold?" he asked, looking for something with which to cover the boy.

"Where is Claus?" Benno asked, voice thick between bruised and swollen lips.

Unshed tears stung Hugo's eyes. "He's here. Don't worry."

The child lifted his head to spy his brother motionless upon the rocks, neck tilted at an unnatural angle. "No," he said, struggling to rise.

Hugo pressed a hand to his chest. "Stay where you are. You're hurt."

Benno looked at him, eyes pleading. His mouth moved, but no words came out, and then his small, dirt-smudged face crumpled and a heartrending wail broke the silence.

Hugo cradled the child, stroking his hair. "Shh," he whispered, throat tight with anguish. And what were they going to do to help him?

A sudden shower of stones skittered down the incline. Hugo leaned over the boy, letting his own back shield Benno from the cascade.

"Sorry," Simon said from above.

Hugo watched the young man alter his course, hanging on to bare roots and tufts of sparse grass while he made way down the embankment. Hugo stood by the time Simon reached them. Benno whimpered on the ground at his feet, grief and pain muffling his sobs.

"Can you fix him?" Hugo asked quietly.

Simon's eyes widened, and he shook his head. "No. How can I fix him?"

"You're the monk."

Irritation strained his features. "I was a scribe. I know nothing about healing."

Hugo blew out a breath. "Fine. I'll carry him up."

"You can't carry him like this. What if he starts bleeding again? We need to bind his wounds."

"I thought you didn't know anything about healing."

"I know that much."

Hugo stepped to where Claus lay. Kneeling beside the child, he took his knife and slit the fabric of the boy's tunic. The child's torso felt heavy for one so young when Hugo slid the cloth from underneath.

"Here," he said, holding out the shirt.

Simon took it and returned to Benno.

Hugo lifted Claus. The boy's head dangled from the crook of his arm. He heard a sound and turned to see Simon retching beside a scraggly bush that hugged the cliff face.

Benno lay unconscious.

"Wrap his leg while you can," Hugo said before searching out a suitable route up the precipice. "We can spare him that pain at least."

Kateline met him at the top, eyes red. "Oh, poor child," she said, leaning in to kiss the boy's cool, pale forehead. "And Benno?"

"Alive."

"Praise be to God."

Hugo shook his head. "Don't praise him yet."

Her lips trembled, but she laid a tender hand against Hugo's cheek. "We'll do what we can. And we'll pray."

Hugo felt like the blood had drained from his body. His arms seemed so weak, and Claus so heavy. "I have to bury him."

Kateline nodded. "I sent the children away. I'll help you."

"No." He would do it. Why hadn't he warned the children not to leave camp? He should have issued an order, set up a watch. Anything could happen to them. Why hadn't he thought of it before?

"Simon's with Benno?" she asked.

Hugo nodded. "He'll need my help getting him up."

"Then lay down the child. We'll watch over him."

It was only then he realized Elisabeth sat nearby, knees upright, head on her arms atop them.

He laid the boy beneath a tree where Kateline could sit protected from the heat of the sun and returned to find Simon with Benno, the child's leg wrapped in his brother's tunic.

"Still unconscious?"

Sorrow etched Simon's face. "Yes. He cried out once."

"Let's move him, then."

A litter awaited them at the top. Kateline's doing. Or, rather, she'd told the children to prepare one. Hugo hadn't even thought of that. They placed the boy carefully upon it. A red spot appeared in the bandage, growing bit by bit.

"Claus." Benno's voice crunched in his throat like gravel underfoot.

"Shh." Hugo gave the child's arm a gentle squeeze, realizing as he did so that blood stained his hands.

"Take him back to camp," he said to Simon and Kateline.

They nodded, and together lifted the litter and dragged it away. Elisabeth trundled after them, wiping her tears, leaving Hugo to his solitary task.

"Benno needs more help than we can give," Simon said later.

Hugo had scrubbed the blood, dirt, and sweat from his hands and face, but he felt them there still, like burning nettles upon his skin. "Where is he now?"

"In Elisabeth's care."

Hugo gave him a look.

"She insisted on tending the boy."

Hugo's head throbbed. He rubbed his neck, pushing against the pressure that radiated down his spine. "What do you propose we do for Benno?"

"We need to get him to Geneva. Quickly. There will be healers there."

"And how far is that?"

Simon pulled the map he'd acquired in Heidelberg from his leather pouch and unfolded it. Hugo crouched beside him, watching the young man trace their route with his finger, stopping at a crease in the sheepskin.

"This is roughly our location," Simon said.

Sweat trickled along Hugo's temples.

Simon slid his finger to another spot. "Geneva is here. Two days, perhaps."

"There are no villages along the way? No monasteries?"

Simon shook his head. "No monasteries. And likely no villages of significance."

Hugo sat back on his heels. "Will he live that long?"

"I don't know. He's young. That's in his favor."

"And undernourished." Hugo palmed the sweat from his eyes. "What possessed them to go wandering off in the dark?"

"Benno said he had to relieve himself. He was afraid to go alone." The knot in Simon's throat bobbed up and down when he swallowed. "They found the ridge and walked along it for a distance, fascinated by the moonlight on the valley below. The ground gave way. They had no warning."

Hugo stood and took a deep breath, exhaling slowly. "To Geneva, then. Let's not waste time."

Simon rose beside him. "Nicholas is ready."

A humorless laugh escaped Hugo's chest. "Of that, I'm certain."

Their eyes met and held.

"Thank you, Hugo."

He raised a brow at Simon.

The young man offered a sad smile. "I admire what you've done this morning."

Hugo stood for a moment, heart balking at Simon's words. Finally he clapped the scrawny fellow on the shoulder. "And you, my friend."

That night Hugo sat alone atop a boulder in a meadow several yards distant from the company of children who grew drowsy and quiet. Worms of uncertainty burrowed into his chest.

"You are disturbed," Kateline said as she approached.

He stood at her words. Golden hair, almost white in the moonlight, framed her face in graceful swells like gentle waves upon a tawny river.

"Your presence quiets my soul," he said.

She smiled and raised a hand to stroke his brow. He caught it and pressed it to his lips, then gazed into her tranquil eyes.

"Such heartache in your face," she whispered.

"Benno fares poorly."

"Simon thinks we might reach help by tomorrow afternoon."

Hugo shook his head. "I should have—"

"What?" She offered a compassionate smile. "Hugo, it's not your fault."

"These children—" his voice broke, and he searched the sky. "Who takes care of these children?"

"You do."

He started to protest, but she gripped more tightly the hand that still held hers.

"You do, Hugo. And me. Simon. Nicholas, in his own way. Elisabeth, even. There are many of us. But we can't prevent every misfortune along the way."

"I fear I can't prevent any." He ran a hand through his hair. "I want so much to protect you, Kateline. To protect all of us, but I don't know what I'm doing."

She sighed. "Dear Hugo, do not doubt that our Lord guides and strengthens you."

His eyes must have betrayed him.

Kateline smiled. "Your abilities have been tested and confirmed. I trust you, Hugo. I will always trust you."

He did not mean to embrace her or place his lips upon her hair, but when he did, she leaned against his chest, peaceful in his arms. He held her there, the curves of her body conforming to his.

They stood thus for a long time, Hugo's mind battling with the words on his tongue. Caution lost. "Kateline," he breathed. "Love for you slays me."

She lifted her head, perfect face only inches from his. "Then let my love give you life."

He bent to close the small distance between them. Her mouth tasted like honeyed mead, sweet and intoxicating. She did not pull away, but returned the kiss, setting his blood on fire. He stopped before the flames consumed him. There would never be another like her. Hugo saw only one way to honor the virtue, strength, piety, and uncommon beauty she possessed. The thought surprised him, but he hesitated no more than a moment.

"Wed me, Kateline."

Chapter 8

Mid-July AD 1212, Geneva, Holy Roman Empire

Elisabeth walked beside Kateline along a street that twisted between tall houses. The people of Geneva—elegant ladies with their hair bound up under veils and grim-faced old men with arms crossed in front of their chests—crowded their balconies and windows to watch the column of young commoners. A servant girl grinned and leaned down to touch the upraised hands of those who passed, and a flock of young aristocrats made bawdy comments to the older maidens who giggled with pleasure.

"Couldn't we have stayed on the lakeshore?" Elisabeth shouted above the calls of the crowds and the enthusiastic signing of the children. At least in the countryside she could breathe freely and see for a distance. "I don't like this place."

Kateline's cheeks had gone rosy with excitement. "Have you never been in a city such as this?"

Elisabeth shook her head. Where was Benno? She tried to look behind, but the swarm of children jostled her forward. She'd been beside him until they reached Geneva, but the press of two hundred young crusaders quickly separated them. Surely Simon had managed to stay close to the litter that bore the injured child.

"You shall walk through greater cities before our journey is finished," Kateline said.

"But do the houses never fall down to crush the people below?"

Kateline laughed, but did not answer, for they'd reached the courtyard of the cathedral. The children finished their song. Nicholas began to preach without delay, his voice ringing clear and strong to the people gathered before him.

Kateline dropped to her knees in prayer. She'd said once that she always asked God to grant favor upon the crusaders by giving the listeners good will toward their movement. Elisabeth thought it made little difference. Whether their lords were sympathetic, indifferent, or wholly opposed to them, the people would do whatever they were told.

Hugo squeezed past Elisabeth, brushing her shoulder as he did so. She flinched at his touch, and a shiver ran down her neck. The beast. She could barely tolerate looking at him, so much did he remind her of Wilhelm.

Elisabeth closed her eyes and took a breath to calm the fear and rage that sprang up unbidden. Would that night never cease to plague her?

The sun bore down on her head, and sweat trickled between her shoulder blades. She could smell the tang of unwashed bodies overlaying the stench of decaying refuse and human waste in the streets. How she missed the fragrance of sweet grass and fir. The musty scent of garden soil and fresh mushrooms. The comforting aroma of pottage bubbling over the fire, pungent with cabbage and wild onions.

Her eyes fluttered open, and she squinted against the harsh light of the courtyard.

Ah, there was Simon, dark eyes scanning the square between the buildings. He always watched and listened as though ready to take flight at the first threat. His eyes paused when they encountered hers, and a small, gentle smile touched his lips. She scowled and turned her focus to Nicholas.

After a moment she cast a sideways glance to see if Simon still looked in her direction.

He did not.

She bent low. "Kateline."

The young woman's lips moved in silent prayer for another moment before she crossed herself and looked up.

Elisabeth tucked a rebellious strand of hair behind one ear. "Must we wait until Nicholas finishes before we find help for Benno?"

"Simon will tend to the matter when possible."

Kateline went back to her praying. Elisabeth straightened. *Hmph.* Where had Simon gone now?

He did nothing but skulk off to solitary places at every opportunity. She pictured him loping down the road like a spindly-legged heron along the Rhine.

Bird.

That's what she'd call him. Not to his face, of course, for she had no intention of speaking to him. He riled her with his—

"Elisabeth."

She jumped and let out a squawk. Nicholas faltered for half a moment at the interruption, lobbing an annoyed look her direction.

"Don't scare me like that," she said to Simon, keeping her voice low.

He didn't respond, but started off, indicating she should follow.

His summons had better concern Benno.

Simon made way out of the crowd. It was easy enough to keep him in view while he poked along on his tall, scrawny bird legs. He waited for Elisabeth to catch up at the perimeter of the sloping courtyard, for the square sat on the highest hill of the city.

"Benno?" she asked.

He nodded. "I've instructed Reto and Erich to move him away from the crowd. Would you like to wait with him or come inside with me to seek assistance?"

Why in the name of the Virgin Mary herself would Elisabeth want to do anything with Bird? And come inside where?

Her eyes flitted past his shoulder, framed as it was by the massive doors of the church.

Oh.

The blood went cold in her veins. "I'll take care of the boy."

"Down that street," Bird said, pointing to a cobbled lane beside the church. "Second alley."

Elisabeth pushed through the crowd to reach the road. Even then she had to fight against the flow of would-be onlookers moving toward the commons. "Excuse me. Let me through, *bitte*. Sorry, are you all right?"

At last she broke through to a narrow alley made nearly impassible by the debris and rubbish piled along its edges.

"Go on," she said to the young men with Benno. "I'll care for him now."

"But Simon said—"

"I'll look after him. Join the others." *Where you'll be safely away from me.*

Elisabeth watched the boys go, wondering as they did whether it was too late for them. Too late for all the crusaders who shared the roads and mountains and forests with her. What did it take for a curse to spread to others?

Benno's face had grown pale as death, and he trembled with fever. His breath came in ragged gasps. The sickening sweet odor of infection was discernable even in the fetid alleyway.

It was her fault. It had to be. Why else would Benno and Claus meet with such misfortune?

Elisabeth knelt beside the child. She wiped his forehead with the hem of her apron then took his small hand in hers. *Oh, please let Bird find help.*

§ § §

Simon stepped from the clamor and sunlight of the courtyard into the quiet dimness of Geneva's St. Peter cathedral. It took a moment for his eyes to adjust to the faint light. Beads of perspiration cooled and sent prickles along his skin. He dipped his fingers into the stone font of holy water.

"*In Nomine Patris et Filli et Spiritus Sancti, Amen.*" He made the sign of the cross and lifted his eyes to the vast nave, its columns rising to meet the vaulted ceiling, supports spread like the wings of angels above him.

The church was still under construction and the earthy scent of lime mortar gave him an unexpected longing for the abbey at Villebonne, where tranquility and order formed a secure wall around each day, brick upon brick. Cut off from the stink of the crowds, the odor of his own sweat stood out. Odious past and inglorious present clashed right under his nose.

He approached the altar at the far end of the cathedral, the soft drone of a cleric's voice growing more distinct with each step. The noon office was just concluding in the prayer of mercy. He whispered the words along with the priest.

Lord, Purger of sin and Almoner of grace, we beseech Thee; abandon us not because of our Sins, O Consoler of the sorrowing soul, have mercy on us.

"We haven't a hospital, as such," the cleric said when Simon presented his case.

"Surely there is an infirmary. A healer. Someone trained in the art of medicine."

The man of God looked Simon up and down. "The bishop is not pleased by Nicholas's movement."

"Benno is simply a child."

"We are not to give aid to your cause."

"But surely you can show compassion to an injured boy?"

The young man pressed his lips together. He seemed not much

older than Simon. Had he, too, been forced into the service of the church through a vow made by his parents? In any case, the man hadn't broken that vow by climbing over a forty-foot wall in the dark of night, a leather pouch of smuggled parchments slung across his chest.

"Please," Simon said. "He needs help."

The cleric looked at the stone floor and gave a small shake of his head. Simon despaired until the young man lifted eyes bright with resolve.

"Brother Andri studied with the Benedictines. He'll know what to do."

Simon accepted directions to Brother Andri's house with many thanks and then went to fetch Elisabeth. Together, they wrestled Benno's litter through the streets to the narrow timber-framed townhouse where Brother Andri resided and worked along with three other monks. Why Elisabeth had dismissed Erich and Reto, he had no idea—and she'd balked when he wanted to find other crusaders to help—but she'd been adamant, and he didn't have the energy to argue with her. Or the time.

The monk said little while he tended Benno's wounds.

"Will the boy live?" Simon asked Brother Andri.

The monk rinsed the blood from his hands in a shallow basin, wiped them dry on his tunic, and frowned. "If God so wills it."

"But you set the bone," Elisabeth said, voice tight. "Surely he'll recover."

Brother Andri shrugged one beefy shoulder. "We can only pray now."

Benno lay unconscious from the pain of the man's manipulations, breath coming in shallow bursts. The acrid scent of vinegar used to cleanse the wound and the stench of a comfrey poultice hung heavy in the air. Elisabeth had already taken up a damp rag to wipe the perspiration and tears from the child's face.

"We need to find Nicholas," Simon said to her. "The boy requires time to heal."

"I'm staying here." She didn't bother to look at him.

Simon cast a glance round the open hall where the sick and dying curled upon rush-filled pallets. Despite the oppressive heat of the room, a chill ran down his spine. "I'll return."

She didn't respond, but murmured words in Benno's ear. A prayer, perhaps.

Locating Nicholas proved more difficult than he expected, but at last he found him lounging in the shade at the confluence of the Rhone River and *Lac de Lausanne*—the large lake upon whose shores Geneva perched. The setting sun hung low in the sky, its summer glow turning the waters of the Rhone to liquid gold.

"We'll have to delay our departure while Benno recovers."

Nicholas used the back of one hand to wipe the juice of a pear from his chin. "No. We move on tomorrow."

"He can't travel."

"Then he stays behind."

"And who will care for him?"

Nicholas finished off the core of the pear and tossed the stem into the water before focusing his dark brown gaze on Simon. "You've taken him to the monks, have you not? Let them worry with him."

"He's a boy, Nicholas. We can't leave him."

"There are ten thousand behind us. He can join one of the other companies when they pass through."

Simon bit the inside of his lip. "I don't know . . ."

"Do you expect God's campaign to wait? Bruno might never recover."

"Benno." Simon sank down beside him. Prayers aside, Benno probably wouldn't survive. That his leg was streaked red and the wound rank with infection was bad enough, but why did the child wheeze and cough so? Brother Andri had bled him, but balancing the humours was always a precarious business. Still. "There would be no campaign without the children you're so hasty to abandon."

Nicholas's eyes flashed like lightning in a storm. "God called me to *lead* his army of innocents. It's people like you and Hugo and Kateline who've been entrusted to care for them. What would happen if I let every tragedy divert us?"

He made a good argument. Who was Simon to question Nicholas, callous as the child might be? Hadn't God appointed Nicholas to lead the crusade? Simon swallowed back his irritation. "You're right. But I can't bear to see Benno left behind."

Nicholas motioned away three approaching children and leaned back on his elbows. "There might be another way."

Simon cocked an eyebrow at him.

Nicholas steadied his gaze. "The parchments."

Simon's heart snapped along for a beat or two while the meaning of Nicholas' words sank in. "You—you want to *sell* them?"

Nicholas nodded. "You said they're worth a lot of coin. We could pay a physician to accompany us."

"The manuscripts are worth far more than one man's wages." Simon's cheeks flushed hot with panic. "Surely no one here could pay their worth."

Nicholas sat up to lean close. "You would rather Bruno die because you might find a wealthier tradesman elsewhere to line your pockets?"

Simon drew back as if he'd been stung. "No, of course not." Did he?

No.

Then why did he feel reluctant to sell the manuscripts if doing so would help Benno?

Because helping Benno is up to God now.

He shook his head. "I've never contemplated peddling the holy texts for a price. I copied them in secret, at risk of punishment, because I craved their living words."

Nicholas moved closer still. "Give me the parchments, Simon."

His voice sounded smooth as a strummed lute. "I'll keep them safe and only sell them when necessary."

"I think we should talk to Hugo first." Did Nicholas's eyes narrow? "If selling the manuscripts will preserve Benno's life or the lives of the children, then I will gladly surrender them. Otherwise, I fear you act in haste."

Nicholas sighed. "Very well. Don't mention it to Hugo. I'll discuss it with him myself if I decide to do so."

He said nothing after that, but only sat with his arms crossed over his chest, a frown upon his face. Simon rose and walked away, the leather pouch tight under his arm.

He came upon Hugo and Kateline gathering the children, bedding them down for the night.

"Surely the townsfolk will take them in?" Simon said.

Hugo only looked at him before instructing two of the older girls to lead the younger to a grassy hillside above. Then he moved on, calling directions to the others as he went.

Kateline shook out a blanket, pieces of dry grass flying off in every direction like bees disturbed at the hive. "He wants them close." Her eyes followed the stocky young man, a gentle glow upon her face. "He feels responsible for what happened to the twins."

She smiled. "He has the heart of a noble knight, don't you think?"

Ah, so she was in love.

Simon felt a twinge of regret. Had he ever hoped for more than Kateline's sisterly affections? Perhaps. But for so long now she'd been mother to them all.

He watched Hugo.

Maybe not to all of us.

"Hugo." Simon strode after him. "We need to speak."

Hugo lifted one powerful arm, indicating to a boy of about sixteen where he should take the group assigned to him then turned his attention to Simon. "The child?"

"The bone's been set." No need to say more. Only a miracle would save Benno.

Hugo nodded, face grim. His eyes swept the nearby hillocks like a shepherd scanning his flock. Twilight wrapped itself around them, a blanket of cool tranquility.

"Nicholas wants me to sell the manuscripts," Simon continued. "To provide for the children."

The muscle at Hugo's jaw tightened, and he turned toward the lake. Nicholas was lost in the shadows, or perhaps no longer there, but Hugo remained rigid.

"The thought of parting with them grieves me," Simon said, "but I told him I would do so if you thought it necessary."

Hugo swung his head back to Simon. "No. Though that day may come, you need not offer them yet." He looked through the dusky light into Simon's eyes. "Keep them close."

Simon nodded his understanding.

Hugo took a breath to speak, but seemed to think better of it. Simon waited a moment, then dipped his chin and started to move off.

"I fear the worst for the children behind us." Hugo's words came low and strained.

Simon halted. Turned.

"The runner is late," Hugo said. "I'm afraid it was unwise to separate into companies."

Simon looked down at his too-long feet.

"Ten thousand of us, Simon."

"That number gnaws at me, too."

"I'd hoped many villages would line our route across the Alps, but your map says otherwise."

"We should talk to Nicholas."

"He won't know what to do."

"He's been divinely appointed. Surely God has given him a

plan."

"Ah, yes." Hugo scratched his neck and lifted one corner of his mouth. "Such as selling your manuscripts."

A night bug darted toward Simon's face. He waved it away as he stalked off. "Good eve."

"Will you read to me sometime?"

Simon looked over his shoulder. He didn't take Hugo for a religious man, but the request pleased him. "I will."

A cool breeze came in off the lake to tug at Simon's hair with mischievous fingers, like Conon in a playful mood.

Where had the boy gotten to? Simon hadn't seen him since morning. He was tempted to fret, but no, someone would have said something if the child had gone missing.

So many things to worry about. So many children.

He met Elisabeth on his way back to Brother Andri's. He spoke to her, but she pushed past him without acknowledgement.

"Elisabeth," he said again and caught her by the wrist.

She jerked her arm from his grasp and spun on him, eyes hard, face contorted.

"Benno?" Simon said. "Is he improved?"

Like a flower wilting under the noonday sun, her shoulders sagged and her colorful head drooped. "Dead. An hour ago."

She swayed, and he reached out to steady her. She stiffened at his touch. Though he half expected it, she didn't slap away his hand.

"Go rest," he said, and lowered his arm. He should offer words of comfort, but had none to give. "I'll see to him."

She looked at him with something like bitterness in her green eyes. Had her face been so gaunt when she joined them?

"When do we march?" she asked.

"Tomorrow, I suppose. Nicholas is eager to move on."

"And how far until Jerusalem?"

How long until I can be rid of you, she might as well have asked. Though he should have been used to it by now, the coldness in her voice took him by surprise.

"Weeks, still, at least." Nicholas had refused to tell him how he expected to secure passage across the Mediterranean, but they were headed to the Italian coastal city of Genoa. From there, another fortnight or more.

Lines of worry crossed Elisabeth's brow, but she said nothing, only sighed and turned away. She looked so forlorn that Simon found himself trying one last time.

"Elisabeth."

She stopped.

"Will you sit with me a while?" Her blank stare made him fidget in place. "I—I have more supper than I can eat." He lifted a small loaf he held in one hand. "We could share it."

Her lips parted in surprise before a scowl took over. "Eat it yourself, and quit pestering me with your company."

She hurried away, bare feet silent on the cobblestones.

Chapter 9

July AD 1212, the Alps, Holy Roman Empire

Simon awoke with a rock lodged against his back. Perplexing, since there hadn't been one there last night when he went to sleep in the pouring rain. He cracked open one eye and looked behind him. Ah, Conon. Curled tight as a newborn kitten beneath a sodden blanket. Wringing out his own waterlogged mantle, Simon covered the boy, then made way to the small wagon to ration out breakfast. The old draft horse they'd been given to pull the cart stood close by, shaking her head in protest now and then.

"Seems like autumn, doesn't it, girl?" Simon glanced up the hill. Clouds hovered so low he couldn't see beyond the alpine slope on which they camped. "Makes me shiver," he said. Not from the drizzle or the coolness of the morning, but at the thought of the high mountains they had yet to cross.

A deep voice interrupted his worrying. "Enjoying a bit of conversation with your horse?"

Simon turned to see Hugo, rain running in rivulets down his face and dripping from his fingers. Mud was slick upon his leggings from knee to foot. The humor faded from Hugo's eyes, and he nodded toward the children. "Let them sleep. We can breakfast later."

"Are we not traveling today?" Simon asked.

Hugo shook his head. "The clouds hang heavy, and the path is slippery. I fear the children will struggle too much for any ground they'd gain."

Simon glanced at the cart, then back to Hugo. "Our provisions will soon spoil in this rain."

"You don't think we should wait for the weather to turn?"

"Geneva gave us no help. Returning would be folly. Our only hope is to reach Mont Cenis Abbey before our supplies run out."

Hugo lifted his chin. "Very well. Let's get the children going."

Nicholas was not happy with their judgment. "I thought I was in charge," he said when Simon told him what they'd decided.

Simon swallowed the retort on his tongue. "My apologies, Nicholas, but our need for food leaves us no alternative. We must reach the monastery in good time, and in these conditions it will take us longer than we hoped."

The boy turned his back to Simon. "At least find me some dry clothes before we start."

He chuckled at Nicholas's humor, but the boy cast a villainous look in his direction. Simon raised his eyebrows. "Nothing is dry," he said after a moment. "And even if it were, do you not realize you would be soaked through immediately?"

Nicholas drew close. "Don't speak to me as if I were a child."

Simon only dipped his head to acknowledge the words before Nicholas walked away.

They made slow progress that morning. Rain dripped from Simon's nose and ran into his ears. The crusaders grew ill tempered, snipping and snarling at each other if they bothered to talk at all. Half a dozen times Hugo called several older boys forward to dislodge the cart when its wheels sank into the mud.

Around mid-afternoon a voice called out from behind Simon where he slogged along the road.

"Hugo," Artur said, running past Simon to catch up with the young man.

Hugo gave Simon an uneasy look before turning his attention to the boy.

"Hannah stumbled," the youth said, wiping the water from his eyes with his good hand. "I think her ankle is broken."

It was. Nothing like Benno's injury, praise the saints. Simon immobilized it as he'd seen the monks do, and Hugo placed her in the cart near the soggy bread.

"It hurts," Hannah whined.

"I know." Kateline reached over the side of the wagon and took the child's hand. "But you'll feel better soon. I'll walk with you. Can you sing a song for me?"

"I don't want to."

Kateline smiled, her lips stiff and purple with chill. "Then I will sing for you."

An hour later they started up a steep incline, the mare snorting and grunting in resistance. Simon commiserated with the poor old thing while Hugo coaxed her along.

"How much farther?" Conon asked, the closest he'd come to complaining.

"As far as we can go before nightfall," Simon said. "Here, take my hand." He smiled down at the boy who put frosty fingers in Simon's own cold grasp, then shuddered from tip to tail. Simon chuckled, but a frantic squeal swallowed the sound.

In horror, he glimpsed the scrabbling feet of the mare. Heard the moan of the cart rolling backwards. Hannah opened her mouth to shriek, eyes wide with terror, but the screams of the mare drowned her out. Mud flew from under the beast's thrashing hooves as the other children scrambled away in fear.

"Kateline, watch out!" Simon cried, and hurled Conon to the safety of the grass.

Kateline stumbled, fell. The wagon slid from the path, one heavy wheel lodging against a boulder with a loud crack. Simon couldn't see her, hidden as she was between the cart and a tumble of scraggly rocks, though he could just make out the blue of her tunic between the wheel spokes.

The mare let out one last high-pitched screech, then shuddered and snorted. At last she calmed.

Hugo rushed to the far side of the cart, Simon on his heels.

"Kateline, are you hurt?" Hugo said.

"I'm fine." Her voice came from behind the wagon wheels.

Hugo lifted the young woman to her feet, the blue tunic torn and black with mire, splotches of mud upon her face and hair. He pulled her to his chest. Whispered something in her ear before he released her.

Simon shook from the aftermath of fear. "She's not fine. The wagon barely missed her."

"I'm all right," Kateline insisted. "Was Hannah harmed?"

Simon checked the girl in the wagon. "Only frightened." And squalling like a cat in heat.

Hugo pulled his concerned gaze from Kateline to several boys standing nearby. "Put the cart in the rear of the company," he said. "Forbid anyone to walk beside it."

The rain never let up. Come nightfall, Simon sat with Nicholas at one of the pitiful, sputtering fires, and listened to the boy grouse about the weather. As if no one else suffered its effects.

"We have no choice," Simon said. "Mont Cenis is our best hope now. If we turn back, we might not be able to breach the pass for days. At least the ground grows rockier and less muddy as the elevation rises."

The boy-leader only scowled at him.

"Nicholas," Hugo said, towering above the two of them.

The child peered up, his hair plastered in tight swirls against his forehead. "What is it now?"

Hugo seemed to swallow his irritation. "The risks of this journey weigh heavily upon me—more so each day. It's time we discuss your plans for reaching Palestine. That way Simon and I can strategize our needs and—"

"You know our plans."

"I know we're heading to Genoa on the coast." He glanced at Simon. "Simon's told me that much. But even he doesn't know how you expect to get us across the Mediterranean."

"We'll walk," Nicholas said.

Simon resisted the urge to roll his eyes heavenward at Nicholas's insolence.

Hugo dropped down on his haunches. "I'm not in the mood for jokes. Simon and I can fashion a plan if you don't have one."

Nicholas's brows came together. "I'm serious. No, listen," he said when Hugo's lips thinned. A smile eased across his young face. "The Lord has given me a vision. He will part the waters of the sea for me just as he did for Moses. We'll walk, Hugo."

Simon felt his jaw drop. "What?"

"A vision?" Hugo's nostrils flared.

Nicholas nodded.

"A vision's not good enough," Hugo said, voice barely controlled.

"Do you question God?"

"I question *you*."

Nicholas's arm shot out, and his palm met Hugo's cheek with a crack.

Simon reached for the boy, but Hugo snatched Nicholas's tiny wrist between thick fingers. They tightened in a squeeze. "Don't ever do that again."

"Kateline believes me," Nicholas said. "If you don't have faith, you don't belong with us."

"Enough," Simon said with more strength than he felt.

Hugo snarled and released Nicholas, leaving the boy to sulk and rub his wrist.

Simon woke two mornings later to more of the maddening drizzle. He prayed briefly then nudged Conon with his foot. "Come on, you lazy boy," he teased. "Help me distribute our bread." Porridge, he should have called it, soaked as it was.

When Conon ignored him, Simon squatted down and placed a hand on the boy's back, feeling every bone beneath the thin clothes and blanket. The lad trembled. Simon rolled him over, put knuckles to Conon's hot brow, then lowered his head and fought back tears.

§ § §

"Simon," Kateline said, "you can't keep carrying Conon. Hugo says he can ride in the cart alongside Hannah."

"Thank you, but no." The child nestled against Simon's chest, arms around Simon's neck, head on his shoulder. "There, there, *mon petit*," he whispered as he walked. "You'll be all right. We'll find help for you soon."

They would. They had to.

Kateline and Elisabeth checked the others when they stopped at noonday, only to find four more whose eyes dimmed with fever.

Hugo ran a hand through his hair when he learned the news. "By the saints, I don't know what to do. We've got to keep moving."

Kateline laid a hand on his arm. "The children cannot go any farther."

"Our supplies are low. We should have reached Mont Cenis by now. The rain..." He looked into her eyes. "We can't afford to camp while we wait for them to recover."

"Would you have Simon carry them all?"

Simon looked from them to Conon. The boy shivered, his small teeth clicking together like rattling bones. *Lord, Purger of sin and*

Almoner of grace, we beseech Thee...

Hugo lifted his eyes to the low clouds, his jaw tight.

Kateline stepped closer. "Let's think together," she said, voice soft.

"Put them all in the cart," Elisabeth snapped.

Simon had forgotten she was there.

Hugo scowled, and his voice dripped with disdain. "And what of the food?"

She sighed. "There are two hundred of us. I think we can carry it."

Hugo's face reddened. Elisabeth tossed her braid over her shoulder and walked past him.

In short order, they dispensed the food, wrung out several blankets, and loaded the children into the wagon beneath them. Except for Conon. Simon refused to let the lad out of his arms. By the time they stopped for the night, seven more had succumbed to fever.

The next day Simon bound Conon to his back with a blanket because the child had lost the strength to hold on. The ground seemed to tilt when Simon stood. He put out a hand to steady himself, closed his eyes, and planted his feet firmly in the pine needles until the dizziness passed.

"Don't your muscles sting under the boy's weight?" Elisabeth asked.

"I won't put Conon in the cart to worsen with the rest of the children."

The rain finally stopped mid-morning, though clouds lingered. Such a relief to feel the air lighten. In fact, Simon might have been elated had Hugo not approached with a grim expression.

"Things don't look good," Hugo said.

"When we reach the monastery, we'll find provisions and herbs to help those with fever."

"How soon?"

"I—I'm not sure. I can't remember any landmarks from the map to indicate how close we might be." He reached for the leather pouch at his waist.

"Never mind. Let's just keep moving."

§ § §

That evening Simon hunted from tree to tree for fallen limbs that had been spared the rain by thick fir needles. Other children fueling their own fires had picked the area almost clean, but he found a few missed branches.

He gathered three small limbs—hardly more than sticks—and turned to make his way back to Conon.

Kuno stood in his path. Though the youngster looked on the verge of puberty when he first joined the movement, his small muscles had wasted away in the weeks since.

The boy sniffed and rubbed his nose with a grimy hand. "Dead."

"What?" The kindling spilled from Simon's hands. He'd left Conon not five minutes ago, breathing. "No," he said in a voice he hardly recognized as his own. A great emptiness seized him. "No…"

The boy nodded. "She cried for her Mama before she went." He hiccupped, and tears began to flow.

Simon grabbed the boy's shoulder more forcefully than he meant to do. "She? Who died?"

"The girl with the limp. I don't even know her name." Tears dripped down the boy's face. "I should have known her name."

Relief almost dropped Simon to his knees. "It's all right." He patted the boy on the back, appalled that he could find relief in knowing one child died while another still lived. "Let's take this wood to Conon's fire then we'll bury the girl."

Simon saw to Conon and then went to inform Hugo and Kateline. "The fever took Anna," he said, for that was her name.

Hugo turned anguished eyes toward him. "Gone?"

"They just found her." He wiped a hand over his face and looked across the grass to the fire where Conon lay.

Kateline saw his concern. "How's the boy?" she asked, her voice as weary as her countenance. Her exhaustion didn't prevent her rising to tend to the bleak matter at hand.

Simon shrugged and shook his head. "He's not spoken for a full day."

Elisabeth joined them, lips pale with strain. "Eleven more down with fever."

Forty-nine, now.

"We must get to the monastery," Simon said through an aching throat. "They can help us."

Hugo's face twisted. "And how are we going to do that? There's no more room in the cart and not enough strong ones to carry the sick. We can't leave them behind."

Elisabeth glowered at Hugo. "Will you simply watch these children die? Do *something*."

The muscle along Hugo's jaw pulsed. He tipped his face to the sky.

Simon did likewise and prayed for wisdom.

The mare.

His heart leapt. "The mare."

"What?" Hugo said. "What about her?"

"Unhitch her. Send riders ahead to the monastery. Perhaps the monks will be able to return with help."

At first light, two boys left on the horse for the monastery and Nicholas headed up the path with the healthy crusaders—those still able to walk.

Simon, Kateline, and Hugo remained behind to nurse the sick. Nicholas seemed glad to be rid of them, but maybe that was only Simon's imagination.

"I'm staying too," Elisabeth said, her chin jutting forward in defiance. "I won't leave these ailing children."

Hugo sighed. "Just go. Nicholas can use your help."

Simon wondered if Elisabeth could tell that Hugo simply didn't want her close by.

She glared at Hugo for a moment before grabbing an empty bucket. "I'm staying." She headed in the direction of a swollen brook that splashed down the mountainside.

Hugo's brows met low above his nose, and Simon thought he heard a small growl deep in the young man's chest, but he said nothing. It was just as well that Elisabeth remained with them. Without the help of a hundred or more young workers, the task of keeping the fires going, distributing water, and wiping blood-tinged sputum from small chins kept the four of them moving at a frenzied pace.

"Here, let me help you," Simon said to Kateline. She struggled to pull a child closer to the warmth of the fire.

"Thank you."

Simon grabbed the foot of the child's thin blanket while Kateline took the head. Together they eased the boy over. Kateline coughed, let down her end, coughed again. Cleared her throat.

Simon didn't like the sound. "Are you all right?"

"It's nothing." She managed a smile through her fatigue. "Only the damp air sitting heavy in my chest."

Two more crusaders died that afternoon.

Chapter 10

Late July AD 1212, the Alps, Holy Roman Empire
Night closed quickly upon them there on the mountain. The gloom of low-hanging clouds muffled the gasps and moans of children who lay fighting to survive. Hugo took Kateline's hand and led her to a secluded spot.

"If only for a few moments," he said, "let's pretend there is no sickness, no mountains, no one but us."

Her fingers were icy. He drew her into the warmth of the blanket around his shoulders, settling his chin upon her flaxen hair when she pressed her cheek against his chest.

"I'm so cold," she said, voice coarse with exhaustion.

"Don't think about it. Imagine we're in the Holy Lands. Simon says Jerusalem will be hot as a baker's oven."

She pressed closer, snuggling into him like a rabbit in a burrow.

"See?" he said. "Already I feel you warming."

So relaxed did she become that he felt if he should release her, she would fall to the ground. "Kateline?"

She didn't answer. When he loosened his hold, her legs buckled, and she slumped against him. He lowered her to the ground. "Kateline," he cried, and put a hand to her moist, hot brow. Her head rocked on the spongy grass when he gently shook her, hoping for some response. Nothing.

"God," he whispered from a throat so tight he could barely swallow. It was the only prayer he could form.

Or perhaps it was an accusation.

A shrill voice cried out. "What have you done?"

Elisabeth stood at the edge of the clearing, gaping at Kateline's unconscious form on the ground.

What did she *think* he'd done? "She's ill." He scooped Kateline into his arms and rushed past Elisabeth, heading to the light of a low-burning fire.

"If you've so much as laid a hand on her, I'll—"

"Quiet," he ordered, in no mood for her sharp tongue.

Elisabeth followed him to the campsite. "Put her down," she snapped. "See if you can find extra blankets. And bring more wood."

She swung her blanket from her shoulders to Kateline's torso, cradling the sick young woman's head in her lap. Hugo hurried away.

What had he been thinking? He shouldn't have allowed Kateline to tend the diseased children. Why did he not send her with Nicholas?

Because he wanted her nearby.

Hugo groaned at his selfishness. What had he done, indeed.

He retrieved his blanket from the spot where only minutes before he'd held her close, using her slim, perfect body to comfort himself.

Blinking back tears and willing himself to be useful, he looked around for firewood. Nothing at hand, and he knew from earlier foraging there was precious little in the vicinity. A tree sprang out of the rocks nearby, a misshapen, ugly thing, growing more horizontal than upright. Sparse greenery dotted its lower boughs, but the bare upper branches scrabbled toward the sky like dead men's bones.

He sprang to the rocks, his right foot barely touching before he launched himself left toward the trunk and slammed into it with a grunt, then pulled himself up the twisted torso of the tree. He climbed, ignoring the scrapes and scratches, thankful for them, even, as they kept him focused on the mission rather than on the wavy-haired maiden unconscious by the fire.

Two or three of the topmost limbs broke off easily in his hand, but they'd burn to ashes in a few minutes. What he needed was that thick bough over there. He straddled a lower branch, locked his fingers around the one he wanted, and pulled on it to no avail.

Kateline lay shivering in the night, and he couldn't even defeat a dead branch.

Scuttling higher to reposition himself, he kicked at the bough, felt it crack, and then yanked as if he had an enemy by the throat. The wood fractured. One more powerful tug, and it fell to the ground, leaving him breathing heavily with the fight still in him.

Kateline can't die. He punched the limb on which he perched.

I won't let that happen. I can't. Again his fist smashed into the wood, the pain a welcome penance for his powerlessness.

Hugo looked to the sky. Not one glimmer of hope twinkling in the heavens. He swung himself down, landing with a thud on the sparse grass and gravel, picked up the blanket and the wood, and headed back to the firelight.

Kateline choked and sputtered against the thickness in her lungs while Elisabeth held her upright, then finally gasped for breath and quieted.

Elisabeth's eyes narrowed when Hugo offered the blanket. She snatched it from his hand before he tossed the small branches into the fire. He placed one end of the larger piece into the flames. If fed into the fire bit by bit, it would last the better part of two days.

"Go check on the others," Elisabeth said. "Leave us be."

Hugo ignored her and knelt beside Kateline. All he wanted was to cradle Kateline in his arms, but what good would that do?

Simon stepped into the circle of firelight. "Not Kateline, too?" His eyes reflected Hugo's own fear. "Is she bad?"

Hugo rubbed his neck with one hand. "*Ja*, I think so."

The breath escaped Simon's bony chest. "We'll pray," he said, as if that would solve anything.

Hugo eased himself down and leaned against a rock. Kateline rested peacefully for now. Elisabeth moved to sit on the other side of the fire, eyeing him with disgust.

Simon brought a cup of water and a rag.

Hugo dipped the cloth into the cup, squeezed away the excess, and used it to moisten Kateline's fevered lips.

"What'd you do to your hand?" Elisabeth asked, suspicion in her voice.

He looked at it, knuckles bloody and swollen from pounding on the tree like an imbecile. "Nothing." He jerked his chin toward the fire pit. "It happened when I got the wood."

Elisabeth continued to glare at him. "Why don't you go?" she finally asked. "I can take care of her."

"Thank you, but I'm fine," he said, settling back against the boulder.

"You misunderstand me. I don't want you here. Kateline doesn't want you here, either."

His brow furrowed. He leaned toward Kateline's sleeping form, the cool evening air slipping past the open neck of his tunic.

He turned at Elisabeth's sharp intake of breath.

"Give that back," she said.

What's gotten into the girl now?

She stood. Stepped close, teeth clenched. "I said give it back."

Simon spoke up. "What are you talking about?"

Her eyebrows met low over her nose and she pointed with one long finger. "He stole Kateline's medallion."

Hugo lifted a hand to the pendant at his throat. Rubbed its raised surface between his fingers. He looked at Simon. "Kateline gave it to me."

Elisabeth trembled, fists clenched beside her. "You vulgar, lying brute."

Hugo rose to his feet, heat in his chest.

"Elisabeth," Simon said, "what's gotten into you?"

"Me?" She rounded on him. "Don't you care we have a thief in our midst?" Her eyes flashed at Hugo. "Take that off your filthy neck. It belongs to Kateline."

The muscle along Hugo's jaw tightened. "I don't know what you think I'd gain by stealing it. I told you, Kateline gave the medallion to me."

"She'd never do that," Elisabeth said, trembling. "It's the thing she holds most dear." She faced Simon. "Look at his hand. He took it from her by force."

And there it was, a bloody testament, but it wasn't true. Simon's eyes lifted from Hugo's hand to his face.

Hugo ran his fingers through his hair. Shook his head. He and Kateline weren't going to say anything to the others yet, but—"It was a gift to symbolize our betrothal."

Simon and Elisabeth both gasped in surprise.

"You're lying," Elisabeth said. "She'd never marry the likes of you."

Simon's voice came soft amid the hostility. "He's telling the truth, Elisabeth."

She rounded on him. "How would you know?"

He looked at her. "Can't you see what's between them?"

Hugo flushed. *So it's that apparent.*

Elisabeth's mouth hung open then snapped shut in a wavering grimace. Hugo didn't care. And he didn't bother to watch her stomp away.

The next dawn saw no improvement in their situation, save no one else had died.

A headache pounded against the inside of Hugo's skull, but despite his weariness, he felt strong and very much alive. Too much so, perhaps. He deserved worse for letting Kateline fall ill.

He, Simon, and Elisabeth spent another day tending the sick, fighting back dread, and wondering out loud when help would arrive. At all times, Hugo and Elisabeth kept their distance from one another. Simon spent as much time as he could over Conon. Elisabeth hung close to Kateline as if guarding her from Hugo.

Their stores dwindled, though they weren't much to begin with. Soggy, blackening bread.

Come evening the three of them gathered around the fire where the lovely young woman lay. Simon had moved Conon nearby.

"No matter what you think," Elisabeth said to Simon, "Kateline is not promised to that swine."

"Elisabeth," Simon said in a stern whisper. "He can hear you."

"What do I care?" She looked Hugo's way. He met her gaze. "When Kateline recovers, she'll tell the truth, and he'll run off with his tail between his legs like the mangy cur that he is."

Hugo pressed his lips together, exhaling hard through his nose, but said nothing at her taunts.

Simon ignored her, too, feeding a bit of bread to Conon with a shaky hand. The child said not a word, but snuggled into Simon's arms when he finished, drifting back to sleep.

"Are you sick?" Elisabeth asked Simon.

He looked up, then back to Conon. "I'm fine."

Sure and Simon's face was pale, and dark circles hung beneath his eyes. The same could be said for Elisabeth. For that matter, Hugo doubted he looked any better.

"You're not fine," Elisabeth said.

Simon looked up. "And what would it matter to you?"

A corner of Hugo's mouth lifted at Simon's pluck.

Sometime later, Hugo made the rounds checking on children, then stirred the fire to new life, and settled in beside Kateline. Soon Simon's voice broke the silence of the night.

"And we know that in all things God works for the good of those who love him, who have been called according to his purpose."

Hugo's eyes snapped up from where he sat stroking his beloved's brow, her head on his lap.

Simon's lips quivered into a smile and he looked back to the parchment he held unfolded between wobbly hands. "What, then, shall we say in response to this? If God is for us, who can be against us? He who did not spare his own Son, but gave him up for us all—how will he not also, along with him, graciously give us all things?"

Warmth spread through Hugo's chest. "Is that really the Scriptures you read?"

Simon nodded.

"The very words of God?"

"Yes."

"May I see?"

Simon eased himself up from beside Conon's sleeping form and closed the short distance between them. Elisabeth, who had been dozing before Simon spoke, sat up on one elbow. Simon knelt next to Hugo and pointed to the marks on the stretched and treated sheepskin.

Hugo swallowed and moistened his lips with his tongue. "Please continue."

Simon read silently for a moment then began again. "Who shall separate us from the love of Christ? Shall trouble or hardship or persecution or famine or nakedness or danger or sword? As it is written: 'For your sake we face death all day long; we are considered as sheep to be slaughtered.' No, in all these things we are more than conquerors through him who loved us."

Doubt covered Elisabeth's bewildered face. She probably hadn't known about the manuscripts.

Simon continued, but he looked neither at the parchment nor at Hugo or Elisabeth. To the sky he turned, reciting the rest of the passage from memory. "For I am convinced that neither death nor life, neither angels nor demons, neither the present nor the future, nor any powers, neither height nor depth, nor anything else in all creation, will be able to separate us from the love of God that is in Christ Jesus our Lord."

Kateline smiled in her sleep.

§ § §

Hugo woke suddenly. Clouds scudded across the sky, obscuring the moon. A breeze made his scalp tingle, and an unnamed fear rose in his chest. Did something move on the path beside which they camped?

Elisabeth had awakened, too, and her rasping throat pushed out terrified words that creaked like wagon wheels. "Death angels."

At the warning, Hugo jumped to his feet in front of Kateline, dagger in hand, searching the darkness. The night congealed into hooded figures that bore down upon them in eerie silence. Hugo's blood ran cold.

Simon sat up and looked over his shoulder. He turned back to Hugo, a smile on his ghostly face. "Praise God, the monks have arrived."

Chapter 11

Late July AD 1212, Mont Cenis Abbey, Holy Roman Empire
Hugo hit the rough-cut stone of the abbey's courtyard wall with his fist, thankful for the pain that coursed through his already injured hand. It redirected a small portion of the anguish that plagued him. He pressed his forehead against the damp rock so that it threatened to puncture his skin, and thought about all they had lost.

Seventeen children died after reaching the monastery. The monks said they were too far-gone upon their arrival. Several more had fallen ill, though Hugo hoped they might survive with the care they received in this place. Simon, sick indeed, lay dying in one of the chambers, and Kateline—

Hugo increased the pressure against his forehead until a trickle of blood ran down to mix with his tears. He wiped them away then stared at the stain on his fingers in the early morning light. How much blood did he have on his hands? How many young souls had he led into the mountains to die?

They still hadn't heard from the companies behind them.

§ § §

Elisabeth paced at the foot of Kateline's bed in a small room off the main courtyard of the monastery. A monk gathered the bowl, cloths, and potions he'd used to tend the sick young woman.

"Linger here no more than a few minutes," he said to Elisabeth before leaving them alone.

Elisabeth moved to Kateline's side and knelt down on the edge of the bed, taking the young woman's hand in her own. "You're looking better."

Kateline tried to smile. "I do not think I shall recover."

"You will."

"How are the others?"

"Doing very well." It wasn't true. Few of the afflicted would leave the monastery. But she didn't tell Kateline this. Or that Simon shook with fever, unaware of his surroundings. That Conon wasn't expected to make it through the hour.

"And what of Hugo? Is he well?"

Elisabeth spoke through clenched teeth. "He is."

Kateline raised her head, fear in her eyes. "You're not being truthful. He's sick, isn't he?" She struggled against the blankets tucked around her.

Elisabeth gently pushed Kateline back against the mattress. "No. He is healthy."

"What troubles you, then?"

Elisabeth feared to speak lest the news upset her. "Hugo stole your medallion and claims it symbolizes your betrothal."

Kateline relaxed and smiled. "We weren't going to say anything yet."

"It's true?"

"Of course, it's true. Don't you rejoice with us?"

Elisabeth felt as if she'd been struck. "I—I can scarcely believe it."

Kateline smiled again. When she spoke, her voice slurred from the potions the monk had used. "I love him. I've promised to marry him when our crusade ends in victory."

"You don't have to give into him, Kateline. He is wicked and cruel."

Kateline pushed herself up on one arm and wrapped the other around Elisabeth's shoulders. "No," she said, barely above a whisper. "He is noble and kind."

Dazed, Elisabeth nearly forgot to breathe. She inhaled. Shook her head. "But he stole your medallion."

"He stole my *affections*. The medallion I gave freely."

Elisabeth leaned back. "No."

"Yes."

"But he's—"

"—he is my betrothed." Kateline's eyelids fluttered, heavy with exhaustion. "And I pray you will come to see his good heart, my friend."

Never. But Elisabeth didn't say so, for Kateline was overcome by an episode of coughing. When the fit passed, she sank into a drugged sleep.

Elisabeth stood and stepped to the doorway. She paused to look back at Kateline, peaceful now on the straw bed. The moon shone through a window high in the opposite wall—surprising her with its appearance after so many nights away—and cast a glow over Kateline's face and golden hair.

Elisabeth returned to the mattress, bent low to place a kiss upon Kateline's cheek, and then slipped out of the room.

Several monks walked noiselessly across the open space of the courtyard, off to the chapel for Compline—the last holy service of the day. She hoped they would pray for the children whose lives were still in question. Perhaps the purity of the monks would outweigh her curse.

A movement near the wall caught Elisabeth's eye. Hugo. Like a half-wit, he stood facing the wall, forehead against the stones.

She clamped her mouth shut and bit back the insults. The monks had been adamant—silence would reign through the night. Far be it from her to stir the wrath of a disapproving God.

She retired with the other young women and girls, and spent the next day and a half tending the sick as the monks would allow, careful to follow their instructions. She coveted their prayers in the hope they would prevent her curse from causing more trouble. And perhaps her efforts found fruit, for slowly Bird and the others began to improve.

Elisabeth sat with Bird on the second morning, wiping his brow with a moist cloth. He opened his eyes, but let them drop shut at once.

"Ah, Bird. Try again," she said.

He shifted on the mattress, burrowing in like a cat. Then he smiled.

She chuckled. "You're just being lazy now. Wake up."

Bird struggled to lift his lids.

"That's it," she said. "Come on."

He cracked open one eye and peered at her, his face twisting in confusion.

"Here. Have some broth. It will help."

She supported his head and put a cup to his lips. Slowly, carefully, he opened his mouth and swallowed. A moment passed. He took another taste. And another.

"All right," she said. "Not too much at once."

He peered up at her. "Elisabeth?"

"Yes, Elisabeth. Who did you think I was? The Blessed Mother?"

He cocked an eyebrow at her. "Definitely not."

She smiled. A small smile. "How are you feeling?"

He took a deep breath. Worked his jaw. "Very tired. But better."

"You've no right to feel tired. You've slept for two days."

A horrified looked swept over his features. "Conon. Is he…?"

Elisabeth shifted so Bird could see beyond her. On a mattress against the far wall, little Conon slept contented as a kitten. "His fever broke earlier this morning," she said. "Same hour as yours."

Tears gathered in Bird's eyes.

She swallowed down the lump in her own throat. "They wanted to separate the two of you. I wouldn't let them." She looked down at her hands. "Many have died," she whispered.

"And what of Kateline?"

The fear in his voice came through clearly. Elisabeth pushed back her own fear and raised the cup to his lips once more. "Pray that God heals her."

He finished the broth before she stood to leave. "I'll bring solid food later. Sleep now."

"Elisabeth."

She stopped, turned to him.

"Why did you call me 'bird'?"

She felt the heat of a blush move up her throat. "I didn't."

"Yes, you did."

"You must have been dreaming."

She hurried from the room, wondering if Bird had noticed her cheeks full of color. Bird. *Had* she said it aloud?

A dazzling sun lit the sky, chasing the morning chill from the air. It would be a cloudless day.

§ § §

"God loves you, Elisabeth," Kateline said.

Elisabeth didn't know how to respond. She wouldn't argue with the sick young woman.

Kateline had coughed and shaken with fever most of the day, but now, as the sun sank in the sky, she spoke calmly.

Kateline persisted. "Tell me you know it's true."

"It's not his love I need, but his forgiveness."

105

"Then one of the priests can take your confession."

Elisabeth shook her head. "I have been refused penance."

"Why, sweet friend?"

"Do not call me your friend, Kateline. I am . . ." she could hardly say it out loud, " . . . cursed."

Kateline laid a frail hand on Elisabeth's arm. "Only by your fears. I *will* call you my friend. And in time, you will know not only God's love, but his forgiveness as well."

Elisabeth bent her head to Kateline's side while the girl stroked her hair.

"Where is Hugo?" Kateline asked after several quiet moments.

"He's been sleeping in the courtyard all day long."

Kateline sighed and smiled. "He watched over me during the night. He must have been exhausted."

Yes, Hugo tended Kateline last night while Elisabeth looked after Bird. Elisabeth had napped a little throughout the day, but spent most of her time scurrying between the two sick rooms, checking on Conon and Bird—who'd managed to stand for a few minutes this afternoon—and her beloved Kateline. Elisabeth resisted the temptation to raise her eyes to the ceiling. "I suppose tending you was too much for Hugo."

"Think kindly of him, Elisabeth."

She couldn't possibly. "I will try."

Kateline coughed into a rag. When the fit passed, a troubled look crossed her features, causing Elisabeth's heart to stop for a moment until the young woman's countenance eased.

"Will you send Hugo to me?" Kateline said. "I—I need to see him."

Elisabeth touched Kateline's forehead. It surprised her to find it still hot with fever—she'd seemed so much stronger the past hour. "Perhaps you should rest first."

Kateline shook her head, worry in her eyes. "No. Please." She forced a smile. "I need to see him now."

§ § §

Hugo looked up to find Elisabeth standing in front of him, arms crossed, foot tapping the ground.

The girl's mouth contorted in disdain. "I said Kateline's asking for you."

Pink clouds edged the sky. Hugo stood, wiping the sleep from his eyes. "Is it morning or evening?"

She stared at him as if he were crazy. "Eventide."

All day. He'd missed an entire day with Kateline. "Has she improved?"

Elisabeth's foot stilled. "I'm not sure. She seems at peace, but the fever burns."

Hugo stepped around Elisabeth.

"Do her no harm," Elisabeth said, her voice cold.

He turned to see her glaring at him with hard eyes. He shook his head and made way to Kateline's bedchamber.

"Kateline," he said from the doorway.

The woman he loved lay quiet, and he thought perhaps she slept. "Milady?" he whispered to be sure.

She opened her eyes and turned her head toward him. A beautiful smile lit her face. Hugo dropped the curtain behind him and entered the room to kneel beside the mattress.

Kateline stroked his cheek with a delicate finger. He clasped her hand and brought it to his lips.

"Hold me," she said, breath rattling in her chest.

He moved to the mattress, gathering her in his arms like he would a child. "How's that?"

She closed her eyes and smiled. "I could stay like this forever."

"As you wish."

She chuckled, but the effort choked her. He held her upright until her breath returned.

"I've asked the abbot to marry us as soon as you are strong enough," he said.

She opened her mouth to speak, but he continued on.

"We'll settle in the closest village we can find. Forget about the crusade."

Kateline felt so light in his arms he thought she might float away like a feather upon the breeze.

"Hugo—"

"Shh. Don't try to speak."

It seemed difficult for her to focus on his face. "I love you, Hugo."

He closed his eyes and pressed his lips to her hair, feeling the heat of her fever. "I love you."

She seemed to sleep, but only for a moment, then her face tipped up to his. "I'm dying, my love."

"No." A sweat broke out on his brow and his stomach wrenched. "You're recovering. Surely your fever will break tomorrow. Tonight, even."

Kateline gave him a look of tremendous compassion. Tears blurred his vision, and he drew her closer. She lay limp in his arms as he rocked her back and forth, his torso shaking with grief. When his tears were spent, he relaxed his hold and looked at her. Her own face was wet.

"Promise me something," she said.

"Anything."

The color drained from her cheeks. "Finish the journey."

How could he continue on without her? "I won't."

Her eyes flickered in the darkening room. "You must, Hugo." She drew a ragged breath. "Promise you'll finish your journey."

He kissed her forehead, cheek, lips. "I promise." Perhaps he, too, would fall ill. He couldn't be blamed for breaking his vow if he joined her in death.

At his words, a faint smile curved her lips. She touched the medallion that nestled against his throat, and a contented sigh escaped her perfect breast.

Soft. Sweet.

Final.

Chapter 12

Late July AD 1212, Mont Cenis Abbey, Holy Roman Empire
Elisabeth sat on the edge of Conon's mattress and felt her face heat. She tried to answer the boy, but nothing came out.

"Conon," Bird said sharply. "Why would you ask such a thing?"

"Mama told me they have hair that color." The little boy turned to Elisabeth with innocent eyes. "But I think if you were a witch, you wouldn't have taken care of me and Simon."

Bird looked as embarrassed as she felt.

"Of course she's not, Conon," he said. "Now apologize."

"Never mind," Elisabeth said, deciding to make light of it. She faced the child. "But perhaps you'll help me find my cat. He's black as midnight."

Conon gasped, and his mouth formed a perfect circle while little brows arched up to touch the hair that fell over his forehead. Elisabeth and Bird laughed until tears came to their eyes. They started all over again when Conon joined in.

Conon, still trying to catch his breath, wrapped his arms around Elisabeth. The gesture startled her, but she returned his embrace.

"I like you 'Lisbeth," Conon said. "You're funny and nice."

The simple words warmed her, but she didn't trust herself to speak. She patted his back with one hand, felt his ribs through the thin tunic. At last she lifted her eyes to Bird, whose tender expression made her blush again.

No longer did he seem a strange, knobby-kneed heron. He was strong, determined, but controlled. Much like a falcon.

Some of the men in her village practiced falconry with their goshawks, training the powerful fliers to hunt prey. She loved to watch the birds in steep descent, swooping down to pluck a rodent from the grass. The falconers thought they'd tamed their pets, but Elisabeth knew better. Intelligence glowed in their dark eyes. One could tell the birds had simply chosen to comply. She admired that.

Bird?

She'd have to start calling him Simon again.

He returned her smile before his eyes moved to the doorway. In the space of a second, every trace of humor left his face. Elisabeth followed his gaze.

Hugo stood there, eyes swollen, shoulders bent. She once saw a dead tree that had been struck by lightning, its torso scorched and twisted. Hugo looked as forlorn as that tree.

"No." Her voice came out low and quiet.

Hugo shifted hollow eyes her direction.

Elisabeth would not accept it. She shook her head. "No."

"What's wrong?" Conon said.

She released him and stood up. Her voice grew stronger, and she pushed past Hugo at the door. "No."

Bird called after her.

She was out of the room, running toward Kateline's bedchamber. Her feet on the paving stones kept rhythm with the only thought in her head. *No, no, no, no, no.*

At the room, a monk muttered indiscernible words over Kateline's unmoving form. His bald head reflected the light from a single candle. Even the stink of the tallow did not overlay the stench of death.

She dropped to her knees at the end of the mattress. Kateline's feet lay exposed. Cold. Elisabeth rubbed them in her hands, but they did not warm. How beautiful those feet should have been, not calloused and dirty.

"Enough, my dear," the man said gently. "Leave her be."

He took Elisabeth's arm to help her up, but she jerked from his grasp and rushed from the room.

She stopped in the courtyard, looked at the walls that surrounded her. There was no place to run.

Bird approached, aided by Hugo.

She moved toward the young men until she stood before them, her breath coming in sharp bursts.

Pain registered on Hugo's face like a raw wound. Elisabeth hated him for grieving Kateline. For being loved by Kateline. She struck his chest with both fists. He winced in surprise, but didn't move. She hit him again. And again.

Bird pulled at her. "Elisabeth, no." He was too weak to stop her.

Her fury boiled over, and she pummeled Hugo's chest, swearing at him. Hugo stood there and let her do it until she sank to the ground, exhausted. Bird covered her with his blanket and sat beside her without a word. Just sat there. She never knew when Hugo walked away.

§ § §

"It's a pity Elisabeth is not stronger," Hugo said to Simon the next day. He deserved her rage. *How could I have let Kateline die?*

"I'm sorry I couldn't prevent her from striking you, Hugo."

"Her curses and blows were fitting. Except that I deserve much worse."

"That's not true. Kateline's death is not your fault."

Hugo rounded on him. "It is. At least Elisabeth is honest about it."

Simon looked at the ground for several silent moments. "The monks have taken care of Kateline's body."

He sighed. "Good. I couldn't have borne putting her in the ground."

Simon nodded his understanding.

"Where's Nicholas?" Hugo said.

"I don't know."

Hugo had seen little of him since they arrived at the monastery. "Our *leader* has probably shut himself away from anyone who would disturb his peace. Compassionate sort." He stood up.

"Where are you going?" Simon looked like he feared what Hugo might do.

"I've got business to take care of."

Whether Nicholas wanted to be found or not, Hugo had to try. He needed to tell Nicholas that he'd not be continuing on with the group. Then he'd make his own plans.

A tinge of guilt snaked through Hugo's chest as he walked under the portico. Who would look after the children with both him and Kateline gone? Simon could do it, but the young man still needed tending himself. Despite her efforts of the past week, Hugo didn't think Elisabeth had it in her.

Well, it wasn't his concern anymore. He was done with this journey.

He halted at the thought. What had Kateline said before she died?

"Finish the journey." Her sweet lips had formed the words. "Promise you'll finish your journey."

Hugo slammed his hand on a nearby pillar and swore under his breath. Why had he promised to do so? He had no reason to go on, had lost his zeal for killing Muslims in the dry heat of the Holy Lands. Some crusader he turned out to be.

He put his back to the column and slid down until he sat upon the ground, head between his hands. Kateline's medallion swung forward and tapped his chin. He grasped it. *God, why did she ask this of me?*

There was no response.

If it had been anyone else—

A sob rose in his throat. How could he go on without her? A vision of Kateline's lovely face formed in his mind, like a guardian angel promising strength and comfort. He gripped the medallion tighter. Had she promised to go with him, even in death? He thought maybe she had. Just before she died. He remembered that she smiled.

Hadn't she promised to be with him forever?

His thoughts turned to what Simon had read from the Scriptures. Something about love. He searched his memory for the words.

Nothing can separate love. Isn't that what Simon had read? Something like that.

Hugo repeated the quote to himself. First silently. Then as a whisper. Finally in full voice.

The words strengthened him. Kateline's love flowed in his blood. She'd asked him to make a promise. Surely she intended to help him keep it.

He'd finish the journey all right. Lead the children safely to the sea. Walk them through it if Nicholas's vision was correct. Kill a thousand Saracens in Kateline's honor.

Hugo stood. There was much to do.

Chapter 13

Late July AD 1212, Mont Cenis Abbey, Holy Roman Empire

The passion filling Hugo's eyes surprised Simon. Two days ago he thought Hugo would give up on the crusade.

"But you have to come with us," Hugo said.

Simon shook his head. "Conon is too weak to travel. If you insist we continue now, I must refuse."

"We need you."

"Conon and I can follow with one of the other groups. You and Nicholas are competent to lead without my help."

Hugo stepped close and spoke into his ear. "The other groups? We've not heard from them in a fortnight. And you know Nicholas is not trustworthy. His motives are selfish at best. But you, Simon, are the reason any of us have survived thus far."

Simon knew what Hugo was trying to do. Still—

Hugo's voice softened. "Who else can obtain and administer our supplies like you?"

Simon cast his eyes to the ground. He did seem to have a gift for management.

Hugo continued. "Who else can speak a dozen languages?"

"Four languages."

"Four, then. Who else?"

Simon met Hugo's gaze. "But Conon . . ."

Hugo looked pained by what he had to say next. "Conon won't be stronger in a week. He won't be stronger in a month. He'll never be strong enough to make the trip."

Simon exhaled. He knew it was true, had seen it happen to others. Hearts so weakened by illness that they lived forever pale and breathless, just short of death. "I can't leave Conon behind."

Hugo picked up a couple of pebbles and rumbled them around in his closed fist like a pair of dice. "You once told me that God called you to use your knowledge and abilities to reclaim Palestine for the Lord and make it accessible to Christian pilgrims. To rid the earth of Islam."

Simon stared at the mountain peaks beyond the walls of Mont Cenis.

"The world, Simon, or one child?"

He looked hard at Hugo. "That's not fair."

"No," Hugo said. "It's not." He laid a hand on Simon's shoulder, squeezed it once, and then walked away.

Is this what he left Villebonne for?

A quarter hour passed before he rose. He found Conon alone in their chamber, lips pale.

"Simon," Conon said, "I walked all the way around the courtyard with Elisabeth and only had to stop twice."

Simon forced a smile. "Excellent. You're getting better every day."

Conon beamed. "I'll be ready to march when Nicholas says it's time."

"I—I think he'll be ready before you're quite strong enough, little one."

"I'm getting better. You said so."

"You are, but . . . "—*oh, God help me*—". . . not strong enough to come along."

"So we'll just wait together for the next group?"

"You won't be strong enough then, either."

The child's face fell, and tears welled in his eyes. "You won't leave me, will you?"

"I must."

Conon ran to Simon. Wrapped his arms around Simon's legs. "No. I want to come with you."

"You cannot," Simon said, stroking Conon's dark curls. He would not cry.

"Please, Simon," the little boy begged. "Please don't leave me."

Don't leave me. Simon remembered pleading with those very words the day his parents took him to the monastery at Villebonne. His mother, round with her eighth child, wept into her apron.

His father had bent in front of him, hands on Simon's shoulders. Lean, leathery face even with his. "It's for your own good, boy."

"No, Papa," Simon said. "I don't want to stay here." The massive gray walls terrified him almost as much as the cowled monks with their brooding looks.

"You're smart as they come, Simon," his father said. "You can make something of yourself with an education."

"I promise to be good!" Simon said. "Please don't leave me."

His father cleared his throat. "You're a fine boy. A very fine boy." A tear formed in his eye, but he blinked it back. "We've just too many mouths to feed. You understand?"

Conon's sobbing interrupted Simon's thoughts. The boy gasped for air around the moisture dripping from his nose. "I promise to be good, Simon." Tears ran down his cheeks unhindered.

Would Conon ever forgive him?

Simon hugged the boy, his voice catching in his throat. "You're a fine boy, Conon. I'll come back for you. When the crusade is over, I promise I'll come back."

§ § §

The day of their departure emerged bright from the dark of night. In the glare of the morning sun, Simon watched Elisabeth place something at the head of Kateline's grave. How his heart ached at the loss of one so dear. With his eyes still on her, Elisabeth knelt to kiss the mound of earth before picking up her blanket and trudging away. She moved towards the courtyard where the children were waiting for Nicholas to start the day's procession.

What had Elisabeth put at the grave? He drifted over to find out.

A stone, small and pink. He picked it up, turned it in his hand.

Ah, Kateline, how could you leave us?

He looked after Elisabeth. A riddle, she was. *What is hard yet soft, unbreakable yet broken?*

Hugo and Nicholas conferred with a monk near the gate. Simon wandered back but kept himself separate. He had no heart for their conversation.

"Hello," Elisabeth said softly.

He looked down at her, unable to conjure a response.

She touched his arm. "You're doing the right thing."

He squinted toward the sky.

Nicholas called to the company, and they quieted. With words Simon dismissed and Elisabeth ignored, Nicholas did his best to renew the children's hearts for their quest. At last the gate was opened, and he marched forward, crucifix aloft, leading them south to the sea.

Ten, twenty, thirty children passed by, but Simon did not move to take his place at the head of the column. Elisabeth stood watching him, worry upon her face. He looked from the little ones, to the mountains beyond the walls, to the doorway of the room he'd shared with Conon.

Finally, he adjusted the strap of the leather pouch on his shoulder and merged with the flow of crusaders. Elisabeth followed.

"No!" a small voice cried.

Conon threw himself into Simon's arms. "Take me with you. Don't leave me."

He gathered the boy close and wept into his brown curls. The child's hair had the salty smell of a young pup, and he breathed it in deeply, his heart aching. "You can't come."

Simon lifted his face. He pleaded silently for Elisabeth to do what he could not. She gently pulled the boy from his arms.

"Simon," Conon called over and over, his voice weakening with each step Simon took.

"There, there." Elisabeth's voice drifted across the courtyard. "Be a strong boy. Simon will return for you."

Simon had no words to speak that day. When they stopped for the night, Elisabeth sat beside him while he stared into the flames.

Chapter 14

Early August AD 1212, the Italian Peninsula, Holy Roman Empire
Four days later, the mountains parted to reveal the Italian Peninsula spread out below them, a green and gentle land, ripe with the pungent sweet scent of fruit and flower. The afternoon light reflected like gold upon the fields and vineyards, but Simon hardly cared.

The crusaders descended to make camp on the rolling plain as the sun sank low in the sky. When the work was done, Simon spied Elisabeth walking his way. She plopped down beside him just as Hugo came into view, checking on the children. A tall, blonde maiden followed him like a duckling after its mother.

"See that girl?" Elisabeth said to Simon. "She pines for Hugo, and rumor has it they were kissing amongst the trees. Her name is Geizbart."

Simon stared straight ahead. "The tongue is a small thing, but what enormous damage it can do. A tiny spark can set a great forest on fire."

She showed no regard for his Scripture quoting. "Geizbart? *Goat-beard?*" She covered her mouth with one hand.

"It's probably a family name."

Elisabeth giggled.

"Stop it." He tried unsuccessfully to hold back a chuckle. "You're being unkind."

She snorted through her hand, and then cackled out loud. It broke down his last resistance, and he laughed too.

In spite of himself, Simon had to admit the laughter did him good. Reminded him that God indeed heals the brokenhearted.

He tried to give Elisabeth a stern look, but suspected she noticed the way his lips still tugged upward.

She tapped her temple. "The girl's dim-witted, you know."

He tried to curb her slander with a look.

"Dumb as a stone."

"Elisabeth."

"Oh, all right." That impious grin stayed put.

Simon shook his head. Elisabeth was like a rosebud—thorny, but full of promise. He liked her more and more. He tore a portion of bread in half and handed a piece to her.

"Hugo truly loved Kateline," he said after several minutes.

Elisabeth's face snapped up, but she didn't speak.

"I wish you would try to get along with him. He's not your enemy."

Her countenance grew cold. "What do you know about it?"

"Why do you hate him so?"

"He is too much like another," she whispered.

Simon unwrapped a bit of cheese from a cloth, and held it out to her. "But he is Hugo. Not someone else."

She shook her head. "I don't want to speak of it."

"Then let's speak of something else."

Relief spread over her face, and she put on a cautious smile. "Like what?"

"Birds."

Elisabeth tipped her head back and laughed. "It's the nickname

I have for you."

"Why a bird? What does it mean?"

Elisabeth played with a piece of grass. "I just think you seem a bit like . . . " She stopped and looked away. " . . . like a falcon."

"A falcon?"

"You know. A proud hunter. Smart, capable." She stood up and brushed the dirt from her dress as though dismissing the subject. "Anyway, it's better than being a heron, is it not?"

Simon smiled to himself. A falcon. While he'd harbored unkind notions toward Elisabeth, she'd thought of him in noble terms. He would've felt worse about it, but the secret nickname was flattering enough to overrule his conscience. He smiled again then straightened his face. If he didn't stop his preening—the play on words amused him— he'd have to ask God's forgiveness for the sin of pride. He resolved not to think of it any longer.

Imagine. A falcon.

Hugo called to them. "It's the children," he said, approaching. "Some have fallen ill again."

Simon's gut tightened. "God in heaven."

Elisabeth frowned. "It's your fault," she said to Hugo. "You rushed them from the monastery before they fully recovered."

"Me?" Hugo said. "The monks said it was safe."

Simon had no taste for their bickering. "There's an abbey," he said. "Probably no more than five miles ahead. It's on the map."

Elisabeth sighed in relief.

Hugo pursed his lips, thinking. "Then let's break camp and continue on. It will be dark before we reach it, but we dare not wait 'til the morrow."

§ § §

Sant'Antonio di Ranverso possessed a mill and a hospital—

these things Simon glimpsed through the abbey gate, though he and the other crusaders had not yet been permitted past the wall. The abbot had been summoned and demanded they give an account of themselves.

Simon explained their situation, and then dipped his head to his chest. "We humbly request your assistance."

The man did not respond, and Simon looked up. Through the sputter of torchlight, the priest stared at him with cold eyes.

"Please, Father, we are mostly children," Simon said in Latin, motioning to the weakest among them. "These few are unwell and need tending."

"I know who you are," the abbot said at last. "Your crusade is not sanctioned by Pope Innocent, and I will not give it credence by harboring you here." His eyes shifted. "Is that the boy?"

Simon followed his gaze to Nicholas, who stood glowering at them. So even this cloistered man had heard about their charismatic young leader. "Yes, that's him. Please, I beseech you, give us shelter this night."

The abbot matched Nicholas's glare for a moment longer before his face broke with a derisive chuckle. "Off with you," he said to Nicholas, motioning him away like a dog.

The boy didn't need to know Latin to understand the scornful words. Simon feared Nicholas's response, so he dropped to his knees before anyone had a chance to speak. He grabbed the man's hand and kissed his ring. "Please, Your Holiness, at least accept the sick. They need your help."

The abbot withdrew his hand. Simon kept his head bowed and prayed that both Nicholas and Hugo would remain in their places. The silence lingered.

"Bring in the sick, then," the man said. "But the rest of you riffraff must camp outside the gate." He pivoted and strode back inside the abbey. The monks advanced toward the ailing children.

Simon stood and looked at Hugo, who shook his head. Elisabeth trembled in rage. Nicholas ranted about being insulted, but did not attempt to force his way beyond the gate.

At least the sick would be tended.

Elisabeth, Simon, and Hugo moved to assist the weakened children inside the abbey wall, while Nicholas only pouted and hovered nearby.

"We'll leave at morning light," Nicholas said when the job was done.

"What?" Simon stopped in his tracks. "We can't leave them. They've come this far. They only need a few more days to recover."

"We're going on."

"Look, Nicholas," Hugo said. "These children are our responsibility."

"Well, you convinced Simon to leave that boy at Mont Cenis, didn't you?"

Hugo avoided Simon's eyes. "We have twenty-three children inside those walls. Conon can stay at Mont Cenis, but these people will turn the young ones out as soon as we leave."

"And what if they do? Are these crusaders not God's responsibility? He's provided for them thus far, and he will continue to do so."

"Don't bring God into this," Hugo hissed.

"Someone has to," Nicholas said. "You are all faithless."

Hugo looked at Simon, threw up his hands, and stomped away.

Simon tried another tack. "You can preach here for a few days, Nicholas. The road is frequently traveled. There may be some who want to finance our movement."

The boy seemed tempted by that. Simon smiled at him.

But Nicholas's face scrunched up, and he shook his head. "No. God has spoken to me. We must move on tomorrow."

"What do you mean, move on?"

Simon and Nicholas turned at Elisabeth's words. She stood

clenching her hands as if to stop them from going around Nicholas's neck. "Do you mean to say you're abandoning the sick?"

Nicholas looked at her with annoyance. "Don't be troublesome, Elisabeth."

"But we can't leave them. They must make it to Jerusalem. Everyone must." Her face had gone unusually pale. "I won't go without them."

Nicholas's lips curled up in a humorless smile. "Stay with them then. I don't need you. Or Simon or Hugo, for that matter. The children will follow me and be better off without your faithless hearts slowing down our movement."

Her face went red. Simon shook his head at her, but she unclenched her fingers and advanced upon the boy. "I'll pluck you like a chicken, you gutless scoundrel."

Nicholas bared his teeth, eyes ablaze.

Simon stepped between them and grabbed Elisabeth's shoulders. "I'm sorry, Nicholas. She's not herself. It's the loss of Kateline. I'll see to her."

Elisabeth looked like she'd just as soon clout Simon, but he half-pushed, half-dragged her to the perimeter of their camp. She twisted to give Nicholas a murderous look.

"Calm down." Simon pulled up and grabbed both her wrists.

She twisted free. "Stand up to him, Simon. If we don't comply, he'll change his mind."

"Hugo and I have tried, Elisabeth. He'll just go on without us. And the children will follow." Nicholas was right about that.

"Then let them be fools."

"How long would they last under his care?"

Elisabeth bit back her response.

He could tell she knew he was right. They had no choice.

Chapter 15

August AD 1212, Genoa, Holy Roman Empire
Genoa, a dizzying jumble of hills and buildings, sloped toward the Mediterranean. It was the water, though—glistening like green glass under an azure sky—that stole Elisabeth's breath.

Reaching the outskirts of the seaside town seemed a bittersweet achievement in her mind. Kateline and so many others should have been with them.

Hugo approached. "Help us settle the children. Nicholas wants to address them." He didn't look happy about it.

Elisabeth knew why when she saw the posture Nicholas took once the children were seated and quiet.

Standing above them in the wagon, the twelve-year-old leader lifted the carved cross while he scanned the group in silence. He wore his cloak like a royal robe and someone—perhaps Nicholas himself—had woven together young olive branches and sat them on his head. Pompous idiot.

"My friends," he finally said in a voice deeper than his natural pitch. He paused to offer a benevolent smile. "Yes, I call you my friends, for that is what you are. Everything God has given to me, I have shared with you."

Simon's quick intake of breath made Elisabeth turn to him. "What's the matter?" Besides the obvious, of course.

Simon didn't take his eyes off of Nicholas but leaned down to whisper. "He's speaking the words of Jesus from the gospel of Saint John."

Elisabeth glared at Nicholas. So he thought himself divine, now, did he?

"Under my leadership," Nicholas motioned toward Genoa, "God has graciously granted us passage to this city."

His leadership? Elisabeth glanced at Simon again, who stared straight ahead at the boy in the cart. She looked past Simon to where Hugo stood sulking and silent, a grimace on his face.

Nicholas continued. "I've seen you through danger, hunger, death, and despair. I've led you across the continent of Europe." His voice rose with excitement. "And soon we shall cross the Great Sea to Jerusalem and victory." He waved the crucifix in the air like a standard, and the crowd of children erupted into cheers.

Elisabeth's mouth fell open in dismay. Several crusaders jumped to their feet and began to dance and clap their hands. Someone yelled Nicholas's name. Others joined in until they were all chanting, "Nicholas. Nicholas."

"He's gone mad," Elisabeth said.

Hugo shook his head. "He isn't crazy. He's arrogant."

They distanced themselves from the others who continued to chant and dance. Nicholas remained in the cart, both arms raised above his head as if embracing the adoration of the crowd.

"I can't abide this." Elisabeth gritted her teeth. "Did you hear what he said?"

Simon spoke softly. "They were only words."

"Only words?" Elisabeth said. "Look at them."

Every boy and girl, every young man and maiden, jumped or

swayed or clapped. Some linked arms and skipped through the group. Many still cried Nicholas's name, though a number of simple folk songs could be heard coming from different directions.

"Let the children celebrate today," Hugo said. "I fear few will see the victory Nicholas promises."

Elisabeth turned to him in surprise. Simon's face reflected her astonishment.

Indignation pitted her stomach. "How can you say that?"

Hugo's blue eyes flicked between her and Simon. His hand went to Kateline's medallion at his throat. It reminded Elisabeth that she hated him.

But at that moment, she hated Nicholas more.

Hugo spoke in a firm voice. "We'll make it. And I'll do everything I can to get the children safely to Jerusalem."

For several seconds, none of them stirred, though their eyes moved from one to the other.

"As will I," Simon said solemnly.

It wasn't that she disliked Hugo any less—she couldn't bear his company—but everyone had to reach Palestine. It was the only way they could be free from her curse. "And I."

Simon pulled at his ear. He felt ill at ease at the thought of entering Genoa, but of course, Nicholas required a translator. The boy also insisted that Hugo accompany them to request a meeting with the town consul, and for this, Simon was grateful.

According to Nicholas, they would demand shelter within the city walls for up to a fortnight. The young leader fully expected the other companies to join them in that length of time. Never mind that it had been nigh upon a month since they'd had contact with any of them—Nicholas claimed another vision. This one assured him that thousands upon thousands still followed.

At the end of fourteen days, if not before, the boy intended to gather every child at the coast to wait for God's miraculous parting of the sea. Simon hated to admit he didn't believe the event would occur, but more fantastic things had been known to happen.

Simon looked at Hugo standing beside him.

"Ready?" Hugo said.

Simon ignored the tight feeling in his gut, nodded, and walked with Hugo toward Nicholas.

"I should ride to the city in the wagon," Nicholas said as they approached.

Hugo appraised the rickety cart and the half-dead mare that pulled it. "It is not likely to impress."

"It's better than walking into Genoa," the boy said. "*Barefoot.*"

"You say you go with God," Hugo reminded him.

Nicholas frowned. "Of course I do."

Hugo motioned with his hand. "Then *go.*"

Nicholas scowled and started walking. Hugo's eyes cut to Simon. Matching grin for grin, they stepped onto the road behind the child.

Upon reaching the gate, Nicholas pushed Simon toward a guard.

Simon's mouth went dry, but he spoke to the armed soldier in the soft, lyrical sounds of the language. "Nicholas of Cologne requests an audience with the chief magistrate."

The guard's face split into a derisive grin. He lacked two front teeth, but the uneven sneer only increased Simon's concern. The guard jabbed a nearby sentry in the ribs and pointed to Nicholas. "He's a pretty lad, no? We should dress him up like one of those dancing girls that come on the ships."

The other man chuckled.

Hugo's fists clenched at the obvious ridicule.

Nicholas apparently didn't have the sense to feel self-conscious. "What are they saying?" he asked in a loud voice. "When can I see the magistrate?"

Simon hesitated. "I—I don't know."

"Well, ask them."

Simon took a deep breath and assumed a stern expression before speaking again. "I doubt the *potestat* wants you to anger the boy. Don't you know the pope himself has given Nicholas of Cologne the power to castrate a man with his eyes alone?"

The smile faded from the first guard's face. The man shot a look at Nicholas and then to the other soldier, whose laughter intensified until he doubled over. Snarling at their small delegation, the jagged-toothed fellow turned on his heel and indicated they should follow him into the city.

The streets of Genoa teemed with merchants, bejeweled women in colorful clothing, and donkeys pulling carts. Shops of every sort lined their way, and open stalls displayed fabrics, pottery, fresh fish, and dazzling trinkets. An unruly crowd mingled in a spacious courtyard— raucous commoners watching masons at work on a tall tower, offering unwelcome suggestions and observations. Pigs ran wild through the open area while vendors cried, "Fine figs from Malta!" or "Peas in the hull, I have peas in the hull!"

The strong odor of unfamiliar spices soured Simon's stomach. Or maybe it was anxiety over the crowds that pressed close upon them.

"Stay alert," Hugo whispered and patted the spot on his belt where he hid his dagger. Simon breathed a little easier knowing Hugo was keeping his eyes open, too.

The guard escorted them toward the sea and deeper into the heart of the city. They passed through another square where brown-skinned slaves were being auctioned. Some of the miserable creatures maintained defiant stares, but most hung their heads at the humiliation they suffered. Simon's focus drifted to the shackles on their wrists and ankles. He guessed they were Mohammedans, and while his heart tugged in compassion, he supposed their fate to be a suitable, even merciful, reward for their ungodly ways.

A second inner wall gave way to a clutter of immense palaces and soaring cathedrals. They were in various stages of construction, and many were decorated with a curious pattern of black and white stripes. They hid from view the city's most valuable asset—the natural harbor around which Genoa was built. Its brackish odor wafted on the breeze.

At last the guard stopped outside an arched entryway. He raised his hand and muttered something before disappearing inside, leaving them at the bottom of the steps.

"What did he say?" Nicholas's tone drew close to a whine.

"To wait here." Simon said. "I daresay we'll have our interview with the *potestat* before long."

"The magistrate?"

Simon nodded.

Nicholas straightened his back, a satisfied smile on his face. "Excellent." He gazed up at the door of the building and then climbed to the top step to appraise the town with both hands on his hips. He looked for all the world like a king surveying his land.

Simon glanced at Hugo, who seemed content to remain with him on the street.

They were indeed ushered to the magistrate quickly. The man, dressed in red velvet embroidered with gold thread, clapped like a child when the three of them stood before him. He smiled at Nicholas then sat down in a wide chair and clasped ring-adorned fingers over his sizeable stomach. "So this is the boy."

"It is, sir," Simon said.

Nicholas basked in the clear approval and, for the first time that day, did not demand that Simon interpret.

The magistrate continued to study Nicholas. "He's very small, is he not?" The official began to chuckle. "How is it that so many would follow such a little mouse, eh?"

Though Simon had been wondering the same thing lately, he said, "Nicholas has been appointed by God. Does the Lord not choose the weak of this world to shame the strong?"

The man stopped laughing.

Simon feared he'd insulted the *potestat*—the powerful one— and hastened to make amends. "Bow down," he whispered to Nicholas and Hugo. Simon lowered one knee to the ground, and the others followed.

"Your Excellency." Simon spoke the word with great emphasis. "We humbly seek the shelter of your city for our poor and defenseless children. Genoa is the crowning jewel of the Holy Roman Empire, and we ask that you, its most powerful citizen, grant our request."

The magistrate deliberated for a moment. "I want to hear from the renowned Nicholas."

"He speaks only the German tongue."

The man's eyebrows lifted. "I won't consider your appeal until I converse with him." He motioned for them to stand. "Translate."

Simon turned to Nicholas. "He wants you to speak."

Nicholas didn't need further invitation. He launched into a lengthy and flattering speech, which Simon translated to the increasingly delighted magistrate. The man plied Nicholas with questions about their adventures and intentions. Nicholas's answers generally rang true, though shaded with language that exaggerated his role and extolled the virtues of the man seated before them.

They were two of a kind, Simon realized, conceited as a pair of strutting roosters. Hugo began to fidget, probably wearied by the obvious self-adulation of both, but he kept quiet.

At last the magistrate promised the hospitality of Genoa.

"Good," Hugo said when Simon informed them. "Let's get out of—"

The magistrate interrupted. "You will be my guests for the night. Tomorrow you may return to your companions."

When Simon explained, Hugo shook his head. "No. We leave now."

Nicholas protested. "I want to stay."

Hugo sighed. "The longer we're separated from the children, the more vulnerable they are."

Nicholas frowned. "They're fine. We deserve this man's generosity. And I'm going to take it."

Hugo's eyes flashed. "Not until the children are within these walls."

The magistrate's voice broke in. "Is there a problem?"

Simon swallowed. "We want to ensure the safety of the children before we partake of your hospitality."

"Don't you trust me?"

The way the man's lips thinned guaranteed that Simon did not. He looked at the guards positioned near the doorway and felt captive in the room. "I agree with Hugo," he said to Nicholas. "We need to leave immediately."

That was all the support Hugo needed. He took Nicholas's arm and headed for the door, infuriating the boy. Ignoring their young leader's objections, Simon turned back to the magistrate. "Thank you for your gracious offer, but we cannot trouble you on such short notice. We will tend to our companions tonight and call upon you tomorrow, if you so choose."

The man's eyes narrowed, but Simon didn't wait for further response. He gave a respectful nod and hurried to catch up with Hugo and Nicholas.

Hugo still pulled Nicholas along by the arm. "Because the magistrate is devious, that's why," he was saying. He looked to Simon. "You know what I'm talking about."

Simon nodded. "If the man changes his mind about trusting us, I don't think he will let us go come morning."

Nicholas made a face. "If his intentions were evil, he would've stopped us leaving now."

Maybe. But Simon let Hugo and Nicholas argue it out. His mind turned to the task of getting the children settled inside the walls before nightfall.

An hour later, the company of crusaders stood before a gate blocked by hostile soldiers, some on horseback.

Elisabeth glanced up at one of the huge black beasts stomping the ground nearby and moved closer to Simon.

"This is outrageous," Nicholas said. "A German plot to overtake Genoa? I don't even know what they're talking about. We're holy crusaders of God."

Hugo stood with his legs spread wide, hand to the belt of his tunic. His eyes never left the soldiers. "I knew the Genoese couldn't be trusted."

Nicholas ran fingers through his hair, leaving it standing in small tufts around his skull. He turned to Simon. "Tell them again. Tell them the magistrate assured us admittance."

Simon shook his head. "It was the *potestat* who gave the new order to prevent our entering the city unless we choose to settle here permanently. Seems he had a change of heart after we left."

Nicholas snarled at Hugo. "We should've agreed to stay the night. This never would have happened if we hadn't offended him."

Hugo stepped in front of the boy and tapped his finger on Nicholas's chest. "Your self-indulgence would've found us in a dungeon by morning. I say it's a good thing we discovered the man's true nature this side of the wall."

Nicholas bristled. "Or we could have had our bellies filled and slept upon down mattresses covered in fur. You always worry about the children. Can't you see they'd have been fine for one night? From now on, *I'll* make the decisions around here."

"I'd like to see you try."

Nicholas's fists tightened.

"Stop it," Elisabeth cried out.

Simon and the others turned wide eyes in her direction.

She lowered her voice. "It does no good to squabble here in front of everyone. The magistrate's made his decision. If you want to see him about it tomorrow, fine. But tonight we sleep outside the wall. It's not like we haven't done it before."

She turned without waiting for a reply and began to direct the children. There were a few groans of disappointment, but they complied, and soon she had them moving back up the hill.

Simon stood for a moment with his mouth open, a slight curve to his lips, and then hurried to help.

Hugo and Simon strode ahead to catch up with her and help the children bed down. Hugo mumbled something as they passed her.

Elisabeth paused mid-stride. "What did you say?"

Hugo lifted his chin. "Well said, Elisabeth." He nodded downhill. "At the gate."

The compliment surprised Simon, but Elisabeth simply gave a small shrug and walked away.

Chapter 16

Late August AD 1212, Genoa, Holy Roman Empire
Two days passed, but still an increased contingent of soldiers guarded the wall surrounding Genoa. Hugo wondered if the ruler truly thought the children would rush the gates on behalf of German kings. The thought was so ridiculous that, had it not irritated him, he would've enjoyed a good laugh over it.

Instead, he stood with his arms crossed over his chest, lips curled at the guards while they watched the young crusaders upon the hill.

"We must seem very threatening," Simon said.

Hugo turned, unaware that the young man had drawn near. Elisabeth was there, too.

"Yes," Hugo said, "undoubtedly these half-starved children camping on the hillside intimidate the fine armed forces of Genoa."

Even Elisabeth cracked a smile at that, though she smothered it at once.

Simon's brown eyes met Hugo's. "The children *are* half-starved. Our supplies are low. I don't know how long we can wait before seeking a more charitable location."

"What is your estimate?" Hugo said.

"Not a fortnight as Nicholas wants. If we're careful, our provisions will last five or six days. I don't think we should wait here more than two before traveling on."

Elisabeth looked toward the sea. "Plenty of food there."

They followed her gaze.

"We'd need a boat," Hugo said.

"Nets, at the very least," Simon said. "I don't imagine the Genoese fishermen will be loaning them to us. And they certainly won't let us fish their waters."

Hugo sighed. "My instincts tell me to move the company along."

"But Genoa is our meeting place," Elisabeth said. "We must give the others time to reach us."

"Are there any others?" God help him, Hugo didn't believe.

"There have to be."

Simon shook his head. "The best we can do is decrease rations. And pray."

That last bit sounded like an afterthought.

Elisabeth's eyes sparked at both of them. "Pray? Is that the best you two can come up with?"

Hugo didn't think he could take her criticism much longer. "And what would you have us do?"

She looked him square in the eye. "You get the nets. We'll go fishing."

"You and Simon?"

She simply dipped her chin and glared at him like he was an idiot.

§ § §

Elisabeth didn't ask or care how Hugo and the other young men managed to get the nets. It only mattered that they succeeded.

At first Simon worried over their pilfering, but in the end, even he agreed the children must eat. And that Elisabeth's plan might work.

"You're sure you can do this?" Hugo said for the fifth time.

Sweat trickled down her back, and she lifted her plaited hair to allow the salty breeze to cool her neck. "Don't ask me again."

He held up his hands in mock surrender, and then walked away.

She glanced at the Mediterranean and tried to imagine those waters parting. They stretched as far as she could see. How long would it take to reach Jerusalem? Two days? Three? She had so many questions, but hadn't asked anyone for fear she'd sound dim-witted. Or faithless.

Her eyes turned to the more than forty girls in their company. "Ready?"

They nodded, and though several of them stood wide-eyed with fear, most of them wore a bit of mischief in their smiles.

"Let's go. Stay close together."

Single file they walked, each with the walls of Genoa on their left and a section of net in their arms to the right. Away from the city and down to a shallow protected bay they went, like so many maidens off to bathe.

"Are we really going to get in the water?" little Giselle said.

Elisabeth cast a glance over her shoulder. "Sure, and how else will we catch our dinner?"

"Maybe Nicholas could work a miracle?"

She sighed and turned her face back to the sea. Could he? That was the hope, now, wasn't it? So desperate was she for the Holy Land and the forgiveness it held, she didn't dare question the validity of Nicholas's claim that the waters would part. Hugo doubted. She could tell. But despite her feelings against Nicholas, she wouldn't allow herself to consider the improbability of his assertions.

Simon believed, didn't he? He was one of the most truly religious persons she'd ever met. And the smartest. Surely he would say something if Nicholas was wrong.

They made it out of view of the city guards and down to the small bay.

One of the crusaders came from a line of fishermen—granted, they fished the Rhine—but he'd tutored Elisabeth and half a dozen of the older girls so they'd know how to handle the nets. "It's not the way we fish the river," he'd said, "but it ought to work."

"All right now," Elisabeth said when they reached the shore. "Sofie. Geizbart." She looked from one to the other. "Remember, start on opposite sides of the bay and swim toward each other with your nets. Get as close as you can. Narrow the gap. Thora, Ute—hold steady your ends in the shallows." The four girls nodded and headed off to do as they were told.

Thank goodness they had two who could swim and that Geizbart wasn't quite as dull as Elisabeth had made her out to be. The two swimmers made quick work of it, despite the unfamiliar weight they pulled behind them. They had to come a bit nearer the shore than she'd hoped in order to stretch the netting all the way across, but nothing could be done about it.

When all four girls were in place, she looked at the others. "Ready to play?"

With squeals and laughter, they splashed into the water, slapping and paddling with their arms, driving the fish into the nets. At least she hoped.

It worked to some extent. They caught two large and five small fish on that first attempt then lounged on the shore for half an hour, waiting for the fish to return, before giving it another try.

By the fourth time, they'd improved their method, and had managed to pull in a total of thirteen large fish and nearly sixty small, dragging them to shore for the boys to retrieve come nightfall. Not a bad day's work.

They hid the nets among the bramble bushes near the shore in case they needed them again, then straightened their tunics, tightened their braids, and filed back to the hill outside Genoa, waving to the guards when they passed by the wall.

§ § §

Simon couldn't believe they pulled it off. Pinching nets and fish right out from under the nose of the Genoese.

Elisabeth's ingenuity surprised him.

Throughout the night, a crusader contingent led by Hugo smuggled fish from shore to camp, using their upturned tunics to ferry the creatures.

Simon borrowed Hugo's knife and went to work while the dawning sun was still only a blush on the horizon, scaling the fish from tail to head, slipping the tip in through the vent and slicing upward toward the jaw. Scooping out the guts, liver, and white sac, removing the gills, handing off the carcass, and reaching for the next.

Hugo squatted beside him when he was almost finished. "You butcher cows and gut fish nice and neat for a monk."

Simon smiled. "I know how to handle a knife."

"They teach you that at the monastery?"

"No."

Hugo raised a brow, waiting for more.

Simon rinsed his hands in a bucket, the smell of fish strong on his skin. "Earned my keep in a butcher's yard for several weeks after I left Villebonne. In Paris, on the banks of the Seine River." Sometimes it seemed he could still smell the dung and offal littering the ground, turning the dirt into a fetid, slippery muck that caused him to retch if he breathed too deeply or considered it too long.

"You're full of useful tricks, then, aren't you?" Hugo said with a laugh.

A commotion to the east interrupted them. Children ran toward the road, crying out.

Simon's stomach twisted. What now?

A moment later he laughed with joy, barely able to believe his eyes. Hugo slapped him on the back, and both of them jogged toward the faraway hill. Hundreds of small heads were just cresting the rise, a cacophony of voices shouting hello to their comrades.

The lost crusade parties, rejoining the group at last.

By the next morning some 5,000 commoners emerged from the mountains that bordered the coast. They continued to arrive in droves as the day sped on, erasing every doubt Simon harbored about Nicholas's visions.

Hugo told Simon to coordinate the groups as they appeared, take a count, and manage their provisions, but by noon the hills sloping down to Genoa were a chaotic mess of young crusaders. The city's soldiers lined the walls, and their horses pawed the ground nervously. Simon paid them scant attention.

"How are we doing?" Hugo asked him.

He grinned. "Completely disorganized."

Hugo laughed. "Well, then, you'd better get Elisabeth on it. She'll whip everyone into order."

Simon coughed and indicated the space immediately behind Hugo's shoulder.

Hugo turned to find Elisabeth standing there.

"At least now you respect my authority," she said with a hint of humor in her voice.

"Just your fists," Hugo said.

She smiled in satisfaction, and it brought a certain beauty to her face that Simon hadn't expected. "Are the children healthy?" he asked her.

Her eyes grew serious. "As far as I can discern." She lowered her head. "They suffered great loss, as we did. More, perhaps."

Simon nodded. When the weather deteriorated, many companies

waited at the foot of the Alps for the skies to clear and then traveled together, reaching Genoa all at once. But they did not escape the hunger and illness that plagued the route. Hundreds, maybe thousands, lost their lives.

"Where is Nicholas?" Hugo said.

Simon motioned with his head to where Nicholas stood in the back of a wagon as he'd done a few days earlier. Rather than inciting the crowd gathered round, he looked to be—blessing them.

Hugo's jaw clenched, but like Simon, he said nothing. The companies behind them had endured, just like Nicholas said they would. Perhaps the boy had some foresight after all, had the right to bless the children.

By the following day, Simon's final count neared 7,200 children. Amazing as that was, they'd still lost a third of the young souls who started out from Heidelberg. Perhaps he should thank God that Conon remained behind at the monastery. At least the child lived.

He sat on a verdant knoll some distance from the activity where he could look out to the water and breathe and pray.

Elisabeth dropped to her knees beside him, winded, green eyes glowing. "It's time."

His forehead twitched. "Time?"

She nodded, lips quivering. "Nicholas says to take the children to the beach."

Simon's heart thumped. "Today?"

"Now."

He inhaled and looked toward the sea. Did he believe? He wanted to, and yet—

No. He wouldn't give in to doubt. Jesus performed miracles only in the presence of faith. Simon did believe. He'd come all this way because he believed.

He looked at Elisabeth, her face filled with hope, eyes full of uncertainty.

"I tell you the truth," Simon quoted from Scripture, "if you have faith as small as a mustard seed, you can say to this mountain, 'Move from here to there' and it will move. Nothing will be impossible for you."

Elisabeth's countenance relaxed and she smiled. "Then we are in luck. Only the sea must part."

Simon chuckled. He took Elisabeth's hand and helped her to her feet. They stood that way for a moment, hands clasped, and he wondered if she gained as much confidence from his touch as he did from hers. He squeezed her fingers and released them.

"Let's go."

Had there not been a breeze off the water that day, Simon thought the crush of thousands of children on the narrow strip of rocky beach would have suffocated them all. As it was, a hundred or more collapsed while Nicholas offered up long prayers and the sun bore down.

All morning and into the afternoon, Nicholas made speeches and shouted prayers until he grew hoarse. Simon, on the other hand, chose to dedicate himself to silent meditation and entreaty. It had been difficult for him to focus on spiritual things, what with children everywhere and rocks cutting into his knees. Nicholas, he could ignore.

Except for now.

The boy ranted about something. Simon cracked open one eye to see the child arguing with Hugo, arms waving. He tried to disregard their bickering until Nicholas called out to Elisabeth some distance away. The boy's words were lost to Simon, but he could see that Elisabeth turned an angry face to their leader. The dispute was going to get worse.

Simon sighed and lifted himself from the ground, marveling that the stones could pierce feet as calloused as his.

Coming from the opposite direction, Elisabeth reached Nicholas and Hugo before Simon did. Her cheeks glowed bright like her hair, and

Simon heard her say, "But you can't make the children sit in the heat any longer."

Nicholas's chin jutted out. "I won't allow them to desert me. They must be ready for God's miracle."

"I told you, they're not going anywhere," Hugo said, wiping his brow. "They simply need a reprieve from the sun."

The boy shook with rage. "Am I not bearing the full force of the sun, myself? Why, then, should they scatter to the trees?"

Simon spoke. "What will it hurt, Nicholas? We've been sitting here for hours."

The child rounded on him. "You are all faithless! I'll show you what God will do."

Simon looked to Hugo. The young man's face reflected his own impatience with Nicholas's temper.

Nicholas splashed into the water then turned and raised his arms. "Crusaders," he yelled.

The waves muted the sound of the boy's voice. Nevertheless, a hush grew over the crowd, and all eyes strained to see him.

"God has delivered us," he cried when they stilled. "He brought us to this place and this time for his glory."

Despite everything, Simon couldn't resist the excitement that swelled his chest. Nicholas was right—God had brought them to this point. And when the Lord opened the sea for them, the world would never be the same. God's mighty work included Simon. The blood rushed through his ears, a dizzying roar.

Nicholas continued. "Many have fallen in sacrifice to the Lord's call. Many will fall yet. But he has for us this day a hope. A crown. A *miracle*."

Simon smiled. *Yes, Lord.*

"We will march to the Holy Lands," Nicholas shouted. "Do you believe?"

"We believe," several called out.

"We will walk on dry ground. Do you believe?"

Simon joined in with hundreds. "We believe."

"We will dance in victory. Do you believe?"

Thousands exclaimed, "We believe."

Simon swayed, lightheaded with anticipation. He watched Nicholas move into the sea until water reached his waist. Simon and the entire company of children cheered when Nicholas lifted the carved cross and slammed it into the waves like Moses striking the rock.

But nothing happened.

Nicholas struck the water again. The waves rolled past him, lazy, undisturbed.

He beat the top of the water again and again with the cross, to no avail.

Simon's head cleared. He watched Nicholas flail, thrashing the water like a child throwing a temper tantrum.

Nicholas turned toward the beach, wild eyes moving from one crusader to another. "Who disbelieves?" It was more roar than shout.

No one answered. Simon's mind reeled, and he glanced at Hugo. Shock and grief etched the young man's hard face.

Nicholas made way to the shore until he stood thigh-deep in the sea. He pointed the dripping crucifix toward the crowd. "Whose doubt betrays me?"

No child moved to confess. Simon's eyes shifted to Elisabeth. She trembled, and devastation sat evident upon her features.

Eyes bulging in a mottled face, Nicholas took a deep breath to bellow out his next words. "Who—"

"You lied!" Elisabeth splashed into the water. "You lied to us all!" She neared Nicholas. "Thousands died for your vision, and you've led us here for nothing."

She stood six inches taller than the boy, but he took advantage of her fragile footing and swung her into an approaching wave.

Simon took off running towards them. Elisabeth popped out of the waves, gasping and spitting seawater.

"This is our traitor," Nicholas shouted. He grasped her tunic and pushed her under the water.

Elisabeth twisted beneath the surface, trying to escape Nicholas's hold. Loose strands from her braid fanned out around her head.

"No, Nicholas!" Simon slipped on the rocks and went down with a splash.

He regained his footing while Hugo lumbered past him to grab Nicholas by the scruff of the neck. He lifted him off Elisabeth just as Simon reached her. He pulled her upright, and she drew air into her lungs, then coughed and sputtered.

Hugo looked ready to drown their leader himself, and he might have had Nicholas not suddenly shouted to the children on shore. "Stop! Wait where you are. You cannot leave."

Simon supported Elisabeth as she continued to struggle for breath, but he and Hugo both followed Nicholas's gaze.

Hundreds of children quietly trudged over the hill and out of sight like weary ants at the close of a fruitless expedition. Simon's mouth slackened.

It was over. In little more than a heartbeat, all their dreams had died.

Hugo looked at Nicholas, dripping like a wet rat beside him, and released the boy's tunic.

The child dropped to the water, but found his feet at once. "How dare you handle me like that?"

"You're lucky you're still alive."

"I'm not afraid of you," Nicholas spat.

"Stop," Simon said from behind them. He led Elisabeth from the water and eased her to the ground, brushed back the hair that clung to her cheeks, then stood and faced Nicholas. "You should be hung for trying to kill her."

Nicholas recoiled. "H—her doubt prevented God's miracle. I thought—it was simply trial by water."

Simon moved to tower over the boy. "Trial by water? You were *holding* her under the surface."

Nicholas must have noticed his own lips quivering, for he pinched them together before speaking. "I meant no harm. She's fine."

Hugo interrupted. "And what of the sea, Nicholas? What's your excuse for that?"

"My vision is true, but God showed me only the day and the place. In your impatience, you've tried to force his almighty hand. He will divide the waters in his own time."

"If your words prove false, we will part company this very day."

"Then you'll go alone." Nicholas swirled his cloak in their direction and stomped away.

"I'll follow you," Simon said to Hugo when Nicholas had gone.

Hugo swallowed and nodded. "Let us see what God will do."

Chapter 17

25 August AD 1212, near Genoa, Holy Roman Empire
Though hundreds left the shore, thousands still remained.

Hugo spent the rest of the day looking out to sea, pleading with the Lord to remove his doubts and begging him to part the waters as Nicholas's vision had promised.

God did neither.

As the afternoon wore on, streams of children departed from the beach. When the sun dipped toward the horizon, Simon sat down beside him.

"Do you have a plan?" Simon said.

Hugo nodded to the east. "We'll head down the coast to another port city. See if we can find passage on ships."

Simon rubbed his chin. "There are few good harbors on the Italian Peninsula." His mind seemed to study some invisible map. "It's probably two hundred miles overland to Venice." He spoke slowly, still thinking. "Brindisi is much farther, as is Amalfi. Pisa is close, but there's no guarantee any of those cities would view us more favorably than Genoa."

He drummed against his leg for a moment, then paused and

looked toward the sinking sun. "Marseilles." He grinned. "We can follow the coast westward. Marseilles rivals Genoa—even Venice—in trade. There'll be plenty of ships there."

Hugo smiled at Simon, grateful for the knowledge he brought to their partnership, but more so for the unity of heart they shared. He placed a hand on Simon's shoulder. "Thank you, my friend."

Simon looked at him with dark, steady eyes. "I'm honored to stand by you, Hugo."

Hugo tipped his head in acknowledgment, and then motioned to the children on the beach. "How many remain?"

Simon's eyes flicked to the group. "Fifteen hundred. Maybe two thousand."

So few. "And will Nicholas let them go with us peacefully?"

Simon shook his head. "I don't know."

"Then let's find out."

Hugo swallowed hard as Simon tagged behind to where Nicholas sat amid a group of young followers.

"Nicholas," he said, softening his voice. "May I have a word?"

The boy narrowed his eyes. "Say what's on your mind."

"Simon and I have decided to find passage on a ship to the Holy Lands," Hugo said. "You inspired us to embark on this crusade, and we are eager to continue without delay. Is there any way we can assist you with your plans before we leave?"

Hugo glanced at Simon, whose eyebrows rose in astonishment, before returning his gaze to Nicholas.

"I'm going to Rome," Nicholas said as if he'd just made up his mind to do so. "I'll gain an audience with the pope. Persuade him to finance our movement—give us ships and equipment." He smiled. "You should come with us instead of going off on your own."

Hugo bowed his head. "Thank you for your offer, Nicholas. Your proposal is a fine one. But I believe the Lord is calling us to do this. Perhaps he requires that we prepare the way for your arrival."

Simon gasped at the suggestion, and apparently choked on his own saliva. Hugo thumped him on the back. "Are you all right, friend?" Simon glared at Hugo while he struggled for breath.

Nicholas, unperturbed by Simon's interruption, smiled. "I see what you mean."

Hugo returned the smile, but said nothing else.

The boy put a hand to his chin. "Yes," he drawled. "I think that must be what God has planned."

"Very well," Hugo said. "I am at your service."

"Is there anything you need?" Nicholas said.

Simon started to protest, but Hugo raised a hand as though he required silence to consider his response.

"There is one thing," he said after a moment.

"Name it."

"I am ashamed to admit that Simon and I do not constitute a notable forward party."

Nicholas's eyebrows crinkled. "You're right." He sat there, thinking. "I'll send fifty others with you."

Instinctively, Hugo's gaze narrowed at the pompous little twit, but then he cast his eyes down in submission. "Very well. Not so grand a delegation as you deserve, but surely someone in Palestine will take notice." He paused and lifted his gaze. "Maybe."

Nicholas's eyes widened. "No, you're right." He bit his lip and glanced at the boys beside him before transferring his focus back to Hugo. "Take as many as will follow you. You have my blessing. I can raise a new army in Rome."

§ § §

Elisabeth felt a hand on her shoulder and turned to see Simon squatting beside her.

"Are you all right?" he said.

The sun was low in the sky, so she must have been staring out across the water for hours. "I have to get there, Simon. How am I going to do that?"

He smiled. "Come with Hugo and me."

Her brain felt muddled. "To Palestine?"

Simon nodded. "Hugo is leading a second group with Nicholas's blessing. We're going to Marseilles, Elisabeth. We'll sail from there."

She turned toward the beach. Only a fraction of the children from the morning remained. Her curse would never be lifted. "We're doomed. There aren't enough of us."

Simon took her by the shoulders. "We're not doomed. God has used a smaller army than this. Don't you remember how Gideon routed the Midianites in the Valley of Jezreel?"

Elisabeth had no idea what he was talking about, and her face must have said so.

"The Lord used only 300 Israelites under Gideon's command to send the enemy running scared. They slaughtered 120,000 Midianites."

The story was unfamiliar, but surely Simon knew what he was talking about. "You really think God will go with us? That he will give us success?"

Simon grinned. "I *know* it, Elisabeth."

"What's Nicholas going to do?"

Simon looked crestfallen. "Head to Rome to seek the pope."

That meant Simon's group would be under Hugo's leadership. Elisabeth balked. Could she follow that swine's direction?

Simon caught her hesitation. "You'd rather go with Nicholas?"

No, she wouldn't. She sighed.

Two options. Both bad.

But Simon was going with Hugo. Elisabeth studied him. He'd changed a lot since they met. Or perhaps she had done the changing.

Well, she couldn't just sit on the beach forever.

"I'll come."

Chapter 18

Mid-September AD 1212, Marseilles, Region of Provence

"You say the man paid for your ale?" Simon said to Hugo, doubt in his eyes.

"Yes, and insisted on buying my dinner." The uncommon hospitality shown by the citizens of Marseilles still amazed him.

Their company arrived in the city two days previous with little difficulty on the road from Genoa. Marseilles, clean and white against the backdrop of sandy hills and Mediterranean blue, dominated the north bank above a narrow, three-sided port. Its residents welcomed the crusaders and offered shelter within the city. In fact, many of them opened their homes to the thirteen hundred children that followed Hugo. One would have thought it a festival week with so many young, joyful faces in their midst.

"This Monsieur le Ferreus," Simon said, "do you think him sincere?"

They walked together up the public road from the port, past Fort Saint-Jean. "I believe he truly wants to help," Hugo said. "What harm can there be in meeting with him? It puts no one at risk."

"I've prayed that God would provide generous hearts to aid our travel to the Holy Lands, but thought at least we'd have to search them out."

"Well, Monsieur le Ferreus tracked me down," Hugo said, grinning, "entertained me last evening with tavern food and merchant tales, and invited me to his offices today. Those are some prayers you offer up, Simon."

Simon sighed. "Perhaps I'm just being skittish after our experience with the Genoese."

"The Genoese are pigs. Assistance is what we hoped for, was it not?"

The scrawny young man shrugged and grunted his agreement.

Hugo stopped and surveyed the building across the street. "That's it."

Simon's left eyebrow rose. "You're sure?"

He was sure all right. Ferreus had given detailed instructions. The offices sat on the east side of a winding street between a four-story home pitched precariously toward the sea and a workshop displaying the woodcarver's symbol of a crossed hammer and chisel. Ferreus's place boasted a red door, just as the man said, though in truth it had faded to a disappointing mud brown.

"It looks vacant," Simon said.

Hugo ignored him and strode across the street to bang on the sludge-colored door. In a moment, a small man with bent shoulders and restless eyes summoned them inside. He muttered something in French and left them standing in the dim, musty room. The space was bare except for a trestle table and four stools.

"He said he's going to find the captain," Simon said. "You suppose he means Ferreus?"

"I guess." A peculiar tingling began at the back of Hugo's scalp, but he attributed it to the sudden coolness of the building. It was a warm September day, and the sun shone intensely as the noon hour approached.

Soon the nervous man reappeared and led them upstairs to well-appointed living quarters.

Hugh le Ferreus stood near a window fitted with a thick piece of glass. "Ah, my young friend," he said to Hugo. "I'm glad you found me." He smiled and motioned to Simon. "Who is this?"

The large man's genial tone put Hugo at ease. He introduced Simon then accepted Ferreus's invitation to sit at a table sanded smooth as marble. The servant brought refreshments on pewter platters and poured wine into fine goblets. Simon sipped the drink with caution, but Hugo's throat was dry, his business important, and his relief at finding a moneyed supporter so great, he swallowed the beverage like a man accustomed to such things.

After they partook of the almonds, raisins, and pastries on the table, Ferreus got down to business. "Tell me, young Hugo, how might I serve the needs of your campaign?"

"We are in want of transport to the Holy Lands, good sir."

Ferreus's bushy eyebrows lifted, and he smiled. "You are in luck, my friend. I own two ships."

Hugo's heart raced at the news. "But we cannot afford passage."

"Then it will be my gift to you."

Hugo could hardly believe their good fortune. A smile stretched across his face. "God bless you, sir."

"Excuse me," Simon interrupted.

Hugo had almost forgotten his friend was present.

Simon continued. "Monsieur le Ferreus, please sir, why would you do this for us?"

Ferreus sat back in his chair and stroked his long, graying beard. "After living eighteen years as a merchant, I have decided to devote to charity—for God's honor and service—the goods which I have so painstakingly acquired. I am determined to sell my possessions and distribute them among the poor, that I might follow Christ more freely."

Simon's eyes widened.

Hugo cleared his throat and spoke. "But first you will convey us to Jerusalem?"

Ferreus's long beard bobbed up and down as he nodded. "That is correct. If you will permit me, of course."

The proposal was outstanding. They'd be fools to turn it down. Hugo smiled at Simon, who signaled his agreement.

"It seems God has brought us together, sir," Hugo said. "We would be honored to accept your offer."

Ferreus took his seat with a grin. "Very well. Tell me, then, how many of you are there?"

"Thirteen hundred," Simon said.

Ferreus's eyes darted to Hugo. "Thirteen?"

Perhaps they were too many. "Can it be done?" Hugo asked around a lump of worry in his throat.

Ferreus smiled and licked his lips. "Oh, yes, of course, but I had no idea you were so many. We will need more ships. I shall consult with William Porcus, an old partner of mine."

The tightness in Hugo's throat diminished. "You think he will help?"

Ferreus stood. "I'm quite certain of it. I'll go see him right away."

"Shall we join you?" Simon said as he and Hugo rose to their feet.

"No." Ferreus's voice was firm. "I will speak to Porcus alone. Present your cause in words that will appeal to his—ah—tender nature."

The man ushered them out of the room and down the stairs.

His smile no longer reached his eyes, but Hugo could tell Ferreus's mind already formulated the line of reasoning he would take with his old partner.

"Would you like us to wait here?" Hugo said.

Ferreus shook his head. "Come back tomorrow at this time."

"Yes, sir." Hugo moved to exit the building, but Ferreus stopped him with a firm hand to his chest.

"My friend is not so benevolent as myself," Ferreus said. "Do you have anything of value among yourselves?"

Hugo's shoulders drooped. "No. Nothing. We are as beggars before God and man."

Ferreus's mouth twisted, and he let out a sigh. "Well, then, I'll do what I can."

"We will pray for you, monsieur," Simon said.

The man's eyes shifted to the street beyond the doorway. "You do that, young friend." He stepped over the threshold, looked up and down the road, then motioned them out. "Be off with you now. Don't speak of my intentions to anyone."

Simon was quiet as they returned to their lodgings.

"Ferreus is a man of great humility, don't you think?" Hugo said. "The children will soon rejoice at our good fortune."

"Elisabeth should accompany us tomorrow."

"Ferreus said not to tell anyone his plan."

"But she is trustworthy and will know what arrangements the children require."

Hugo considered Simon's words. Surely Ferreus wouldn't mind Elisabeth's knowing. And Simon was right about her—she'd offer valuable recommendations. "Speak to her straightaway, then."

§ § §

Despite Hugo's elation the day before, it seemed to Simon that he now steamed like a pot about to boil. Elisabeth's temper was no better. They'd waited almost three hours, but at last le Ferreus and Porcus showed up for their scheduled meeting.

"You've kept us waiting an intolerable—" Hugo began, but Ferreus lifted a hand to cut him off.

"This is my dear ally, William Porcus."

Porcus blinked, adjusting his eyes to the dim offices, then shifted his gaze to Simon. Without introduction, the man squinted at him, then belched. "He's too skinny," he said in German laced with a heavy French accent.

Ferreus pointed to Hugo. "Look at this one, though. Strong as an oarsman." He suddenly noticed Elisabeth. "Who's this?"

"A trusted member of our company," Hugo said.

Le Ferreus looked Elisabeth up and down, and then pulled her forward. "She'll be a beauty when she gets some meat on her bones, eh?" he said to Porcus. "Do you see her hair?" He lifted Elisabeth's long copper braid, to her obvious embarrassment. She twisted away to stand near Simon, trembling with anger, but silent.

Porcus's eyes moved back to Simon. He grunted. "Very many like him, and they won't survive the trip. It'll be a complete loss."

Simon felt himself redden. "It's true we're underfed, but the citizens of your city have been gracious to us. We grow stronger and healthier every day."

Ferreus smiled. "Porcus, tend your tongue." He did not invite them upstairs, but motioned for them to be seated at the trestle table in the common room.

There were only four stools, so Simon stood behind Elisabeth, hands at his hips, conscious of his gangly form, the way his bony elbows poked through the sleeves of his threadbare tunic. Though he rarely considered such things, he wished he had Hugo's broad chest and powerful arms. Even with the rigors of their journey, Hugo still looked like a man, not an undernourished child. Simon shook his head to push the vain thoughts aside.

Hugo looked at Porcus. "Will you help us or not?"

Ferreus laid a hand on Hugo's arm. "Patience, my young friend." He turned his attention to Porcus. "William, as my colleague and brother in Christ, won't you consider our petition? These young people have traveled far, blessed by the hand of God. Think of the treasure you will store up in heaven by aiding them."

Porcus frowned. "You can't buy ale with heavenly funds."

Ferreus glanced toward the crusaders then leaned close to Porcus. "God's reward is all you need," he said in a firm voice.

Porcus sat still for perhaps a full minute, and then rubbed a hand over his face. "Oh, all right. You can count on one of my ships."

Simon's heart beat faster. "Thank you. God bless—"

Ferreus lifted a palm in the air, quieting Simon's gratitude. "William, you own three ships. There are more than a thousand children."

Porcus bounded to his feet, bellowing out a stream of curses. "You expect me to let you use all three? What if I can't make a profit?"

Elisabeth jumped up to lean across the table and point a finger at him. "What kind of profit do you expect to receive, taking a group of children to the Holy Lands? Would you have us sell ourselves to the Mohammedans to line your purse?"

Simon reached for her. "Careful, Elisabeth."

"*He* needs to be careful. I've had enough," she said. "Surely Monsieur le Ferreus has other partners. If not, I'm ready to leave."

Ferreus stood. "Don't be rash, girl. William only hopes that his ships will return from Palestine with enough goods to cover his expenses." He turned, towering above Porcus to speak terse words. "We do not serve God for profit. Would you abandon the children to other traders who would steal from you the blessing of providing for God's chosen ones?"

Porcus screwed up his face as the two men stared each other down. Finally, his eyes turned toward the floor. "It's a crazy wager. We're likely to lose everything, but I'll do it."

Ferreus smiled and clapped a hand on Porcus's back. "A worthy investment, my friend."

Simon felt relief course through his veins. At the same time, Elisabeth relaxed under his grip on her slender shoulder.

"How soon can we get under way?" Hugo said.

Ferreus chuckled. "Three weeks perhaps. Two, if we're lucky."

"So long?"

"We must hire on fresh crews. Make sure the vessels are seaworthy."

"And stock them with plenty of food for the children," Elisabeth said.

Ferreus's face went flat. "Yes. Of course."

"How will they be lodged aboard ship?" Elisabeth was nothing if not persistent. Simon hoped she wouldn't offend the man.

"These are merchant ships, my dear. Though they are of the newest design—with decks that offer protection from the elements—I'm afraid conditions will be cramped and uncomfortable."

"How cramped?"

"She's like a bulldog, that one," Porcus grumbled.

Simon couldn't help smiling.

Ferreus ignored his partner. "There's space on each ship for about two hundred souls. We'll carry crews of at least fifty."

Simon calculated. "That means your five ships will hold only seven hundred fifty of our number. We have almost twice that many."

Porcus snarled. "Children are small."

Elisabeth shook her head. "Not that small. And we've many young men and maidens. We'll need more ships."

Ferreus nearly sneered. "We don't have any more."

"Then hire them."

"With what? Neither we nor you have any assets."

"Wait," Simon said. "That's not true."

Hugo and Elisabeth turned to him in surprise, even as a slow smile spread across Ferreus's face. Porcus stepped close, one eye squinting, the other studying him below a raised eyebrow.

Simon looked to Hugo. "The parchments."

"Parchments?" Ferreus said.

Simon matched Hugo's gaze. At last Hugo nodded. "If you are willing to make this sacrifice for your companions, then I approve."

The very words of God. Words Simon copied with his own hand. It crushed him to think of it, but the time was right. In faith, he would do this. "It is a worthy cause."

Taking a deep breath, he withdrew the small books from his leather pouch and extended them to Ferreus.

The man's eyes lit up like a bonfire as he reached to take them.

Simon licked dry lips. "They are the Holy Scriptures. Not in their entirety," he clarified, "but valuable all the same. I hope it is enough to secure more ships."

Ferreus's hands trembled with excitement. Porcus just smiled and scratched his throat. The *scritch*, *scritch* of nails against whiskers reminded Simon of the rats that used to scuttle about the wattle and daub hut of his early childhood.

Ferreus cleared his throat. "They might suffice, though I doubt we can engage more than two ships with these alone. Are there more?"

"No. This is everything."

Porcus snorted. "Don't expect more than two additional vessels, then. We aren't made of gold, you know."

"Seven ships will do," Hugo said, taking Elisabeth by the arm and lifting her to her feet. "We trust you'll make the necessary arrangements in a timely manner."

Ferreus dipped his head. "But of course. Come back in a fortnight, and we'll collaborate on final details."

Hugo's eyes flashed. "With Simon's contributions to your efforts, we expect to sail in a week. I'll be back tomorrow to check your progress."

Simon followed Hugo and Elisabeth to the street. He did not tell them how his knees quivered or the degree to which his heart ached.

§ § §

Eight days later, Elisabeth waited for Simon outside Saint Laurent's Church. They were to set sail the following day. He emerged with a peaceful smile.

"Simon," she said.

She liked how his face brightened when he saw her.

"What are you doing here?" he said.

"Waiting for you."

"You should have come inside."

Elisabeth glanced at the massive church door and shook her head.

Simon took her hand and led her around the building where the steps gave view to the sea. They sat in silence for several minutes. "What's wrong, Elisabeth?"

She bit her lower lip, but did not answer his question. "Hugo said farewell already."

Simon nodded. "To me also."

"He thought we might not have the opportunity to speak in the morning since we're each assigned to different ships."

"He's probably right."

She buried her head in her hands. Simon didn't say a word. At last she spoke through her fingers. "Aren't you afraid?"

"No, Elisabeth. I'm not."

She looked up at him, at the confidence in his eyes.

"We are called by God," he said. "He will not leave us or forsake us. You must believe that."

"What of Kateline and the others? Did he not forsake them?"

"No, they are with Jesus in Paradise. And our faith has been tested and refined."

Elisabeth straightened. "I don't know why I feel so frightened. I want this, but so much could happen on the sea."

Simon smiled. "Trust in God. He has *chosen* us, Elisabeth."

"Must we be on separate ships?"

"You and I?"

She nodded.

"It's only a few weeks," he said.

"But what if—what if something happens?" she whispered through trembling lips.

Simon chuckled and wrapped a brotherly arm around her shoulders. "It won't."

For a moment she felt the urge to pull away, but in truth, his touch calmed her. She sighed. "I wish I was brave."

"You are."

She shook her head. "No. I'm a coward just tagging along in the hope I'll find favor with God."

"You've already found his favor, Elisabeth. He loves you." He cocked his head at her. "You don't believe me, do you?"

She got to her feet. "I should make sure the others are ready for tomorrow."

Simon stood on the step below, still taller than Elisabeth by three or four inches. "So we take our leave now?" he said.

She smiled and nodded. "May God grant you a safe journey, Simon. I'll miss you."

"It is only for a time."

"I know."

They looked at one another for a long minute. She wanted to cry, wanted to change all the unkind things she'd said and done. Wanted to stay with him.

He touched the tip of her nose with one knobby finger. "Go with God."

Chapter 19

Late-September AD 1212, the Mediterranean Sea

"Where are the other ships?" Elisabeth demanded.

The sailor stared until Elisabeth's skin crawled. He gave her a crooked grin and a shrug.

Fine. She'd look for Porcus, much as she hated speaking to the man. She found him on a raised deck at the rear of the vessel, digging in one ear with his finger.

"Where are the other ships?"

He grimaced at her. "Don't trouble me, girl, or I'll tie you up below."

She ignored his threat. "There are six other vessels. Why can't I see any of them?"

"Look." He leaned close enough for her to observe the hairs in his nose. "I listened to your caterwauling and let you on deck—"

"Only a dozen of us at a time, and only for a few minutes."

The veins in his neck bulged. "You're lucky to get that."

"Well, we haven't gotten much to eat. You should at least give us a decent meal. I know there's plenty. I saw the men loading the ship."

He grabbed her and pressed a filthy hand to her mouth. "Hush up, now," he growled. "Don't push me too far."

Fear snaked through Elisabeth's chest at the meanness in his eyes. His grip hurt her, but she resisted the impulse to strike him. She relaxed her body and gave him a nod instead.

Porcus released her. "Get below deck. If I hear you complaining again, no one comes up top, and I'll reduce your rations. Understand?"

A strong gust of wind blew loose strands of hair into her face. With a shaky hand, she pulled them away. "I was only concerned for the others. Shouldn't we be able to see them?"

His face turned red. "Do you understand me?"

She narrowed her eyes at him. "I understand."

"Then get below."

§ § §

"Let me speak with Monsieur le Ferreus," Simon said, hand on the ladder that led to the deck.

The toothless seaman paused on the steps and grinned. "Guess you'll have to make an appointment." He laughed, then scurried up the ladder and slammed down the hatch before Simon could follow.

Simon ran a hand over his face. He spoke to the children crowding near. "At least we've got a candle now." Little good it would do. The air in the hold was already stifling and smelled like sweat and vomit. The smoke from the small putrid flame would hardly be worth the illumination it provided.

He pried open a barrel of water, then measured out a small portion in the single cup they had and handed it to the first child. "Someone pass along the loaves of bread. Don't take too much."

"There's mold on the cheese," a small voice said.

Simon sighed. "Scrape it off."

What was Ferreus thinking? That two hundred children could go untended in the entrails of his small ship? They needed fresh air, better food. A place to relieve themselves. Perhaps the man feared that one of the young ones would fall overboard, but Simon would watch over them.

Dread tickled his throat. Something wasn't right. He wasn't the only one to think so.

An older boy moved next to him. "We're practically prisoners," he said quietly.

Simon nodded and dropped his voice to a whisper. "I'll wait at the top of the ladder. When next the hatch is opened, I'll force my way above and insist—on behalf of the children—that Ferreus give me an audience."

"It'll be a long wait," the boy said.

Simon moved about the hold, encouraging the others. Perhaps if they rearranged the cargo, they'd be less cramped. "You, and you," he said to two of the bigger boys, "help me move some of this."

They began to stack the sacks and barrels.

"Not too high. We don't want them falling down on top of us." Several bundles lay against the hull of the ship. "Here, we can place some of the sacks on these."

Simon stepped close to push against the goods, testing their stability. They gave. "Bring the candle."

One of the boys carried out his request. Simon moved from bundle to bundle, examining the contents. Wool. Linen. Furs. He swallowed back his anger.

That Ferreus decided to profit on this voyage after all was the man's own business. But that they were so cramped in the hold they sat on top of each other was infuriating.

Simon staked out his place on the ladder and instructed that the candle be blown out. He wasn't sure they'd get another anytime soon and didn't want it wasted. While he perched on the steps in the dark, his concern grew. He wondered how Elisabeth and Hugo were getting along on their ships. His mind conceived all sorts of potential hardship and suffering for the crusaders, and he sought to stave off his sinister imagination with prayer.

For a time, he felt comforted. Then he discerned an exaggeration in the movement of the vessel. When he heard the crack of thunder and felt the boat rock violently with the waves, he banged against the door of the hatch for some news of their circumstances.

It never opened.

§ § §

Hugo stopped struggling against the man who pinned his arms behind him and looked at the captain of the ship.

"What's this?" the captain said.

"He's gettin' a bit unpleasant." The beefy sailor holding Hugo's arms gave them a twist.

Hugo panted after the short struggle. "There's no need to lock us below like captives. Monsieur le Ferreus will hear about this when we reach Palestine."

The captain and his mate laughed, and the sound made Hugo's stomach turn. These men were scoundrels. For the first time since boarding two days ago, he truly feared for the safety of the children in his care. "We won't tolerate these conditions any longer."

Humor left the captain's face. "And what will you do about it?"

Hugo thought of the dagger at his waist. "There are many more of us than there are of you."

The captain's eyebrows rose. "Mutiny, is it?" He smiled. "I can't be risking that, now, can I?" He nodded to the man holding Hugo.

To Hugo's relief, the man released him. Perhaps the captain finally saw reason.

Something slammed into the back Hugo's head. Pain sliced through his skull, fading his vision. He dropped to his knees. When he strained to get to his feet, something pressed sharp against his throat.

The captain's dark eyes glowered down at him.

"You're a fool," the man said, a sword extended.

Hugo had no time to respond before a blinding punch landed against his temple. He felt the deck rush up to meet him, busting his lip. Then nothing.

When he came around, his head throbbed, and his stomach churned with the motion of the ship. A roar sounded in his ears. He tried to roll over, but something restrained his hands and prevented him from doing so. Cracking open one eye brought a sharp pain to his head, but soon his vision focused on a small opening in the hull. Seawater sprayed in through the little window, misting him.

He was in a storage room of some sort. Near the cook's galley, if his nose told him anything. His hands were tied in front of him and bound to a narrow plank that spanned the space between the wall and floor. A look at his waist confirmed the dagger was gone. With great effort, Hugo got to his knees and tugged at the beam, but neither the wood nor the rope gave. On closer inspection, he realized the timber passed through the flooring to some area below. He guessed he'd been thrown into one of the raised regions of the craft, above the main deck.

The vessel rocked unevenly. Hugo lost his balance, banging headfirst into the wooden beam. The impact sent slivers of light across his vision and doubled the agony in his skull, making him retch.

He refused to kneel in his own vomit, so when the surge of pain subsided, he grasped the beam and pulled himself to his feet. Dizziness threatened to send him back to the floor, but he leaned against the timber and held on as the ship bucked the waves. At last he raised his eyes to the rectangular window—not more than a slit in the wood, really—and noticed for the first time that it wasn't night, as he had thought.

A storm raged outside. The roaring that filled his head was the wind, driven down from black clouds. No wonder the ship roiled in a frenzied dance. He licked the mist from his lips. It was rain, not seawater, that spewed into his tiny prison.

Lightning blazed at the same moment a tremendous crash shook the boat. Shouts, though muffled by the storm, confirmed that they'd been struck. Hugo smelled smoke somewhere close by.

He yanked at his bonds to no avail then slid the rope that bound his wrists up the beam until he reached the joint at the wall. He shook the timber, attempting to loosen it. The movement made his head spin and ache, but did no good. He rubbed the rope back and forth over the edge of the wood, hoping to break the fibers. After several ineffective tries, arms quivering with the effort, he stopped. Sweat dripped into his eyes.

"God, help me," he groaned. Not exactly the sort of prayer Kateline would have voiced, but the best he had to offer.

The ship came to a violent halt. Like a rider thrown from an obstinate horse, Hugo pitched over the beam to hang from his wrists. Objects flew across the room, smashing into him, glancing off his head and shoulders. He fought another wave of nausea and struggled to find his feet. The remnant of light from the slit of a window disappeared, leaving the compartment in darkness.

What had happened?

His mind barely had time to form the question when the craft slammed against something again, knocking him off balance. When it happened a third time, he clung to the beam to keep from being battered to unconsciousness.

The sound of snapping wood accompanied a fourth, jarring impact. Against what, Hugo had no idea. He felt along the beam. His heart leapt when he discovered it had splintered. Ignoring the pain in his arms and head, he yanked against the weakened section until it broke apart. Slipping his bound hands from the restraint, he moved to the door. Locked. He kicked until it burst open.

Beyond the door, a lantern rocked from a hook in the deserted galley. He located a knife, dropped to the floor, and wedged the handle between his knees to use the blade like a saw. Minutes later, the fibers severed, Hugo shook his hands free of the rope and ran through a dark passageway to the deck, the vessel trembling under the force of the wind and sea.

The ship had been driven into the side of a cliff. Even now, waves continued to crush it against the rocks. The sheer mountain of stone offered little hope of abandoning the craft for land, but still the crewmembers attempted to scramble upward. None got high enough to reach safety before losing their footholds; they plummeted to the water below or fell to the deck like wounded birds. One man lay impaled on the jagged remains of a broken mast. Hugo had no time to consider the horror, for the sound of two hundred voices rose above the noise of the storm. Racing past timbers charred by the lightning to the barred hatch, he gripped the lever and released the door.

Water flooded the cargo area below. Frantic faces looked up at him, small hands clinging to the ladder. Several treaded water. Hugo feared some had already been overcome. Boys and girls scurried onto the deck, but not fast enough. Hugo braced his leg against the far side of the opening and reached into the hold to help the exhausted and frightened children to safety.

His muscles burned with the exertion, but he pulled young bodies from the would-be grave, even as waves washed over the deck.

"What do we do now?" a girl cried out.

It seemed the entire crew had either abandoned ship or perished. Hugo called to the children nearby to help the remaining young ones from the hold, and then ran to the bow of the vessel to peer down at the rocks. Perhaps they could find safety on the narrow ledges that met the sea. Risky, but they had no better alternative. The ship would go down, of that he was sure.

Screams raised the hair on the back of his neck, and he turned in time to see ten or fifteen children wash overboard with a retreating wave.

He wouldn't let the storm win. "Get ropes," he shouted, head spinning, light prickling his vision. "Lower them over the side here, near these outcroppings."

Several crusaders acted upon Hugo's instruction while he returned to the hold. Descending the ladder until the cold water rose chest-high, he squinted through the dark space. Barrels and parcels floated by, but he saw no one. "Anyone here?" he called.

Something soft bumped his leg below the water, causing his heart to pound. Reaching beneath the surface, his hand became entangled in fine hair. Hugo clenched it. There was resistance—the child's tunic was probably caught on something—but then he lifted a small girl up and over his shoulder, limp as a half-empty bag of grain. Retreating to the deck, he laid her out.

He thought her name was Cristina. She wasn't breathing. He shook her, hoping against all odds that she lived. Pressing his hands against her stomach, he tried to force the water from her lungs. Nothing.

No time to grieve. He left her there and ran to the bow to check the children's progress.

Many climbed down the rigging. Some had missed the ledge and slipped into the water. Young bodies floated face down in the deep, but still the others persisted, desperate for escape from the sinking ship. He feared there wouldn't be enough room for all of them on the narrow outcropping. And the waves. It seemed they crashed higher upon the rocks now.

Hugo trembled. Too many lives were lost already. Too many still counted on him.

A child cried out beside him. Hugo glanced down to find a golden haired girl. He thought of Kateline and wondered for an instant if she'd looked so vulnerable at such an age. The girl stepped close and wrapped her arms around him, burying her face in his stomach. He patted her back and lowered himself down to one knee so they gazed into each other's eyes. "Be brave."

His words were lost on the wind, but she nodded. He helped her onto the rigging then turned to rush past the crowd of evacuees, looking for another rope to aid them.

"Here," he yelled to a boy big enough to help. "Throw this over the side after I get it secured."

The boy grabbed the thick rope, pulling it toward the front of the vessel while Hugo worked to fasten the other end to an iron ring on the deck. He cursed the rain and waves that wet his hands and made him fumble with the knot.

Sudden shrieks caused him to look up. Water ran into his eyes. He swiped at them to clear his vision. Pandemonium had broken out among the children remaining on board. They crowded the bow, scrambling over each other in terror like lambs fleeing a monster from the deep. Some flung themselves over the edge to the waves below. One small boy dropped to the deck, tiny arms covering his head. A girl faced the sea, a hand over her mouth, the other pointing behind Hugo.

He spun around.

Another craft approached, driven by the storm to that very spot. He recognized the markings on the sail. One of the seven that had departed Marseilles. Hugo's stomach squeezed when he realized it was set on a collision course with them. The vessel plunged from the summit of a mountainous swell, and he could see it no longer.

Perhaps it had capsized. Dread and relief mingled in his chest. Was it Simon's boat, or Elisabeth's? To witness the loss would be excruciating, but it might mean the survival of these children in his care. He hated being forced to such thoughts.

The next wave proved the ship remained afloat. It drew perilously close. He saw   crewmembers jumping overboard to escape certain impact, but discerned no children. Were they held captive below decks, too? Mesmerized by the impending calamity, he watched as the nose of the other ship rose high above him on the crest of a wave. Almost too late, he ran to the bulwark and threw himself toward the water.

The clash of the two vessels came louder than any thunder

he'd ever heard. Just before he hit the sea, something struck him from behind. Searing pain pushed the air from his lungs as he plunged far below the surface.

§ § §

"Yes, I can," Hugo said to Eginolf.

"Prove it, then."

The last time Eginolf bested Hugo was two summers ago when they were twelve. Hugo stood and stripped off his tunic. "Start counting."

Eginolf shook his head. "Not until you're underwater."

Hugo grinned, took a deep breath, and dove into the pond.

He could hear Eginolf shouting. "One. Two. Three—"

Belatedly, Hugo wondered if his friend could count to a hundred. He should have thought about it before he took the dare. Sorry shape he'd be in if Eginolf got mixed up around forty and had to start over.

As it turned out, Eginolf seemed to have it mastered, but Hugo's lungs were burning long before the boy reached fifty. Only stubbornness kept him underwater to hear sixty-five. By ninety, he was fuzzyheaded and angry with Eginolf for counting so slowly, but he'd resolved to win the wager or die.

"Ninety-nine. One hundred."

§ § §

Hugo burst above the surface of the deep, gasping for breath. His lungs seemed paralyzed, and he couldn't get air fast enough. Each inhalation tortured the ribs beneath his right arm.

A wave thrust him close to the mangled mountain of wood that had been two ships only moments before. Frantic, he kicked away, unwilling to die amid the wreckage.

Bodies floated everywhere. Cries for help sounded here and there, but he could do nothing. He swallowed seawater, then gagged and spit it up.

A split plank floated just beyond him. He swam toward it and grabbed hold. Heaving his chest out of the water, he laid across it. His vision blurred with the effort.

The vessels were nearly submerged now. The cries quieted. He could see no one on the rock ledges, no one alive anywhere. The billows that ran the ships together must have washed the children from shore. The rain continued, but the strength of the waves seemed to have diminished.

He aimed himself parallel to the cliff and kicked. With excruciating slowness and almost unbearable agony, he inched his way past the small islet to the open sea.

Did he imagine a voice calling out?

It was, perhaps, the echo of screams that would haunt him forever.

The cry came again.

He looked up and saw a small head bobbing in the water.

"Hold on," he shouted.

The boy bled from a jagged wound at his temple, but he stayed afloat long enough for Hugo to help him onto the small wooden sanctuary.

Hugo must have passed out then.

When he awoke, the boy was gone.

Chapter 20

Fall AD 1212, the Mediterranean Sea
Simon calculated it'd been more than two weeks since they left Marseilles.

He'd long ago figured out that Hugh le Ferreus was a brigand and a fraud. In all this time, they'd been offered no reprieve from their captivity below deck. The food had been meager, the air in the hold foul, and the filth intolerable.

On the one occasion Simon attempted to force his way above, he'd been beaten and tossed back to the children. They wept over him, but were as powerless as he.

For Simon, the worst part of their wretched circumstances was discovering his own foolishness.

He'd thought himself wise.

Favored by God.

He shook his head. Vain was more like it. Proud of his intellect and arrogant before the Almighty.

He tried to explain it to Reto one day. "In my conceit, I determined that God had chosen me to help lead this crusade against the Saracens. A crusade. Now the idea seems preposterous."

Reto looked at him in fear. "Your faith has grown weak."

"It remains strong," he said. "But this whole scheme reeks of Satan's lies."

"Then we are doomed."

"No. There has to be a better way to carry out the Lord's will."

The young man's face twisted in confusion.

On another day, he sat talking to a fellow his age with a good mind and a fair knowledge of Scripture.

"Remember?" Simon said. "Though the Israelites were sent to wage war against the Lord's enemies in the days of the Old Testament kings and prophets, Jesus established a new law of love."

The young man scrunched up his mouth in skepticism.

Simon quoted. "'You must love the Lord your God with all your heart, all your soul, and all your mind.' This is the first and greatest commandment. A second is equally important: 'Love your neighbor as yourself.'"

"But the Mohammedans aren't our Christian brothers."

"I don't think it matters, does it?"

The fellow nodded. "Sure, and it does. Whoever heard of extending the love of God to the dark heathens?"

Simon spent the next few days in the blackened hold considering Christ's command from every angle. "All men are our neighbors," he tried to tell the others when the candle was lit. "How does slaughtering Mohammedans in the name of Jesus fit with this perspective?"

They stared at him, but did not answer.

"To bring them to faith in Christ, now that's the thing to do. And not by force or fear, but by love. That's the true call of God—to be messengers to the Saracens."

Several turned their backs to him. A few of the bigger lads eyed him and talked amongst themselves.

"Do you not see?" he said. It had become painfully clear to him.

One of the young men stood. "We've left our families and homes to wage this war. What you're preaching is wickedness and stinks like devil's dung. Keep your thoughts to yourself if you have so little faith."

Simon drew in a slow breath. The sputtering candle illuminated weary faces filled with fear, bitterness, anger, and hatred. They'd be more likely to listen once they reached the shores of Palestine. He could wait.

One by one they left him sitting by himself.

No wonder you discipline me aboard this ship, Lord. In my arrogance I've led these children astray. Forgive me.

He lowered his face to the grimy floor of the hold. *Even if I stand alone, use me to carry your message to the lost. I want no weapon but your divine power. No sword but your Spirit. Remove pride from my heart and evil from my motives. Instruct me in your way so that I might be your witness to the world.*

Three days later, Simon and the others were ushered onto the deck. Weak from hunger, eyes squinting against the glare of the sun, legs trembling at the unaccustomed activity, they were defenseless as their captors bound their wrists and shackled them together at the ankles.

Slaves, Simon's shocked mind realized.

Please, God, no.

In all the deprivation and misery of the voyage, Simon had never contemplated that possibility.

They were transferred to a Muslim pirate ship. Simon swallowed back his panic and dismay and shaded his eyes with his arms. The ship soon neared the port of a large city that hugged the flat coastline. In spite of everything, he marveled at that first glimpse of the land of his Savior. Until he saw the lighthouse soaring above the harbor. His eyes snapped to the white marble palaces and temples on shore, then back to the lighthouse. He'd read of this place.

Alexandria.

Egypt, then. Ferreus's treachery extended deeper than he imagined.

§ § §

You have heard that it was said, 'You shall love your neighbor and hate your enemy.' But I say to you, love your enemies, bless those who curse you, do good to those who hate you, and pray for those who spitefully use you and persecute you, that you may be sons of your Father in heaven . . .

Simon's mind kept repeating Jesus' words.

It was either that or weep, and he had no tears left.

The slavers divided the boys from the girls and the youngest from the oldest. As far as Simon could tell, only two shiploads of them were being auctioned off in Alexandria. Ferreus's ships. Neither Hugo nor Elisabeth was among them. Perhaps the others still made way to Palestine.

Simon thought it ironic that he sat in the center of this ancient city of learning, a dream come true under other circumstances. But stripped to his baggy leggings and tied up in a holding pen suitable for farm animals made it nothing but a nightmare.

A bear of a man—dark, hairy, and ferocious—shook the timbers that formed the stall, yelling at them in his native tongue. Coptic, perhaps. Probably Arabic. Simon knew both were spoken in northern Africa, and he understood neither. It was easy to see, however, that the man wanted them to stand and be quick about it.

Simon got to his feet with the others. The guard opened the gate, cursing at them, no doubt, and motioned them forward. He goaded them with a whip. They shuffled out of the pen and trundled toward a platform in the center of a market square, prodded along by an occasional blow to the head or shoulders.

There seemed to be great interest in the fair skinned slaves being offered. Some of the young women were already on display. Simon bowed his head when an auctioneer ripped the bodice of one maiden's tunic to expose her womanly assets. She screamed in protest, but a slap silenced her. Simon's chin trembled.

Beea was the first Arabic word he learned. *Sold.*

From what he could tell, one turbaned man bought all the young women. Then Simon and the young men tied to him were hustled up the steps. He lifted his head. The man who'd purchased the girls seemed interested in a number of the smaller boys in his line. In short order, they were cut from the rope that bound them together and guided to another holding area.

Simon surveyed the crowd. An older man standing near a fountain caught his attention, calm and quiet amid the raucous assembly. It startled Simon to realize the graying one appraised him. He looked the man straight in the eye, willing his torso to stop trembling. The man returned his stare for a moment before a smile broke across his face, and he nodded.

Simon didn't respond, but for some reason the peculiar interaction eased his spirit. He watched the man closely. When it came Simon's turn to be auctioned, he was not surprised to hear the older man call out the winning bid.

The auctioneer appeared to take issue with what the man said, but at last the seller nodded in agreement. Gray Hair spoke to a scribe at a nearby table while a guard cut Simon from the line and led him to the man's side.

"*Tah al,*" the man said, beckoning to Simon. *Come.*

The gray-haired one spun around and started off across the square, not looking back to see if Simon trailed behind. It crossed his mind to turn and run, but his hands were bound and it would be impossible to blend into the crowd with his height and bony, white limbs. So he did the only thing he could do.

He followed.

§ § §

The man lifted Elisabeth's flowing hair for the crowd to inspect. She jerked her head, trying to pull the tresses from his grasp. The spectators laughed.

When she learned that Porcus had taken them not to Palestine, but to a city called Damietta at the mouth of the Nile River in Africa, she wanted to murder the man. Once she realized they were to be sold as slaves, she wanted to murder every dirty Mohammedan she saw.

But she didn't see any now. She refused to look at the infidels ogling her. By focusing on a single, white cloud in the midst of the bluest sky she'd ever witnessed, she found it easier to ignore the screeches of the mob, the putrid stench of the strange city, and the anguish that tore her heart in two.

Bidding came fast and with great spirit. The auctioneer suddenly shouted a single word, and the crowd cheered. Rough hands grabbed her arms and jerked her from the wooden stand, yanking her back to the horror of her fate.

Elisabeth struggled against the handler, shouting curses and kicking at him. He slapped her, then grabbed her hair and pulled her close to his ugly face. His lips parted in a vile grin and dark eyes mocked her. Saliva landed on her cheek when he laughed.

She spat at him. The man raised his arm to strike her, but someone shouted to him. He paused—foul breath hot upon her face, mouth twisted in anger—then muttered some insult and thrust her into a holding pen.

He used such force that it sent her sprawling. She could hear him snickering as he locked the high gate. She'd bitten her lip and knocked a tooth loose. Blood came away on her hand when she wiped her mouth.

Elisabeth got to her knees and pulled the hair from her eyes. A dozen or more small crusaders huddled against the far side of the pen. Most were quite young, and a good number of them were crying.

"Don't let them see your tears," she snapped.

They looked at her in bewilderment.

"Hate them," she said. "Curse God. But don't ever show weakness."

"I want to go home," a little girl wailed.

"Shut up," Elisabeth said. "You'll never see home again."

Fear and astonishment distorted their features, but Elisabeth kept her own expression firm. No sense giving the children false comfort. The sooner they recognized the hopelessness of their future, the better.

Part II

Chapter 21

June AD 1217, near Rome, Italy

Hugo wiped his mouth with the back of one hand and set down his fourth cup of ale. Where was Orry? They were supposed to meet at this God-forsaken tavern on the Appian Way more than an hour ago.

A woman smiled in Hugo's direction and sauntered toward him, holding his gaze. "You look lonesome." Her voice purred as she knelt beside him.

"Just waiting for a friend."

She shifted to German as he had. "Really?" She smiled again and traced his muscled forearm with one finger. "*I'm* friendly."

"I can see that."

The young woman chuckled. She was still pretty, unlike most of the women that sold themselves in this area. Hugo took in the fair skin, blonde hair, and pale eyes. She didn't look more than seventeen. He briefly wondered if she'd been part of the failed crusade five years ago. Out of habit, he shut down that memory.

She placed a warm hand on Hugo's arm and moved it slowly to his shoulder. He didn't resist, so she eased herself onto his lap. "There, now. That's nice, isn't it?"

Yes, it was. Instinctively his arm moved around her waist, and his heart quickened at the feel of her. It'd been a long time since he'd indulged in gentle human contact.

The young woman giggled softly and leaned into him, wrapping her arms around his shoulders, nuzzling his temple. He pulled her closer and put a hand on her thigh. She was so young and fresh. Perhaps she wasn't a prostitute after all. Just lonely like himself.

"I love soldiers," she whispered, flicking her tongue at his ear, and sending flames down his neck.

"Why is that?" he forced himself to reply. He wanted to throw her over his shoulder and carry her upstairs.

She looked at him with sultry eyes. "Because they— " she put a hand to his chest, "—*you* are handsome and strong and fierce."

Hugo swallowed. She made him feel more like a lad than a twenty-six-year-old soldier of the Holy Roman Empire. But he imagined he'd be man enough when it mattered.

She leaned to kiss his neck once. Twice. A third time. Hugo's pulse raced, and he knew he wouldn't resist her.

"Ooh," she said, sitting up suddenly and lifting the medallion he wore at his throat. "What's this?" She focused on the pendant, and a fire lit her eyes.

Hugo grabbed the medallion from her grasp and pushed her roughly from his lap. She stumbled, but managed to stand and look down at him in confusion. He rose to his feet, fished a coin out of his money-belt, and dropped it on the table.

She caught his arm. "What's wrong?"

"Get away from me." He pushed past her and rushed to the door. To daylight. To sanity.

The sun burned down hot and bright. Hugo leaned against the plastered building, head pounding, and breathed in great gasps of scorching air. Sweat beaded on his face.

Kateline. How had he almost forgotten her? She was the only

reason he'd stayed afloat when he found himself adrift at sea. Devotion to her wishes brought him to Rome to find Nicholas after a fishing crew rescued him from the waters. His promise to her was the one thing that allowed him to tolerate the boy leader, who'd obtained the pope's favor. And now—because of the charge she had bestowed upon him— Hugo stood in place of some whimpering nobleman's son in the army and trained with honor for the next crusade. He owed his very life and purpose to Kateline.

His disloyalty to her made Hugo want to vomit. He'd dishonored her by even touching another woman with lust in his heart. He gripped the medallion and prayed. *Kateline, my dearest, forgive me. Let nothing deter me from my devotion to you and the vow I made.*

Hugo tipped his face to the sun and let its heat purge the transgression from his body.

"What are you doing, Hugo?" a cheerful voice said. "Worshiping the sun god? The pope will have you quartered."

Orry.

Hugo squinted at his friend. Tall and lean, but well-muscled, Orry wore a perpetual grin. He was dark-eyed and French like Simon had been. Maybe that's what drew Hugo to Orry in the first place. They'd formed a fast friendship—both training as impoverished soldiers, both quiet about what brought them to Rome. "You're late."

Orry's smile broadened. "Perhaps, but I cannot help it if the young ladies of the empire need an escort home from the market. It is my duty to protect their honor."

Hugo harrumphed and pushed himself from the wall. "And where are their fathers?"

Orry fell in alongside him. "Praise the saints, I have no idea. Drinking, perhaps. Like you."

Hugo ignored the comment. "It'll be dark by the time we get to Pelagius's estate."

"Nonsense," Orry said. "But even that would not keep Nicholas from showing off his cow."

"Horse, Orry. Practice your German."

"I meant horse. And what happened to your learning French?"

"I'm smarter than you," Hugo said, beginning to enjoy the banter.

"How's that?"

"I've taught you German so well that now I don't have to speak your language."

"Very good, *mon ami*," Orry said with a laugh.

They made their way through the countryside toward Albano, Orry jabbering away like the baker's wife, Hugo chiming in every now and then. Mostly, he let his thoughts wander.

He didn't like spending time with Nicholas. The boy, seventeen, was more arrogant and self-centered than he'd been five years ago.

When Nicholas reached Rome, he gained an audience with Pope Innocent. His Holiness listened to Nicholas's plea for troops, ships, and supplies, then patted the boy on the head and told him to come back when he'd grown up.

Those accompanying Nicholas had dispersed, some to attempt the journey home, most to settle into the streets and alleys of Rome. Rumor had it that many of the girls turned to prostitution, unable to support themselves by respectable means.

Like the young woman at the tavern.

Hugo shook the thought from his head and grunted his agreement with whatever Orry was saying before his mind returned to Nicholas.

The boy told the story in grander terms, but Hugo suspected Nicholas had blabbered like a baby before Innocent until the pope requested that his friend and representative, Cardinal Pelagius, give Nicholas a home and a liberal allowance. Now Nicholas, fuzz embellishing his upper lip, indulged himself like a heathen.

Much as Hugo hated to admit it, he needed Nicholas. Or at least he needed the connections the boy provided. How else would he have found himself in one of the best regiments in the empire? And now that the truce between the Christian Kingdom of Jerusalem and the Mohammedans had ended, Innocent's successor, Honorius, had managed to rouse the Empire to launch a new crusade. By the end of the summer, Hugo expected to set sail once again for the Holy Lands.

Until then, he studied the finer strategies of warfare and learned to handle a sword as skillfully as any knight. His body had become stronger, harder, bronzed like one of the ancient pagan deities. There was only one thing left.

"Do you think Nicholas is here?" Orry asked, breaking into Hugo's thoughts.

They'd passed the outer boundary of the estate.

"He said to come today." Hugo wouldn't have bothered at all if it weren't for the hope of riding one of Pelagius's magnificent horses. If Nicholas didn't show—

The thunder of hooves sounded from behind them. They both scrambled from the road to avoid being run down by a massive auburn stallion.

Nicholas pulled up the reins and turned the animal to face them. Still slight of build, he looked out from under long, dark curls. "I could have sliced you both in half just now," he said triumphantly, arm raised as if holding a sword.

"Impossible," Orry said. "You'd have to have chosen one of us."

Nicholas scrunched up his lips and thought about that for a second. "You know what I mean."

"No, Orry's right," Hugo said, hiding the smile that tugged at his mouth. "At that speed, with only one imaginary sword, you couldn't have sliced us both."

Nicholas sighed, lowered his arm, then circled Halveron around to lead the way up the hill. Orry and Hugo exchanged quick grins and followed the boy.

"You should be nice to me," Nicholas said over his shoulder. "I'm your personal benefactor. And very generous toward you, too."

At that, the stallion lifted its tail and let his droppings hit the ground.

Hugo's thoughts, exactly. Instead, he asked, "Can you get Halveron to do that trick for us again?"

Orry smirked, but Hugo ignored him.

"What?" Nicholas said. "You mean jump? That's not a trick, Hugo. Any worthy mount can do it. It's the rider's skill that's put to the test in such a maneuver."

"You handle the animal so well," Orry said. "Won't you show us, then?"

Nicholas feigned a sigh at the supposed inconvenience, but Hugo saw his eyes light up. The boy fancied himself an expert teacher and never tired of showing off his skills to a couple of poor foot soldiers. As usual, it took only a quarter hour before he'd given up his seat to Hugo.

"No," Nicholas called. "Keep your calves on the horse."

Hugo tugged on the reins, bringing Halveron round to Nicholas and Orry. "I'm trying."

"It's hot," the boy said. "I'm getting tired of this."

"But you haven't taught us to jump yet," Orry said.

Nicholas scowled then wiped a trickle of sweat from his temple. "You're never going to jump if you can't get the basic techniques right."

Hugo was careful not to smile. "Let us practice a little longer. I think I've almost got it."

A grunt escaped Nicholas's arrogant little throat. "Very well, but you'll have to do it without me." He turned his steps toward one of Pelagius's shaded courtyards. "Take Halveron to the stable boy when you're done."

"Should we come back again next week?" Orry said.

Nicholas didn't bother turning round, but lifted a hand as if to shoo them away. "Yes, but not so late in the afternoon. I don't enjoy this heat."

Hugo made a silent vow to arrive at Pelagius's estate at the warmest hour of the day next time.

He and Orry waited until Nicholas was out of view, and then got down to the business for which they'd come. Nothing matched the thrill of jumping. Hugo lifted his seat, bent low over the horse, grabbed the mane, and held on. Halveron left the ground with a powerful thrust of his hind legs. Hugo kept his focus straight ahead, between the stallion's ears, but sat upright too soon, landing heavy in the saddle. He pulled the horse around for another go at it.

Ja, and he loved riding.

§ § §

Two months later Hugo stood with Orry at a warped barricade on a strip of land overlooking the sea near Split, Croatia, and watched a jousting contest.

Pope Honorius's crusade finally got underway when King Andrew of Hungary issued an appeal for troops. Hugo's regiment had responded, along with dozens of others. But now they were stuck on this godforsaken Croatian shore, thousands of men piled up waiting to board the few available Venetian ships. It would be weeks before the main body of soldiers could sail for Acre on the Palestinian coast.

The warriors groused like fishwives at the inactivity while poor planning held them up in Split, and so their commanders had organized this week's mock battles for training purposes. Or for entertainment, depending upon one's point of view. Hugo and Orry's regiment, under Giovanni of Rome, faced off against the soldiers of Vittorio of Solerno and Sibratus of Bavaria. Hugo never had liked Bavarians, neighbors to his native Swabia.

Four of them stood nearby, loud and blustering. Almost worse than Nicholas's intolerable boasting. At least that little peacock still strutted his feathers back in Albano, whereas these braggarts had been issuing vain threats to Orry and Hugo all morning.

Come to think of it, he'd had enough. He winked at Orry, then turned to the Germans and made his voice a growl. "Why don't you fellows pick on someone your own size?"

Orry smiled and raised his voice. "But they can't, Hugo. There are no women present."

One of the Bavarians started toward them, but his companion held him back.

"Jesters, are you?" the second man said. "We thought you to be soldiers. Must have been all that dirt on your necks. I see now that you're nothing but court fools, pale and gutless."

Hugo's fists clenched. He'd punch that donkey first then start in on the others.

Orry sidetracked Hugo's strategy. "So you think you can outlast us on the battlefield, do you?"

They grunted their agreement.

"Then lay coin to it," Orry said.

The Bavarians consulted each other. "Our fifteen silver pieces against yours."

"Done," Orry said.

Hugo grimaced at the challengers then stomped away with his friend.

"We don't have fifteen silver pieces," Hugo said to him.

Orry smiled, untroubled by the reminder. "You think we'll need them?"

He had a point. Normally, Orry served as an archer—a fine one at that, capable of shooting an astounding fifteen arrows a minute—but today he would do quite a bit of damage with a war hammer, to say nothing of the mace. Hugo trained as a foot soldier, adept in the use of pike, axe, and sword. They made a lethal pair.

By noon the knights' jousting contests were over and the scrimmage was set to begin. Hugo adjusted his chain mail and scrutinized his steel cap, thankful to have found an armorer to beat out the dents it received during his last training round.

"Tell me again why this isn't a tournament?" Orry said.

"Because the pope has outlawed them." Hugo selected a blunted sword and tested its weight.

Orry straightened his leather jerkin. "So we're only training."

"Exactly. No pomp. No spectators. No ladies fair."

Orry sighed and picked up a mace. "I knew I wasn't having any fun."

"Just wait," Hugo said with a grin.

A knight cantered by on a powerful destrier. Two soldiers argued over a pike. A third swung a war hammer up and back down in a series of loops. The pungent scent of sweat and horses hung heavy in the humid air.

Hugo felt more alive than he'd been since Kateline left him. Since the children perished at sea, and his soul died along with the disastrous crusade. He knew Simon, Elisabeth, and the others had failed, too, for no word of them ever reached the empire. Certainly there'd been no victorious defeat of Islam, no liberation of Jerusalem.

Nearly five years, and he'd become an expert at pushing aside the guilt and agony of those memories. Only one thing occupied his focus now—the promised journey to Palestine. His quest still lay ahead, and today's *mêlée* would demonstrate which skills needed to be strengthened before the real battles began.

But he had no doubt he'd beat the arrogant Bavarians before dusk.

Previous games served to disqualify Vittorio's troops from the event. Now only two teams faced one another on a long field, ropes restraining the formations of infantrymen and mounted cavalry.

Marshals on raised platforms edged the perimeter, intent upon guaranteeing that no one was killed—at least intentionally. Hugo, Orry, and the others who gathered under the banner of Giovanni of Rome stood ready to the south. Sibratus and his Bavarian mongrels positioned themselves to the north.

Hugo's limbs tingled. He gripped an eighteen-foot-long wooden pike, willing his palms dry, and wishing that it carried its spearhead. He had a taste for blood today.

Trained soldier that he was, though, he knew his job, even in this mock battle. Protect Giovanni's cavalry. Of course, should he also happen to dismount a Bavarian knight and force the man to surrender, he'd win a ransom—perhaps a half-dozen silver coins or a finely crafted weapon.

He lifted his nose and sniffed the breeze. The musty smell of soil mixed with the salt of the nearby sea and the heady tang of five hundred men in armor. Hugo planted his feet in the spring mud. The powerful coursers stomped the ground behind him.

At the command, "Let them go!" the rope dropped, and both sides charged.

Hugo's powerful legs propelled him forward. A primal roar escaped his throat, joining the war cries of hundreds of others. The earth trembled at the pounding of their feet. Exhilaration washed over him. Carried him up the field.

The clash of pikes sounded like thunder in summer. The force of the collision threw Hugo back as if he'd been hit by lightning. He tasted blood, all right. From his own tongue.

Hugo gritted his teeth and angled the next strike to snap the spear of a squatty opponent. Swung his weapon round and clouted the man's helmeted head. The thickset soldier dropped face-down in the mud. With no time to cheer the small victory, Hugo raced ahead and shoved through the first wave of attackers. Flying splinters from shattered pikes stung his face, doing more damage than the blows of his rivals.

At last he joined eighty or so of his cohorts and broke through the Bavarian line. Sibratus and his warriors faced them, solid and unyielding. Their warhorses pawed the dirt. Giovanni's men rushed the cavalry. The knights dug their spurs into the beasts.

The horsemen were sixty paces out. Thirty. Fifteen. Hugo lowered his pike to fend off the charge.

A dappled stallion bore down on him. He thrust his headless spear into the armor of the advancing combatant. His weapon exploded on impact. The breath of the animal heated his neck when it passed by.

Hugo cursed the loss of the pike and his failure to unseat the rider, but had no opportunity to think further. Ducking low and spinning to the side, he barely escaped the sweep of a second knight's weapon. He pulled his sword from his belt and turned to meet the battle, now behind him.

The opposing forces interlocked like fingers in prayer, though there was nothing meditative about the exchange. Hugo let out a whoop and sprinted to the fight.

Though men fell all around him, he somehow maintained his ground. Eventually he caught sight of Orry, swinging a mace as gracefully as a dancing partner. Hugo fought his way toward him.

"What happened to you?" Hugo panted with exertion.

Orry held his left arm close to his torso, the other arm wielding the mace with ruinous aim. "Shoulder." Orry grunted, felling one of Sibratus's infantrymen. "Dislocated." Wood fragments pitted his face, leaving thin trails of blood.

Hugo parried blows from a hefty, sandy-haired German. Not more than a boy, but strong as a draft horse. He beat back the blond and tried to spot Orry again. A sword caught him unprepared, smashing broadside across the stomach. The blow pushed the air from Hugo's lungs. He doubled over.

"Sorry," Orry called. "Was just going to warn you."

Hugo lifted his head to see one of the wagering Bavarians jump out of the reach of Orry's weapon. Two of the man's cronies joined him, circling like wild dogs.

"You haven't turned tail and run yet?" one of them said.

"Run? When we're at full force?" Hugo straightened, adjusted his grip on the hilt of his two-handed sword. "I see you're down by a man."

Another challenger sneered at him. "We still outnumber you."

Hugo felt Orry's back against his. "We'll see about that."

The Germans swooped in for the attack. Swords and maces clashed. Blinding light flashed into Hugo's eyes. Dirty Bavarian had over-polished his shield. Hugo growled and dropped to his haunches. A sword glanced off his steel cap. He stood, swung round, and caught the fellow with the flat of his blade on the back of his helmeted skull. The man wavered for a moment then crumpled.

"Looks like you're half the men you used to be," Orry said. He lunged at one of the remaining adversaries, cracking the man's leg with a single blow of his mace. The Bavarian dropped to the ground, howling in pain. "Oops. My apologies, man. Didn't mean to be so heavy handed." He turned to stand side-by-side with Hugo, their chests moving in tandem, both winded from the exertion. Hugo shook the sweat from his eyes.

The last of the gamblers faced them, mouth agape like a dead fish. Then fury reddened his features. With bulging neck muscles, he charged Hugo, sword lifted high. Hugo sank to one knee and thrust his blade upward. It plunged into the exposed, fleshy underside of the man's arm. The Bavarian screamed once, then passed out. Hugo retrieved his weapon.

"I hope they're not dead," Orry said. "Otherwise, who'll pay us?"

"They're fine," Hugo said, and wiped the steel on his leggings. "Having fun yet?"

Orry nodded, eyes sparkling. He dodged a mace when a

shrieking rival ran by. "I've got my sights on that knight over there."

Hugo followed his friend's gaze. Two poor foot soldiers against one heavily armored knight sounded fair to him. He grinned. "Let's go earn a ransom."

§ § §

Hugo scrunched up his mouth while he examined the dagger he'd claimed as ransom in last week's game. Finally, something to replace the one he lost—a lump formed in his throat—the one he lost that day on the ship from Marseilles.

Hugo swallowed, sheathed the knife, and tucked it into the belt at the small of his back. A glance around the encampment revealed throngs of soldiers still milling about. They all itched to board one of the Venetian ships that waited in the harbor.

"Come on, Hugo," Orry said. "Let's get something to eat."

Hugo rubbed Kateline's medallion between his fingers. "I don't want anything."

"You can't stare your way aboard, you know."

Hugo looked at his friend and raised his brows. Orry knew him well. "Do you have a better idea?"

Orry thought for a moment before his face brightened. "You could sleep with the King's daughter. Or the King, himself, perhaps, though I don't think he'd be interested in the likes of you. Maybe the King's cow. He's magnificent, don't you think?"

Hugo lifted his eyes to the clouds. "*Horse.* The King's horse. I'll keep your suggestions in mind."

"Glad to be of service. Are you coming or not? I'm starving."

"I'm coming."

They made way to an area of Giovanni's camp where several cooking fires burned. Twenty or more women tended them, preparing meals for a price while their children ran among nearby tents. For a small charge, Hugo could get a wooden bowl of pottage and a round loaf of bread. Orry, on the other hand, often charmed one of the cooks into giving him a discount or a free loaf as he did today.

They took their food and returned to the shade of a tree that overlooked the harbor.

"The commander said we'll know something soon," Orry said.

Hugo lifted the bowl to his mouth and let the broth flow down his throat then wiped his chin with the back of one hand. "From what I hear, Giovanni's attempting to make a deal with King Andrew to get our men on board. And he's reminding the Hungarian who triumphed over Sibratus's soldiers in last week's contest."

Orry smiled. "Giovanni would do well to let you address the king. As desperate as you are, I'm sure you'd make a persuasive argument."

"Don't you want to fight?"

"Of course I do. But there's something in your eyes when you speak of the crusade, Hugo. Something both dark and light. You've a passion one rarely sees."

Hugo bit into his bread, the inside of the coarse, brown loaf still hot. If only it could warm his soul.

Perhaps the blood of a thousand Mohammedans could redeem him for letting Kateline perish at Mont Cenis. The blood of ten thousand might begin to compensate for his unsuccessful leadership of the children's crusade. It was the only passion he held close to his heart now, for there was no woman to take in his arms. No luminous hair in which to bury his face. No chaste lips to place his mouth upon.

But he would not tell Orry this.

A trumpet sounded in the distance. A long, low note followed by several short repetitions. Hugo jumped to his feet. "That's for us."

Orry rose beside him. Grinning. "We're going."

Hugo couldn't stop his own lips from turning up at the corners. He stroked Kateline's pendant. *At last.*

Chapter 22

Early September AD 1217, near Alexandria, Egypt

Simon looked up from the plow when he heard Jabir's voice.

"*Simon al-Nasrani,*" Jabir called again. *Simon the Christian.* It was a name Jabir used in private with a small dose of humor and a large degree of affection.

The ox tugged at the thick leather straps that bound her to the wooden device Simon maneuvered through the soil. "*Kafaa!*" he said, ordering her to stop with a snap of the leads.

Wearing only a *mi'zar* wrapped loosely around his waist, Simon lifted his tunic from where it hung over the handle of the plow and used it to wipe the sweat from his face and chest while Jabir scurried toward him. He'd come to love the old man who'd bought him at the slave market five years ago. Such emotion came as a genuine surprise, as did the fact that he'd been unable to convert the overseer from his heathen beliefs.

Nevertheless, Simon's love for the man remained strong. It was liberating, really, to love without expectation. Liberating even for a slave in a foreign land.

"How are you, my father?" Simon said in Arabic, bowing

slightly.

"Well, my son." Jabir's russet face split into a smile, revealing startling white teeth that matched his beard. His forehead remained dry.

It amazed Simon that Jabir never seemed affected by the heat. He accepted the fresh water pouch Jabir held out.

Simon lifted the bag to his lips, letting the cool liquid course over his tongue and down his throat. When he finished drinking, he found Jabir eyeing him with a grin. "What brings you to see me today?"

Jabir pulled a handful of dates from the folds of his robe and held them in an outstretched palm. Simon took them, popping one of the soft, sweet fruits into his mouth.

"I have business in this region of Harun al-Rashid's estate," Jabir said. "Your supervisor showed me where to find you. You are looking good after so many weeks."

Jabir once said he recognized the depth of Simon's intellect when he stood at the slave auction. That Simon quickly learned Arabic delighted the man. And now Jabir planned to acquaint Simon with every section of Harun's land and tutor him in the specifics of administering the master's holdings. It was Simon's calling, he said.

Simon tossed another date into his mouth. "And what does my supervisor report?" The man had groused when Simon was placed under his management. Didn't trust Christians, he'd complained.

"Hisham cannot find fault with you, though he has tried."

"That much is certain." It took every bit of Simon's resolve not to balk under the harsh treatment he'd received. It was with God's help alone that he served with diligence, going beyond what Hisham demanded of him each day.

"He means you no harm." Jabir smiled. "He simply possesses the heart of a child, jealous of one much younger than himself who is as strong, mystifying, and dark as the Nile."

It was true that Simon's once-scrawny arms and legs had muscled out. Cultivating the land did that to a man. And his skin had browned under the Egyptian sun. But mystifying? He lived an uncomplicated life. "Flattery is against your beliefs, is it not, Jabir?"

Jabir chuckled. "It is, my friend. And so I do not use it. Now put your tunic back on before your flesh turns to leather."

"It's too hot today. Not a breath of wind."

"Never mind that. Only discipline will preserve your French skin. You are a handsome young man, Simon. You can rise above slavery as my father did, but not with the scales of a crocodile covering your bones."

Jabir had explained that under Islam, slaves could hope to purchase freedom from their masters, but that didn't interest Simon today. He shook out the sweat-stained tunic and pulled it over his head. "Any word from your last visit to Alexandria?"

Jabir's eyes grew soft. "None."

The overseer proved to be Simon's most trusted source of information concerning the lost crusaders. With Jabir's help, Simon had pieced together the story of four of the ships from Marseilles.

Apparently upon leaving Europe, one ship quickly strayed to the shores of Bujeiah in northwest Africa. Rumor had it that a sultan bought the entire shipload of children. Whether Hugo or Elisabeth suffered their fate, Simon had no way of knowing.

Then, of course, there were the two vessels that landed in Alexandria. Close to ninety of their number—the girls and younger boys—had been purchased for the governor's palace. The rest had been auctioned off here and there, as Simon had been.

A fourth boat deposited young crusaders in Damietta to the east. Slavery for all of them, it seemed. No word of a spirited redhead or a blue-eyed bull-of-a-young-man ever reached Alexandria. Of course, what were a few hundred slaves to the Mohammedans of Africa?

Three ships remained unaccounted for. No marketplace gossip suggested what became of them. What was certain was that no Christian crusade had emancipated Jerusalem or overcome Islam.

"You've been much help," Simon said. "Thank you for trying."

"Though I enjoy a measure of respect and authority as the overseer of Harun al-Rashid's estate," Jabir said, "poking my nose into the whereabouts of Christian slaves leaves me suspect in the eyes of my people. I wish I could do more."

Simon looked to the hills stretching out low and purple in the distance. His chest rose and fell in a cheerless cadence.

"Why do you do this to yourself?" Jabir said after a silent minute. "It is time to leave the past behind. Look to your future."

Perhaps the old man spoke with wisdom. But Simon couldn't get Hugo and Elisabeth out of his mind. Or his prayers.

He sighed. "I'll try."

"Very good," Jabir said, slapping Simon's back. "It is all you can do. Now, about your reading lessons—"

"I've been practicing with the text you gave me."

"And how do you like the poetry of al-Jahiz?"

"It is vivid. Musical. And it articulates an exceptional moral commentary. But I prefer David the Psalmist," Simon said.

Jabir chucked Simon's chin. "Of course you do. We will break you of that soon enough."

Simon smiled and looked over Jabir's shoulder. The supervisor approached, face red and eyes bulging. "It looks like Hisham would like to break my neck." He lifted the leather leads and returned his hands to the plow.

"I will deal with Hisham," Jabir said, moving off. "You, Simon al-Nasrani, keep working and learning as you are doing."

Simon clicked his tongue. The ox began to tread the field with heavy steps. His arms skillfully controlled the plow, forming straight lines that ran perpendicular to the squat hills on the horizon. The tedium allowed his mind free reign, and soon his thoughts returned to his lost friends.

How could he forget them? They'd shared his hopes and

sorrows. They still shared the depths of his soul. Were they even alive?

Every now and then a storm brought inland the salty aroma of sea air, and Simon would remember their last day in Marseilles, sitting with Elisabeth on the steps of St. Laurent's, patron saint of sailors. He could still see her eyes, the same green as the Mediterranean, intense and compelling.

"I don't want to be separated from you," she'd said. "So much could happen on the sea."

He should have listened to her concerns. Should have protected her. And Hugo? Well, he was always man enough to fend for himself, but Simon missed him all the same.

A sudden breeze lifted the hair that hung even with Simon's ears. He looked north to see dark clouds forming over the sea. They mirrored the turmoil in his chest.

The rain came late in the night—a bitter, pounding storm. Simon hunched under the woven bramble shelter, pulled a goat-hair *aba* over his head, and tried not to remember Elisabeth's eyes.

By mid-morning the next day, he'd all but forgotten the storm. Shielding his eyes from the morning sun, he surveyed the flocks that grazed as far as he could see, and felt his temper rise.

Before Hisham rode off with Jabir yesterday, he'd warned Simon about the nomads who tried to infiltrate the master's territory to the south. Now, here they were, destroying Harun al-Rashid's crops directly under Simon's nose. What right did they have to use these fields?

He took a deep breath and purposely relaxed his muscles. As much right as the master. Simon scratched his chin, rough from a full day's growth, remembering what Jabir had taught him.

In this part of the world, the relationship between farmers and shepherds remained fragile. No one owned the land or, more importantly, the water that fed it. Dominance tended to shift in favor of one group or another, depending upon the strength of the leader.

Harun al-Rashid came from a powerful heritage, Simon speculated, for his family had worked this region for decades with little challenge to their authority. They'd accumulated immense wealth in the process. And now these uncivilized tribesmen sought to destroy all that.

"Not if I can help it," Simon said out loud. "And not if I follow Hisham's instructions to sound the alarm now that you scoundrels have shown up."

All Simon had to do was rally the other workers to intimidate these grazers, and off they'd run. He sighed. If Harun's men presented a threat, violence would ensue. Simon pictured farmers battling shepherds. Perhaps he should try to reason with them first.

Simon walked upstream from the flocks, shaved, rinsed out his tunic, straightened his skullcap, and then made way toward the herdsmen.

It didn't go as well as he'd hoped. An hour later, he knelt with his hands bound behind his back by thick cords. His left eye had swollen shut, and fresh bruises sprouted on his arms and legs, judging by the ache. Above him stood the *shaykh*—the tribal leader—studying him with a grim expression.

The grizzled elder interrogated Simon in the bowels of his colossal tent. "Who are you?"

"Simon."

The man scowled. "What kind of name is that?"

French, sir hardly seemed the most discreet response. "I am Simon, servant of the master of these lands."

The *shaykh* narrowed his eyes, studying him. Perhaps that answer had been imprudent as well. "I am now the master of these lands," the man said, voice grainy as desert sand, "and I do not know you."

It sounded like a death sentence.

Simon bowed his head. "Forgive me, father of your people, if I have offended you. I meant no disrespect."

He seemed to consider Simon's apology. "Who is your master?"

"Harun al-Rashid." *Aaron the Rightly Guided.*

The man chuckled. "Well, See-mon, I've decided to spare your life, despite your insolence. Leave me now, and tell al-Rashid I'm rightly guiding him off his land."

"Please, sir, may we come to a satisfactory agreement?"

The *shaykh's* eyebrows rose in surprise, and Simon hurried on. "My master is a powerful man. Like you, he commands many who would fight and die for him. If you send me away to deliver your message, I fear bloodshed upon this land. Won't you wisely reconsider your path?"

The *shaykh* seethed before Simon, broad shoulders quivering with rage.

Almighty God, in your great mercy, I plead with you to intercede.

The man, eyes bulging, finally took a deep breath and bellowed, "How dare you insult and challenge me? Your foolishness has brought ruin to Harun al-Rashid."

He spun around and strode toward the opening of the tent, barking an order to one of his servants to see to Simon's beheading. Sweat broke out on Simon's forehead. How had he insulted and challenged the man?

Two burly sentries grabbed Simon's arms.

"I did not mean to offend!" He struggled against them in vain while they dragged him outside. "Wait, please, let me talk to your master."

They tossed him to the ground. His vision blurred, speckled black. "This is a misunderstanding." His voice cracked. "I can explain."

A sword seemed to appear from nowhere. It hovered high above his head. The hands of the executioner trembled with eagerness. Simon's ears rang. Sweat coursed down his face. He smelled his own fear, salty and sharp.

Never again would he see France. Never find Elisabeth or

Hugo. Never return for Conon. *Father in heaven, I entrust my soul to you.* He clamped his lips together so he would not cry out and waited for the deathblow.

A crowd had gathered. Eager onlookers thirsty for blood.

The *shaykh*, mounted upon a gleaming black horse, pulled up in front of Simon. "May you be the first to know the wrath of the house of Zanata."

Simon gasped and blinked back the drops of sweat that stung his eyes. "Zanata? Then we are brothers!"

The crowd murmured. Shock drained the elder's face of its color. The man swayed on his horse.

The swordsman grunted and pulled his arm back to strike.

Simon hurried to speak before the *shaykh* passed out cold from astonishment and the executioner completed his duty. "Please, my master is a descendent of Zanata."

The older man's face went from pale to red with fury. "You lie." Nevertheless he stretched out a hand to give the swordsman pause.

"No, noble son of Zanata. I speak the truth." The elder narrowed his eyes, and Simon rushed on. "Zanata was the father of Idris, the father of Ma'bad, the father of Sinan, the father of Dirar, the father of—"

"Enough!"

Simon trembled with dread and hope, but struggled to straighten his shoulders. Looked the man square in the face with his one good eye.

"Master?" the executioner prompted, arms still poised for the deathblow.

The elder glared at Simon then swung his gaze toward the swordsman.

And nodded.

Chapter 23

Early September AD 1217, the home of Harun al-Rashid

"What should I do?" Simon asked Jabir while a servant led them to Harun's banquet room. His stomach had been spiraling since they'd entered the master's palatial home.

"Just bow, pray God's blessing upon him, and answer his questions," Jabir said.

Simon swallowed and nodded. Bow, pray, and answer questions. He could do that.

When Jabir first told him of the master's invitation, Simon had been delighted. To dine with Harun was an honor he never expected, but al-Rashid insisted on hearing first-hand the full account of Simon's negotiations with the agitated tribesman. Now all Simon could think about was meeting the man who held sway over his future.

No, God rules your future, he told himself. *Never forget that.*

They entered a pillared room bright with white marble and copper oil-lamps. A refreshing night breeze laced with jasmine drifted in through unshuttered windows. Decorative porcelain adorned silver trays on low wooden stools at the far end of the space. Jabir motioned for Simon to stand still when the servant left them alone. A moment later, two female servants—one older, the other young—entered through a second doorway. They filled glass goblets before kneeling in the corner of the room, heads bowed.

Simon looked at Jabir and was about to ask what they should do next, when a man entered the room dressed in a dove-colored robe, belted and trimmed in cobalt blue. Jabir sank to the floor, and Simon imitated him, bowing low before Harun al-Rashid.

Jabir spoke first. "May God spread your power, my lord, as fruit is scattered from a shaken tree."

Simon eyed the carpeted floor not an inch from his nose and followed suit. "May God in his great mercy defend, protect, and keep you, my master."

"Rise, please," Harun said. They stood, and Harun embraced Jabir. "My friend, it is good of you to join me this night." He looked at Simon with eyes like Egyptian soil, dark and full of life. "This is the young man?"

"Yes, Harun. Simon al-Nasrani."

"Al-Nasrani?" Harun raised his brows at Simon. "A follower of the Nazarene? A Christian?"

He managed a nod. "Yes, master."

Jabir spoke up. "He is European, Harun, but he serves you well."

Harun's face creased into a warm smile that slowed Simon's racing heart. Fine lines around his mouth and eyes indicated he smiled often. "So I hear."

Before they ate, the master appealed to Simon to share the details of his recent adventure, which he did. He got to the part where he claimed brotherhood with the house of Zanata.

"And how did the *shaykh* respond?" Harun grinned beneath tented fingers resting against his nose.

"I thought he might faint," Simon answered honestly. "I only hoped he would call off his executioner before doing so."

Al-Rashid and Jabir laughed out loud, though Simon had not been joking.

"Go on," Harun finally wheezed. He snapped his fingers and the servants began to move.

"When the shock passed, he was angry." The women placed aromatic dishes of meat and vegetables on the table, and Simon's stomach rumbled in anticipation. "He thought I lied, but I explained that you are likewise a descendant of Zanata, listing your lineage as I had practiced with Jabir."

The master looked impressed.

At twenty-two, Simon's appetite made him impatient to finish his own story and get to the food. "He dismissed the executioner, but seemed still unconvinced. I appealed to the corporate spirit—"

"The *'asabiyya*?" Harun said.

"Yes, I appealed to the *'asabiyya* of the Zanata name and the loyalty that has existed with it for centuries." Now that he was less nervous, Simon found himself distracted by the younger servant's slim arms and small hands when she placed a bowl of fruit in front of him. Her nose was petite and straight, her brows arched just so above dark-lashed eyes.

"And then . . . " al-Rashid prompted.

"The *shaykh* climbed off his horse, embraced me as a servant of the house of Zanata, and apologized for trampling your wheat."

Harun clapped his hands. "Very good, young Simon. Your quick thinking, despite enormous stress, saved your life *and* my fields."

Simon looked at Jabir, then back to al-Rashid. "Not entirely, my lord."

The master's eyebrows floated up. "No?"

Simon cleared his throat. "I took leave to offer him use of the land his flocks grazed, as well as the portion of river that passes through it."

"The crops were already destroyed," Jabir hastened to explain.

"And I thought," Simon said, "that such a gift from you would guarantee fidelity from the tribesman should you ever be in need."

Harun's silence lingered long, but he finally took a deep breath and spoke. "You have accomplished a considerable deed, Simon al-Nasrani, and proved both your loyalty and wisdom. Feast with me now."

Harun motioned toward the tempting meats and dishes the women supplied. "Do you favor well-seasoned foods?"

"Yes, master, though most of these are unfamiliar to me."

"The diet of a slave is simple," Jabir said to Harun before turning to Simon. He pointed to a bowl of cooked vegetables. "This is flavored with cinnamon and cloves, and it is one of my favorites."

"I've read of such spices," Simon said. "And I recognize the couscous, but have never seen it so long and yellow."

"That's rice," Harun said. "Colored with saffron. Try it."

Throughout the meal, the older men educated Simon on the fare of a wealthy table. It was difficult to listen, though, so taken was he with the young servant girl. She had uncommonly beautiful skin—light brown, like toasted almonds, and smooth as cream.

"So you like the feast I offer?" Harun said, humor in his voice.

"Very much, sir." Simon drew his eyes from the girl and took another bite.

"And how long have you been my slave?"

"Five years, master."

The girl ventured a look at Simon, and he thought perhaps she blushed.

"Tell me, Simon al-Nasrani, how it is that a young European slave would show such knowledge of our ways and devotion to his master as you have recently done?"

Simon considered his response for only a moment. "I am indebted to Jabir's patient tutelage, for I would not otherwise understand your customs."

Jabir smiled, and Simon continued, settling his attention solely on Harun. "But my dedication to you, master, is a reflection of my allegiance to God. I seek to honor him by keeping his command to work as though serving him alone."

Harun held Simon's gaze for several seconds, weighing his words. Simon feared he had displeased the master, but he could not have answered differently.

Then al-Rashid smiled and snapped his fingers. "Would you care for a taste of our sherbet? It is made of fruit juices cooled with snow from the southern mountains."

Simon smiled in return. "Yes, please."

"Good," Harun said. "And then I want you to tell me why you follow the Nazarene."

Chapter 24

October AD 1217, outside Damietta, Egypt

Elisabeth sprinkled marjoram over the roasted lamb and placed the meat on a silver platter. She no longer took the trouble to sample the food she prepared, but simply trusted her instincts to produce meals appetizing enough to preserve her life. Though most days, preserving her life didn't seem worth the bother.

But, I haven't found forgiveness yet.

A person couldn't die unpardoned by God unless she was willing to spend eternity in the flames of hell. She glanced around her.

If she wasn't there already.

In all her years of slavery, she'd come to hate everything about living, about this land. Relentless heat. Dry winds. Brown-skinned servants who jabbered their stupid language. Nighttime.

Especially nighttime.

At first the hours after supper provided Elisabeth a sanctuary from the misery of her circumstances. The master favored her culinary skills, but when her duties were done for the day, she walked the garden path or retired to her pallet in the back room. Either choice allowed her to block out the sights and smells and sounds that disgusted her with their foreignness. Flowers were flowers. Sky was sky. Sleep was blessed escape.

Then everything began to change. For years she longed to resemble her sister Methild with round hips and full breasts, but even the pregnancy failed to alter her straight, girlish lines. When the growing pains finally came a year or so ago, she suffered them without much consideration. What difference did it make that her body now curved, as a woman's should? Even had she been a virgin, there were no village boys to take notice. No potential husband to dream of her at night.

But there was the master.

Elisabeth wiped her hands on her apron and pushed those memories away. "Here," she said in her native tongue to the slave who served the master's dinner. "Take it, and may he choke to death on it."

From the beginning Elisabeth refused to utter one word in their ridiculous language. She spoke only German. And often. It pleased her to discover that fact aggravated them all.

The slave looked at her with brows askew, but took the tray.

Elisabeth picked up a cauldron and began to scrape it out.

The master had first noticed her transformation during a feast he and the mistress held last fall. Nearly every servant or slave tended the guests, pouring drinks and replacing empty dishes with full. He ogled Elisabeth all night, eyes drifting where they shouldn't, vulgar tongue licking his thick lips. She had avoided him the best she could that night, but he motioned to her often, fat arm brushing against her every time she bent to refill his goblet or lower a tray overflowing with one delicacy or another.

A figure moved in the kitchen door way. The slave, back after only minutes. He shook his head and uttered the name they called Elisabeth—*Moshkelah.*

The other female servants grew agitated, spoke their gibberish, and motioned with dark hands. The oldest servant stood and moved toward Elisabeth. She took the pot and then gave Elisabeth a push, nodding in the direction of the doorway. *"Roah."* *Go.*

Her palms began to sweat. "No." *Not again.*

The old woman fought to remove Elisabeth's apron. Pointed to the doorway. *"Roah."*

When Elisabeth failed to move, the woman's voice rose. All at once the others began to chastise her. Urge her. Warn her. The woman finally shoved her roughly toward the door.

Elisabeth should have expected the summons, for the mistress had left this morning. She gritted her teeth and walked to the master's private quarters. Fabric hung from the ceiling, draped in soft folds. Candles glowed throughout the room, and the air reeked of incense. Always the same.

"Does this stench and stifling heat emanate from you?" she asked with a quiet voice, knowing the master would think she spoke of nothing more than the food.

The master lifted a knife from the dinner tray and approached her. He traced the outline of her throat with its edge, and then used the tip to loosen the laces at the neck of her garment.

He didn't attack. He never did. Just watched as she obediently began to undress.

His repulsive eyes glowed like a demon's when the last of her clothing fell to the floor. He led her to the cushions. His dinner rested on a nearby low table. He waited for her to settle next to him before indicating that she should feed him.

The same thing had happened every time his wife was gone. Three trips so far. A total of twenty-five nights naked before him—the object of his heathen lust—retching into the bushes before returning to her pallet.

He had only touched her once. Drunk on wine, he sidled up in front of her one night when she failed to remove her undergarment. His clammy hands grasped her quivering arms. His fetid breath assaulted her nostrils. With excruciating slowness, he fondled her upper torso, and then bent to lift the chemise that hung to her knees.

"No," she said, but he ignored her.

Elisabeth held down the linen fabric. She would not permit him to see. "No."

He yanked the garment high enough to expose the rags between her legs, stepped back in surprise and disgust, then slapped her hard across the cheek.

She fled the room and had not been sent for since.

Until tonight.

Elisabeth pulled a piece of meat from the roast and touched it to his tongue. "I wish I had the nerve to reach down your throat and rip out your heart," she crooned.

He made obscene sounds of pleasure as he savored the lamb.

"I hate you," she whispered.

A huge bite of this. A grotesque mouthful of that.

"I hate you all."

A slurp from the goblet she held to his mouth.

"I hate myself."

He took her hand and licked the grease from her fingers with his rancid tongue.

She wanted to plunge the carving knife deep in his chest. "Maybe I should take the knife to my own breast."

The thought started to take shape, but, no, she had to live. Had to survive the torment she now experienced. If she ever managed to win God's favor, her misery would end. Then maybe the curse that had befallen those she loved would be lifted.

The master kept eating while she imagined the lives that would be set right if her curse ended. Crusader slaves being freed. Simon spinning her around, a wide grin on his face. Did he live? Hugo marching by, the sign of the cross emblazoned on his armor. Mama's tears gone forever. Her baby in heaven.

A shriek brought Elisabeth's attention back to the bedchamber.

She turned to see the mistress standing just inside the arch, shaking with rage. The master pushed Elisabeth away and stood up, trying to speak, but managing little besides a choking sound.

Elisabeth crawled to her clothes and pressed them to herself. She tried to edge past the quarrelling couple, when suddenly the woman's wrath turned upon her. Elisabeth shrank under the blows, though in truth she did not feel them much. Not as much as the shame. Not as much as the relief that her ordeal with the master had ended. Not as much as the fear of what would happen next.

She did not have to speculate long. The following morning she stood in Damietta on the auction block. It occurred to Elisabeth that there was at least one place on earth that God did not roam.

And she'd found it.

Chapter 25

Early November AD 1217, the village of Bet She'an, Syria
Hugo shifted on the dirt, stiff and chilled. No fires tonight. A thick
fog coated his face with moisture, and his legs ached from the forty
miles of hilly terrain they'd covered since daybreak. He glanced to
where Orry snored beside him. Thank goodness Orry was there, or this
reconnaissance mission would be little fun.

Muffled sniffs and grunts and the occasional noisy flatulence
signaled that the others drifted off for a scant few hours' sleep before
dawn. Four hundred Hungarians, two hundred fifty of Giovanni's men,
and a hundred Austrians hugged the hill above Bet She'an. It was a
wonder their nocturnal music didn't wake the Mohammedans inside
the walls.

Hugo rolled to his back, tossed an arm over his eyes, and wished
he could sleep. But too much rest had plagued him since arriving in
Palestine two months earlier. He'd long grown weary of inactivity.

John of Brienne—the so-named King of Jerusalem—and the
masters of the three military orders of the temple continually met in war
council, but made no decisions, gave no campaign orders.

A large army of crusaders arrived in the Christian-controlled city of Acre throughout the autumn months. Too many, in fact, for the food at hand. Poor harvests left the Holy Lands in famine conditions. Troops were advised to return home, but Hugo wasn't going back.

He didn't hesitate when Giovanni announced the operation to Bet She'an. Frustrated by the lack of action—and in his opinion, leadership—he leapt at the chance to flex the muscles of his finely honed battle skills. Not that the mission looked to be anything more than a supply raid. Nevertheless, if necessary, he'd fight vigorously. No one would ever call him a coward.

Something rustled the scraggly bush that grew close by. Hugo put a hand to his sword and lifted his head, straining to see through the darkness. Hedgehog, probably.

He sighed and relaxed. Clasped his hands over his chest.

Bet She'an sat at the convergence of three valleys and two rivers. Underground springs and the nearby Sea of Galilee made the soil fertile and guaranteed a plentiful harvest despite shortages in other regions. For centuries the city prospered at the junction of major trade routes.

Hugo tapped his fingers against his breastbone and reviewed the morrow's strategy.

The city walls were low and surprisingly unprotected. Forward scouts reported few lookouts. Siege works were unnecessary because the Christians would easily plunder the city by noon. They'd head out in the morning in staggered formation, Hugo and Orry contributing to one of three frontal infantry screens made up of archers and foot soldiers. Barring an improbable Muslim ambush, the forces would surround the city in quick order. The Mohammedan tactic of using mounted archers to harass an army on the move would prove useless against the Christians this time, for the infidels would still be abed when they discovered their foe's presence. Hugo grunted and rolled over, disappointed by the prospect of an enemy surrender.

The crusaders were on their way before daybreak lit the valley.

Silent, grim-faced soldiers and armored horsemen streamed down from wooded hills as a faint glow paled the eastern sky. Hugo strengthened his grip on his pike and navigated the rough ground. The city sat mute below them.

Night relinquished its hold on the heavens by the time the army reached the valley floor where their three companies separated into diamond-shaped attack units. Hugo advanced with forty-nine other foot soldiers in Giovanni's front line. Somewhere behind him, Orry joined one hundred archers. Fifty knights on powerful warhorses comprised the main body. Another fifty pikemen brought up the rear.

The crusaders encircled the city. The place appeared vacant, but Hugo sensed the Mohammedans inside the walls. The tang of unfamiliar spices wafted from their darkened homes.

Thwish! A volley of arrows lobbed from inside the walls broke the quiet of the morning. The hair on the back of Hugo's neck stiffened, but he marched forward with his comrades, unhindered by the surprise assault. His eyes darted to the left. By the saints! Arrows protruded from the chain mail of a half-dozen infantrymen. He turned his head to the right and saw the same baffling sight.

He looked down, only to realize he, too, bore evidence of the attack. The light weapon hadn't penetrated beyond his armor. Hugo grinned, jerked the arrow from his chest, and dropped it to the ground without breaking stride.

By then Orry and his fellow archers had begun to let loose their own offensive. The sky dimmed as if storm clouds had moved in, but a quick glance told Hugo it was merely the barrage of arrows overhead.

The city gates swung open and mounted archers charged forth like ants from the nest. Their swift little Arab horses split formation to surround the Christian ranks. The horsemen loosed their arrows without halting or dismounting. Some even shot backwards as they swooped away, circling around for another attack.

Their indirect methods angered Hugo. "Fight like men!" His

voice was lost amid the sudden noise of battle. He ran toward the gates with the other foot soldiers, pikes lowered to strike oncoming Mohammedans. Another wave of mounted Muslim archers emerged from the city to engage Hugo and the rest of Giovanni's determined front line. More than a few of the heathen's undersized horses fell to the ground to thrash under the menace of Christian pole arms. Hugo plunged his pike deep into the chest of an Arab pony when it dashed by, preventing the archer from reaching Orry and the others. The stricken animal reared and dropped its rider to the ground, then collapsed with an unearthly squeal.

Hugo pulled his sword, surprised by how quickly the small Mohammedan gained his feet. The man's black eyes burned with vengeance. In one smooth motion, the pagan drew his own sword from his belt and swung it in a wide arc. Hugo dodged, then lunged. The clash of their weapons reverberated up his arms. He held his sword too tightly, stiffening his limbs. Hugo secured his grasp, but relaxed his arms, and allowed the weight and design of the blade do its deadly work.

Chaos surrounded them. The screams of wounded men and dying horses filled the air. Sweat drops blurred Hugo's vision. He jerked his head to fling them away. The Mohammedan persisted with astounding agility, determination, and stamina. Hugo felt a momentary stab of concern, but then the man stumbled. The warrior touched a hand to the ground to regain his balance, leaving his chest exposed.

Hugo hesitated. For a fleeting second he thought to show mercy to his enemy. To wait until the man could face him fairly. But this was a real battle. No more contests. It was kill or be killed.

Too late, the Mohammedan's eyes flashed up to Hugo. The man knew his mistake, and despite the certainty of his demise, his face registered a hatred so caustic Hugo's eyes stung.

"*Allah il*—" His shrill cry broke off when Hugo's sword plunged through his heart.

Even though the scene had played out with agonizing slowness—

each movement embedded in Hugo's mind as though performed over a lifetime—the skirmish took only moments. Hands trembling, he pulled the sword from the man's lifeless body and turned to survey the conflict around him.

The Christian archers had switched to their maces and war hammers, their longbows ineffective at close range. Knights barreled through the ranks on their coursers—trampling downed friends and foes alike—and swung swords with fatal precision. Hugo pushed his way toward a foot soldier whose face and tunic was covered with blood. Not his own, Hugo surmised, for the fellow battled heartily. But the crusader stood alone against two enemies. Hugo charged one of the aggressors, running his sword through the man's back just as the second received a jab to the stomach.

Hugo's comrade-in-arms looked up to grin his thanks, then suddenly flew backward, an arrow to the throat.

Head spinning at the sudden loss, Hugo dropped to his knees.

Blood drenched the ground. It was not yet time to grieve his dead ally. Or the men still to die. He stumbled to his feet, dodged a Roman warhorse, and took to the battle again.

It seemed a strange thing later, to have fought and killed and hardly been aware of it. After those first moments, his training took over, as did his natural instincts. Power surged through his arms, and he felt invincible, striking down dark infidels and deflecting blows from Arab swords.

All in all, the Christians fared well. The Muslim forces soon faltered and then surrendered. By nightfall the city had been plundered, and the raiding party made its way across the Jordan River, south of the Galilee. They intended to circle the great sea rather than return to Acre directly, hoping their circuitous route would confuse those Mohammedans who might attempt retribution.

Hugo paced beside the shore. "What do they call these again?" he asked Orry.

"Pomegranates."

Hugo popped several plump seeds into his mouth. Their skins burst between his teeth, spilling tart juice over his tongue. "I'm not sure I like them. What do you think?"

"I think you're much too concerned with fruit after a day of fighting and looting."

Hugo grinned and squatted beside his friend. "Fighting and looting *Muslims*. That's enough to make any decent Christian feel agreeable."

Orry tested his shoulder, rotating his arm forward and then backward. "Is that what you are? Agreeable?"

"Admit it. You had fun." Hugo sat down and rested his forearms on his knees.

Orry raised an eyebrow at him. "Men died today."

"*Their* men."

"And ours. What's gotten into you?"

Hugo was painfully aware that some of their own forces had fallen, and he'd grieved their loss, but the day's victory was a boon to his spirits. He met his friend's gaze. "Didn't you feel it, Orry? Didn't you feel life coursing through your veins as you swung your weapon?"

Orry averted his gaze, but Hugo knew his friend understood.

Exhilarating is what it was.

Hugo tugged at the medallion hanging at his throat. Despite his words to Orry—and he meant them wholeheartedly—it'd been more disturbing than he expected, taking the life of another man. But the act carried with it a peculiar sense of redemption. In Kateline's honor, he would gladly do it again.

Chapter 26

December 5 AD 1217, Mount Tabor, Syria

Another thick splinter gouged Hugo's palm. He swore, used his other hand to steady the scaling ladder upon his shoulder, removed the fragment with his teeth, and spit it to the forest floor. He looked up too late to prevent a branch from plowing a furrow across his left cheek.

A growl started low in his chest, but he held it back and kept tromping, panting, silently cursing the trees, the solitary mountain rising high above the plains, and the Mohammedan fortress atop it.

Jerusalem sat empty, abandoned by the heathens who had scrambled behind the massive walls of this hulking stronghold. Its numerous towers sat like so many horns on the devil himself. But were the Christian armies taking Jerusalem?

No.

Instead, day after day, Hugo and the others climbed the mountain through woods too thick to move catapults and trebuchets. Protected by a deep trench and superior height, the fortress on Mount Tabor stood unyielding to their futile attempts.

Hugo scowled in the general direction of the stronghold, the heads of the men in front of him barely visible in the predawn gloom.

They were good men, these. Determined as he, despite the massive ladder they strained to carry uphill.

Mount Tabor.

He understood well enough why the Mohammedan forces occupied its heights—and why the Christian army wanted it. For more than a decade, Muslims had controlled the Valley of Esdraelon and threatened, from their secure perch, the forces at Acre. Now, after destroying the walls and ramparts of Jerusalem, the heathens retreated here, waiting for the crusaders to move into the city where they'd be vulnerable to attack.

So the Christians were going after them instead. If they could route the Muslims at Mount Tabor, Jerusalem would be theirs for the taking.

The squat little Arabs were fighters, though, he had to give them that.

Just two days ago the Christians got closer than ever to the stone walls, thanks to a cloaking fog. Nevertheless, the Mohammedans routed them from the mountain, swarming out of the fortress in a stinging counter offensive.

It was a wonder nearly all of the Christian force survived, really. Orry took an arrow deep in the thigh, but the bleeding had been light and he'd no fever, so Hugo stopped worrying over him.

This morning, under the command of John of Brienne, the Christian troops set out again from their camp along a nearby spring, leaving the wounded behind. So far, they climbed the mountain undetected. Hugo, near the front of the line, could see little more than a few feet ahead. The fortress remained silent, its occupants unaware of the Christians' boldness.

The trees thinned, and without warning, the ground dropped off. The ditch. Hugo looked to Gaspar behind him, matching the fellow's grim smile with his own. They hurried down the slope and up the other side, coming to a halt a few yards farther when they met the high stone wall of the citadel. The troops in the rear circled the fortress and organized themselves for attack. Near the tree line crossbowmen and archers would be readying their weapons. Hugo felt the dagger at the small of his back and the comforting steel of the sword behind his shoulders.

He and his companions maneuvered the ladder into place and leaned it against the stone. His blood raced as he and some twenty others scrambled upward in quick succession, the ladder swaying under their weight. His arms itched for a chance to unleash his wrath inside the enemy stronghold.

He was high above the ground, nearly tasting the sweet fruit of revenge against the dark-skinned foes, when something shattered above him. A tremendous blast shook the ladder and rattled his teeth. Hugo flattened himself to the wood and grasped the edges to keep from being pitched over the side.

Flames engulfed the bodies of the men above him and leapt down the wooden beams. Confused cries broke out among the ranks.

"Move it!" he yelled to the men behind, pushing at Gaspar with his feet. Gaspar froze in place, white-knuckled hands clutching the ladder.

Earthen vessels sailed over the wall and cracked on the ladder or among the men below. Each jar broke with a roar, lighting the sky like the sun at midday. Screams filled the air.

Hugo climbed over Gaspar and pulled him by the tunic. "Come on. We'll die here. Move."

"Stop! We'll never make it down." Gaspar swung a powerful arm at Hugo, knocking him off balance.

Hugo lost his hold, clawed at the ladder, slipped several inches before finding his grip with raw hands. No time to argue. "Stay there, then."

Gaspar didn't answer, but flung himself off the ladder head first, arms paddling the air. His skull split upon a jagged boulder, blood and brains sprayed the rock. Bile rose in Hugo's throat.

Fire consumed the wood like a hungry beast. The weakened structure began to crumble. Burning men and timber blocked Hugo's escape above and below. He twisted left and right, calculating his options. Most of the soldiers on the ground forty feet beneath him fled downhill. A few tried to assist their dying comrades, but found themselves ablaze when they attempted to beat out the flames.

Hugo's skin blistered from the heat. His nostrils filled with the stench of burning flesh. He turned, balancing himself on a single rung. Crouching chest to knees, he concentrated on a smooth, grassy area beyond the devastation. Beyond the men, blazing like torches.

With a strength born of panic, he hurled himself through the air to meet the ground.

Chapter 27

February AD 1218, the home of Harun al-Rashid

"I will gladly do so, my lord," Simon said to Harun. It was his fourth trip to the master's home in five months. Each time, the man commissioned him with a special task somewhere on his vast estate—a test, it seemed. And each time Simon visited, he sought out the beautiful young servant Fazila.

"Very good," Harun said. "And when you are done, return to me. We will dine again and continue our conversation."

Simon smiled. He enjoyed the friendly debates they had over a dozen different topics. This particular discussion concerned the finer points of al-Ghazali's *Ihya 'ulum al-din*, the *Revival of the Sciences of Religion*.

"Surely you agree, then" Harun had said, "that a single sin does not deserve eternal punishment?"

"But I believe it does, unless one is within the grace of God."

Harun waved his hand. "You speak in riddles."

Simon laughed. "I speak poorly, then, my lord. It is not my intention to puzzle you."

"Explain your meaning."

Simon took a breath, lifted his eyes to the ceiling, paused to choose careful words. "As Ghazali correctly concluded, man cannot purify his soul by good acts." He returned his gaze to the master. "And virtue does lead toward our goal of knowing and serving God."

"Then in what way do you disagree with the teacher?"

"Let us suppose, sir, that you asked me to purchase a slave for you at the market, sell a hundred bushels of wheat for you while there, deposit the proceeds with a banker, and bring back a cluster of grapes for your supper."

Harun smiled beneath tented fingers, but said nothing.

"And let us say, master, that I carried out your commands, except for one point. What if I never deposited the funds with the banker, but kept them instead?"

Al-Rashid raised his brows. "Then you would be a thief, young Simon."

"That, I would, master. And a disobedient servant."

Harun's eyes narrowed, and Simon could see that the man weighed his words. "By a single act, you would have rebelled against me."

"Yes, my lord. With one sin, I would become your enemy."

"And grace?"

"God's grace is beyond human reason, master." Simon smiled. "He seeks to make sons out of his enemies."

"Through the Nazarene?"

Simon nodded.

"I have a job for you, Simon al-Nasrani," the master said. "I want you to oversee the export of my stored grain. Make way to the harbor in Alexandria and coordinate arrangements for the transport. Jabir will provide you with the information you need to carry out your mission."

"It will be my pleasure, master"

Jabir provided not only information but also a heady dose of encouragement when he heard the news.

"This is a good sign." The old man rubbed his hands together with the soft swish of skin against skin. "Harun would not give you so much freedom and responsibility if he did not trust you."

Jabir proceeded to carefully explain where Simon should go and to whom he should speak. "You will stay in the guest accommodations tonight and leave tomorrow at first light."

The announcement surprised Simon. "A guest room? Are you sure?"

"It is within my power to offer it to you. Your master would approve."

So it was that Simon found himself wandering the gardens alone at eventide. He'd been to his room and tested the plump cushions on which he would sleep that night, but excitement about the next morning's adventure propelled him outside.

Prayer came naturally. He sank to his knees in the soft dirt beneath a flowering bush. "Thank you, Father, for your care and provision. For the conversations I've been allowed to share with the master. For the beautiful Fazila who works in this household." His heart swelled at the thought of her.

Simon soon ended his prayer and wondered where he might find the young woman. Near the servant's quarters, of course. He went in search of her.

He took a sharp breath when he spied her coming toward him down a narrow passageway lit by torches. She had not seen him yet, for she watched her step while she carried a basket heavy with dirty linens.

"Fazila."

She looked up, a light brightening her lovely eyes. Her footsteps slowed and a blush moved across her face before she bowed her head. "You have returned." Her voice rose barely above a whisper.

He smiled and drew close. She reminded him of a doe, shy and cautious. "I have. The master sends me on his business tomorrow, but tonight I'm staying here."

Fazila cleared her throat. "Excuse me. I must finish my chores."

"Won't you walk with me in the garden?"

Horror crossed her features. "Oh, no. I cannot. We should not even speak to one another." She didn't move, despite her protests.

"Why not?" Simon took a step forward.

"It is not allowed." She focused on the ground. "You know the law."

"What I know," he took the basket from her and set it down, "is that every time we see one another you say the same thing."

She lifted soft eyes to his. He wanted to touch her smooth skin, pull her into his arms. "You are beautiful, Fazila." He could not resist caressing her jaw with one finger.

She dropped her gaze. "Simon," she breathed. "We mustn't be together."

"It's all right."

"But I will be punished if we are discovered. So will you. Someone could come at any moment." She did not pick up the basket to leave.

Simon felt weak at her nearness. He didn't understand what could be so evil about talking to her. About kissing her. That's what he wanted, and he knew it. The thought surprised him, warmed him, spurred him on. He bent toward her, lifted her chin. She turned her face so that his mouth brushed her cheek.

They seemed paused like that for eternity, her warm, fragrant skin beneath his lips, his heart pounding. He drew her close, and she leaned against his chest. Tiny and fragile, a little sparrow. He wanted to protect her.

A door creaked open and closed. Voices. Fazila stooped to grab the basket then ran away without a word.

Simon stood in the hallway looking after her, dazed and sporting what was probably a ridiculous grin.

The glow of meeting with her lasted for days, carried him through until their next encounter at a formal dinner with Harun and Jabir. This time Fazila fluttered in the background, serving. He was careful not to look at her, though, for he knew he would gaze too long, divulging to Jabir and the master the secret of his affections.

"If it pleases you, master," Simon said, "I will finalize the arrangements tomorrow." The trip to Alexandria had been successful, if he did say so himself. He'd spent two days bartering with ship owners until he secured a fair deal that would profit al-Rashid immensely.

"It does please me," Harun said. "As it pleases me to promote you to the position of overseer."

Simon nearly choked on the flavorsome vegetables he'd just placed in his mouth. He looked wide-eyed toward Jabir, who chuckled at his surprise. "What about—"

Harun held up a hand. "I've decided to alter the responsibilities of my trusted friend. Jabir is more than capable of serving me as an advisor." Al-Rashid looked at the gray-headed man. "In fact, he has been doing so for some time now."

Jabir leaned forward, brown eyes twinkling. "I am old, Simon. That is the simple truth. You are better suited for the travel and toil of managing Harun's estate. I will retire to my own house near the river, give my opinion on this and that, and let you and Harun suffer the stresses of administration."

"Don't think you've outlived your usefulness, Jabir," Harun said. "I will continue to rely heavily upon you. This young man, however," he nodded in Simon's direction, "has proven himself wise, loyal, and conscientious. We need him, friend."

Simon's head spun. He was a twenty-two-year-old Christian slave in Mohammedan lands. Surely God had done this thing. "I am honored beyond words," he finally managed. "I don't know what to say."

"Nonsense." Harun snapped his fingers at the serving girls.

Simon wondered what Fazila thought of the news.

"I did not make this decision without warrant, Simon," Harun said while the servants refilled their glasses and replaced empty dishes with platters of fruit. "I am a shrewd man. Your youthful vitality is to my advantage, your skills in management an asset to me, and your intelligence astounding. I would be a fool to make any other choice."

Simon forgot the food. Forgot Jabir and Fazila. He bowed before Harun al-Rashid. "In the name of the Most High God and His Son Jesus Christ, I will honor your confidence. May the Lord punish me severely if I do not prove true to you, my master."

"And what of God's grace?" Harun said. "Would it not reach so far?"

Simon, nose to the ground, thought about his answer. "It would, my lord. Which is why I would entrust myself to his wrath over yours."

Harun laughed out loud, a low, rich sound that spilled over to Jabir. Simon lifted his head to see both men doubled over, their faces contorted with humor, both gasping for breath. What was so funny? He'd spoken truthfully. His eyes cut to Fazila who bowed in the corner. Was she smiling, too?

"Ah, Simon," Harun finally said with a chuckle. "Your faith might make a Christian of me yet."

Chapter 28

May AD 1218, 'Atlit, Syria

Hugo wiped grit and sweat from his brow and turned his face toward the sea. He didn't care that he toiled long hours in backbreaking labor on the Templar castle. At least most of his strength had returned.

Built on a small piece of land jutting into the Mediterranean, the new fortress would hold over 4,000 people during a siege. More importantly, it would serve as a base of operation for Templar knights protecting pilgrims traveling between Acre and Jerusalem. That is, at least once Jerusalem was retaken.

Hugo couldn't wait to fight. When two brave comrades rescued him from Mount Tabor—his skin blistered and peeling from the Greek fire the infidels had launched, bones broken and vision blurred from the impact of his life-saving jump—he feared he'd never swing a weapon again. He pushed himself to persevere through the process of recovery, even now when his shoulder throbbed and a recurring dizziness forced him to plant his feet firmly. The inconvenience was nothing compared to those whose lives were lost in the fire or to the 500 who were slaughtered in the mountains of Sidon two weeks later, while he recuperated in Acre, useless as a baby.

"Are you well?" Orry asked.

"Of course." Hugo stirred the mortar used to secure the stones of the six-feet-thick walls.

"I've heard good news."

"They're bringing Christian women to 'Atlit?" Hugo knew his friend pined daily for the fairer sex.

Orry grinned. "Perhaps not that good." His eyes remained bright. "Fresh troops have been arriving in Acre for almost a month now."

Hugo didn't understand what benefit that held—other than to speed along construction of the Templar castle. His look must have said as much.

"Don't you see?" Orry said. "Soon our number will be great enough to invade Egypt."

King Andrew had given up on Jerusalem and returned to Hungary, but Giovanni attached their unit to Oliver of Cologne. It hadn't meant anything, so far, but word had come lately that John of Brienne convinced the war council to attack Egypt instead.

"We're going, then?" Hugo tried to keep the irritation from his voice.

"So it would seem." Orry looked pleased about it.

How could Hugo be so close to Jerusalem—to fulfilling his promise to Kateline—only to change course now? "It makes no sense."

"Of course it does," Orry reasoned. "We'd be fools to go after Jerusalem at this point. Cairo's the seat of Muslim power. With Egypt under the control of Rome, we can pluck Jerusalem like a ripe grape."

Hugo scowled at him. "That's what they said about Mount Tabor."

That night, bellies full and limbs aching, Hugo and Orry made their way through the camp set up close to the shore. The moon shone bright, and the surf broke noisily upon the rocks. Hugo's thoughts jolted back to that day outside Genoa when Nicholas's sea failed to part. He forced himself to listen to Orry's joke telling.

A laugh exploded from his friend's mouth. "Get it?" Orry wheezed. "*A Hospitaller.*"

Hugo was about to confess he'd only heard the last few words, when a small turbaned man stepped out of the shadows in front of them. Orry went silent at once, pivoting to position himself back-to-back with Hugo. Both of them drew their weapons and scanned the darkness for more intruders.

The man's hands flew up. "I am alone and unarmed." His voice squeaked like a woman's. One hand moved cautiously toward his neck, and he lifted a silver cross that glistened in the moonlight.

"See?" the man said in a singsong voice. "I am a Christian."

Hugo's eyes narrowed. A Christian *today*, at least. "What do you want?"

The man pulled open his outer robe to reveal an assortment of baubles sewn into the lining. "I am but a businessman. May I interest you in a souvenir from the Holy Lands?"

Orry lowered his sword, but Hugo kept his aloft.

"It's a dangerous thing to be slinking around in the dark."

The man grinned as he shook his robe, jingling the trinkets. "I've been in 'Atlit for a week. Everyone knows me except you brutes. Look, here is a pretty bracelet for one of your lovers."

Hugo's jaw tightened. "Be off with you, scoundrel. Your goods are probably stolen anyway."

"For you, I'll sell them cheap," the dealer persisted.

"Come on, Hugo, let's take a look," Orry said. "Jewelry never fails to win a lady's heart."

Hugo slid his sword back into its sheath. "What lady, Orry? Have you not noticed we're all men?"

"It never hurts to be prepared," he said, fingering a bangle.

"Yes," the man said to Orry, his whining voice irritating Hugo. "You are a handsome one. I'm sure you have many maidens waiting for you back home."

Orry tipped his head. "The man is brilliant, Hugo. Who cares if he's honest?"

"You are a man of love," the peddler crooned to Orry. "Light-hearted, appreciating true beauty wherever it is found."

Hugo sighed and folded his arms in front of his chest.

The man shot a glance at Hugo. "Not like your dark-tempered friend there. He has the look of death in his eyes. Like the lost children."

Hugo's heart lurched. "What are you talking about?"

"The light-skinned children," he said, pointing out a delicate chain to Orry. "Christians, all of them."

Hugo rushed the man, grabbed him by the shoulders and hauled him to the tips of his toes. "What do you know of them?"

Orry stood open-mouthed, watching the exchange.

"I—I know little," the man said.

Hugo's grip tightened. "Where are they?"

Terror mingled with indignation in the man's eyes. "How am I to know? I saw them on the auction block in Damascus years ago."

The breath came hot through Hugo's nostrils. Slavery? He released the man, who rubbed his undersized arms. "How many?"

"A hundred, perhaps. Maybe more."

One ship's worth, then. A sharp pain sliced through Hugo's head as the news lodged there.

"Some say they were taken to Baghdad," the man whispered. He seemed to enjoy how his words punished Hugo. "That they were martyred there, and their blood still stains the streets of that great city."

Hugo's eyes felt heavy—he could barely lift them to the peddler's face.

The man sniffed and shrugged his narrow shoulders. "But how am I to know?"

Hugo turned and walked toward the water, hand to the medallion at his throat. Orry called out to him, but he didn't answer.

§ § §

Sure enough, within the week they were bound for Egypt. Hugo kept close to the bow of the ship to feel the spray on his face.

"Why is it you stay here, soaked by the sea?" Orry asked him the second day out.

Hugo glanced at him, then back to the horizon. "I like to see what's up ahead."

Orry laughed. "Up ahead? There's nothing but more water up ahead, my friend."

Hugo gripped the rail. "You never know."

Orry leaned upon his forearms and offered Hugo a biscuit.

He turned it down with a shake of his head. "So, it's Cairo, is it?"

Orry was sociable enough to have gleaned a few details from one of the officers. "In due course," he said, "but first we have to take a town that guards the Nile River just a couple of miles inland, otherwise we'll never reach Cairo."

It already felt that way. "Alexandria?" Hugo said. He'd heard soldiers speak of that great city before.

"No." Orry scrunched his brows. "Dama? Dametta?" His face brightened. "Damietta. That's it."

Hugo sighed. Damietta it was, then. With any luck, they'd defeat the city quickly and be on their way to Cairo. Then back to Jerusalem.

He thought of all those who perished trying to get there. Of the missing children. Of those slaughtered in Baghdad. His gut tightened.

Had Simon been among them? Elisabeth?

He wasn't sure he wanted to know.

Chapter 29

May AD 1218, Damietta, Egypt

Elisabeth looked at her sleeping mistress and hoped the woman would live. Not because she had any affection for the witch. The old crone had been ruthless as a scorpion—all sharp words and stinging blows. No, Elisabeth wanted the lady to live because the ailment that left the woman's speech unintelligible and the right side of her body paralyzed also provided Elisabeth with her first measure of freedom since arriving in this loathsome place.

Elisabeth's second encounter with the auction block months ago—or was it years?— taught her to prefer familiar horror to unknown terror. Trembling, she'd heard the auctioneer voice her name. *Moshkelah.* He laughed at her along with the crowd, while the sneering overseer who'd taken her to market berated him and ordered him to shut up.

That was one command she knew well. The overseer had said it whenever she answered him in her native tongue. She delighted in speaking nothing but German to the heathens, for it annoyed them. And it reminded her that she used to have a home and a people of her own.

Bidding had been slow that day, but at last a weasel of a man bought Elisabeth and led her to a large house in an elegant part of the city. The only free occupant was the old woman. A dozen slaves tended her. Elisabeth had no idea why the lady needed another. Perhaps to cook, for none of them could roast meat like Elisabeth. "*Moshkelah*," they still called her, laughing at her with their filthy mouths.

The mistress was healthy at the time, and her son and his family often visited. At first Elisabeth couldn't figure out why, for they bristled and hissed like ill-tempered cats. Then she began to notice things. The son's sandals had been re-stitched many times. His wife always wore the same robe, frayed at the hem. They arrived without attendants. Though they carried themselves with arrogance and rudeness, Elisabeth knew it was her mistress who possessed the family wealth. She wondered what sort of legal arrangement had made the mother master of the household.

Elisabeth was sure the son didn't like the old hag. Hated her, in fact. His eyes, while always cold, hardened like marble when his mother entered the room. His mouth twisted in disdain when she spoke. He let his brats run wild, and smirked at her complaints.

One night last winter, Elisabeth found the woman on the floor, saliva dribbling from her open mouth, face slack, eyes panicked. Elisabeth knew with sickening certainty that life would change once again. What she hadn't anticipated was the son's reaction. He'd cleared his mother's home of every valuable thing—statues, tapestries, items of gold and silver—leaving only the mistress's private quarters intact. Then he'd rounded up all the slaves except for that weasel of a servant and herself, and marched them through the gate that led to the streets of Damietta.

Whether they were sold or taken to serve in the son's home, Elisabeth could only guess. And why should she care about any of it? The bedridden woman probably didn't know the difference anyway.

Or maybe she did.

Elisabeth saw malice in her mistress's eyes. She hated the woman herself, and wondered sometimes why she stayed and cared for her when it would be easier to slip away to the city or smother the lady with a cushion and feign tears at her mistress's death. Except where would that leave her? At the mercy of unknown terrors again.

The truth was, she suffered enough guilt already. And no matter how low she'd sunk, she could never take a life. Though in this case it might be merciful to do so.

The mistress's breath rattled in her chest, and she'd grown exceedingly frail. Her skin resembled that of an onion, thin and transparent. In the rare instances she awoke, Elisabeth offered broth, but the woman took little before she choked and pushed it away with her one good hand.

Malice was not the only thing Elisabeth read in the mistress's eyes. Fear smoldered there. And loneliness. Despair. Death.

Good.

That even one Mohammedan shared Elisabeth's lot gave her some satisfaction. Very small, though, and it shamed her to admit her soul had become so calloused.

The woman's eyes fluttered open, and Elisabeth leaned forward.

"*Aaanshhhha*," the mistress groaned, distorting the word. *I thirst.*

Elisabeth looked at her. Pity, alone, kept her from pretending she didn't understand. She poured a portion of diluted juice into a cup, then lifted the woman's head and brought the drink to her mouth.

The mistress sipped, but most of the liquid spilled onto the cotton chemise she wore. She lay back, exhausted by the slight effort. "*Sh . . . shgrnnng.*"

Garbled as it was, Elisabeth knew what the woman tried to say. *Thank you.*

She dared to show some bit of kindness or gratitude at this late point in time? Elisabeth said nothing in response.

An hour later, the old lady's eyes opened. Her body shook, and then went rigid. Elisabeth jumped to her feet, breath coming in shallow bursts. She stilled her chest. How quiet the room seemed. She stretched out a hand to touch the woman, putting her fingers to the wrinkled, brown neck.

After a moment, Elisabeth exhaled and wondered what unknown terror lay ahead this time.

She found the Weasel.

"The old lady is dead," Elisabeth said.

He looked at her, understanding, she guessed. Elisabeth followed him back to the mistress's room. He didn't even glance at the woman, but opened a lacquered box and removed a small coin. Ah, so that's how he managed to bring food from the market each week.

The man made way to the front gate and pulled it open. He called to a young boy passing by. The child hesitated, but his face brightened when he saw the coin. Weasel issued instructions, and the boy ran off.

Two men with a cart came that night and took the body.

"We've been abandoned," she said to Weasel, though of course he ignored her German. "I know slaves are killed for less than running away, but if no one comes before sunset tomorrow, I'm leaving." To where, she had yet to decide.

She needn't have worried. The following morning, the mistress's son arrived, smiling broadly and surveying the home as if he'd just bought it. Elisabeth supposed he had. Yes, she thought, he'd purchased the place with patience born of spite, biding his time until the woman died.

Within two days the household belongings were back in place. A few pieces were missing, and Elisabeth imagined the son had sold them off.

In addition to several new slaves, most of the previous servants returned to the house with the son, taking up their former duties. Except for Elisabeth. The new master installed in the kitchen a woman she'd never seen before, skin as black as the kohl that had lined the old mistress's sunken eyes.

Instead of roasting meats or baking flatbread, Elisabeth was forced to clean out the sewer trenches. On hands and knees, she crawled through narrow tunnels under the foundation of the home, mucking out the drains that ran the length of the house on both the east and west sides. She gagged despite the cloth she wrapped around her mouth and nose, and almost relished the greasy smoke from the candle that lit her way.

What had she done to deserve such humiliation? Discarded, like the dung she was forced to remove. A vile, worthless nothing.

It was the curse.

Elisabeth finished the backbreaking job by late afternoon. She washed out her tunic, cleaned the filth from her arms, face, and legs, and pulled on her everyday chemise and robe—a dingy, rough-woven garment that fit poorly and made her skin itch.

She started in the kitchen after that, washing dirty pots, and collapsed with a thin blanket on the hard earth of the servants' quarters sometime after midnight.

She dreamed of Hugo.

Elisabeth saw herself scrubbing the courtyard, knuckles raw and bleeding. The dream intensified, grew more vivid. A horse thundered up to the gate. The thick wooden doors crashed open. A moment later a brawny soldier stood in the sunlight of the courtyard, dust motes glittering around his form. She thought at first it was Wilhelm, and she screamed.

"Elisabeth," he said, and she saw the man was Hugo.

She fell to the ground in relief. He picked her up and carried her to freedom. No one protested, not even the master. She was nothing, after all.

"How did you find me?" she said when they boarded a ship for home.

"I've been searching for you. For all of you," he said gently, his eyes as blue as the morning sky.

She could hardly get her questions out fast enough. "Where is Kateline?"

"Gone, remember?"

Elisabeth felt confused. "Oh, yes. And what of Simon?"

Hugo's face clouded. "No one else is left. Only us."

She bent to the deck of the ship and wept for their loss.

§ § §

Panic tasted bitter in Elisabeth's mouth and left it dry as the summer air. Awakened an hour ago, she was now burdened with possessions that wouldn't fit on the master's two carts that trundled ahead of her.

Whatever caused the family to flee the city with dozens of other residents terrified her. Or, rather, whoever caused them to flee. Invaders of some sort—she'd guessed that much.

"*Moshkelah, Moshkelah,*" the slaves had cried nonsensically while they ran back and forth through the house. At first she feared they blamed her for the catastrophe. Her hands still shook as she gripped the bag of silver goblets.

Who threatened the city? Elisabeth couldn't imagine a fiercer people than those she'd suffered under these many years. She trembled at the alarming thoughts that swirled through her mind.

Three days later, her bag of treasure traded for passage through the canals, Elisabeth wondered why the master bothered to preserve her life. Surely, she'd outgrown her usefulness to him. She and most of the other servants who followed the wealthy refugees of Damietta were certainly more hindrance than help. Perhaps they were to be offered as ransom to the enemy. The idea sickened Elisabeth.

It was no use holding out for God's mercy. She should have given up on it long ago and taken a knife to her wrists.

Her eyes drifted to the brown water rippling past the barge on which they traveled. If she jumped, she'd likely drown or be attacked by one of the scaly, sharp-toothed creatures that inhabited the river.

But then again, that was the point.

Elisabeth got to her feet, swaying under the weight of what she was about to do. She inched toward the edge of the deck. Water churned under the barge, and a stray droplet landed wet and cool upon her foot.

She thought of the Rhine. Of *Vati* rubbing her cold feet between his big hands.

A tear spilled from her eye, for she would not see him in heaven. Elisabeth wiped the moisture from her cheek. She would never see heaven.

"*Moshkelah!*" A rough hand pulled her away from the edge. The muscular servant struck her across the face, and the master yelled angry, unintelligible words.

They tied her hands to a ring in the center of the boat, but she did not let them see her tears.

Chapter 30

June AD 1218, the home of Harun al-Rashid

Simon's gut wrenched. "Does Jabir still live?" he asked the servant who led him through the courtyard.

He'd received news a full day ago that Jabir suffered pains in his chest, leaving the man struggling for his life.

"Yes, but he's very weak," the servant said.

Simon soon stood in one of the guest chambers, looking down upon the sleeping form of the man he loved like a father. He could not help the tears that brimmed in his eyes. He turned to Harun. "I came as quickly as I could." Word had reached Simon while he consulted with workers on a distant section of the estate. "I feared myself too late."

Sorrow dulled Harun's features, but his eyes remained dry. "He is not long for this world, I think."

"Has he spoken?"

"Little." Harun sighed then offered a weary smile. "It is good you are here."

Simon nodded and kneeled on the cushions beside Jabir, taking the man's hand in his. "My father," he said softly.

"Simon?" Jabir's eyes opened and then closed. His mouth

trembled into a worn smile, and his voice came low and faint. "Why are you not working?"

Simon almost choked on the chuckle that escaped his throat. "I came to see you. How are you feeling?"

Jabir opened his eyes again. "Not good, my young friend." His breath came in sharp jabs. "But I am ready to meet Allah."

Simon's heart twisted, and a tear dropped to the bedding. "I wish you would know the Nazarene."

Jabir licked his dry lips. Harun lifted the man's head to offer him a sip of water. When he was done, Jabir turned his face to Simon. "But I do know him, my son." His eyelids closed, and he mumbled a few more words. "I see him in you."

Simon bowed to pray while Jabir drifted off to sleep and Harun sat silent. When he raised his head, Harun was watching.

"Wash the dust from your feet, Simon," Harun said. "And get something to eat."

"I want to stay with Jabir if I may."

The master stood. "Very well. Someone will tend to you." He nodded to the male servants who waited nearby. One of them left the room to carry out his unspoken order. "The doctor will return soon, and I will join him."

Jabir died two days later, early in the morning. They buried him before sunset according to custom, his body wrapped in white linen and placed in the ground on his right side facing Mecca. Simon mourned the death of one so dear, mourned that his rescuer should fail to confess the Lord Jesus, and mourned anew the family and friends he'd lost in one way or another so long ago.

He wondered what had become of Hugo. Did Elisabeth still live? And little Conon? The boy would be eleven or twelve now, if he survived. Practically a young man.

Simon looked down at his hands, which used to be smooth and too large for his gangly frame. Now they fit him perfectly, strong and calloused. A workman's hands, not a scholar's. How different life had become in the six years since he'd left the monastery at Villebonne. And though the years had been filled with great pain and loss—and even greater foolishness and failure—God remained faithful. Such knowledge humbled and soothed him.

Why had Jabir not confessed Jesus as the Christ? The man could have rested for eternity in the arms of a patient and loving Savior. Simon could hardly think on it, so heavy was the sorrow he carried.

"Have I disturbed your prayers, my friend?" Harun asked.

Simon got up from the bench in Harun's garden. "No, master. I am just thinking," he said, bowing down.

Harun motioned him to his feet. "Thinking of Jabir, *rahimahu Allah?*"

May God have mercy, Harun had said. Everyone who spoke Jabir's name uttered the same phrase. Simon nodded, hoping indeed that God would have mercy on his friend.

"It is a sad loss," Harun said. He settled on the bench and indicated Simon should join him. "He served my family since before I was born. As did his father before him."

Simon knew this, but had not considered how great Harun's attachment to Jabir must have been. "I'm sorry, master."

Harun did not respond, but sat quietly. "Why is it," he said at last, "that our friend did not accept your Jesus?" He settled his dark eyes on Simon.

Simon was taken aback by the question. "I don't know, my lord. I've asked myself the same thing."

"He was well-favored by the people of Alexandria," Harun said, "wealthy for a man in his position, and he delighted in reading and studying."

"Those are all good things," Simon said.

"Yes, yes." Harun stared straight ahead. "I would say I have excelled in each of those areas myself."

"Certainly, my lord."

"Jabir, *rahimahu Allah*, was a kind man."

"One of the kindest."

"A man who lived virtuously."

"Yes, master."

"I loved and respected him deeply."

"As did I," Simon said.

Harun looked to the night sky. "But why did he reject the Nazarene?"

Simon had no response.

Harun continued, "I think Jabir, *rahimahu Allah*, contented himself with this life." He paused then looked to Simon. "I was married once, many years ago."

Eyebrows aloft, Simon listened while Harun talked on.

"My wife was a beautiful woman, intelligent and gentle, and I loved her with great passion. She died of fever after five years, having never borne children."

"You have suffered great sorrow, then, my lord."

"I have," Harun agreed. "But even before, when life was as sweet as date sugar and the future bright as the summer sun, there was something unsatisfied within me. A part of me that searched for something more. Don't misunderstand, Simon al-Nasrani, I have enjoyed my life."

"I can see that, master."

"But I have wondered as I've seen your faith these many months, if you have not discovered something that exceeds all I have accomplished and acquired."

This was not the moment to be speechless, but Simon found himself tongue-tied.

"I don't want to be a man who grows content with this life," Harun said, "and thinks not of the next."

"No, my lord."

"When Jabir, *rahimahu Allah*, said that he saw the Nazarene in you, I knew he spoke the truth." Harun laid a hand on Simon's shoulder. "I want you to teach me earnestly of your Jesus, my friend, for I recognize something eternal and true in your young life that is lacking in all men I have known before. Especially myself."

§ § §

A flush of heat spread across Simon's face.

"Ah. So you *have* thought to take a wife, young Simon." Harun grinned like a child at the end of Ramadan, the Islamic holy month of fasting.

Nearly three weeks had passed since Jabir took his last breath. Four days since Harun had confessed faith in Christ and been baptized in a courtyard fountain. The master permitted Simon to teach his household the way of Christ, and many followed, including Fazila.

Simon cleared his throat. "The thought of marriage has occurred to me."

"I should like to act as your agent, then," Harun said. "I'm sure I can find a suitable young woman for you among the households in Alexandria."

"Alexandria?" Simon's voice betrayed the alarm he felt, but the master seemed not to notice.

"I would consider Damietta if necessary." Harun popped a grape into his mouth. "I have a relative there, you know."

"No. That won't be necessary. I . . . " He cast his eyes toward the servants in the room, thankful at the moment that Fazila was not among them.

Harun sat up from the cushions where he reclined. "What is it, Simon?"

Swallowing, Simon ventured to speak his heart. He leaned close. "I am in love, master."

Harun's eyebrows shot up. "In love? With whom?"

Simon glanced toward the servants again then back to Harun, who dismissed them with a wave of his hand. When they were gone, Simon spoke. "With your maidservant, Fazila, my lord."

"Fa—" Harun could not even complete the name. "She is but a child!"

"She is seventeen, master. A young woman of marriageable age."

"Seventeen already?" Harun asked, eyebrows askew.

Simon nodded.

Harun considered the information, and then narrowed his eyes. "You have not trifled with her, I hope."

Simon's ire rose. "Never, master. She is the purest among women."

"I'm glad to hear it." Harun grunted. "In love? Since when does that have anything to do with choosing a wife?"

"You said you loved your wife passionately."

"I did come to do so, but I never beheld her until the day we wed."

"I didn't intend this to happen."

Harun scratched his head. "She *is* a lovely young woman."

"And mild and graceful and—"

A chuckle burst from the master's lips. "All right, young Simon, I see that you are quite smitten. Have you shared your intentions with her?"

Simon shook his head. "She knows of my affection, but I would never be so bold without your blessing."

"Very well, then. I will speak to her on your behalf."

Simon smiled and began to articulate his gratitude, but Harun cut him off.

"If she is willing to accept you, then I insist upon a lengthy betrothal. In cases such as this, when the couple has made their own decision, time helps to test their wisdom. She shall not marry until she completes her eighteenth year."

"But—"

"That is my decree, Simon. You will abide by it."

The two men looked each other in the eye. Disappointed as Simon was by the prospect of waiting nearly a year to marry, his heart soared with joy that the beautiful Fazila would one day be his bride.

Harun matched the grin that broke across Simon's face.

Two days later Simon walked toward the marketplace, satisfied with the world and his place in it. The citizens of Alexandria treated him with respect. They no longer saw a young Christian slave, but a man of position and power in Harun al-Rashid's household. God had fit Simon well into this new life—giving him a gift for the language and an appreciation for the customs of these people. Strangers even thought him an Arab, albeit an exceptionally tall one, with his dark eyes and hair, deeply tanned skin, and perfect local dialect.

But more important matters contented him today. He'd successfully negotiated a contract on behalf of his master this morning. Now he searched the bazaar to find a small gift for his beloved Fazila. She'd accepted his offer of marriage, and yesterday they'd taken vows in front of Harun in a tradition the master's family held for more than a hundred years. Though the betrothal would not be consummated until Fazila's birthday the following spring, their bond was sacred, and could be broken by Simon only in the case of infidelity. Of course, Harun had insisted that Fazila retain the right of retraction until she turned eighteen, but Simon knew she would not exercise it.

He scanned the crowded stalls, inspecting silver jewelry, porcelain figurines, and finely woven fabrics. Nothing seemed suitable, so he continued to browse.

A man bumped Simon's shoulder, snapping his attention from his thoughts to the bustle of the market. It seemed busier than normal for the hour and day, and Simon looked around him. The crowd rustled with excitement.

"What news is there in the city today?" he inquired of a basket weaver.

"Invaders surround Damietta."

"Seljuks?"

The basket maker shook his head. "Europeans."

Simon's breath caught in his chest. "Christians?"

The man nodded. "A few prosperous citizens escaped before a siege could begin. Some arrived here this morning."

Crusaders in Africa? Of course. Jerusalem no longer served as seat of the Muslim empire. Cairo did. Simon's heart began to race. If the Holy Roman army liberated the cities of Egypt, then Christian slaves would be freed. The children who'd been betrayed by le Ferreus and Porcus would be freed. *He* would be freed.

Simon's eyes darted to the figures hurrying toward a large square in the center of the merchant district. He moved to join them. "Are the refugees from Damietta addressing the crowd?" he asked a portly shopkeeper who pushed past him.

"Slaves," the man said, panting as he waddled ahead. "They're selling off servants to finance their resettlement."

Simon stopped in the street. It only took him a moment to realize why the Alexandrians were excited by the news. The price for slaves would be down today, the refugees eager to recoup some of their financial loss. No telling what else they were hawking in the square. Perhaps he could find something for Fazila.

The street opened into a large, public area. The recent immigrants displayed a few items for sale, but most of their belongings, along with their women, were hidden from the view of the masses swarming the vicinity. As he always did when in town, Simon glanced over the slaves huddled around the auction block, looking for fair-skinned Europeans. He'd long since given up hope of rescuing crusaders from the failed campaign, but the habit stuck with him.

No, none of the missing children were among them. Not that he expected any. He turned his attention to an intricately carved bottle of perfume being offered by one of the refugees.

"Let me go, you heathen pig!"

The hair on Simon's scalp stiffened when the shrill words rang out across the courtyard. In German.

He spun toward the crowd. Where had the voice come from? He searched the faces of the people, the faces of the slaves.

Simon's eyes snapped back to the auction block as a torrent of German curses sounded above the noise of the bartering and bickering going on in the marketplace. There, struggling between two handlers, was a woman whose once-fiery hair had deepened to a rich, warm hue. It hung loose around her face, hiding eyes he knew to be green as the sea.

Elisabeth.

He couldn't move, so stunned was he by the discovery. Joy displaced every moment of regret. Every sharp stab of grief. Every tear he'd shed over the past six years.

Elisabeth.

If she lived, perhaps Hugo did as well. And Conon. And hundreds of others.

Simon realized the bidding had started. He tried to elbow his way through the throng, but hopeful buyers pressed together in front of him, blocking his path. Desperate to reach his friend, he began to shove aside merchants and businessmen.

"Watch it," someone snarled.

Head spinning, he stumbled toward Elisabeth, every thought and movement centered on her rescue. The bidders gasped when he shouted out an enormous sum. No matter that it would take all of his small savings to make the purchase in Harun's name—she was worth every coin. Heads turned his direction, including Elisabeth's. Those eyes, green as a summer meadow, met his in a moment of sheer surprise before she turned her face to the heavens, praising God, no doubt, for his salvation in the person of Simon.

Quickly finishing his business with the auctioneer, Simon raced toward Elisabeth who'd been brought forward for inspection. Elation filled his chest, and his lips spread into a wide grin. His reached out to embrace her.

"Touch me, and I'll send you straight to the devil, you filthy Muslim dog."

Simon stopped short. But of course, she could not see him clearly, for the sun was in her face. He stepped to the left, brows lifted in anticipation of her great delight when she realized who had saved her. She followed his movement, eyes narrowed, mouth set in a hard line.

He bent so that his nose was even with hers. Smiled. "It's me," he said softly, not thinking to speak her native tongue. He lifted a finger to touch the hair he'd remembered so often, strands glowing in the afternoon sun like low-burning embers in the hearth.

Something struck his face, and he jerked back, realizing she'd spat upon him. Bystanders laughed as she let loose another stream of expletives. Anger and humiliation surged through Simon's chest.

She didn't even possess the decency to see beyond his Muslim garb. To see past the painful years that marked their separation. To see the friend whose very existence should have sent her heart rejoicing. He'd rescued her at great expense, and all she offered him were German vulgarities. How little she'd changed in all this time.

He turned to the auctioneer and spoke to him in Arabic. "Have her delivered to the residence of Harun al-Rashid."

Then he straightened his turban and pushed past the onlookers.

Chapter 31

September AD 1218, Damietta, Egypt

Hugo strained to see through the crowd at the dock. He wanted to know what kind of men disembarked from the Italian vessels. What kind of men had come to help them take Damietta.

Following a fierce battle last month, the Christians gained control of the city's chain tower—from which iron chains could be raised to block the passage of ships—and were poised to attack Damietta itself. But then the gutless Frisians abandoned them, delaying the planned siege.

The Italian reinforcements that came to replace them looked very fine, indeed.

A number of counts and other lords came ashore with their forces, fully armed and well supplied. Hugo couldn't take his eyes from the warhorses, palfreys, and hot-blooded destriers being led from the ships.

Orry jabbed Hugo in the ribs.

"What?" Hugo said absently.

"There."

Hugo followed Orry's nod, his gaze alighting on a man who

walked the gangway with a regal air. Cardinal Pelagius, Nicholas's old patron.

"What's he doing here?" The disdain in Orry's voice was obvious.

"Representing the pope, of course." Hugo's lip curled. "Sticking his nose in military affairs where it doesn't belong."

"He'll ruin everything, to be sure. I hope the war council resists him."

Hugo drew in a breath to reply, but it stuck in his throat.

A young man followed the cardinal. Slight of build. Dark hair. Head aloft. Arrogant eyes ignoring the onlookers.

Nicholas.

Orry saw him, too. "I'll be a horse's—"

"No," Hugo interrupted. "That's *his* job."

Orry laughed out loud.

Hugo expected a summons, but not so quickly. Only three days passed before he received an order to meet Nicholas. Hugo walked through the camp toward the boy's tent. The *young man's* tent, he corrected himself. Nicholas must be eighteen or nineteen by now, but Hugo doubted he'd ever see the former crusade leader as anything more than a pompous little brat.

Hugo entered the tent.

"There you are!" Nicholas reclined on cushions. "This foul heat is unbearable. I shouldn't like to be here at all if it weren't for seeing you." He tilted his head. "You've become a beast of a man, haven't you?"

Hugo dipped his head. Was that perfume he smelled? "You're finally on your crusade."

Nicholas frowned and waved his hand. "Some crusade. I don't understand this business about Egypt. Jerusalem is what we're after."

Hugo cocked an eyebrow at him. Nicholas was smart enough to realize that what happened here determined who possessed the Holy

Lands in the future.

Nicholas must have read his thoughts. "Oh, I know. It's just that all the political squabbling bores me."

At least they agreed on one point.

The young man sat up, damp curls clinging to his forehead, and crossed his legs beneath him. "Sit, Hugo. Tell me of your battles."

Hugo reluctantly lowered himself to the ground.

"I'm a squire now, you know," Nicholas said without giving Hugo a chance to speak. "Though in truth, everyone treats me as a knight. I'm very well respected and am not required to serve like most squires, grooming horses or polishing armor."

Hugo clamped his jaws tight. Nicholas had to be lying. He had neither the breeding nor social position to be considered for knighthood, despite his place in Pelagius's household. Some decaying old soldier probably tutored him in swordplay. Doubtful the young man would be truly fit for combat when the time came. "Well done, though I'd think you'd value all aspects of training."

"Oh, I'm sufficiently skilled. All that really matters is keeping one's seat on a horse and knowing how to handle a weapon. I'm an expert at both."

"You've partaken in a *hastiludium* then? A training exercise?"

Nicholas's brows knotted. "Of course." He lifted his chin and smiled. "It was not so difficult as learning the proper way to carve meat and the correct term for each type of carving. Did you know a deer is *broken*? A duck *unbraced*? A hen *despoiled*? It's all so very dull."

"Yes," Hugo drawled. "I'm certain it is."

"Now the hunt is another matter. I find it—"

"Nicholas."

The young man closed his mouth for the first time since Hugo entered.

"The siege of Damietta will soon begin," Hugo said, and stood. "I must sharpen my sword and clean the rust from my chain mail. Is there anything else you need?"

A pout shaped Nicholas's lips and perspiration glistened in his pores. His eyes drifted to Hugo's throat. "I see you wear Kateline's medallion even now. You're not still pining over her, are you?"

Hugo wanted to *unbrace* the little duck in front of him, but it was hardly worth the effort. He returned to his own tent where men smelled like men. Where they weren't afraid to sweat or sleep on the ground. Where they didn't care a scrap about the carving of meat, except when it came fresh from the fire, dripping and succulent, pierced by the tips of their knives.

It would be a long crusade with Nicholas there.

Chapter 32

September AD 1218, the home of Harun al-Rashid

"Yes," Simon said to Harun. "It's very bad business, indeed."

Although Simon had at first been glad to hear that crusaders landed in Damietta, the past months spent managing remote sections of Harun's estate had given him time to reconsider. Thousands were sure to die in that city, including the innocent, be they slave or free. And while he hoped to continue spreading the gospel of Christ among the Mohammedans, he knew the crusader strategy would do little to win converts.

Harun nodded. "I am concerned for my young nephew and his wife there. Now that al-Adil has died and al-Kamil is sultan, the invaders won't wait long to lay full siege to the city."

"Won't al-Kamil sue for terms of peace?"

"Perhaps." Harun sighed, and his brows knit together. "But I fear the Europeans are determined to fight."

"Master, is there some way I can serve you?" Simon asked. "I could travel to Damietta. Seek out your relative. Secure his escape, perhaps."

Harun tapped his fingers together. "No, young Simon, I will not yet ask you to go to Damietta, though the time may come when you can help."

Simon bowed his head. "Then is there anything else before I leave for your southern lands tomorrow?"

"Only one thing."

Simon lifted his eyes in question.

"It's the servant you purchased, my friend. She is exceptionally troublesome. The household staff has been most kind and patient with her, but she proves unmanageable. I've thought many times to sell her, but first I want to know why you bought her."

Simon's throat went dry. "I—I know her, master."

"Ah. I suspected as much. And has she always been difficult?"

"I'm afraid so."

The master drew a deep breath and leaned forward. "Do you desire her?"

"What?"

"Come now, her beauty is striking. My question is a simple one—did you have an improper motive for buying her?"

"No, master. I am faithful to Fazila. In fact, I have not seen Elisabeth since the market. She doesn't even recognize me."

Harun straightened. "Then why haven't you revealed your identity?"

"She insulted me, my lord. And I found her to be as mulish and vulgar as ever. I wanted nothing to do with the woman once I'd discovered her."

Harun lifted an eyebrow. "So you brought the woman here and left my servants to deal with her?"

Simon felt the blood rush to his face. "Master, please accept my apology. I didn't think about—"

Harun held up a hand. "You must speak to her immediately. She disrupts my household and will be sold if her behavior does not improve." He paused. "I'm sorry, Simon."

"Yes, master. Forgive the trouble I've brought to your home."

A smile played at Harun's mouth. "That's what they call her, you know. *Moshkelah*."

Trouble.

§ § §

Elisabeth didn't know why she'd been directed to the garden, commanded to sit on a stone bench, and then left alone. Not that she cared. Every moment away from the dark heathens was heaven to her. The only heaven she ever expected.

A movement along the path caught her attention. In the next instant a tall turbaned man stood before her. She knew him. He'd purchased her in the market, leering like a fool. She put him in his place and hadn't seen him since. Why had he come for her now? She sat on her hands to keep them from shaking, swearing that if he led her to auction, she'd find a way to kill herself before standing on the block again.

Elisabeth stared straight ahead, determined to ignore him, but he watched her for so long, she risked a glance his direction. The expression on his face held her. To her astonishment, moisture brimmed in his eyes. He had to be crazy. Her heart began to pound.

He moved to the bench, sat beside her, pulled off his turban. She wanted to flee, but all she could do was return his peculiar gaze.

"Elisabeth, don't you know me?"

She jumped from the seat with a yelp. Her name. How did he know her name? No one had spoken it for years.

She couldn't breathe, and her torso began to quiver. Was he a specter from the past? A demon? What evil had God sent her way?

Her paralyzed lungs finally loosened, and she took a great gulp of air. The man stood to grasp her shoulders between his hands. With great effort, she resisted the blackness that threatened her vision.

"Elisabeth," he said again, his voice firm.

She focused on his face, on the lips that formed her name.

"I am Simon."

Her heart squeezed in anguish, his words an agonizing lie. Simon? No, this man before her was an infidel. A vile, brown-skinned—

She'd gone mad. God had taken her sanity along with everything else.

A moan started deep in her chest, in the foul pit of her guilt. Moving up her throat, it strangled her as sure as hands upon her neck. With a wail that sounded otherworldly even to her own ears, grief burst from her mouth to proclaim her misery to the world.

The man shook her. "Elisabeth, look at me."

Unwillingly, she lifted her face to his. Tears flowed down his cheeks from eyes so dark and warm she shrank from their intensity. Those brows. The line of his jaw. That chin.

Eyes dark and warm.

"S—Simon?"

"Yes."

Fear ran its chilled hand down her spine. "Am I dead?" she whispered.

He laughed, and all at once she knew it was truly Simon. Knew she was very much alive.

She flung herself into his arms, weeping and repeating his name over and over. He picked her up and swung her round. She hardly felt her feet touch the ground when he set her down, but burrowed into the security of his arms, fearing he should disappear if she broke the embrace.

"How is it you?" she managed to ask.

He lifted her chin and smiled then led her, trembling, to the garden bench. She dared not let go of his strong hand.

Simon searched her face, trying, she thought, to see the young woman he'd once known. How many years had passed, she had no way of knowing, but guessed they'd been numerous. Fifteen. Twenty. She must look an old hag by now, a witch as gray and withered on the outside as she'd become inwardly.

He tucked a stray lock of hair behind her ear before speaking. "I, too, am a servant of master Harun al-Rashid. *Your* master, Elisabeth. God has prospered me, giving me authority in our master's household and allowing me to rescue you from the pain you may have suffered in slavery."

"*May* have suffered?" Had he not suffered, too?

She scrutinized him, noting his fine, Arab clothing. His tanned skin. He'd been unrecognizable to her until moments ago. Had spoken the heathen gibberish to her in the marketplace. Walked the master's domain with apparent freedom. She released his hand. "You've become one of them. A Mohammedan."

"No, my friend. I've simply learned their ways and come to love these people."

Horror and disbelief swept over her. "You're a blasphemer, Simon. A *traitor*. How could you?"

"I am neither, Elisabeth. The master has accepted Christ. He allows me to preach the gospel among his servants here and throughout his estate. He's a *believer*."

She shook her head. A Christian master? Was it possible?

"Do you understand, Elisabeth? I've not forsaken our Lord Jesus, but have come to love even those who do not serve the Holy One of God. These people have inherited a rich culture. They mourn and rejoice as we do. They are clever and gentle in heart."

She flinched as if he'd slapped her. "I've known nothing but cruelty among them. Abuse and degradation so loathsome I cannot speak of it."

His eyes softened, and he cupped her cheek with his hand. "I'm sorry."

Her chin quivered as she fought back another onslaught of tears.

"I hate them all, Simon. Every one of them. I cannot do otherwise."

"Have you been mistreated in this household?"

She opened her mouth to speak then closed it and shook her head.

"You're safe here, Elisabeth. These are good people, I tell you, and many of them are Christians." Simon smiled for a moment before he grew solemn. "But it is reported that you are difficult and disobedient. The master insists you be sold if you continue this behavior. I can't bear to lose you again."

Elisabeth felt a tremor of dread snake through her limbs. "Oh, no, Simon, please. I promise to work hard. Don't send me away. Let me serve here with you."

He swallowed, and she thought he struggled against more tears. "Tell me where I shall place you amongst the staff so that you can be happy."

Her shoulders sagged. Happy? She'd given up hope of that long ago. Being near Simon would have to be enough. Something fluttered in her chest as the reality of his presence settled there. Could it be her heart coming to life again? She looked to his honest, gentle face and saw the young man she remembered. A mature man now, strong and handsome, but her friend and brother all the same.

A small smile—unfamiliar after so long—curved her lips. "Put me in the kitchen."

Chapter 33

Late October AD 1218, Egypt

"I won't do it," Hugo growled.

"You can't object," Nicholas said. "It's been decided. You're to serve as my personal attendant and trainer here in Damietta."

Hugo paced the luxuriously appointed tent. "Giovanni agreed to this?"

"Not yet, but he will. Pelagius promised. Besides, you've got nothing else to do."

The old dizziness returned—a reminder of Mount Tabor. Hugo steadied himself, planting his feet in a wide stance. Nothing else to do? The Christians had fought off two deadly Muslim attacks against their encampment this month alone. How the imp could make such a request mystified him. "I refuse to nurse a spoiled child when there's a war to fight."

Nicholas reddened, and his eyes burned with a heat so intense it bordered madness. "How dare you? You forget who I am."

"Oh, no. I'll never forget. Neither will the thousands who perished or disappeared thanks to you."

The young man sprang to his feet. "Who took responsibility for their safety, Hugo?" He pointed a slim finger in accusation. "You."

Pain throbbed against Hugo's temples, and he stormed out of the tent.

"You," Nicholas called after him.

Hugo tramped along the muddy riverbank, brown water soaking his flat-soled leather boots. The boy's emergence in Damietta served to snap the frail thread of disregard Hugo had stitched around his grief.

Kateline, how can I bear the burden of this guilt unless you release me from it?

He'd gladly kill ten thousand Mohammedans in her honor if only she would heal the wounds she left him. The wounds he suffered for all of them.

He thought of Claus and Benno who fell from the precipice near their campsite on the road to Geneva. And of the children who sickened and died in the Mont Cenis Pass, along with his beloved. Of those who drowned off the European coast. The hundred martyred in Baghdad. The shiploads of children unaccounted for. Of Simon. Elisabeth.

Upon her deathbed Kateline bade Hugo continue his journey, but for what purpose? To tend Nicholas in Egypt? Certainly she had more in mind than that. With Hugo's help, Jerusalem would one day be in Christian hands again, his promise fulfilled.

In a moment of brutal honesty, he didn't imagine his guilt and grief would lessen one jot.

Yes, surely the crusade would be over sooner than later. And what, in the name of God Most High, was he supposed to do then?

§ § §

Elisabeth walked the garden pathway with Simon. She loved his visits. Only a week had passed since his last report to the master, and this time he planned to stay four days conducting business in Alexandria. Simon always sent word to her of his arrival, and in the evenings after his supper meeting with Harun they walked and talked as they were doing now.

"Master Harun commends your culinary skills, Elisabeth. So do I."

She dipped her head, but couldn't help smiling, something she found easy to do in Simon's presence. "And how was your recent journey, my friend?"

Simon rubbed the back of his neck as they went. "Productive, but tiresome. Negotiating with tribal leaders along the borderlands is always complicated."

Elisabeth tilted her face up to him. "I don't understand how you've done it. How you've come to be so powerful."

He chuckled. "Didn't think I had it in me?"

She hadn't meant it that way. "You've always been uncommon, Simon. Extraordinary, really. I wish I possessed even a small measure of your talents."

He stopped and put a hand to her shoulder. "I've tasted your cooking, Elisabeth. And I've always known you to be intelligent, tender-hearted, nurturing—you'll be a fine mother some day."

A lump formed in her throat at his words. She moved out of his gentle grasp and continued walking. While she ached to hold another babe in her arms, she'd lost hope of a family long ago. Besides, her heart yearned for more than even that. Something she couldn't express, but felt deeply. She tossed her hair behind her shoulders. Fruitless dreaming was all it was. "I miss you when you're gone, Simon," she said to change the subject. "I wish you didn't have to travel so often on the master's business."

"You won't be lonely if you'll make friends here. Why won't you let me teach you their language?"

She scowled. "I've picked up enough of their words to function among them. What more do I need to know besides a few commands and the name they call me?"

"Uh, yes. I—I will tell them your Christian name tomorrow. I think it best if they used it." He led her to their favorite bench, and together they sat down.

"I'm not sure I want to hear my name on their lips."

Simon looked pained and unsure whether to speak.

"What is it?" Elisabeth asked.

"Trouble," he finally said. "*Moshkelah* means *trouble*."

The information took a moment to register, then her face flamed. Though glad for the darkness, she feared the moonlight still revealed the extent of her humiliation. Wretched Muslims.

The following night brought another shock, but this one more welcome. "Only six?" she said to Simon.

"Yes."

Her mind spun with the news even as joy coursed through her limbs. "I thought I'd lost so many more years."

He smiled at her.

"Simon?" She hesitated to ask her question. "Do I look—" She cleared her throat. "Am I—"

"You're beautiful, Elisabeth."

She bowed her head, not believing his words. "I don't care to be fair, Simon, only young. After all this time, I feel my soul coming to life again. I should so hate to be old."

Chuckling, he took her hand in a brotherly fashion and tucked it into the crook of his arm. "Well, my friend, you certainly are not."

Elisabeth enjoyed the security of Simon's presence while they strolled in silence for a few minutes. How confident he'd become. Of course, he had reason to be so. Had he shared even a portion of her misery, things would be different for him. That he didn't chafe under the curse of slavery bewildered her.

"How do you do it?" she said at last.

Puzzlement settled on his face. "Do what?"

"Tolerate the heathens."

He stopped and released her hand. "The master and his household?"

Well, who else would she speak of? "You act like they're your friends."

"They are my friends."

She laughed. "Godless infidels?"

Simon's face grew rigid. "Some of them know a good deal more about faith in Christ than you do."

Her lips parted in surprise at the insult. "What do you mean by that?"

He shook his head and strode forward. She hurried to catch up. "Answer me, Simon. What do you mean by that?" She heard her voice rising, but couldn't stop it. "I've worked for years trying to earn God's favor. Which of these infidels have done that? How can you say they know more than I about—"

He stopped short, and she almost bumped into him. "Don't you understand, Elisabeth?"

"Understand what? That I don't like the way you're speaking to me?"

Simon's nostrils flared. "That you can't earn God's favor. What he requires is that you die to yourself—to your own selfish desires—in order to pursue the way of the Lord Jesus."

Her eyes stung, but she was too angry to cry. "What does the way of the Lord have to do with me? He knows nothing about what I've suffered—the loss, the grief."

"Yes, he does," Simon snapped. "Jesus knows everything about it, Elisabeth."

She'd heard enough of his preaching. Her voice pushed its way through clenched teeth. "Don't you dare talk to me about dying to myself. I've been dead for as long as I can remember. You've no idea what I've been through."

His eyes flashed. "I've lost everything, too. I'm a slave in a foreign land just like you. It's time to quit feeling sorry for yourself."

Before realizing what she intended to do, she raised a hand and slapped him.

His eyes were darker than ever when they met hers again, matching, it seemed, the fury boiling inside her. He gave one slow shake of his head then left her standing alone.

She hated him in that moment.

Chapter 34

November AD 1218, Egypt

Hugo heaved the rope, the muscles of his arms burning with the effort. Senseless it was, using men to dredge the canal that bordered their camp when powerful horses were available. "Why must the knights pamper their steeds and make us work like draft horses?"

Orry grunted, his own arms straining at the rigging. "Be glad you're here instead of tutoring Nicholas."

He had a point. At least Giovanni had refused the outlandish request, offending Pelagius's considerable ego and infuriating Nicholas. Hugo pulled the rope with renewed vigor at the thought. "How many more Muslim ships do you think we have to clear?"

"No idea," the team member behind him grumbled, "but next time I get my hands on a heathen neck, I'll be sure to ask."

Hugo grinned. "A clever tactic, really."

"Strangling infidels?" Orry asked, panting.

"Blocking the Nile with sunken ships." Leveraging his powerful thighs to strengthen the effort, Hugo pulled with the team until his muscles threatened to fail. Like a storm from low, ponderous clouds, the craft broke free from the sludge of the river bottom, the ropes groaning, crunching with the strain. Hugo dug the balls of his feet into the mud and lumbered along the bank. "The Muslims are smart enough to know it doesn't matter that we possess the Chain Tower if our own vessels can't approach Damietta."

The man behind Hugo spoke again. "You sound like you admire the pagans."

"Good strategy is always commendable," Hugo said. And unlike ours, he added to himself.

He hesitated to voice his annoyance with the war council to anyone but Orry, but had the Christians pressed their advantage immediately after taking the tower, Damietta would have fallen by this time.

With winter floods approaching, he feared the delay might cost them dearly.

§ § §

Simon swatted a fly that pestered him while his donkey trotted along the road, releasing his frustration on the hapless insect. Two weeks had passed since the argument with Elisabeth, yet he still fumed. Selfish, hotheaded, and caustic, she was. So unlike his sweet-tempered Fazila.

Elisabeth had abandoned their evening discussions for the remainder of his visit to the master's home, leaving Simon to stroll the garden paths alone. Not that he'd been in a social mood, but he thought perhaps she'd offer an apology for her outrageous behavior. Most likely that endless pride of hers had kept her in hiding. Very well, he was done with her.

The donkey slowed to a steady gait, and Simon noticed the gathering shadows. Blast the woman. Even now she so irritated him that he'd passed the spot where he intended to stop for the night.

He halted the beast and studied the landscape to determine his exact location. Apparently he'd seethed over Elisabeth for so long that he'd traveled much farther than planned. Only recklessness would force him to make camp now—thieves were known to inhabit this portion of road where it snaked through low bluffs. He nudged the donkey's flanks to get it moving again.

He had befriended Elisabeth when no one, save Kateline, would do so. Apparently it meant nothing to her. He spent these past years praying, agonizing, *seeking* her even, yet it made no difference to the woman's obstinate heart. He'd rescued her from the marketplace, and still she clung to bitterness like an old shawl. How he despised her moods and temper.

A small question wormed into his thoughts. As the sky darkened, it writhed and grew until he couldn't ignore it. Which upset him more? That Elisabeth insulted him and those he loved, or that she resisted the Lord Jesus?

A tight hand seemed to grip his chest, and he sighed. In all honesty, his anger toward Elisabeth stemmed from injured pride, not righteous indignation. Hadn't he told her to pursue the way of Christ? Yet he'd failed in being like Christ toward her.

She bridled at his condemnation, and rightly so. In his mission among the Mohammedans, he demonstrated patient love, but not toward Elisabeth. Why did she rile him so? What was it about her that drove him to the edge of—

The skitter of rocks caused the donkey's ears to stiffen. Simon ran a soothing hand along the animal's neck. Its fur bristled with nervous energy. Simon held his breath as they continued forward, both of them listening for hints of danger. His eyes scanned the deepest shadows among the crags.

An unseen stone, knocked loose from its perch, clattered against the surface of a broad rock face.

Simon gripped the reins and jabbed his heels into the beast. "Hie," he cried.

The donkey broke into a run as five or six riders streamed out of hiding from a narrow pass. Simon goaded the creature on, but the little animal was no match for the horses bearing down upon them. One rider, eyes glinting between folds of fabric wrapped around his head and face, drew even with Simon, sword drawn.

Simon ducked. In that instant the donkey let out a shrill cry. The world lurched as the animal stumbled, and Simon pitched over its head. The beast struggled to its feet and left him in the dust as the bandits circled round. He rolled to his hands and knees, wheezing from the impact that sent the air from his lungs. Prayed they'd take the pack animal and leave him unharmed.

The thieves circled close and drew their knives.

§ § §

Elisabeth needed a reprieve from the heat of the kitchen. Meat sputtered and hissed above the coals, vegetables simmered in thick spicy gravy, and flatbread had just come hot from brick ovens. She lifted an empty jar from the shelf and indicated to the supervisor that she was heading to the well.

Outside, she set the jar down and made way to the garden instead, confident the women in the kitchen wouldn't miss her for several minutes. She decided to take a shortcut through the front courtyard. If she kept to the shadows of the surrounding portico, no one would take notice.

A great commotion stirred at the main entrance. For a panicked moment she wondered if invaders had reached the master's home. Slipping behind a marble column, she peeked out to see Harun al-Rashid rush toward the entry. She pressed close to the pillar's cool surface. Only a moment passed before curiosity emboldened her to take another look.

A weathered man led a donkey into the courtyard, a ragged bundle thrown over its back. The master barked orders to his attendants, and they gently lifted the form from the beast—a man, she realized with a start—and laid him out, long and limp, upon the stones. The servants shifted, giving her a clear view of the scene. Blood and dirt stained the man's tattered clothes and streaked his face, which was tranquil as death. Elisabeth cocked her head and squinted at his features beneath the grime.

"No!" Forgetting the safety of her hiding place, she crossed the yard at a run and dropped to her knees. She wrapped her arms around the lifeless body. "Simon, no." Her tears fell to his face, making tracks in the filth.

Weeping, she put her forehead to his chest, the searing pain of his loss crushing her with savage strength. She'd never had a chance to say goodbye, to apologize for her hateful temper. "How could you do this, God?" she said, voice shattered by sobs. "How could you punish him because of me? Bring him back, I beg you."

The master's servants pulled her from Simon. She struggled in their grasp, wanting only to hold his broken body one last time. Tears coursed from her swollen eyes, but she lifted her face to meet Harun's gaze.

Compassion filled his countenance, and the servants released her when he uttered but a few words. Gratitude could be expressed to the master later. For now, she turned toward Simon. No matter who or what had done this to him, she bore the guilt of his death. She alone would suffer in the depths of hell on his account.

Yet her real grief lay in the thought that her good, true friend died because of her curse. Because he dared to love her like a brother. She kissed his forehead, her lips lingering on skin that had not yet cooled.

Too soon, men came running with a litter and transferred Simon's sagging body to its narrow frame. Her heart broke to see them bear him away. The master motioned that she should accompany them, and she gratefully did so.

They carried Simon to a large bedchamber furnished with finely upholstered cushions. Additional servants hurried to remove his outer garments and wash away the dust and blood that covered him. To her dismay, they tenderly cleansed his wounds with aromatic water.

She stepped close to watch, touched but confused by the care they took. Someone gave a low moan as a wet cloth was pressed deep into a large gash at Simon's side. Elisabeth searched the faces of the men ministering to him, but they remained focused and untroubled. Another quiet moan sounded, and Simon's head rocked to one side.

Joy consumed her disbelief. She knelt to the cushions and laid tingling fingers against his hair. Bending low, she brought her lips close to his ear. "Simon, don't leave me. Fight this evil that has come upon you. And forgive me, my brother."

She sat up to see Harun studying her, anxiety thick upon his features. He issued quiet commands to the servants and signaled for Elisabeth to leave the room.

She shook her head. "Please don't make me go," she said in her native German. "What if he—"

The master had no patience for her protests. He snapped his fingers.

Elisabeth stood to leave, stopping to bow to the master before looking back at her friend. *God, I have no right to ask, but please . . .*

Chapter 35

Late December AD 1218, the home of Harun al-Rashid

Simon eased himself down to Harun's table, wincing inwardly at the pain that still plagued him. That he'd survived the attack at all was evidence of God's gracious favor. That he'd largely recovered from his wounds was a testament to the superior skill of the Muslim doctors who cared for him.

"It is good to see you up and about, young Simon," the master said with a smile.

"Thank you, my lord. I have, indeed, grown weary of my bed. I pray you will let me return to work again soon."

"You mustn't be impatient. Your doctors tell me it will be at least a month yet before you resume your normal activities."

"Surely I can supervise accounts and carry on your correspondence."

Harun chuckled. "Many a servant would welcome a forced holiday."

"You show me your favor, master. I have no need for one."

Harun appraised him for a moment then lifted a morsel of food toward his mouth. "Eat, Simon. You need to regain your vigor if I am to increase your workload."

Relieved, Simon joined the master, wondering momentarily which part of their meal Elisabeth had prepared.

"Tell me." Harun cast a knowing glance his direction. "Have you enjoyed your frequent visitor?"

Simon warmed at the thought. "She has done much to cheer me in my recuperation. I think I might have gone mad without her company."

Harun lifted a goblet to his lips, drank, and then nodded as he set it down. "I hoped it would be so, though I wrestled with the wisdom of letting you enjoy her company so often."

"But why, my lord?"

"She is your betrothed, Simon. I feared it unseemly."

"My betrothed? Fazila?"

"Hasn't she visited you thrice during your recovery?"

"Yes, my lord." Simon shook his head and smiled. "I thought you spoke of Elisabeth, for she visits me daily." He bit down on a sweet piece of fruit. Harun's gaze pierced Simon, causing him to pause his chewing. "Master?"

"You have nothing to say of your betrothed? You speak only of Elisabeth?"

Simon felt the heat spread up his neck as he swallowed. "I'm sorry, master. I'm very grateful that you allowed Fazila to see me, but her visits have been brief. She is shy, and we speak little."

Harun lifted his chin. "As you know, young Simon, I represent both your and Fazila's interests. Tell me truthfully — what is the nature of your relationship with my servant Elisabeth?"

"My lord," Simon said, throat constricting, "I swear that we are as brother and sister."

The master eyed him for a long moment then exhaled slowly. "I will not allow you to dishonor your betrothed."

"Never, master. Nor will I dishonor my friend and sister,

Elisabeth. Only let our time together continue. Her heart becomes more tender toward the Lord Jesus every day."

"She should spend time with the Christian women in my household."

"But she doesn't speak your language, my lord."

Harun pressed his lips together before coming to a decision. "Very well. If you were not so trustworthy, I would forbid you to meet as you have been doing."

"Thank you, master."

"This is a singular situation, you understand."

"You have no need to worry."

That evening when Elisabeth came to Simon's quarters, he suggested they walk the garden.

"Are you sure?" she said, worry in her eyes.

He chuckled. "Exceedingly so. My doctors have encouraged me to exercise in order to reclaim my strength." He did not tell her of the master's concerns, unfounded as they were, but thought it prudent to resume their conversations in a less private setting.

They arrived in the garden, and he drew a deep breath of the fresh night air, ignoring the ache in his ribs. "I've been thinking about something you said last evening."

Elisabeth smiled up at him. "About you becoming fat and lazy? I was only jesting."

He grinned and shook his head then spoke softly. "That your very soul is tired. What did you mean by that?"

§ § §

Elisabeth looped her arm through Simon's, glad for the peace between them. Thankful that Simon's life had been spared, that their closeness had returned. They ambled in silence for a minute or so as she thought how to answer his question.

"You once said the heathe—the *people*—here know more about faith in Christ than I do."

"Elisabeth, I'm so sorry. It was wrong of me to make such a statement."

She patted his arm with her free hand. "You've apologized already. Numerous times." She didn't know which of them had begged forgiveness for that argument with more vehemence.

"But still, I—"

"Simon." She gave him a look that made him close his mouth and nod for her to continue. "The truth is," she said, "I don't know how to earn God's favor. And I'm so tired of trying."

"Oh, my sister." He shook his head. "God smiles on you."

How she wished it were so. Tears pooled in her eyes. "No. He has cursed me."

"What?"

Simon's wounds must have pained him, for he angled toward the bench, though it was only their first turn around the garden. "How can you say that?" he asked when they sat.

If you only knew.

She exhaled. "So many people have suffered because of me. So many have died."

"That's not your fault."

She dashed the moisture from her eyes. "Yes, it is."

"Look at me." When at last she did, he went on. "Our journey was by its very nature wrought with great risk. We knew that." He looked past her, to the darkness. "We never should have left our homes."

"I had no choice."

He cocked an eyebrow at her.

She bent her head, watching her fingers where they twisted the fabric of her tunic. "I couldn't stay. I had to find God's forgiveness."

"You could find it only in Jerusalem?"

"The parish priest denied me penance." She'd only whispered

the words, but he must have heard, for he stiffened beside her.

"What do you mean? Why?"

She put hands to her face.

"Elisabeth?"

"I am a fornicator and a murderess," she said, rocking back and forth, the familiar words slipping between her fingers. Simon would hate her now. As he should.

"Stop it." He stilled her shoulders. "You don't know what you're saying."

"I do." How many times had she confessed to God these many years, for all the good it did? She shook off Simon's touch and stood, stepping away from the bench, keeping her back to him. "I deserve no mercy, but I hope for it."

Her secret came spilling out. She spoke over her shoulder, though she dared not turn far enough to meet his gaze. "I thought Wilhelm loved me. You met him once, in my village. He dealt harshly with Kateline."

Elisabeth heard a soft grunt of surprise behind her, but she did not stop her story. "I should have known what sort of man he was. A devil. But I was foolish. He—he cruelly violated me."

"You don't have to tell me this."

"You have a right to know what kind of person I am."

He sighed behind her, and she continued. "The babe died before its time came. 'Evidence of my sin,' they said."

"You did nothing wrong."

Elisabeth rounded on him. "Tell that to God. Tell that to my child. To Kateline. To Benno and Claus. To all the others who died because my cursed soul touched them."

Simon looked at her with such compassion that the fire sizzling in her veins cooled, leaving her weak. She sank to her knees. Put her forehead to the ground. And wept.

He said nothing for so long, she thought he'd left her there in the garden alone, but when at last her tears were spent, she lifted her face to find him kneeling in front of her, his own cheeks stained with tears.

Simon put a finger to her chin, scanned her face with a tender look. "I think, had I been you, I would feel the same way."

"So it's true? I'm cursed?"

His voice cracked when he spoke. "You're not cursed. You were abused. By all the people who should have been taking care of you. By even me, perhaps, for misjudging you. I'm sorry. For everything."

"No, Simon you—"

"All these years, you've been trying to earn God's favor, thinking the sins of others rest on you. But they don't. God loves you. Do you believe that?"

She knew he wanted her to. "Of course. God loves everyone, yes?" She stood, and he rose to join her, flinching with the effort. "You need to return to your quarters," she said.

"No. Not yet."

How could he even look upon her, knowing? "Then I will bid you goodnight."

"Sit down." His voice came low, and she dared not protest.

He fixed sad, dark eyes on her. "You know that God loves you, do you not?"

"I told you, yes."

"Because that's what I want to hear?"

She thought her tears were over, but her lip trembled and moisture spilled onto her cheeks. "He doesn't love me." She shook her head. "Not me. How could he?"

Simon limped back and forth in front of the stone bench.

Her heart broke, knowing she caused his anxious pacing. "I'm sorry. I want to believe the Lord cares for me. I really do."

He knelt before her, taking her hands in his. "I spent years studying the Scriptures, Elisabeth, and I never found one reason to believe that God would remove his love from anyone. He offers it as a free gift to you, just like he does to everybody else. There is no curse keeping you from it. You only have to accept it. God loves you, my dearest sister. I beg you to cast off your unbelief."

She bowed her head, fighting back fresh tears. Simon pulled her to his chest. She didn't deserve his kindness or love, but there it was. Didn't deserve the Lord's love, either, but if Simon was right, then it was just as real. "How do I do it?" she said in a husky voice that must have sounded as forlorn as she felt. "How do I believe? I am so far from God's mercy."

"Are you?"

There were his dark eyes again, warm and sincere. She looked down at the bench, at the lovely, soul-soothing garden that surrounded her. Had it been God who rescued her, brought her here, gave Simon back to her after all this time? Gave him to her twice, returning him from the brink of death only recently? Hope, like an ember, began to glow in her chest. She tried to abandon it lest it forsake her first. "God doesn't . . . he can't . . . ."

Simon took her hands and helped her to her feet. "Accept God's love and mercy as the gift he freely offers, Elisabeth, and give yourself to him in return. Choose the Lord now, sweet sister, and follow the way of Christ."

If God loved her, then why had she suffered so greatly? Yet if he did—if he truly did—then she'd be a fool to refuse him. "It can't be that easy."

"Easy?" he asked. A kind smile softened his words. "Christ died for you. For all of us. While we were still sinners, and because of his great love. In what way, now, would that have been easy?"

She'd never thought of it like that. Jesus had known suffering, pain—just like Simon said the night they argued—but he'd chosen that path. Surely, only love would inspire such a sacrifice.

"He loves *me*?"

Simon smiled, and her heart lifted at the look of love on his wise and gentle face. For the first time, she dared to imagine Jesus smiling at her in just such a way.

She made a terrifying decision. "Then I will believe it to be so."

Simon gathered her in a long embrace, then kissed her forehead and held her at arm's length. "Be baptized, and wash away your sins, calling on the name of the Lord." He smiled. "A new life is yours."

A new life.

Elisabeth could breathe again. She'd never realized until this moment how tightly the fear and grief had constricted her all these years. Ever since the night Wilhelm forced her to the forest floor. Since before, perhaps. She took another breath. Let the air fill her lungs, like a swimmer breaking the surface of the water.

God loved her. She believed.

Chapter 36

February AD 1219, Egypt

Hugo stood on the deck of a ship in the middle of the Nile and shivered—not from the early February air, for it was mild—but from the fever that beset him. Not that he would let such a small thing stop him from securing his piece of ground on the Damietta shore.

Severe winter floods had waylaid their efforts against the city, just as Hugo feared. Provisions and tents were destroyed, a new floating siege engine washed away, and scores of soldiers fell ill. Off and on for two weeks, he battled recurring chills and headaches. He'd experienced far worse.

And it hardly mattered now. Though he'd practically given up hope that a good end would come of their waiting, fortune smiled on them today.

"Did you see the way those Mohammedans on shore ran when we boarded for the crossing?" Nicholas said, approaching.

Hugo barely glanced at him before turning his eyes back to the city walls. "Every last one of them abandoned their camp yesterday," he said. Whatever it was, it hadn't been fear that sent them scurrying. At least the war council had sense enough to take advantage of the

Muslims' flight and claim the Damietta side of the river.

Nicholas leaned against the railing. "How many do you think still defend the city from inside the walls?"

Hugo's head hurt, and he was unwilling to carry on a conversation. "Hard to say."

"Well," Nicholas patted his scabbard, "I'm itching for a fight. I hope I won't be disappointed."

"It'll be weeks yet before we breech the main walls."

"Still, should any infidels try to escape, I'll cut them down."

Hugo marveled that Pelagius had tolerated Nicholas all these years. No wonder the cardinal brought the scrawny brat across the sea and stuck him on the front line.

Within a day—and without a fight—the Christians secured the Damietta shore. Once they possessed both sides of the river, they benefited from the supplies left behind by the vanishing Muslims. Construction on a bridge between the Christian-held shores began immediately.

Later that week, Hugo stood waist-high in the muddy river, trying to repair a portion of the bridge while a comrade struggled with a rope beside him, teeth chattering. Many soldiers worked at various positions along the structure, while others beat the water with sticks, aiming to frighten off the boldest crocodiles.

"You should rest," Hugo said to Pero.

"It'll take more than a minor ailment to make me lounge on shore like a knight after a tournament."

Hugo grinned at the man's pluck and moved to help him with the rigging. "Here, I'll take this end of the rope and tie it off below. Give me plenty of slack."

Hugo swam to a point several feet away and tread water long enough to glance back at Pero. "That's it." He filled his lungs and descended into the murky depths.

He mostly felt his way to the spot where the other rope had

frayed. Fastening the new piece in place with a strong Carrick bend technique, he turned almost upside down to wedge his feet against the bottom of the bridge and tug the knot tight. Satisfied, he let loose the rope and allowed his body to upright itself before he gave two powerful kicks and broke the surface of the water.

With a shake of his head, he flung the droplets from his face then looked to where he'd left Pero to make sure the man secured the other end of the rope.

Pero wasn't there.

Running a hand over his eyes, Hugo turned right and left, then back to the spot where he'd last seen his comrade. Suddenly Pero's head thrust above the water. His arms flailed, and he screamed, though the sound broke off when he plunged below the surface again. A thick reptilian tail momentarily pierced the air.

Hugo propelled himself forward. The river ceased to churn by the time he reached the spot, but Hugo dove anyway, willing his eyes to see through the faint light. He sensed rather than saw a movement to his right. Pushing his way through the silty water, he finally bumped into Pero, who fought against the crocodile with little more than feeble movements.

Hugo wrapped his arms around the man's torso and pulled. The croc tugged back, this way and that until the crusader went limp in Hugo's arms. The creature used the advantage to drag them both along the bottom of the Nile. Lungs burning with the instinct to breathe, Hugo lodged his feet against the animal's snout and pushed.

Nothing.

Hugo released Pero and moved atop the creature in a futile attempt to pry apart its jaws. Lightheaded and desperate, he pivoted once more to batter the animal's head with his heels. The beast thrashed about then released Pero without warning and darted into the blackness. Hugo grabbed his companion and sped toward the surface.

They emerged gasping and retching. Hugo pulled his comrade

toward those waiting at the shore, horror on their faces. A few brave souls met them in the water to help Hugo to his feet and haul Pero from the river.

The lower half of Pero's right leg was gone, his knee a bloody, ragged clump of flesh.

Hugo turned his back, walked away from the injured man, the crowd.

A voice called out. "Hugo."

Hugo ignored Nicholas and moved on.

"Hugo, wait."

Hugo rounded on him. "What are you doing here?"

The boy straightened his shoulders. "I've a right to be anywhere I like. Besides, I'm bored with nothing to do. At least there's activity here beside the river." He grinned and elbowed Hugo. "You provided a bit of entertainment, now didn't you? Lucky I got here when I did. I should have been disappointed to miss the excitement."

Hugo glared at him.

"Oh, come on. You know what I mean. You saved the fellow's life. The men will call you a hero."

The concept lost its appeal long ago. Hugo narrowed his eyes. "He's a soldier. Without a leg, he has no life."

Nicholas shrugged. "It's not like we'll be battling much longer anyway." He turned as if to leave, but Hugo stopped him with a hand to his puny shoulder.

"What do you mean?"

A smirk spread across Nicholas's face. He loved bearing gossip, little girl that he was. "The sultan has offered terms of peace."

Finally the boy spoke words worth hearing.

"Jerusalem?" Hugo said.

"Yes, along with this and that. Al-Kamil proposes a thirty-year truce."

Hugo hardly dared to hope. "And the council has accepted?"

"John of Brienne is in favor, but Pelagius will never agree."

"Why not?"

Nicholas lifted his chin, sniffing as if he'd been insulted. "It would only give John more power in the region. Besides, we can't yield to the infidels. It would be blasphemy to accept anything less than complete surrender."

Hugo took a deep breath. "And how will this refusal end the war?"

Nicholas looked at him like he was an idiot. "The Muslims will give up soon enough when they understand our resolve."

Fools, Hugo thought. The whole lot of them.

§ § §

Six weeks or more had passed since Elisabeth's heart responded to God's. Simon continued to teach her, guide her, but she'd much yet to learn. She liked to have him close by, answering her many questions, stilling her doubts.

Tonight, she hurried to meet him in the garden as they did each evening.

"You're late," he teased.

"The master's nightly dinner guest eats with the zeal of a suckling pig," she said, grinning. "I've only just finished in the kitchen."

Simon chuckled and took her hand, lacing his fingers through hers. "Poor Elisabeth. I'll have to do something about that. Perhaps it's time to take my leave."

Her heart sank at his words. "You're resuming your former duties?"

"Next week. Now, don't look so sad," he said, stopping on the path. "My renewed health is a blessing."

She searched his face. How handsome he was. How much she loved him.

Her breath caught in her chest, and she felt dizzy. She *loved* him. There was nothing sisterly about it.

"Elisabeth, are you all right?"

Releasing his hand, she moved straight toward the bench. "I'm fine. I will miss you, that's all."

He sat beside her. "I'll miss you, too. Are you sure you're well?"

She couldn't meet his eyes, so stunned was she to realize the depth of her feelings. "I was thinking about someone."

Her affection for Simon made sense, really. They'd been through so much together. These past weeks had changed everything between them. She stole a look at him.

"Oh." He sounded disappointed. "Someone here, in the master's household?"

"No," she said too quickly. "No. About—" Who? "—my father."

"Your father?"

She had to think fast, so she told him the story that often came to mind. Of the time she and *Vati* splashed their feet in the Rhine that spring day when the water was much too cold. How he scooped the stone from the river, and she pledged to carry it as her most valued possession. That he chuckled and said, "Always so earnest, my little 'Lisbeth."

Simon spoke, voice soft and low. "The stone—what became of it?"

Her spirit mellowed. "I left it at Kateline's grave." So long ago.

He looked at the ground, ran a hand through his hair.

Something was wrong. "Simon?"

His eyes returned to hers, and he smiled. "I think it's a beautiful story, Elisabeth. A remarkable glimpse into your lovely heart." She held her breath when he caught a lock of her hair and let the strands cascade from his fingers before caressing her cheek. "Always so earnest," he whispered.

She did. She really loved him.

Chapter 37

February AD 1219, the home of Harun al-Rashid

Elisabeth could not sleep. Her mind turned to Simon, knowing he was to arrive late that night. She pictured his smile, the depth of his gaze, the warmth in his voice when he spoke. She rose, dressed, and made way to the garden. Perhaps the coolness of the night would rid her of such juvenile thoughts.

The moon cast its pale light upon the path that wound through the plants and trees. Jasmine scented the air, and Elisabeth drew a sweet breath as she walked. A pebble caught in her sandal. She paused to shake it loose, smiling at the realization that such a small thing could pain a foot that had once been so calloused, she'd tread the Alps shoeless. No, not quite shoeless. Simon had given her leather rags to bind her feet.

Elisabeth chuckled at the memory. She'd recoiled from his touch when he tried to help her, but he was so gentle, so kind, that she couldn't help trusting him just a little. It was hard to imagine ever thinking poorly of him, and she cringed at the girl she was then, that girl who treated Simon so harshly. What was it she used to call him?

Bird.

He'd been a tall and scrawny youth, all hands and knees and

feet. He reminded her of the gangly herons along the Rhine. She had no idea they promised a man of strength.

Now his lean body moved with grace and power. Even his robes couldn't hide the broadness of his shoulders, the firmness of the muscles beneath his tunic. She pictured him standing in the courtyard, talking with Harun, legs planted firmly, strong jaw, lips that—

Elisabeth blushed. She'd hoped to escape the thoughts that made her dizzy. Instead, her pulse beat an erratic cadence and the air seemed suddenly close and stifling. Reaching the bench, she plopped down on its cool surface, lifting her hair to give the subtle night breeze access to her skin.

"Hello."

Simon's voice startled her, bringing the heat to her face again. She dropped her hair, grateful for the darkness, and placed her hands in her lap.

He sat down beside her. "What brings you to the garden so late this night?"

"I—I could not sleep." When he didn't respond, she met his gaze. His dark eyes danced above a mischievous smile, and she could not help the curve of her own lips. "And what about you? Certainly you've only just arrived."

"I was searching for someone."

"Me?"

Simon nodded. "I hoped I might find you here. I have a surprise for you."

She tilted her head and studied his handsome face. "What is it?"

He shook his head. "Not yet. Cover your eyes."

She suppressed a grin and did as she was told.

"Now you can look," he said after a moment.

Elisabeth took her hands from her eyes and gave him a smile before focusing on the object suspended in front of her.

A smooth, pink stone dangled from a delicate silver chain. It looked just like—

A gasp escaped her throat, and her hand went to the curve of her breast. "Simon? Is it really . . . ?"

He nodded, smiling.

"How—how did you . . . ?" She bit her lower lip, unable to speak more.

"I saw you place it upon Kateline's grave. I don't know why I took it, except that I thought you might want it back one day. It's beautiful, really, and somehow I could tell it held special meaning for you. I'd forgotten about it until you told your story."

He unhooked the necklace and reached to place it around her throat. She pulled her hair to one shoulder to keep it from tangling in the clasp. His hands warmed her skin and lingered there a delicious moment. Sent pleasant prickles along her neck.

He sat back and smiled at her. "It's lovely on you."

Warmth spread from her torso to her limbs. *So this is what happiness feels like*. Without warning, her chin quivered, and tears threatened. She looked down.

"Elisabeth, have I grieved you? I'm sorry. I should have left it there that day."

She couldn't answer, but only shook her head.

"If you don't like it," he said, "I can have another chain made. Or we can—"

"Oh, Simon," she whispered, lifting her gaze to take in his concerned face, "why do you treat me with such kindness?"

His eyes nearly melted her with their intensity. "Don't you know you're worth every bit of kindness I can offer?" He lowered his forehead to hers and slipped his hand beneath the veil of her hair, cupping the nape of her neck with a gentle touch that made her stomach flutter. "Don't you know how much I love you?"

Neither of them spoke or moved for several moments. With only the slightest shift, their lips met in a tentative kiss. Then another.

That might have been the end of it, had he not pulled her close. Her arms circled his neck, and his mouth pressed hers, seeking, urgent. Her senses filled with the taste of him, the heat of his hands at her back.

And then he released her with a groan.

She searched his eyes. "What is it?"

He shook his head. "I'm sorry, I . . . "

Elisabeth placed a hand on his chest. "Simon, are you all right?"

He flinched as if her touch held fire and jumped to his feet. "No, I shouldn't have done that, I—" He stopped and put his hands to his head.

She rose from the bench. "I don't understand what's happening."

Simon let out a breath, and then swallowed. He tried to speak three times before the words finally croaked out. "I am betrothed."

Elisabeth's limbs went weak, and she felt her way back down to the bench. "Betrothed?"

Simon nodded. "To Fazila."

Fazila. Elisabeth knew her. Petite, meek, all polite smiles. "When did—"

"Last spring."

Elisabeth drew in a breath. "And you never thought to tell me?"

"No, I—I don't know why."

She hugged her arms to her chest.

"I've been distracted by . . ." His words trailed off.

How could this be? Simon betrothed to another, and all this time she thought—he seemed— "What are we going to do?"

Anxiety stretched across Simon's face. He searched the sky. "The only thing we can do." His troubled eyes returned to her. A small smile touched his lips. "I must beg forgiveness for the pain I will cause."

The blood resumed its journey to her limbs. She smiled in return. "She will give it."

"I meant from you, my sister."

Her heart squeezed until it crumbled inside her chest like broken pottery. Was she even breathing? He didn't mean it. She misunderstood. "I'm not your sister." Her chin trembled. "There is more between us. You said you loved me."

"Fazila is my bride in all ways but one."

"No." It couldn't be. She shook her head, refusing to cry. "Tell her you've changed your mind. Tell the master."

Simon raised his voice. "We took vows."

She could not speak for a moment, and when she did, her words dripped with anguish. "Why were you so foolish?"

He lifted mournful eyes. "I'm sorry to hurt you."

All she wanted was to lie down and sleep. To awaken and discover this was nothing but a nightmare. She exhaled slowly. "Do you love the girl?"

Simon cast his gaze toward the darkness. "She's a young woman. And, yes, I do."

Elisabeth recognized the resolve in his voice. Her chest felt open to the night air, and a chill ran through her. She hardly remembered leaving the garden, leaving Simon standing there with his head bowed. In fact, she didn't quite realize she'd done so until she curled upon her mat and felt something cold press against her cheek. The necklace. She pulled it back into place and thought of her father.

Always so earnest, my little 'Lisbeth.

Her ragged breathing gave way to silent, choking sobs.

Chapter 38

March AD 1219, the home of Harun al-Rashid

Simon looked over the rim of the goblet to his bride while the banquet room reverberated with the sounds of music and dancing. Fazila sat quiet and shy amidst the festivities, offering a timid smile every now and then, but generally avoiding his gaze.

The marriage contract had been signed and registered earlier in the day. Fazila, wrapped in a simple pink *aba*, hands and feet hennaed from the women's gathering the night before, kept her eyes to the floor during the ceremony. After sunset, the wedding party began. A gift from Harun, it followed Egyptian custom, though modestly as befitted their station.

Fazila had since changed into a blue robe, trimmed with green silk thread. Her translucent skin glowed warm and creamy, and her dainty lips flushed to a deep rose red. She hardly touched the cooked meats, vegetables, and fruit enjoyed by the guests. Simon pretended not to know who had prepared them.

The party would not end until dawn, but long before that, he took Fazila's hand and led her to the bridal chamber. Later, he begged God's forgiveness for remembering the fervor of Elisabeth's kisses as he consummated his marriage.

In the following weeks his love for Fazila grew more than he thought possible. She was sweet, calm, and compliant. Kind and gentle toward everyone. Never did she anger him. Never did she confound him with her opinions. Her faith was indisputable. Her prayers, frequent. She listened to his thoughts without interruption. Smiled at his jokes. Soothed him at the end of a long day's labor. Accepted his absences with patience.

One night he came to her, weary from a recent journey, craving her softness. He put his hands to her small waist and pulled her toward him. "I missed you," he said, bending to nuzzle her neck.

She relaxed against him. "And I, you, my husband."

Inexplicably, he wanted her to need him like he needed her in that moment. He kissed her deeply. Scooped up her willowy frame and carried her to bed. Then laid awake for hours afterward, wondering what madness caused him to feel anything less than perfect contentment.

Within two months of the wedding, Fazila announced she was with child.

Chapter 39

August 29, AD 1219, near Damietta, Egypt

Better late than never, Hugo decided.

The war council was finally dealing with the Muslim forces that pestered the crusade army by launching a direct assault on their encampment outside the city. The Christians covered the distance in battle formation, Hugo near the head of the column, Orry somewhere behind. Nicholas rode in the rear, skittish as a virgin bride.

The council spent more time bickering amongst themselves than dealing with the real issues of the campaign, but today would be different. Today, they took action.

The tramp of hooves and three thousand feet advancing upon the heathen camp echoed on the hot Egyptian breeze. The flat plains near Damietta spread out before them with little to break the horizon save a wide ridge that rose to the east. Hugo could see movement among the Muslims. His heart pumped in anticipation of the impending conflict and sweat slicked his palms. He tightened his grip on the pike and marched forward.

Five hundred paces out, Hugo and the other foot soldiers stopped. Crossbowmen behind them wound their bows then let loose a hail of flaming arrows. Orry and the other longbowmen sent a succession of deadly volleys.

Hugo lunged forward with his comrades, legs pumping. The startled Mohammedans grabbed their weapons too late. A few charged the crusaders, but most scattered like the vermin they were.

Maybe it was the strength of Hugo's pent-up anger and frustration that swept him along like the wind. He sprinted into the camp, overtook a Muslim fighter, and flattened him with one strike against the skull. Acrid smoke burned Hugo's eyes and throat, tasted bitter on his tongue. Another foe rounded a tent to face him, teeth bared, disgust evident in his sinister eyes. Christian riders galloped past. Hugo grunted when he plunged the pike through the man's stomach, ignoring the vacant look that dulled the Muslim devil's face in a heartbeat. Hugo left the pike and ran on, pulling his sword as he bounded over obstacles in his path. Blood pounded in his ears, muting the cries and curses of the men fighting around him.

The infidels spilled out of the camp, running through tent rows like water, rushing toward the ridge in the distance. What fools they were, making straight for the natural wall that would hem them in. Knights on their powerful warhorses thundered ahead, wielding their weapons with deadly aim.

A great howling arose like a chorus of phantoms straight from hell. Hugo pivoted at the sound. The blood thickened in his veins. Five hundred mounted Mohammedans charged them from the rear. Hugo spun around. At the ridge, the fleeing Muslims turned to face the crusaders. Swords up. Ready to engage them in battle.

An ambush. Perfectly executed. Mercilessly effective.

Hugo dodged an Arab pony and the swinging blade that accompanied it. Another Muslim rider hurtled his direction, focused on a crusader to the left. Hugo grabbed the man's leg and yanked him from his charger. The jolt wrenched his shoulder, and pain radiated down his arm. Both men fell.

Staggering to his feet, Hugo grasped the hilt of his sword with two hands, and thrust the weapon into the dazed warrior's heart.

Hugo wiped his face with a sleeve then ran to where two foes advanced upon a downed crusader, bloodlust in their eyes. The rider's horse lay writhing on the ground, blood spurting from a wound in its neck. The soldier, on hands and knees, retched into the gruesome mess.

The heathens grinned at each other before lifting their weapons above the stricken fighter. Hugo jumped between them, kicked one aside and felled the other with a lethal swipe of his sword. The first Mohammedan quickly regained his footing and rushed Hugo, roaring with the ferocity of an injured beast.

Their weapons clashed. Hugo stumbled backward, struggled to keep his balance. Strike, parry. Strike, parry. He tripped over a slain warrior and fell hard to the ground. The assailant threw himself toward Hugo, who rolled aside and spun up on one knee to bring his sword down through the man's chest, pinning him to the earth. Hugo heaved a deep breath and retrieved his weapon.

The petrified soldier wiped vomit from his chin with a shaky hand. "Thank you, Hugo."

"You have no business here, Nicholas." He caught the reins of a nearby rider-less horse, calming the frantic animal. Though the steed pulled against his grip, he handed over the leather straps and helped Nicholas into the saddle. "Now get your useless carcass off this battlefield and summon reinforcements."

"I'm fine now."

"Go, before I deal with you myself."

Nicholas scowled then snapped the reins and headed for Damietta.

Though the heart of the conflict had shifted eastward, pockets of fighting continued close at hand. A dozen heathens surrounded four knights—on foot and back-to-back—tightening their circle like a noose. Hugo sighed and loped toward another lone horse. The animal shied away, but he snatched the reins and leapt upon its back. He dug his heels into the beast's flanks and charged the band of Muslims.

They scattered when the destrier plowed into their midst. He turned the animal and took after them again, brandishing his blade while the crusaders made their escape. The horse responded easily to Hugo's handling, and shivers of exhilaration tingled his scalp.

But an arming sword wasn't meant for fighting from atop a stallion. He aimed the beast toward the main battle. The animal crashed into the fray. Hugo slid from its back. His feet barely touched the earth before an infidel flew at him and knocked him to the ground, sending his sword careening into the mêlée. The panicked stallion trampled it, snapping the blade.

The two men rolled through the dirt, snarling, grunting, Muslim breath hot upon Hugo's face. He threw a punch to the man's ribs, felt spittle hit his cheek. The heathen's hands found Hugo's neck. His vision darkened before he pried the enemy's fingers away, but at last he took a great gulp of air through a raw throat and rolled atop the infidel to slam his fist into the adversary's face. Twice, thrice, four times it took before the man lay unconscious.

For a moment, Hugo heard nothing but his own labored breathing. Blood covered his hands and arms.

A pair of dueling swordsmen lurched by.

Hugo dove for a mace dropped by some ill-fated soldier and sprang to his feet, smiting the chest of an attacking Muslim. The weapon stuck fast for a moment, but Hugo pulled it free and turned to swing it at a passing foe. Unaccustomed to it, he scanned the area for something better.

Men began to yell. "Retreat!"

The handle of a battleaxe rose from the chest of a dead Mohammedan. Hugo salvaged the weapon, swung it high in the air, and brought it down to split a man's skull.

"Retreat!"

Another stabbed at him. The thrust went wild. The tip of the sword arced across Hugo's cheek. A sharp sting. He tackled the fellow. Wrestled the sword from his grasp. Impaled the dog with his own blade.

A foot soldier grabbed Hugo by the arm. "Get going, man."

Hugo growled, but jogged toward the Christian rear.

Blood slicked the ground. The odor of vomit and waste soured the air. A pikeman drove his sword into the heart of a dying comrade.

A downed man groaned and rolled to his back. Hugo bent to survey his injuries. Probably wouldn't survive the trip back to Damietta. The fellow cried out when Hugo hoisted him to his shoulders. He pivoted and scanned the enemy line.

The Muslims paced back and forth on their ponies or looted the dead for weapons and equipment, but allowed the Christians to retreat unmolested.

Hugo turned and limped back to Damietta with the others.

Chapter 40

Late October AD 1219, Egypt

Elisabeth forced her gaze away from Fazila's swollen belly to the girl's gentle brown eyes. Surely whoever made the decision to put Simon's wife at work in the kitchen had no idea how troubling the move would be for Elisabeth.

The past eight months had been excruciating as she labored to put aside her thoughts of Simon. To overcome anger and bitterness and grief. How unbearable those early weeks had been, especially after the wedding.

"Sit here," she said to Fazila, testing the limits of her civility with her growing Arabic vocabulary. She gestured toward a pile of vegetables on the table beside a batch of dough. "Do you prefer to knead or cut?"

"To cut, I suppose," Fazila said with a voice sweet and smooth as honey.

Naturally, she'd choose cutting. Fazila's very presence hacked away at Elisabeth's heart like—

She caught herself. No, contempt wouldn't do anymore.

When Simon rejected her in the garden, she plummeted into

the abyss of hopelessness and cursed God for hating her as she always knew he did. But then the strangest thing happened—the Lord of all the earth eased her pain. Certainly, she still railed against him for letting Simon love another. But from some place deeper than the grief, she found comfort.

"Very well." She managed to conjure a smile for Fazila. "I'll move over to give you space."

"Thank you, Elisabeth." Fazila picked up a knife with one delicate hand, pulled a squash toward her, and began to slice it into neat, even segments. "It's a beautiful name—Elisabeth." She lifted her face and smiled. "It caresses the lips like a kiss."

Elisabeth flipped the dough over and pounded her fist into it.

"You know my husband, Simon, don't you?"

Elisabeth nodded and threw a handful of flour into the mixture, sending a cloud of fine powder into the air.

"He thought to dissuade me from serving in the kitchen when the midwife suggested I alter my duties, but I told him that I heard you make everyone laugh by your wit."

In that moment, Elisabeth suffered tremendous regret for becoming a determined student of the language. She squeezed the dough through her fingers.

Fazila's back straightened suddenly. "Oh." She chuckled and rubbed her round abdomen. "The child grows more vigorous every day. He'll be as strong and handsome as his father."

Elisabeth needed a breath of air. "Excuse me." She wiped her hands on her apron and headed for the doorway. One of the other cooks questioned her on the way out, but she pretended not to hear.

She blotted perspiration from her brow with her forearm and stepped into the sunshine. This was madness. What was God doing, placing Fazila next to her? How could she ever manage to stop loving Simon while his wife worked beside her, speaking endlessly of him? She sighed and walked to the shade of a large potted tree.

For months she'd accused the Father of every evil motive in his dealings with her, but each time she severed the cord that bound her heart to his, he drew her closer and re-secured the knot. Finally she could no longer resist him, and, in fact, had lost the desire to do so.

Elisabeth watched a tiny martin hop from branch to branch. She envied its cheerfulness.

God alone knew to what extent she missed her dearest friend. That, in itself, was a loss almost too great to endure. If only Simon had not kissed her that night. If only she hadn't wanted him to. But it *had* happened, ending their friendship, and now she felt she might be the loneliest creature on earth.

Yet, truth be told, Christ had begun to fill a place in her heart she thought would be forever empty. What was the Scripture Simon bade her repeat many times over? *You have made known to me the path of life; you will fill me with joy in your presence . . . .*

She felt it sometimes—joy in the Lord's presence. Too often, though, the old fears and doubts threatened to consume her. So hard it was, walking the path alone. But at least, unlike the crusade she'd begun years ago, this journey promised victory. If she could simply stay the course.

How she missed Simon.

§ § §

Hugo's boots crunched on the gravel outside the wall of Damietta. "Cardinal Pelagius is a fool," he said to Orry.

The moon shone bright.

Orry surveyed the area. "You really ought to mention the Templars and Hospitallers while you're at it."

"Thank you." Hugo nodded at him. "Them, too."

"Glad to be of service."

The Muslim blade Hugo carried weighed less than the one he

lost some months ago. Better for guard duty. "It is incomprehensible that they would spurn the sultan's new offers of peace. At least John and the Teutonics were willing."

"Don't forget the French."

"And the English, for that matter. Why should Pelagius win out?"

Orry shrugged. "Al-Kamil has only offered the Kingdom of Jerusalem, a thirty-year truce, and the return of the True Cross lost at Hattin. What's that compared to the veritable treasure chest we're sitting on here?"

Hugo cocked his head to survey the pitifully disfigured walls of Damietta. The stench drifting from the city didn't bode well for its inhabitants.

Two other sentries approached from the south, and the four of them tossed dice for a time, periodically searching the shadows for suspicious activity.

"Pay up," Orry said after a winning throw.

The others groaned at their losses, but Hugo focused on a nearby tower. "Does something seem wrong to you?"

"I won't be sidetracked that easily," Orry said. "You, too, now. Pay up."

Hugo shook his head. "No, look at the tower. Where did the guards go?"

Three sets of eyes followed his.

"Appears deserted," one of the sentries said.

The other scratched his neck. "Think it's a trick?"

Hugo lifted his chin. "There's only one way to find out."

"You can't mean to go up there?" Orry said.

"Why not?"

Orry raised a brow at him. "Certain death comes to mind."

"Nothing's ever certain."

One of the other sentries piped in. "Let's get back to our game.

If the tower's empty, it'll likely be empty tomorrow when it can be taken by daylight."

Hugo glared at him. "And be called cowards?"

The newcomers exchanged sheepish glances.

"Come on," Orry sighed. "Let's find a ladder and be done with it. Otherwise I'll never get my winnings."

They located a scaling ladder and leaned it against the tower. Hugo went first after pausing to be certain an alarm had not been raised inside the city. The others followed, ladder swaying under their weight. His mind flashed to Mount Tabor, and the Greek fire the Mohammedans had launched.

But tonight there was only the chill November air. Didn't keep his hands from sweating, though.

Near the top, Hugo stopped and motioned for the others to halt.

He stilled his breathing and willed his heart to slow its thunderous pace, then climbed the last few rungs, careful to make no sound. Hovering just feet below the top of the bastion, he instinctively glanced down. With a mental grasp of Kateline's medallion, he prayed he'd pass out before hitting the ground should enemy sentries repel him.

He stretched to lift his head above the battlement. No sound came from the guard tower, and from that vantage point, it looked empty. He hoisted himself up and over in one smooth motion, rolling to a stop with his sword drawn.

Deserted. Could they really be so lucky? An abandoned tower meant a breach through which the city could be taken.

A slow grin lifted one corner of his mouth as the others followed him over the wall.

Orry crouched low and sidled up next to him, war hammer at the ready. "So you were right," he whispered. "But you still have to pay."

Chapter 41

January AD 1220, overseer's quarters, the home of Harun al-Rashid

"Must we speak of Elisabeth?" Simon said, on edge from his wife's talk.

"Forgive me, my husband, but she entertains me so. She has become a good friend, and I thought you would be satisfied to know it. I did not mean to displease you."

Simon shifted on the bedding where they lay and pulled Fazila close, her small body heavy with child. Her warm skin smelled of honeysuckle when he kissed her forehead.

Honeysuckle. The fragrance reminded him of Elisabeth. Her hair always—

"You never displease me," he said, halting the disturbing direction of his thoughts. In truth, he had not one complaint against Fazila.

If only his perpetually serene wife could soothe his tormented soul.

But souls were God's business, and Simon's had begged forgiveness over Elisabeth for so long, he finally quit asking. To do so any longer seemed disgraceful and insincere, despite the enormous guilt and self-loathing he'd brought to bear upon his adulterous heart. When was the last time he'd prayed?

Nearly a year ago he thought it would be a simple thing to put Elisabeth out of mind, but avoiding her hadn't worked. Doting on his precious wife hadn't worked either. He'd become obsessed, a madman. It wasn't that he lusted after Elisabeth, though it would be easy enough to do so. What he craved was her spirit. Her passion and courage and honesty. He cherished the way she challenged him, mystified him, made him smile.

Simon gave an exasperated sigh, but froze when his drowsy wife stirred beside him. Fazila settled, and his mind turned to the baby. Fazila was certain she carried a son, and Simon often pictured himself raising the boy—teaching him, loving him, disciplining him with wisdom and tenderness.

Surely the child would vanquish every disloyal thought in Simon's head. Surely a son would fill his heart with such joy there'd be no room for a beautiful, disarming redhead. Surely when the babe came, he would be able to pray again.

What had become of the young man who wanted to change the world for God? How was it he no longer had the heart to share the doctrines of his faith with the nonbelievers around him? Why did he avoid deep, spiritual conversations with his master?

Simon slid his arm out from under Fazila. She rolled away from him, asleep, and he nestled against her back, reaching around to place a hand on her taut belly. Oftentimes the babe stretched and kicked, but this night the child slept with its mother.

Simon loved Fazila. He really did.

And, God willing, she would never know he also loved another.

§ § §

"Fazila requests that I attend her?" Surprise and alarm mingled in Elisabeth's chest.

"Yes," the young servant said. "She says she needs you."

Elisabeth swallowed back the fear that rose in her throat and followed the girl. "How long has she labored?"

The servant spoke over her shoulder. "Since late last night."

Eight hours at least. Maybe more. Elisabeth breathed a prayer as she hurried along the passageway.

She hadn't wanted to grow fond of Fazila, but every day for the past three months the young woman had showered her with kindness and affection reminiscent of Kateline's. Guileless and godly, Fazila endeared herself to Elisabeth's fragile heart, and Elisabeth knew she was better for it.

The servant stopped at a doorway and motioned Elisabeth inside. The chamber was simply furnished and much larger than the room Elisabeth shared with three others.

"There." The girl pointed to a draped archway on the opposite wall.

Elisabeth headed toward it but stopped short. Simon sat on a cushion against the wall. His knees were drawn up almost to his chin, his hands clenched atop them, eyes stiff with worry. She wanted to go to him. To hold him in her arms and soothe him as she would a brother.

The girl pulled on her arm. "This way."

Elisabeth opened her mouth to speak to Simon, but he turned his head. Of course, his thoughts—his very prayers—were for his wife at that moment. Without a word, she followed the servant into the second chamber of the small apartment.

Fazila lay wilted and pale upon the cushions. The midwife wiped perspiration from her brow. "Elisabeth," Fazila said, voice low and weak. "Thank you for coming."

Elisabeth kneeled beside her. "I am honored."

Fazila offered a feeble smile. "My son is stubborn, and I grow weary. Pray with me, and then make me laugh to take my mind from the pain."

Laugh? Elisabeth could not. "I will pray with you," she said, "but you must use your energy to push the child."

"I have used it all." Fazila's voice broke. "I do not think he lives."

Simon's baby had to live. Elisabeth took the woman's hand. "Shhh. He is only collecting his strength to greet his father like a rambunctious young goat."

Fazila seemed about to speak, but a birth pang gripped her. Elisabeth lifted the young woman from behind, as the midwife instructed, supporting her through the spasm that brought forth a chilling moan and nothing more.

"Can't you help her?" Elisabeth asked the midwife.

"It is up to Allah now."

Elisabeth spent the next five hours praying with Fazila, wiping away her tears, encouraging the young woman. "Do not lose heart, Fazila. God is faithful. Your baby lives."

Sometime around noon, Fazila's spirits revived. Soon thereafter, the contractions intensified. The young woman pushed as they came one behind the other. She bore down with great, soulful cries until the baby's head emerged, followed by its shoulders, and finally its long, slippery body. The child greeted the world with a hearty wail.

"A son, Fazila." Elisabeth shook with relief. "Your son is born."

The exhausted mother took the babe in her arms when the midwife finished and put him to breast. He suckled vigorously as she lay back on the cushions and closed her eyes.

By sundown, she'd bled to death.

§ § §

Simon stared at the platter of food he could not eat.

"I am so sorry, my friend," Harun said again.

"Thank you, master." Had he spoken aloud? Perhaps. Maybe not. He didn't care.

"We will find a nurse for the boy. He is strong, Simon. He will be fine."

Fine? How can a boy be fine without his mother?

It was Simon's fault. He should have known Fazila was not built for childbearing. Wasn't it his duty as a husband to protect her? Instead, he'd failed to do so. Failed to pray for her, as he should have. To love her in the way she deserved—wholly, purely, unwaveringly. Even now he should be paving her path to heaven with his prayers, but he could not utter the words.

A servant entered the room.

"What is it?" the master said.

"It is your maidservant Elisabeth, my lord. She begs to speak with you."

A moment passed before Harun answered. "Admit her."

Simon knew he deserved this punishment—to see Elisabeth and hear her condemnation before the master. Still, he flinched when she walked in.

Elisabeth ignored him and bowed low before Harun.

"Speak," the master said gently.

Simon did not look at her, but even so, the sound of her voice pierced his soul.

"My lord," she said. "You surely know that for many years I have been a friend to your esteemed servant Simon al-Nasrani. Not only a friend, but a sister. Furthermore, I trust you are aware that Fazila, *rahimaha Allah*, lately became my friend as well."

"I know she called upon you in her travail, a testimony to your friendship."

Involuntarily, Simon's eyes shifted to focus on Elisabeth. Would her next words reveal his infidelity?

She kept her face to the floor. "I plead with you and with your servant to let me tend the child. To take him as my own."

Simon's astonishment infected Harun's voice. "But he needs a wet nurse."

"No, master," she said, her own voice firm. "I have seen many a babe suckled with a small jar. A bottle fitted with rags. It can be done. Please, my lord."

Simon could not bear a close association with her. His voice trembled when he spoke. "No."

Harun studied Simon's face, eyebrows aloft.

Elisabeth kept her nose to the ground. "Master, your servant Simon must travel far and often to manage your estate. The child needs someone nearby who will love him not because she is compensated, but because she—because God has put it in her heart to do so."

"And you are such a woman?" Harun said.

"In the presence of God, I swear that I am."

"I won't allow it," Simon said.

"She speaks the truth, Simon. You cannot raise a child. Not alone."

"I won't raise him alone. I'll hire a nurse."

"You prefer a stranger to your old friend?"

God knew he did. "Yes, my lord."

Harun looked from Simon to Elisabeth and back. "I think you are speaking irrationally in your grief, young Simon. As your master, it is my decision to make. I believe it is in the child's best interest to be cared for by one who will love him. By one who has chosen him." He turned to Elisabeth. "Rise," he said.

She stood, tears brimming in her eyes, but still she did not meet Simon's glare.

The master spoke to her again. "You will take the child. However, should he fail to thrive, I will hire a wet nurse immediately. When he is weaned, I will reconsider Simon's wishes in the matter." He turned to Simon. "You are the boy's father. I urge you to see him as often as your duties permit."

Harun dismissed Elisabeth. She bowed to him then turned to Simon, her green eyes so intense he gritted his teeth to keep from crying out in anguish.

"My friend," she said, "I grieve your loss. I, too, loved Fazila. And I will love your son."

Simon cast his gaze toward the floor and did not watch her leave.

Perhaps it was just as well that Elisabeth took the boy. The child would only remind him of Fazila. Of his guilt.

Fazila, *rahimaha Allah*. May God have mercy.

Chapter 42

January AD 1220, Damietta, Egypt

The blow caught Hugo in the temple, sending sparks of light across his vision. He shook his head to clear it and tried to identify the offender among the men rioting in the street. Though it was impossible to tell who'd thrown the punch, he was of a mind to join the fray after all.

"Hugo," Orry called from an alley. "This way."

Hugo growled, evaded a man who stumbled into his path—and another in hot pursuit—then lumbered toward the narrow passage.

"For a moment I thought you were going to have a go at it," Orry said when Hugo reached him.

"I was. Worthless Bavarian cuffed me."

"Purely by accident," Orry said. "They never hit anything they're aiming for."

Hugo snarled then followed his friend down the alley. Riots broke out among the crusaders almost daily now. Hugo and Orry avoided them. With the surprisingly considerable wealth of Damietta available as plunder, regular supplies coming into port on Italian ships, and the largely undamaged interior of the city to house and protect the soldiers, the discord seemed outrageous.

But the crusader army had finally splintered from top to bottom. John of Brienne — the chief military leader — departed for Acre when Pelagius refused to give him control of Damietta. Italian troops brawled with the French, who clashed with the Bavarians. Templars and Hospitallers joined in the hostilities, all for the spoils of the city. Factions and fighting. Hugo was sick of it. Meanwhile, the Muslims were probably strengthening their army, waiting for the opportune time to exact revenge.

Hugo stepped over a stray human thighbone, shuddering at the memory of the grisly scenes they'd encountered less than three months earlier. When he and his companions discovered the abandoned tower, they reported their findings. Commanders had dispatched a full force. The troops secured an entire section of the wall, opened a gate, and charged the city.

Of the 80,000 inhabitants, perhaps 3,000 survived. Dogs fed upon the dead — men, women, children. So many children. Most of the living lay sick. Their suffering turned Hugo's stomach more than the stench of the putrid air. Heathen or not, something within him recoiled at what the Christians had done to these people. What *he* had done. And for what? He glanced over his shoulder to the fighting behind him.

Hugo set his gaze straight ahead, past Orry, past the buildings that lined the polluted alleyway. Past the death and disease, the sand and flies and heat and pain. Past the waterlogged screams of drowning children and the abbey at Mont Cenis to a golden-haired young woman treading the road from Offenstadt on a dazzling June day.

"How are you faring on this journey of ours?" she asked.

Not well, he wanted to reply, but the smile on her pretty face left him speechless.

Hugo's heart ached with a grief that intensified day by day. With a sorrow that grew deeper every time he watched a human life slip away. Every time *he* took a man's life. He'd always dreamed of crusading. Envisioned himself a hero, a chivalrous knight. That dream was dying along with the unity of the pope's army and the survivors of Damietta. Perhaps it had already died. Now all he wanted was to complete his obligation to Kateline and lay down his sword.

Orry stopped ahead of him, near an elderly Muslim huddled against a wall, a tattered blanket covering her head and features. Only her small bent shoulders and scrawny form gave away her gender.

"Move along, old woman," Orry said.

The hunched shape didn't so much as breathe, and Hugo figured her another casualty of their yearlong siege.

Orry stepped close and nudged the woman with his foot. "Come on," he said. "There's only trouble for you here. Go home."

Hugo doubted she had one. The crusaders had taken over most of the dwellings and made slaves of the few captives inside the city.

To his surprise, the figure stirred. With great effort, the aged woman stood, head down, back to them. Orry reached out to help, but the moment he touched her elbow, she spun around, kicked him hard in the shin, and took off down the alley.

That was no old woman. A young thief, more than likely. Orry cursed and bolted after him, gained on the young man and tackled him. But no sooner had he pinned the boy down, did he roll off the young fellow in surprise. Hugo trotted toward them.

His own face must have reflected the same astonishment as Orry's when the culprit proved to be neither elderly nor male. A young female face peered at them from the ragged robes. Anger sparked in her eyes. Anger and fear.

They gaped at her while she glared at them.

"I'm sorry," Orry stammered. He rose to one knee beside her. "I didn't realize. Here. Let me help." He tried to assist, but she recoiled at his touch. "I want to help," he explained again, but she didn't understand.

Hugo was still leery. "She's hiding something beneath the blanket."

Orry looked at him, shamefaced. "It's only bread."

Starving, judging from her bony hands and wrists. Probably tried to make off with a small loaf during the height of the riot, when the crusaders wouldn't notice her pilfering. Or her curving form and lovely face. "Let's leave her be."

Orry looked at her then back to Hugo. "We can't, Hugo. If anyone finds her . . ."

Hugo knew what Orry was thinking. A woman in Damietta didn't have to be beautiful to be savagely used. And this one was breathtaking. "They probably already have. It's not our business."

Orry's expression disgraced Hugo. "I won't leave her to them. Go if you want."

Hugo sighed and lifted his eyes to the sky. "Fine. What are we going to do with her?"

"Take her home."

He had a bad feeling about this. "And where would that be?"

Orry spoke steadily. "Our house."

Hugo's head hurt.

Orry used his charm to coax her back to the house beside the blacksmith's shop. The moment they got her inside, Hugo hurried to bolt the door and latch the shutters.

"*La!*" the woman said, sudden panic in her eyes. Her hands went to her chest. She trembled, shook her head. "*La atşal! La atşal!*"

Hugo rushed to her, pushed her against the wall, put a hand over her mouth. She shrieked and thrashed at him, terror on her face.

Orry shoved an elbow into his side and pushed him away. "What are you doing?"

The woman crouched. Covered her head.

Orry knelt beside her. "It's all right."

Hugo scowled and rubbed his ribs. "She was screaming. What was I supposed to do?"

"Come on." Orry spoke softly to her. "See? You're safe." He narrowed his eyes at Hugo then reached to scoop a fig from a nearby bowl. Smiled. "Eat it. It's all right."

She looked him up and down. Glanced at the fruit.

Orry held it close to her. "Hmm?"

Her face softened. One small hand snuck out from her robe to take the fig.

"There, see?" Orry said. He glared at Hugo. "No one's going to mistreat you here."

Hugo rolled his eyes. "I wasn't mistreating her."

She gave Orry a small smile and took a bite of the fruit.

"What's your name?" he said.

Her brows wrinkled.

Orry tapped his chest. "Orry." Pointed at Hugo. "Hugo." Looked at her. "What's your name?"

She swallowed. Hesitated. Placed a hand to her breast. "Salamah."

Orry grinned. "Salamah."

By evening she slept in the back room with a full stomach.

"We can't hide her here forever," Hugo said to Orry.

"I doubt we'll be here forever."

"You know what I mean. Someone's bound to discover her eventually."

Orry raised an eyebrow. "Then we'll make sure they don't."

Hugo gave a humorless laugh. "What if she already belongs to someone? With her looks, some lord has surely laid claim to her. Don't you think he'll have our heads if he finds out?"

"I suppose you're right." Orry's eyes flashed. "I'll just march over to Pelagius's mansion and ask if he can help us locate her defiler."

"Orry."

"Or maybe we should turn her out and let her scrounge for her supper until she starves." He tilted his head. "Oh, yes. She was already doing that."

Hugo had never seen his friend in such a fit. "Stop. I get your point. She can stay. Just keep her out of sight."

"Of course, she can stay," Orry said. "It was never up to you."

Hugo sighed.

Blast it. Orry was falling in love.

§ § §

Hugo trudged toward the house that sat near the blacksmith's shop, Orry at his side. The tedious twenty-four-hour shift at the gate left him weary. The August heat didn't help matters.

But Orry walked with more bounce in his step than anyone inside the walls.

"Many suspect you've gone mad," Hugo said.

"Why?"

"Because you're as cheerful as a child in springtime."

Orry grinned. "And what's so odd about that? I've always been a pleasant fellow."

Hugo lifted a brow. "Look at us, Orry. Twenty-six months we've been in Egypt. Nine months inside the city, wasting away with the monotony of it."

A twinkle lit Orry's eyes. "I'm content."

"That's just it," Hugo said as they neared the house. He had to pick up his step to keep pace with his friend. "You stand out. There's not one man here as happy as you. People are starting to ask questions."

"Would you have me wear a dismal countenance like the rest of you?"

They arrived at the house.

"It might help."

Orry laughed out loud, looked up and down the street, then rapped on the wooden door. Three hard strikes, two soft. Inside, the latch slid away from its hold. Orry led the way in.

Hugo began to unstrap his sword while Salamah threw herself

into Orry's arms. On second thought, he didn't want to infringe on the lovers after their daylong separation. Didn't want to watch them pretend he wasn't an intruder in their romance.

"I'm going to the tavern," he said, letting himself out the door.

They didn't seem to notice.

The inn likely never served strong drink before the crusaders came along, but Hugo was glad for it tonight. He rested one arm on the trestle table and used the other to lift a pint to his mouth. The ale flowed down his throat, bitter flavor matching his mood. He set down the cup then peered over it to the soldier across the table. The man's head hung irresolute above the wooden planks, eyes unfocused, brow gleaming with sweat. Two slow blinks, and then his forehead dropped to the rough timber. All hail the pope's finest.

The noise and heat and foul stench of the room suddenly soured Hugo's stomach. He left a coin on the table and made way through the crowd to the clear night air.

Stars lit the sky like a million points of hope—small glimmers of faith in a sea of blackness. He focused his gaze on the narrow lane that stretched before him. What good was faith anyway?

His hand moved to the medallion, snug against his throat. The links of the fine chain strained at his brawny neck. He'd thought to have it lengthened, fearful the clasp would break and the charm would be lost to him. That the memory of Kateline would vanish along with it.

The small pendant comforted him—solid, secure, familiar between his fingers.

How he missed her.

He stopped walking. Closed his eyes. Took a slow breath, imagining Kateline's scent. Remembering the love in her eyes. The gold in her hair. Was she still with him as she promised to be?

Hugo opened his eyes to the desolate street and continued on.

He bedded down on a mound of hay in back of the blacksmith's shop, wondering if his crusade would ever come to an end.

Chapter 43

August AD 1220, the home of Harun al-Rashid
Baby Peter jabbered to himself in the storeroom off the kitchen. Elisabeth smiled, finished checking the meat on the spit, then wiped her hands and went to retrieve him.

"When did you wake up?" she cooed to the dark-haired tot.

His whole body quivered with excitement as his pudgy little arms reached for her. She bent over the low reed partition that kept the boy safe while he napped and lifted him from his blankets. He nestled against her chest, gnawing sloppily on one round fist. She pressed her lips to the top of his head, letting the delicate strands of hair tickle her skin and his warmth fill her like a soothing drink. "Come on, you," she said after a moment. "You need changing."

"It's a beautiful day to take the boy outside," one of the cooks said when she passed by on her way out the door.

Indeed. A rare rainstorm the previous night had cooled and cleansed the stifling August air. The afternoon was hot, as summer should be, but perfect for playtime in the garden. Elisabeth changed the boy's wet clothing then tucked a small leather ball and woven mat under one arm, perched the baby on her hip, and headed to a patch of green between the flowering plants.

She dropped the mat and ball in the shade of a sycamore and took Peter to one of the fountains. Sitting him on the edge, she took a firm hold on his chubby tummy and let him splash his feet and hands in the water. He squealed with delight when the shimmering droplets speckled his arms, face, and legs. She laughed. Why did she bother dressing him in dry clothes?

How she loved the boy. Loved him like her own. Every day she thanked God for healing the old wounds—and more recent ones—with this precious child.

She longed for Simon to let God do the same for him.

Elisabeth swooped Peter up before he drenched himself completely and strolled the garden path, stopping to let his curious fingers explore velvet petals and rough bark. To watch birds dart from bush to bush. A tiny mouse scurried across the sod, and the infant threw himself toward the rodent, eager for the plaything.

"No, no." Elisabeth chuckled and tightened her hold on the baby. "That's a mouse." She tickled one of Peter's fat feet. "He'll nibble your toes."

She usually spoke German to the boy, hoping he had his father's gift for languages. He was clever like Simon. She'd known it since his first week of life. He'd awoken her in the middle of the night, crying for his milk, then settled quickly once she put the clay bottle to his mouth. She'd propped up the cushions where she slept and leaned against them, closing her eyes as she held him snugly against her. He sucked noisily for a few minutes then grew silent and still. She glanced down at him, his miniature face only inches from hers, thinking he'd drifted off to sleep.

Moonlight from a nearby window set the room aglow, and in its light, his dark eyes focused on her. The intensity of his gaze made her gasp, but she returned his look while he studied her face, intelligence in his deep brown eyes. They watched each other, and it felt to Elisabeth that their very souls touched. She traced his cheek with her finger, but still he scrutinized her features, memorizing them perhaps. His mother. The only mother he might ever know.

She thought of poor Fazila and felt a moment's guilt that she should reap blessing from the young woman's death. But then Peter had sighed and took to nursing again, and joy swallowed up her sorrow. She could not help it. God had turned all her years of mourning into days of dancing.

She no longer questioned why.

"Your *vati* will be home tomorrow," she whispered to the baby as his plump fingers reached for a moth flitting by. "Would you like to see him?"

The child pumped his legs, sensing the significance of her words.

She smiled. "I thought so."

Elisabeth returned to the sycamore, unfurled the mat, sat Peter atop it, and then got to her knees and rolled the ball to him. He chuckled and grasped at it when it bounced against his legs.

Perhaps this time Simon would visit the boy.

In fact, she would make certain of it.

The next evening she marched with Peter to the building where Simon managed Harun's accounts. A servant blocked her entry.

"Let us in. The child needs to see his father."

"Wait here," he said.

Peter began to fret. She bounced him on her hip. If Simon didn't hurry, the boy would be too tired. Of course, if Simon hadn't turned her away earlier in the day, it wouldn't be an issue now.

Elisabeth brought Peter to Simon daily, whenever he lodged in Harun's home. But only occasionally did Simon see the child. Never with Elisabeth present. Never for long.

The slave returned, shaking his head. "Al-Nasrani says he does not have time tonight."

Her mouth twisted, but there was no reason to be angry with the servant. Simon, on the other hand . . . .

She put the boy to sleep, and then headed to the garden. Simon would be there. Though they no longer walked the paths together, she knew he did so almost nightly.

Stars shone against a clear, sapphire sky. Crickets chirruped softly. The scent of jasmine hung heavy in the air.

There he was, his back to her.

"Simon."

He startled. Turned. "What are you doing here?" he said, his tone sharp.

"I've a right to walk the garden." Which was not what she'd meant to say.

"Very well. I'll leave it to you." He moved past her.

She shook her head at herself. "Please wait. I came to speak with you."

He hesitated. Faced her.

"Simon, you must be a father to Peter. He needs your love."

His face hardened further, if that were possible. "I do love him."

"Then why won't you see him?"

When he did not speak, she looked first to the ground, then to the stars. Put hands to her stomach to still its sudden turbulence. Unable to meet his gaze, she settled for his collarbone. "Do you hate me so?"

He did not answer.

Only looked at her until she finally walked away.

Chapter 44

October AD 1220, Egypt

Simon blotted the page, closed the ledger, and rubbed his eyes. Harun's financial records looked in good order. The latest shipment of grain to Syria was bound to bring a healthy profit. As long as the crusader army controlled little more than Damietta—which they seemed content to do—trade would continue much as always.

Despite the security Alexandrians felt, news from Damietta remained disturbing. Most of the citizens died during the siege. There'd been no word from Harun's nephew, Ahmad, and no way of knowing how he fared without making a visit to the city. For months, Simon had been trying to form a workable plan to rescue Ahmad and his bride from the occupiers.

And now he'd found it.

He hoped.

Simon made way to the master's quarters.

"Is the master at leisure?" he asked a servant.

The slave slipped away and returned a moment later. He beckoned Simon to follow.

"I've found a tailor," Simon said after bowing low in front of

Harun and receiving an invitation to speak.

Harun's eyebrows knit together. "Do we need a tailor?"

"Yes, my lord." He couldn't help but smile.

The master lowered the parchments he studied. "And why is that?"

"Because you and I are going on a journey."

"You speak in riddles, Simon. Explain."

"We're going to rescue your nephew from Damietta."

Harun exhaled. "Thank you, my friend, but we don't even know if he still lives."

"He won't, if he remains there."

The light faded from Harun's eyes, and his gaze shifted to the window. "Then we must pray for Ahmad and his wife."

Simon drew close. "Master, we can rescue them."

Harun shook his head. "There is nothing we can do. I should have acted a year ago, but I waited too long, foolishly thinking the Christian army would accept the terms offered them." He clenched the edges of the parchment sheets until his knuckles grew white.

"I would not respect you half so much, my lord, had you not hoped for peace."

The man's mouth lifted in a small, sad smile. "My optimism could prove deadly, I'm afraid."

"I've formed a fail-proof plan, my lord. Surely you agree we must not give up until we know his fate."

The master looked long into Simon's eyes. The past several years had carved deep lines in Harun al-Rashid's wise face. "Tell me what you have in mind."

Simon took a deep breath and began.

§ § §

After a fortnight of preparation and planning, Simon and the master set out for Damietta. In all honesty, Simon doubted they'd succeed. The news from Damietta was disheartening. But something compelled him to try. To do everything he could to restore the young man to his devoted uncle. To liberate Ahmad from the devastation and decay that surrounded him.

The sun arced high above by the time they stopped on the fourth day for a short rest and a light meal of flatbread and figs. Their horses drank from a narrow canal supplied by the Nile.

Harun sat back against the curving trunk of a date palm. "Why are you doing this, Simon?"

"To rescue your relative, master."

"No, no." He waved a hand. "What is it that drives you to take this mission upon yourself? It is accompanied by great risk, you know."

Simon considered the question. "Though I've never met your nephew, my lord, my soul is pierced by his need. More than anything at this moment, he requires hope. A second chance. Life. We can offer him that."

"God willing." Harun squinted at the sun, and then cast his gaze to the horizon for several moments before speaking. "Ahmad is my sister's son."

Simon said nothing, only listened.

His master continued. "When her first husband died young, I brought them both to my home. Ahmad was only eight."

"He is like your own, then," Simon said. Harun would have taken his responsibilities seriously.

"It is true. His mother married a merchant from Damietta shortly after Ahmad turned seventeen. I sorely missed the boy when they relocated."

"Your sister is no longer there?"

"She and her husband died many years hence. Fever." The glare of mid-day accentuated the creases in Harun's face. "Ahmad was younger, stronger, so he survived."

"And he married."

Harun nodded. "Almost three years ago now. Beautiful girl. I traveled there for the wedding. That must have been just a few months before I made you manager of my estate." Harun tore a piece of bread from a small loaf and placed it in his mouth. He stared at some point in the distance while he chewed. His eyes shifted back to Simon. "You are much like Ahmad, my friend."

"Master?"

"In need of hope. A second chance. Life."

Simon's neck stiffened. "I don't know what you mean."

"I think you do."

Simon said nothing, only looked at the water moving lazily along the ditch.

"Ah, well." Harun rose and started toward the horses. "Let's be off to Damietta, then. Someone besides you needs rescuing."

The pulse in Simon's temples beat a thunderous pace the next morning when they approached the city, though the stallion he rode ambled along with a steady step.

"Are you sure I'm not wearing this backward?" Harun asked. "It feels too tight." The master, beard trimmed close, looked surprisingly European in the crusader garments he wore.

"I'm positive, but you must quit fidgeting with the neck." Simon, too, wore the clothing of a soldier of the empire, the handiwork of a Syrian-born tailor who recently set up shop in Alexandria.

"How do they fight in such restrictive garb?" Harun said.

Simon ignored his master this once while he assessed the details of their plan. He carried in his tunic a forged letter authorizing their entrance into the city. Once they gained access to the streets, they'd blend into the throng of crusaders.

Harun remembered the location of his nephew's home well enough, and they carried additional attire rolled up in their blankets to disguise Ahmad and his wife when they found them. There would surely be less security for soldiers exiting the city, but Simon was prepared to explain the appearance of two additional men with another fake document. The only thing that caused him any great concern was the master. They'd be in trouble if he were forced to speak.

The guards at the gate seemed largely disinterested in a couple of common knights. A burley Italian checked the correspondence with a cursory glance. Simon doubted the man knew how to read and had counted on the fact that he would not. At any rate, the sentry accepted the seal as legitimate and let them pass without hindrance.

Once inside the walls, Harun led the way toward his nephew's home. They found it within half an hour, dismounted, and made way to the door.

Harun pounded on the wooden frame. A scowling crusader opened it.

Disappointment clouded Simon's thoughts. "We've a message for—for Lord Cunrad," he improvised.

"Never heard of him," the man replied.

"My apologies." Simon turned and made way past Harun, who stood beside him, slack-jawed in his devastation. "Come, master."

Simon froze. He'd spoken Arabic.

"What's that you said?" Suspicion prickled the soldier's voice.

Suddenly cognizant of Simon's blunder, Harun moved into action. They both scurried toward their horses.

"Stop! Detain them," the man cried to others in the street. "They're spies."

At once, menacing figures blocked their path. Simon willed his hands to stop trembling and spoke calmly. "I tell you, we are not spies. I have an urgent message for Lord Cunrad. He'll be in a rare temper if he fails to receive it."

The man from the house pushed his way through the growing crowd to stand in front of them. "I don't know what treachery you're planning, but I heard you speaking the Saracen tongue, plain and clear."

"As you can see, we are not Saracens."

"What about him?" A gap-toothed man in the crowd pointed to Harun. "Looks like a black-eyed infidel to me. Let's hear what he has to say."

Harun lifted his chin and narrowed his eyes while Simon calculated their options. There were few. "I daresay you'll all be camping outside the gates if Lord Cunrad learns you've harassed his brother-in-law." He nodded toward the master. "We will not be interrogated by the likes of you."

They weren't falling for his bluff. The circle about them began to tighten.

"I smell a couple of Muslim rats," someone said.

"Dirty, spyin' heathens," said another.

The metallic scrape of swords pulled from their sheaths made beads of sweat pop out on Simon's forehead. "Lord Cunrad will have your—"

He never got to finish his vain threat, for a rough hand grabbed his shoulder and spun him around.

Chapter 45

October AD 1220, Damietta, Egypt

Hugo searched the face of the tall man before him. It *was* Simon. He knew it. Though his friend's voice resonated deeper and his muscles strained against the fabric of his tunic, Hugo had glimpsed something familiar in the soldier being threatened by the crowd.

Simon's features held alarm for an instant before his eyes widened in recognition. Something peculiar permeated his appearance, to be certain—and that of the old man's beside him—but Hugo could sort it out later. The important thing at the moment was to extract them from the clutches of the restless mob.

"You're late," Hugo snapped, resisting the smile that tugged at his lips. "You were supposed to meet me long ago."

A grin split Simon's face. "I had trouble on the way."

Hugo swallowed back the questions that flooded his mind. There'd be time for them soon enough. "Come with me." He pushed through the startled onlookers. They parted for him, confused but quiet.

"Halt," the primary challenger growled. "Those men are spies."

Hugo turned and raised a brow at him. "Spies? Fine. Tell Cunrad you think so. But he's mad as a flea-bitten bull, having to wait on these two. I shouldn't want to be in your shoes when he finds out you've delayed them longer."

The man's eyes darted to the dissipating circle. Men scattered like pickpockets in a crowd. "Uh . . . well . . . they're your responsibility then. I won't be suffering on account of them."

Hugo's fists relaxed, but he kept up his ruse. "Suit yourself."

Simon and the old man led their horses through the streets, heads down as they followed Hugo. He made straight for the house near the blacksmith's shop, fished a key from the pouch he wore at his waist, and slipped it into the lock. The door creaked open. Hugo ushered Simon and the old man through with their gear and slid the latch down behind them.

"Hugo, is it really you?" Simon said.

Hugo's heart swelled. "It is, my friend."

The two of them embraced and laughed, slapped each other's shoulders, and blinked back tears. The old man looked on in astonishment.

"Simon," the bearded one finally said, but the word sounded strange to Hugo.

Simon turned, bowed to the man, and then rattled off a string of heathen gibberish. Hugo's stomach tightened. In the space of a breath, the man took on an air of authority—he stood tall, commanding, and his dark eyes glistened with intelligence. He replied to Simon with a rich, cultured voice. The man's abrupt transformation from a common crusader to a seemingly powerful and sophisticated member of the enemy's camp made Hugo's hand move to the hilt of his sword.

"Hugo," Simon said. "Forgive me. I have not introduced you to my master, the most praiseworthy Harun al-Rashid."

Master? Hugo's head reeled at the disclosure, but an unexpected movement caught his attention. Salamah darted out of hiding and into the room. She threw herself at the old man's feet, sobbing and uttering words that would have been incoherent even had he understood her tongue.

The room filled with a cacophony of voices—Salamah's, the old man's, Simon's. They all spoke at once, unintelligible words. He pulled his sword, nervous in the sudden chaos.

The action riveted their focus on him. The hair on his scalp stood straight.

Simon laughed. "Hugo, put away your weapon. This is a time for rejoicing. My master is this woman's relative."

He interpreted while Salamah explained that her husband— the old man's nephew—perished not long after the crusaders landed at Damietta more than two years previous. With no access to medicines or fresh food, disease had taken him quickly, leaving Salamah to fend for herself while the pope's forces squeezed the city in their merciless siege.

Tears streaked the old man's face, and his chin trembled, but he remained dignified.

Regret—shame, perhaps—snaked through Hugo's veins.

A knock sounded at the door. Three hard strikes, two soft.

Simon and his master tensed.

"It's all right," Hugo said. He went to the door and lifted the latch. "We've visitors."

Fear stiffened Orry's features. "Salamah?" he whispered.

"She's safe."

Orry rushed in, hesitated when he saw Simon and his master, then hurried to Salamah's side. He put a protective arm around her and looked to Hugo for explanation.

Hugo didn't have much to offer. "This is my old friend Simon. And his master, Salamah's uncle. By marriage."

"Marriage?" Orry's eyes widened. "She has a husband?"

"Don't worry. Seems we killed him off."

Orry's face softened. He turned to Salamah, spoke hushed words to her. She responded, stroked his face.

Simon and the old man looked at one another, and then to Hugo, astonishment on their faces.

Hugo shrugged. "You see what I must deal with."

In quick order, Harun, Salamah, and Orry settled in beside the hearth. It surprised Hugo to discover just how much Arabic his friend had learned over the past few months.

Hugo and Simon sat on cushions some distance away.

"So that is how I came to serve the master," Simon said with a lift of his shoulders.

Hugo's lip curled. "You make slavery sound like a privilege."

"Harun al-Rashid is a good man."

"And an infidel."

"No, my friend. He is a Christian."

Hugo's brows lifted at the news.

"He follows the Way," Simon assured him, "as do many in his household. He has appointed me manager of his estate, and I have great freedom and honor as his representative."

Hugo wiped a hand over his face, and then shook his head. "I can hardly believe what you're telling me."

"It's true."

Hugo straightened and examined Simon from head to toe. "In all these years, I never dared to hope you fared so well."

Simon smiled. "I've missed you, Hugo. I used to pray for you often."

The corner of Hugo's mouth lifted. "Used to?"

Simon looked his friend full in the face. "I no longer pray."

Hugo's gaze faltered. "Seems a waste of breath, doesn't it?"

They sat silent for a moment before Simon spoke again. "Tell me of you, Hugo. How you came to be here. What you know of the others."

Hugo's voice grew cold. "There are no others. My ship and one other went down at sea. I, alone, survived."

Horror twisted Simon's face. "When?"

"Two days out."

"How did you—?"

A bitter laugh rose from Hugo's chest. "I floated on a piece of flotsam for a day and a half before Genoese fisherman pulled me out of the water. Headed straight to Rome to find Nicholas. He's here, you know."

"Here? In Damietta?"

"Curried the favor of the great Cardinal Pelagius himself. Ah, I see you know him."

Simon's face had gone stern. "I've heard."

"The little milksop Nicholas lounges on cushions all day long and whines when his supper is late. You say three shiploads besides yours were sold here in Africa?"

"Yes. That accounts for six ships altogether."

"Seven," Hugo said. His teeth ground together. "The seventh landed in Syria. According to a peddler I met in Palestine, the children were sold in Damascus and martyred in Baghdad. All of them."

Simon turned a sickening shade of green. Hugo didn't bother to ask if he was all right. Of course he wasn't.

"How is it that only we three have found each other?" Hugo said. "You, Nicholas, and myself?"

Simon's lips grew tight. "There is Elisabeth."

Hugo's mouth dropped open. "Elisabeth?"

"I found her on the auction block in Alexandria. Her master had escaped the Christia—escaped Damietta before the crusader army arrived."

Hugo looked to the dirt floor.

"She serves my master. Raises my son."

Hugo blinked. "She's your wife?"

"No," Simon said, heat in his voice. His eyes shifted past Hugo's shoulder. "My wife died in childbirth. Elisabeth is but his nurse."

They did not speak for a long time.

§ § §

"A wedding?" Hugo turned to Orry. "Now?"

Orry grinned and nodded. Salamah sat beside him, radiant gaze fixed on her beloved.

The old man—Harun—spoke, and Simon interpreted. "He says Salamah is a freewoman. That's she's suffered so much he will not deny her request to remain with Orry. To be his wife. They've already pledged themselves to one another before God."

Hugo looked at Orry. Raised his hands in question. Orry smiled.

Hugo sighed and turned to Simon. "And in what court will the bond stand?"

"Only heaven's, I imagine."

"Orry, you can't mean to do this."

"But I do. And why do you care?"

Orry would marry one of them? A heathen? "It can't work. Your life will be at stake."

His friend laughed. "And on which day is it not?"

Hugo exhaled.

In the dim light of a tallow candle, Harun recognized the union before Hugo, Simon, and a silent God.

"We must be away tonight," Simon said to Hugo afterward.

"So soon?"

"I fear for the master's safety if we delay." Simon glanced to Harun, who sat talking with Salamah in the corner. His gaze returned to Hugo. "You could come with us, you know. What is there for you here?"

Hugo swallowed past the lump in his throat. "No. Perhaps I'll come find you one day. When all this is over."

Simon nodded at the floor, resigned. "We must pack our things.

I'd like to set out at dusk." He grasped Hugo's forearm, and Hugo returned the gesture. "You know where to find me," Simon said. "When it's over." His arm dropped, and he breezed through the doorway into the back room to gather their belongings.

Hugo stared after him, the burn of disappointment in his throat. For a small space of time today, he'd thought he and Simon might partner together again. Might talk and laugh and collaborate as they used to do. But reality dashed his hopes. No matter what he said to the contrary, Simon was a half-Muslim slave. Simon—once the most fervent of Christians—no longer prayed. If Simon had lost hope, what remained for Hugo?

He looked at the bride and groom. Orry had Salamah now.

All Hugo had was Kateline's ghost.

Chapter 46

October AD 1220, outside Damietta, Egypt

Simon and Harun made a fireless camp a safe distance from Damietta. The master remained pensive while he ate, which suited Simon's mood.

One would think that with the discovery of Hugo—and all the other bitter discoveries of the day—his mind would dwell on the failed crusade.

He thought of it, but it was other failures that harassed him.

He tried not to think of Peter, but images of his son floated before his mind's eye. The boy had his mother's complexion—skin smooth and brown as toasted almonds. How long had it been since Simon had seen him? A month? Probably two.

Peter.

Harun had finally chosen the name, scolding Simon for taking too long to do so. Peter, the apostle. The evangelist. The rock. Such a legacy for a little boy to live up to. Especially without a father who could help. Simon once thought he could do so. Could teach a son the ways of God. But now—

Be careful when you think you stand firm, lest you fall. Isn't that what the Scriptures said? How far he'd fallen. If only the child didn't seem to ridicule his guilt. If only he'd been a worthy husband for Fazila. A worthy friend to Elisabeth.

He remembered the night she'd come to him in the garden. Chastised him concerning Peter. Auburn hair framed her face, glowing warm and rich in the light of the rising moon. It felt a sin to let his eyes linger on her lovely features. Another, in the long list of his sins.

She'd spoken to him, but he could not answer her. Longing tore at him when she finally walked away, fading into the shadows of the garden like mist.

How could she think he hated her?

At last the master spoke again, rousing him from his thoughts. "You are an empty man, Simon."

"It is the loss of Fazila."

"I don't think so."

Simon's head snapped up. "I grieve my wife."

Harun bent his knees, planted his feet flat on the ground, and rested his forearms atop them. "I know you do. But you have been like a leaf withering on the vine since long before she died."

"You imagine things, my lord."

"And now, after all that binds our hearts together, you would lie to me."

Simon bowed his head in shame, and guilt squeezed his chest with a crushing grip. He could not refute the master's words. And then his disgrace deepened, for Harun began to list his sins, one by one, a man hammering nails into a casket.

"You no longer speak to me of spiritual truths," the master said.

Simon confessed. "I am no longer a spiritual man."

"You neglect your son."

"I am an unworthy father."

"You seem to have abandoned your prayers."

"I cannot form the words."

The creases on Harun's face appeared to deepen in the moonlight even as Simon watched. He wanted to tear his focus from the master's distress, but something in the man's rich brown eyes would not let him go. "Ah, Simon. You have become a son to me, but I fear I have lost you."

"You would not claim me if you knew the depth of my transgression."

"Put me to the test."

Simon's mouth grew dry as dust upon the wind. "No, master. Please."

"Then let me set forth my theory."

Simon's eyebrows crinkled.

"You have become paralyzed," Harun said, "not so much by your supposed sin, but by the knowledge of your weakness."

Sin is my weakness. My many sins.

"You were once the most godly man you knew, were you not?"

"No, I . . . ." The protest died on his lips.

Harun smiled. "Just as I thought. And it surprised you when temptation ensnared you, sorely tried you, as if you were a normal human being. Don't bother denying it. I can see by the look in your eyes that this is true."

Simon blinked, trying to clear away any signs of affirmation. Was the master correct? Did such an arrogant heart beat within his chest? "No. I have sinned. Sinned against you, Fazila, Peter. And Elisabeth."

Surprise lifted the master's brows. "Elisabeth?"

Simon struggled with the truth that sought to escape. "*Ohibboha,*" he finally breathed, tormented by the admission. *I love her.* "I always have."

It took a moment for the master to find his voice. "You assured me she was but a sister to you."

"I thought it to be so." Guilt pierced his chest like a fatal wound. "I—I realized the depth of my feelings for her too late to prevent them from happening. I stopped spending time with her. I married Fazila in good faith. I *loved* my wife." His ribs constricted around his lungs, and he struggled for air as the confession spilled forth. "But I could not stop loving Elisabeth."

"And now the woman you love raises your dead wife's son."

Simon nodded. Felt the sting of unshed tears.

"And does Elisabeth love you?"

He exhaled. "I do not know."

Harun rubbed his silver-streaked beard. "So what you're telling me is that your intentions toward your old friend were pure. That you behaved chastely toward her—"

"We kissed." Simon looked toward the ground. "Once. That's when I knew . . ." His eyes flicked back to the master's. "I did not meet her again."

Harun's hand resumed its measured rhythm against his beard. "You fled temptation and kept your vows to Fazila. You loved her and doted on her. Anyone could see that. You gave her a son."

"But she—"

"You are not to blame for her death."

"I should have known she could not survive the birthing."

"How could you? And what right would you have had to deny her a child?"

The silence lingered while the master's words filtered into Simon's soul.

Harun finally spoke. "I stand by my original theory. However, I exercise my privilege to amend it."

Simon lifted his eyes to the master.

"You have sinned, my son. Not against any man or woman, but against God alone. It is my belief that you acted righteously despite your temptation. But, in pride, you've turned from the Father. You've given up your faith, rather than admit your weakness and humble yourself before the Lord."

Simon could not deny it.

When they retired, he tossed upon his blankets until the moon sat high in the heavens.

He wrestled with memories of the failed crusade. With leaving Hugo, whose heart was burdened by remorse and doubt. With the idea of facing Elisabeth and Peter upon his return. With thoughts of Ahmad, for whom rescue came too late.

At last Simon got to his feet and stumbled two hundred paces across the dry soil before sinking to his knees. Who knew emptiness could give such pain? Who knew loss could leave a living man dead? That love could confound and confuse and cut a heart so deeply there seemed no heart left for it?

Simon bowed his face to the dirt and dared God to end his suffering. But instead the ache in his chest swelled until his torso no longer contained it. His arms shook with grief, his legs throbbed with it. Every inch of his body trembled under the load of his guilt, the enormity of his failings, the brutality of his losses.

Harun had been right about him. He was once the godliest person he knew. More fervent than the monks at Villebonne. Purer in heart than Nicholas. Wiser than Jabir. Superior to Elisabeth in both temperament and faith.

He'd thought to change the world, but had learned the world changed one man at a time. And now he was that man. Like dross burned from gold in the heat of the flames, so in that moment did the Spirit's fire begin to sear the blackened edges of his soul.

He lifted his face to the stars. A moan started low in the pit of his stomach, mounting, building. His arms rose of their own accord, extended, like a man crucified. A strange wail—primal and horrible—pierced the silence of the night, and Simon realized the sound sprung from his own breast.

His lament echoed across the land. It faded, and an inexplicable peace filled him. God's peace. God's presence. Tears wet his face. For the first time nearly a year, he bent his head to the ground and prayed.

Chapter 47

October AD 1220, the home of Harun al-Rashid

Elisabeth sat on the mat in the garden and rolled the small leather ball to Peter. She smiled when the nine-month-old chortled and kicked his legs. He reached for the toy, but his plump fingers bumped it out of reach. Lips parting in a wide grin at the game, the baby moved to all fours and crawled to the ball, then plopped himself back on his round little bottom, grasped it in an awkward hold, and brought it to his mouth.

"That's not your dinner, little one," she said with a chuckle. She scooted to where he sat, caressed the curls at his brow, and kissed his smooth forehead. "My turn again." Trading a tickle for the plaything, she pivoted to make her way back to the opposite side of the mat.

Simon stood there, home from wherever his latest journey had taken him.

"Oh." She didn't know what else to say. Never had he come to visit the child on his own. Dread gnawed at her stomach. Surely he didn't intend to take Peter away. The child wasn't weaned yet. She moved to stand.

Simon lifted a hand. "No," he said, gently. "Don't get up." His eyes drifted to Peter. "I—I just wanted to see him."

She let out a slow breath and observed the peculiar look on Simon's face as he regarded his son.

Peter demanded the ball with a grunt. She glanced his way. Saw his sweet arms extend, entreating her to play. She tilted her head up to Simon, whose eyes hadn't left the boy's face. She lifted the ball. "If you're going to stay, you have to join in."

Simon blinked and turned his gaze toward her. For the briefest moment, something in his expression made the breath catch in her chest. Stirred the feelings she'd worked so hard to conquer. Though she would never overcome them, she'd found a safe place for them. A place deep enough to pretend they no longer mattered. The moment ended, and she wondered if she'd merely imagined it.

He shook his head. "I don't want to intrude. I—" His protest broke off as he instinctively caught the ball she tossed his way.

She raised an eyebrow at him. "Your turn now."

He smiled uncertainly, looked at his son, and lowered himself to the mat.

Peter grew shy at Simon's nearness. The baby scuttled toward Elisabeth and climbed into her lap, then pointed toward the ball, babbling a complaint.

"The child is waiting," she prompted.

"I fear he's waited too long."

They rolled the ball back and forth for several minutes. Bit by bit, Peter warmed up to his *vati,* giggling when Simon bounced the ball against Peter's feet or laughing heartily when Simon rumbled his tummy with it.

Elisabeth smiled at the light that grew in Simon's eyes.

§ § §

The *shaykh's* sprawling camp resembled a small village. Elisabeth had not encountered a more exotic setting since coming to

Egypt. She inspected the lavish interior of Ra'zin's tent. Smoky with incense, adorned with animal hides, woven carpets, and gauzy curtains, the space both intrigued and discomfited her. She pressed the baby tightly to her breast. Peter, almost a year old now, wasn't having it. He arched his back and grunted at her, eager to explore.

Simon stood and came forward. "Peter has eaten?" He waited for her nod. "Good. Thank you for bringing him." He reached to take the boy. Peter's arms stretched out for him.

"Elisabeth," Simon said when she failed to relinquish the boy. "Give him to me."

She didn't want to let go. To leave that innocent child with men she didn't know or trust. She looked at Simon with pleading eyes.

"It's all right," he said.

"No, it's not." She whispered, fearful that Ra'zin, of the house of Zanata, might overhear despite Peter's noisy protests. "This is the man that almost beheaded you, Simon."

Understanding softened his gaze. "The *shaykh* wishes only to offer a blessing to Peter. I would not have brought him if I thought any harm would come. I'm his father." He smiled. "I'll take care of him."

She frowned. Simon had explained that the gesture of trust would enhance the bond between Harun al-Rashid and the powerful tribesman. At the time it seemed reasonable, but now that she was actually here in the tent, about to let Peter go . . . .

Simon's dark eyes, full of peace and confidence, was the only thing that loosened her hold on the baby.

"Not long?" she said.

Simon took Peter in his strong arms, smiled at the boy who giggled and curled into his father's chest, then returned his gaze to her. Humor and kindness mingled upon his face. "Not long. I promise."

"I'll just wait here, then."

He smiled. "No. Go back to your tent. I'll send for you as soon as we're done."

"But I—"

"Trust me."

She sighed and moved to comply. Simon caught her hand. He winked, squeezed her fingers then turned toward Ra'zin and his entourage.

Elisabeth stepped into the sunshine. Though tempted to linger outside the tent, she needed to check on the maidservant who accompanied her. The poor girl had eaten something that soured her stomach, and Elisabeth had left her resting in the quarters they shared.

She nearly got lost trying to find her way back among the nondescript lodgings, but at last she recognized the one she was looking for. She lifted the tent flap and ducked inside. Blinded by the sudden dimness, she blinked to regain her sight. Something was amiss. This wasn't the tent she shared with the servant.

The air held the foul odor of sweat, and a quiet moan reached her ears. Her vision still adjusting, she peered into the heart of the shadows.

She spied a woman, skin as black as obsidian. "Do you need help?" Elisabeth asked in Arabic.

A chill ran up her spine when the woman merely whimpered. She stepped closer then gasped. Not a woman, but a girl no older than thirteen or fourteen. Arms stretched between two posts, wrists bound by rope. Face twisted in pain, her lips curled to reveal white teeth clenched together. A groan pushed past them.

"God in heaven," Elisabeth whispered, the only prayer she could manage. The child was pregnant. And in labor.

Rushing to untie the ropes, Elisabeth mumbled what assurances she could. "It's all right. I'll help you." She fumbled with the knots. Growled in frustration. At last one cord fell free.

She pulled the girl toward the second post, relieving the strain on the still-bound arm, then worked to unfasten that rope as well. The girl's arm came free as another pang followed the previous one. Elisabeth remembered what the midwife instructed when Fazila labored, so she lifted and held the girl from behind while the tortuous waves swept through her. Once or twice the child cried out with strange, guttural words, but mostly she panted and moaned under the birth pains.

Within an hour, the babe was born. A daughter, strong and beautiful.

Elisabeth placed the tiny creature in her mother's arms and found a blanket to cover them both. The girl's teeth rattled, and her whole body trembled. "Easy," Elisabeth crooned. "It's over now."

When the girl finally quieted, Elisabeth stormed from the shadows, blinked against the glaring sun, and focused her eyes upon the pinnacle of Ra'zin's extravagant tent where it towered above the camp.

"Elisabeth," Simon said, catching her arm and spinning her to face him. "Are you all right?"

Her breath came in short bursts. "There's a girl, Simon—"

"I've searched for you everywhere," he interrupted, alarm evident in his eyes. "Where have you been?"

"She was tied up."

"When I called for you, the maidservant came instead."

"I delivered her baby."

His lips parted, then closed again. A moment passed. "What?"

"I entered the wrong tent. Found a girl bound with ropes. She was in the midst of childbirth, Simon. *Childbirth*. She's but a child herself."

He drew back. Elisabeth followed his gaze. Blood covered her clothes, her hands.

Understanding seemed to dawn on him. "Where is she?"

"In that tent. We've got to do something. Ra'zin has to be behind this."

Simon ran a hand over his face then settled troubled eyes on Elisabeth. "She's a concubine."

"No, she's just a girl."

He shook his head. "That doesn't matter. I heard him speak of her."

Elisabeth felt her temper rise. "You knew about this?"

"Only that she'd found his disfavor. That he'd disciplined her."

"Help her, Simon."

"What would you have me do?"

"Challenge Ra'zin. Buy her. Anything."

"He'll have our heads if we meddle in his business."

"How dare you bring us here—bring Peter here—to court the favor of such a monster?"

Simon's face hardened. "You don't understand these people."

"I understand what's happened to that poor girl back there. I've lived through that kind of cruelty, Simon. Something has to be done. You can't allow Ra'zin to brutalize her further."

Simon dropped his gaze. "I'm so sorry." He raised heartbroken eyes to hers. "There's nothing we can do."

Her lips quivered. "Where's my tent?"

They didn't speak while he led her back to Peter, to the tent she shared with the maidservant.

"Elisabeth," he said as she lifted the flap to escape him.

She paused, jaw set.

He looked pained standing there. "I can't fix this."

"You could try."

She retreated to the cool darkness. Peter jabbered at her.

She blinked, adjusting her eyes to the dim light. The boy swayed where he'd pulled himself to stand against a heavy earthen jar, lifted one chunky little foot and lurched forward. She dropped to one knee, chest expanding. Peter staggered across the floor, picked up momentum and lost his balance the last few steps, falling into Elisabeth's open arms. She drew the child close, kissing his dark head.

How could Simon do nothing? That he knew what Elisabeth had gone through—what this meant to her—only made it worse.

Peter wriggled from her arms and crawled away.

She wept over innocence abused.

Simon came to her later. Called her from the tent with a hushed voice. She left Peter asleep in the care of the maidservant.

Clouds scudded across the sky. It wouldn't rain, though. It never did.

Elisabeth looked at Simon in the moonlight and didn't bother to hide her pain and disappointment.

Simon's eyes grazed her face and settled on her eyes. "I thought about what you said."

She crossed her arms over her chest.

The corners of his mouth tipped up in a small smile, and contrition crinkled his brow. "You were right."

"I was? I mean—you really think so?"

He nodded. "You can be right about a lot of things."

A chuckle escaped her throat. Then she sobered. "What are you going to do about the girl?"

Simon shook his head.

Elisabeth opened her mouth to chastise him, to urge him to go to Ra'zin, but Simon interrupted her.

"He gave her to me."

"What?" Her pulse quickened.

"I—I couldn't believe it." Even now, his eyebrows rose in disbelief. "I asked to buy her, and he said she would become his goodwill offering to Harun."

"He didn't get angry?"

"No, but . . . " Simon seemed uncertain whether to go on. " . . . he asked for you in return."

Her throat went dry. "You didn't—?"

Simon tipped his head back and laughed, then looked down at her with an expression that made her face heat. "Never."

The girl was free. Without thought, Elisabeth raised up on her toes to throw her arms around his neck. "Thank you, Simon. Thank you."

He chuckled into her hair. His hands were warm at her waist. Warm and firm. She released him. Took a step backwards. "Thank you," she said again.

He shrugged. "We owe Ra'zin five camels in your place."

It was her turn to laugh. "I would have thought more."

Simon said nothing, but held her gaze until both their smiles faded.

She swallowed. "You're staring."

"I cannot help myself."

A nervous chuckle escaped her lips to skitter away in the silence.

Something deep and indiscernible flashed across his face. "Elisabeth."

"Yes?" Her voice registered no louder than a whisper.

"Can you forgive me? Not for today, for—"

"Of course. I did so long ago."

"I'm so sorry."

She stepped to him, put a hand on his arm. "I know, my friend." Her eyes pleaded with him. "Do not trouble yourself a moment longer on my account."

He scanned her face. Lifted a hand to her cheek.

She pressed her skin into his palm, closed her eyes. Inhaled the fresh scent of the Egyptian countryside that clung to his wrist.

His thumb traced her lips. "I love you, Elisabeth," he breathed. "Not as a sister or merely a friend, but as the woman I have always loved, no matter what has transpired."

Chapter 48

August AD 1221, near El Mansura, Egypt

Hugo slapped the donkey's hindquarters. "Hie!"

The beast strained to pull the supply cart from the mud. Somewhere a dam had been breached, Hugo was sure of it. A man splashed by, panicked by the fast-rising water.

"You," he called to the fellow. "Roll that barrel. Get it out of here before it's ruined."

The man ignored him and kept running.

Nearly a month ago, the Christians had marched toward Cairo. John of Brienne, ordered back to Damietta by Pope Honorius III himself, led them unmolested to a location across the river from al-Kamil's troops where they'd delayed for God-knew-what purpose. But today the tributary beside which they camped suddenly flooded, forcing the army into an awkward retreat.

The air resonated with the bawl of pack animals and the shouts of men.

Another soldier, water dripping from his chin and ears, grabbed the donkey's harness and pulled while Hugo pushed. His feet sank in the muck, but at last the wheel came free. The comrade guided the animal to dry ground.

A horse snorted.

Hugo pivoted, growled through his teeth, and slogged toward Nicholas. He didn't have the time or patience for this today. "What are you doing here?" he said. "Move back where it's safe."

Nicholas's horse shifted at Hugo's approach. The young man smiled and tugged at the reigns to steady the beast. "I came to tell you things aren't as bad as they seem."

"No?"

Hugo's gaze swept the chaos surrounding them. The Mohammedans were behind the mayhem, if he'd learned anything about Muslim strategy. A fact that didn't bode well for the pope's forces.

"I've got everything under control," Nicholas said.

Hugo was about to ignore him and tend to the withdrawal, but something in the young man's eyes made him hesitate. "What do you know?"

Nicholas looked to the right and left, then leaned close. "Al-Kamil intentionally flooded the river. When John surrenders Damietta, the sultan will let us go peacefully. The infidels have ships hidden on the Nile to take us to the coast."

Hugo's blood ran cold. "How do you know this?"

Nicholas grinned. "I arranged it myself."

Quick as lightning, Hugo grasped Nicholas's tunic and pulled the scoundrel toward him—nearly dragging him from his horse. They faced each other nose-to-nose. Hugo spoke through clenched teeth. "You'll get us all killed."

"Relax, Hugo. I'm saving our lives. You know it's Jerusalem we want. What awaits us in Cairo? Another eighteen-month siege?"

"What does Pelagius have to do with all this?"

Nicholas looked pleased with himself. "He knows nothing of it. I, alone, managed to contact the sultan's representative. I, alone, will benefit from the gold I've earned."

Hugo scowled. "That's treason."

"It's genius," Nicholas protested. "I've arranged safe passage for all of us out of this god-forsaken land. The pope would thank me if he ever found out."

The water topped Hugo's knees. "And who's to say I won't hand you over to John as a traitor?"

"We're friends, Hugo. That's why I told you in the first place. Besides, I'm willing to give you a share of the booty if it will ease your conscience."

Hugo trembled with rage. Pulled Nicholas from the horse and thrust him under the water.

The boy came up sputtering and gasping, long curls straggling across his face. "What'd you do that for?"

He vacillated between strangling Nicholas at that very moment or helping the men to safety. He lifted a hand to the young man's throat and raised him until he wavered on the tips of his toes. Nicholas's eyes bulged with fear. "If one of our men dies," Hugo said, "you'd better hope the Muslims kill you, or I'll do so myself."

He dropped Nicholas and plowed through the water.

Everywhere men shouted, tugged at the leads of nervous animals, or wrestled cartloads of supplies from the mud. He stopped to help four soldiers pull a wagon from the sludge.

A cry rang out that caused them to hesitate for the space of one heartbeat. "Battle formations!"

The words had scarcely resonated past them before they unfastened their weapons and ran toward their comrades. Hugo's legs strained to reach the front line where it formed near the rear of their camp. Muslim riders pelted the troops with arrows in advance of a massive force cutting off the Christian retreat.

He hurdled over debris abandoned by the pope's army when it scurried to meet the attack. Sprinted past knights organizing their ranks.

Past archers as they let loose their own barrage of missiles.

"Hugo," a familiar voice shouted. "Over here."

An enemy arrow barely missed Hugo as he turned see Orry on one knee, poorly protected by a fallen barrel, rapidly releasing his own deadly volley. Hugo dove for the scant security of the large cask, and rolled to a stop, face up, beside his friend.

Orry yelled above the din. "Giovanni's moving to the east. He hopes to break through their left flank."

"To the east," Hugo repeated.

Orry paused his firing to duck beneath the curved side of the barrel. Their eyes met. "Be careful, my brother."

Hugo nodded then rolled to his stomach. Prepared to spring to his feet.

Orry readied his bow. "I'll cover you." He straightened, rose above the crude refuge.

A hiss in Hugo's ear. A sickening thud. Orry flew backward, an arrow lodged in his chest.

Hugo scrambled toward his friend. Where was Orry's chain mail? Why didn't he have his mail?

Hugo's breath came in ragged bursts. The entire arrowhead penetrated the flesh between Orry's ribs. Blood gushed from the wound and spilled from his mouth. The color drained from Orry's face, leaving it ashen, lifeless. His body shuddered, then stilled.

Tears filled Hugo's eyes. He could see through the watery view that blood covered his hands. Always the blood.

A vicious fury filled him. He staggered to his feet, drew his sword, and headed across the battleground. Muslim foot soldiers and horsemen had broken through the Christian line, but Hugo made his way east toward Giovanni. Dark faces appeared before him. Faded away when he cut them down. He couldn't hear anything. Just the thud of the arrow that killed Orry. His own heartbeat in his ears.

Seventy-five yards away, several mounted Christians fought in vain against an onslaught of incensed Mohammedans who brandished their weapons with a rage born of three year's enemy occupation. With a malevolence nourished by the battered ghosts of Damietta.

Hugo could discern Nicholas among the riders. The infidels pulled him from his horse to slay him in the heat of an Egyptian summer. And just like that, Nicholas — who used to be a boy, lively and disarming — was gone.

With the cries of 10,000 crusader children echoing in his head, Hugo cut to the right to run along the edge of the river and bypass the heart of the fighting. The water churned past him.

Almost too late, he heard the thunder of a Muslim horse in pursuit. He whirled to meet it, used his sword to sever the animal's tendon and bring it to ground. The rider sprung from the beast's back when it fell. He flattened Hugo when he landed, and Hugo felt his sword spin out of his fingers.

They rolled to the brink of the current. The Mohammedan had lost his blade when he fell. Grunting, battling the mud and water, they pummeled one another with their fists. Hugo managed to gain his feet, but the heathen came right behind him. They grabbed their weapons.

Blade clashed against blade. The hilt of Hugo's sword slipped in his wet hands. Escaped his grip.

The infidel's eyes registered neither hatred nor pity. He leapt at Hugo, grabbed him by the neck of his tunic, and plunged his sword into Hugo's side.

It surprised Hugo to experience no pain. Nothing but overwhelming weakness.

He sensed himself falling backwards toward the water. Felt a tug at his throat. Kateline's necklace broke off in the attacker's hand. It glistened in the sunlight as the man flung it into the torrent.

Chilling blackness engulfed Hugo.

Chapter 49

Autumn AD 1221, Damietta, Egypt

The flames of hell burnt deep in Hugo's gut. Excruciating. Consuming. Tremors shook his body while the fire blazed. He couldn't see beyond the blackness, beyond the pain. For a moment he discerned a faint light, but then the shadows bore down upon him.

"Orry?" a plaintive voice asked. "Orry?"

Orry was dead, like Hugo. He hoped his friend had found heaven instead of this horrific place.

§ § §

Locusts were singing when Hugo came fully awake. Soft, soothing lyrics that seemed out of place in his torment.

He could barely work up enough saliva to swallow. Every breath came at an agonizing cost. Heat seared his torso, but he'd never felt so cold in all his life.

When he forced his eyes open, an arched ceiling stared down at him. Without the strength to turn his head, he circled his gaze to take in whatever details he could. Even the rotation of his eyes within their sockets pained him. He spied a shuttered window, moonlight pouring in through the slats. Narrow columns supported the ceiling. Firelight flickered against the walls. Not much else.

The reconnaissance exhausted him, and he drifted into an uneasy sleep.

§ § §

A cool cloth pressed Hugo's forehead. He was already cold enough. "Stop," he said, but the word came out garbled.

"Hugo."

Kateline? No, not Kateline. She was gone. He tried to conjure her face, but couldn't.

"Hugo."

The voice sounded demanding the second time, and it rubbed him the wrong way. Probably Elisabeth. He relaxed at the thought—it would be good to see her, even. The next words were gibberish. Heathen language. He cracked open one eye.

Salamah.

She offered him an unsteady smile. "*Bonjour*," she said in one of the few words they both knew.

He meant to return her smile, but the pain and the sudden reminder of Orry's loss produced nothing but a grimace.

She removed the cloth only to wet it and place it back upon his skin.

"I'm cold," he mumbled.

Of course, she didn't understand. Just sat there giving him a concerned look.

"No," he said.

"No?"

He lifted his eyes toward the cloth. "No."

Comprehension quickly replaced the confusion on her face, but then she shook her head and issued a stream of nonsensical words.

He sighed. Women were stubborn in any language.

They stayed like that for a minute. Him flat on his back with a cold rag on his brow. Salamah looking down at him with authority in her countenance.

Her features softened. She took a breath. Glanced at her hands. Brought anxious eyes to meet his. Her lips parted twice before she asked the question he didn't want to answer. "Orry?"

A lump clogged his throat. With great effort he shook his head. "I'm sorry."

She didn't have to speak his language to understand his grief. Tears filled her eyes at once. She swayed. Put her hands to the neck of her outer robe. Rent the fabric with a noise so bitter, his wounds throbbed at the sound. She sank to the floor. Her muted sobs pierced him more deeply than the shrillest keening would have done.

He could feel his own tears collecting in his ears, but he was too weak to wipe them away.

§ § §

How had he survived? That's what Hugo wanted to know. Mercifully, he'd not felt the blade slice into him, but he'd seen the hilt of the sword meet his flesh. No man could endure that and live. Maybe it had been a dream.

But his pain was too real now. The fever that plagued him served as evidence—infection, it seemed. When he improved, he'd check the wounds himself.

If he improved.

Nights were worse. Mornings, not much better. Salamah tended him almost constantly.

He wished he could remember how he got back to Damietta. Orry's widow had communicated through hand motions that this place was hers—likely the home she'd shared with her first husband before the siege began. Hugo's comrades had obviously stripped it of every valuable thing, plundered it along with the rest of the city.

A city the crusaders had since surrendered and the Muslims reoccupied. He'd figured out that much. He was the one in hiding now, dependent on Salamah as she had been dependent upon him and Orry.

But that didn't explain how he'd kept from drowning in the flooded river while it rushed his unconscious body toward the Nile. How he'd ended up in Salamah's care. The last thing he remembered was falling toward the water.

His thoughts halted.

No, the last thing he remembered was Kateline's medallion, shimmering in the sun when it soared above the current.

Dismayed, Hugo labored to lift one arm to his throat. His fingers searched for the pendant, even as his heart sank with the truth. Kateline was gone.

§ § §

Kateline had always been gone. Hugo knew that now, though the awful fact had taken a week to set in.

He'd lived the last nine years in a fantasy, thinking she came to him every time he called her. Thinking she'd promised to be with him always. Killing men because he thought she demanded it.

Not demanded it. She'd never have done that. It wasn't her way.

But it had become his. Kill or be killed. Isn't that what he'd learned during his first battle at Bet She'an? He hadn't been willing to die with the guilt of ten thousand lost children on his conscience, so he'd offered Muslim souls as sacrifices to appease a just God. The notion that he could ever satisfy God made Hugo laugh out loud. An acrid laugh, harsh even to his own ears.

Salamah looked his direction. Puzzlement settled on her face while she watched him. He turned from her, but in a moment she kneeled beside his bed with a cup of water.

He didn't want it, but she lifted his head with a warm, gentle hand, so he sipped.

Why, in God's name, had Kateline made him pledge to continue the journey?

§ § §

Hugo managed to sit up one afternoon. The pain made him dizzy, but Salamah supported him with an approving look and an arm about his shoulders.

The fever had finally ceased. He could see the gaping hole under his left ribs, a jagged gash the width of his hand. He knew from Salamah's nursing that he suffered a similar wound in his back on the right side. The sword had penetrated all the way through his body.

Hugo pushed the disturbing questions aside and allowed himself to smile his thanks. They sat close like that until weakness forced him back to the cushions much too soon. He liked the warmth of her.

Three days later he was able to sit on his own without the room spinning. Within a week he could feed himself, though he still had little mobility. Salamah cleansed his wounds twice each day.

She worked with the most tender care, pouring diluted wine over his injuries. Patting them dry, examining them closely, repeating the procedure until she seemed satisfied. Afterward, she wet a cloth and blotted away the perspiration that accumulated on his face, his chest, his back. Her gentle touch always eased the agony of the routine. The light caress of her long fingers where they brushed against his skin relaxed his tense muscles.

One night while they ate together, communicating only with hand signals and smiles, Hugo found it difficult to take his eyes from her. She was a pleasant woman, really. And more beautiful than he'd ever realized.

They were just finishing their meal when she clapped her hands together, apparently remembering the necessary cleansing ritual. She stood and gathered her supplies.

The fire burned low in the hearth when she kneeled beside him again. He concentrated on the silky touch of her hands rather than on the pain. On the way he could discern her feminine curves beneath the light fabric of her robe.

He closed his eyes to shake the thoughts from his head.

§ § §

It took two more weeks before he could stand again. He couldn't do it quickly or straighten to his full height, but he could bear his own weight.

A fact that seemed to please Salamah almost as much as it did him, though she couldn't know his plan.

He'd formulated his strategy days ago. As soon as he could travel, they'd head to Alexandria. Find Simon. Hugo would continue recovering there. Salamah would be restored to her relative, Harun al-Rashid. It was perfect.

If only he knew how to communicate the idea to her. If only they had something with which to fund the journey. If only he could escape the city unnoticed.

Salamah helped to ease him down from his standing position. Her very touch sent his blood racing.

His wounds had closed, though she inspected them often, as she did now. Her fingers gently poked and prodded. He winced, but kept his eyes straight ahead for fear they would linger on her face. Or elsewhere. She clicked her tongue and placed a hand on his shoulder when she leaned behind him to examine the laceration on his back. Her nearness drove him to the brink of all that was decent.

He wanted her.

Didn't want her.

She dampened a cloth with the medicinal wine and began to dab at the wounds, balancing herself with a hand to his chest. The intimate touch ignited his passion.

He grabbed her wrist more roughly than he intended, meaning only to break their physical contact. The move startled her. She sat up, forearm trapped in his grasp, her mouth a mere few inches from his.

Instead of releasing her as he planned, he pulled her close, pressed his lips to hers. A real flesh-and-blood woman, not a figment of his imagination.

But she didn't respond. Didn't return his ardor. The kiss ended as abruptly as it began.

He could barely meet her gaze, and when he did, her sad eyes watched his.

She shook her head. Tapped her chest with one hand. "Orry," she whispered.

That was all she said. All she needed to say.

She stood and walked away.

Hugo dropped his head in shame. Some hero he turned out to be, lusting after his deceased friend's wife.

Even chivalry was dead to him now.

Along with everything else.

Chapter 50

January AD 1222, Egypt

Hugo had recovered enough to travel. He just hoped Salamah would understand that. He pointed back and forth between the two of them. Moved his fingers to indicate a man walking. "You, me. Travel."

Salamah's face registered confusion, and she shook her head.

He sighed. Tried the hand signals again. "Go to Harun al-Rashid."

She perked up. "Harun al-Rashid?"

He nodded. "Yes."

She bit her lower lip, and her eyes focused on some point beyond him as she struggled to comprehend what he wanted to do. Then her face brightened, and she nodded in return. "Harun al-Rashid."

Hugo exhaled in relief. "Good. You understand. We need to make plans." He spoke slowly, loudly, but she paid him no heed.

Jumping to her feet, she motioned for him to stand. He did so with difficulty.

"Salamah, we must—"

She left the room.

He hastened after her as quickly as he could. He would need a disguise in order to escape the city.

She waited for him at a doorway, but scurried off again before he caught up.

And he would have to determine their route.

He found her kneeling on the floor in the corner of a long, empty storage room.

They would need funds. How would he ever communicate any of these concerns to her?

She lifted a tile from the floor to reveal a handle in the dirt below. With both hands, she tugged at it until a section pulled away — a trap door. Hugo stepped close and peered down into the hole. Salamah smiled up at him.

So her home hadn't been plundered after all.

§ § §

Salamah seemed to have come to all the same conclusions about their escape that Hugo had. At any rate, he managed to get out of the city undetected in the Arab garb she secured for him. And she'd navigated their travel as far as Alexandria, though his injuries had slowed them.

Now she apparently inquired after directions to the home of al-Rashid. Hugo posed as nothing more than her slave, her protector. Averting his blue eyes from the discerning gaze of men came easy to him these days.

Soon they were on their way. Before sundown they approached the walls of an expansive home. A servant ran to meet them. The young man and Salamah exchanged a flood of Arabic, and then the servant's face brightened. He darted ahead of them to shout open the gate.

The courtyard quickly filled with attendants. Harun al-Rashid appeared, arms wide, grinning to see his relative. He embraced her, kissing each cheek, then turned to Hugo.

Hugo could read the question in the man's eyes. He shook his head. Salamah's husband was dead.

Harun took Salamah's hands in his own, spoke to her in low tones. Her eyes filled with tears, but she did not weep.

At length, al-Rashid snapped his fingers and uttered a few commands. Two servants came forward to take the woman away. The crowd began to dissipate before Harun turned back to Hugo, a sad smile upon his face.

He offered a few words, but quickly perceived Hugo didn't understand him. He finally clapped a hand on Hugo's shoulder—the impact jarred his aching torso—then motioned behind him.

Hugo's gaze followed to a woman, eyes green as a June willow, red hair a deeper, richer shade than the last time he'd seen it. He couldn't read the emotions on her face. Did she still hate him? He unclenched the fists at his sides, stretched his fingers. Loosened his jaw and took a breath. "Elisabeth."

"Hugo." She walked toward him. "Simon will be glad you've come."

And you? "It's been a long time."

She nodded. "It has."

There was so much to be said. He didn't know where to start. Or if he should bother.

Harun spoke. Elisabeth gave heed to his words, bowed to acknowledge him then returned her focus to Hugo.

"My master bids you come and find rest." She began to walk toward the main section of the house. He caught up with her.

"I'll show you to your quarters," she said. "My husband returns home tomorrow, and you will want to spend time with him."

"Your husband?"

She steadied an even gaze on him.

"You mean—Simon?" Who else could she mean?

Her chin lifted, and her eyebrows arched. "That surprises you."

Hugo smiled to discover she'd not lost her pluck. "It shouldn't.

I could tell Simon loved you when he spoke of you in Damietta last year. In fact, I suspected it in Genoa." He chuckled. "I just didn't think he'd ever figure it out."

She turned her eyes straight ahead, but smiled as they walked.

Hugo slept until noon the following day. His injuries wearied and pained him more than he was willing to admit out loud. Apparently Salamah informed Harun of them, for doctors were sent to tend him. After examining his fresh scars, they scratched their bearded chins and shook their heads, then left him alone.

Elisabeth brought food on a tray and stayed with him while he ate. She told him that she was with child—that the babe was due before summer. He choked out his best wishes.

They fell silent for a time.

"Hugo," she said at last. "I fear I misjudged you these many years ago."

Her eyes looked strained. Had she been crying? He said nothing.

She bit her lip. "It wasn't fair, I know. But you resemble— *resembled*—both in appearance and manner, someone who did me great harm."

Ah. So her inexplicable hatred of him wasn't so inexplicable after all. He studied her face, wondering what wound could have pained her so. Whatever it had been, it didn't seem to trouble her now. "It's all right."

"No. I owe you an apology." She met his gaze. "I'm sorry." She nodded. "Kateline truly loved you, you know."

His brow furrowed. He'd long since given up ill-feelings toward Elisabeth. Given up most feelings, in fact. "I'm sorry, too. I made my own judgments against you. You need not speak of it again. Or of Kateline."

She took a breath. Looked at him. "God—God loves us, Hugo. And he waits for us. To be ready."

And what was that supposed to mean?

Their talk dwindled after that. Before she left, she informed him that his next meal would be with Simon.

And so it was.

"I hoped you would come," Simon said after they'd eaten.

"I had nowhere else to go." He didn't mean it. He'd wanted to see Simon. Needed to see him.

"You could have gone to Italy, could you not? Rejoined your regiment?"

Hugo shook his head. "There's nothing for me there."

A full minute passed before Simon spoke again. "I recognize the look in your eyes."

Hugo dropped his gaze.

"It's the look of a crushed man," Simon continued. "I know it well."

Hugo raised his face. "You, too?"

"At one time."

"And now?"

Simon smiled. "Now I am rescued. Restored."

Hugo exhaled. "There's no hope for me, I'm afraid."

"Why not?"

"I've lost everything, Simon. *Everything*."

"We all have."

Hugo's shoulders tensed. "You've a wife. A son. A child on the way." He indicated the luxurious room. "You serve with honor in the home of a great man. How can you understand? I've lost my dignity. My pride. Even my strength."

Simon laughed. "Then you're in a very good position, my friend. For when we are weak, then we are strong."

Hugo ground his teeth together. "You make no sense."

Simon raised his hands in mock surrender. "All I'm suggesting is that you submit to God. Depend upon him if you would be strong."

"God wanted me dead. I would have been better off had he

succeeded." He stood and untied the neck of his robe, letting it drop below the undergarment at his waist. "One thrust," he said as he pivoted. "One thrust of the enemy's blade produced both these wounds. I should have died."

Simon's eyes widened.

Hugo could barely utter the question he'd asked himself a hundred times. "Why didn't I die?"

§ § §

He dreamed that night. Experienced a vision, perhaps. A memory as vivid as the day it happened.

It had been a fine morning. Kateline walked with her arm in his.

"Hugo," she said. "What brings you to this place?"

He didn't know how to answer at first. The words seemed to come from outside him. "I believe God made me for this journey. That he trained me in my youth to lead, to fight for what is right, to carry out a noble task."

She looked up at him as her hand tightened on his arm. Her eyes searched his. "And do you know him, Hugo?"

"God, you mean?"

She nodded, and he knew everything hinged on his answer.

Even as he spoke, his heart stirred in anticipation. "No, Kateline, but I would have you teach me."

Her face lit. "It is a journey like no other. A journey you will never regret."

The dream ended abruptly, and Hugo's eyes shot open. He looked about, reorienting himself to his surroundings. His breath came in quick bursts. Sweat dotted his brow. He eased himself up from the cushions on which he slept and ran a shaky hand through his hair.

Elisabeth's words came back to him. *He waits for us. To be ready.*

Chapter 51

Late spring AD 1222, the home of Harun al-Rashid

Simon bent low to kiss Peter's warm cheek. The sleeping boy was going on two-and-a-half years. Full of energy, he kept Elisabeth both delighted and exhausted. Of course the impending arrival of their second child probably had a lot to do with her recent fatigue.

Simon ducked past the curtain that separated Peter's sleeping area from theirs. Elisabeth did not hear him enter, so he watched her for a moment, unobserved. A certain luminous quality enhanced her already beautiful skin. Her hair cascaded over one shoulder and shone a glossy ginger in the flickering light.

Elisabeth turned. The glow from a half-dozen candles highlighted the wonderful roundness of her abdomen beneath the gauzy fabric of her nightgown. She looked at him. Caught him smiling at her. Smiled in return.

He crossed the small room and settled himself behind her, kissed her neck, wrapped both her and the unborn child in his arms. She leaned against him, covering his hands with her own.

"I'm glad you're home," she said. "The master's new shipping enterprise has kept you in Alexandria too often these past months."

"I'm here now. And I shall remain so until the child comes."

"You don't have to worry, you know," she said.

"I'm not worried."

She turned in his arms. "Yes, you are. I see it in your eyes when you look at me."

Elisabeth took his hand and placed it low on her womb. Within a moment he felt the unmistakable outline of a small foot where it pushed hard against the skin.

She gave a small gasp then chuckled. "Your child is strong and healthy. And so am I. Otherwise how could I tolerate this rough treatment?"

Simon smiled and bent to kiss his wife, pulling her as close as her belly would allow. Her lips responded eagerly to his, set his blood afire, and rendered his fears powerless.

§ § §

Simon walked back and forth under the portico. His head hurt. "What do you know about it?" he said.

Hugo resisted smiling, but mirth danced in his eyes.

Irritating, it was.

Hugo crossed his arms in front of his chest and leaned against the wall. "Elisabeth loves you too much to let a small thing like this keep her from you."

"She's in childbirth as we speak. She could die."

"Not her. Too strong-willed."

Simon recognized the logic in Hugo's statement. "That's true."

Hugo grinned. "She'll be fine. You've prayed. We've all prayed."

Simon took a deep breath. Let it out slowly. "So you pray now, do you?"

"A little."

Well, this was new. Simon raised an eyebrow at him.

Hugo continued. "Kateline bade me start a journey many years ago."

"A journey?"

"Yes." Hugo's lips twisted. "But I traded it for a crusade."

Simon opened his mouth to reply, but the midwife interrupted from the hallway that led to his apartment.

"Your wife is ready for you," she said with a toothless grin.

Simon's scalp tingled. "Ready?"

The old woman nodded. "She's safely delivered."

His limbs went weak. "The baby's come so quickly?"

"A daughter. Your wife's an impatient sort, I gather."

"You could say that."

Hugo punched Simon in the arm.

"What was that for?" he asked, rubbing the sore spot.

"Quit standing there like a novice on the training field," Hugo said, humor on his face. "Go see your wife."

Both females were in fine moods when he entered the birth chamber. Elisabeth's lovely face and tranquil expression sent his heart soaring. Baby Kateline looked at him wide-eyed and unblinking. He took her fragile hand in his and examined her dainty nails, translucent and tiny as dewdrops. Caressed her downy red hair. She yawned, and her pink lips formed a perfect circle.

His eyes turned to Elisabeth. "She is beautiful like her mother."

"We can only pray she is wise like her father."

"And happy like her brother."

"Is Peter awake?" she asked. "I want to see him. Introduce him to his sister."

Simon retrieved the boy and watched him carefully kiss Kateline on the forehead like Elisabeth instructed. The newborn caught his dark curls in her fingers, but he did not cry, only waited patiently for his mother to rescue the captured strands. When they were released, he nestled against Elisabeth's shoulder while she leaned upon the cushions, Kateline cradled in her arms.

A servant came to the room. "Simon al-Nasrani."

"Yes?" Simon half-turned, but paid scant attention to the man in the doorway.

"I have a summons for you from the master."

The man had his full attention. "Now?"

"Go," Elisabeth said. "It's all right."

Simon kissed her. Kissed the foreheads of his children.

He bowed low when he came into Harun's chamber. "Yes, master?"

"Congratulations on the birth of your daughter, Simon. God is good."

"He is, my lord."

"It took me months to decide what gift I could bestow upon you and Elisabeth in honor of this child."

"None is necessary."

Harun smiled. "Perhaps not, but it is my choice."

Simon bent his head in deference to his master's will. When Harun did not speak, Simon lifted his eyes, concerned by the sudden silence. "Master?"

Harun grinned. "Rise, Simon, and call me master no longer. I grant freedom to you, Elisabeth, and your children."

"Freedom?"

"Yes." He laughed. "Now get up. I've an offer to make."

Chapter 52

August AD 1222, on the Mediterranean Sea

Elisabeth stood portside and inhaled the salty breeze, relishing the moisture that caressed her face and stroked her hair. She smiled when Simon laid a hand on her shoulder.

"The children are asleep?" he said.

"Yes, though Peter fought valiantly against slumber."

Simon chuckled. "Afraid he'd miss something?"

Elisabeth nodded. "The boy doesn't understand we'll be aboard ship for more than a fortnight before reaching Genoa." She paused. "The sky is the loveliest blue, is it not?"

Simon squinted toward cloudless heavens bright with the light of a gilded sun then glanced to the south where the white marble buildings of Alexandria faded into the distance. "I've always thought so. It's one of the things I'll miss about Egypt."

Her eyes searched his. "Will we come again?"

"Is that what you want?"

"I don't know." She bit her lip, thinking for a moment. "I've yearned for the forests and hills of our homeland, but after all this time, I fear there won't be a place for us there."

"I promised Harun I'd see that our shipping contacts are well established in Genoa. By then we should know whether we want to remain in partnership with him or sell our portion of the venture and build a life in Europe."

Elisabeth gazed out over the deep. "I can't imagine what that life would look like. I'm a different person than I was a decade ago."

"We've both been changed," Simon said. "And while it may seem strange, I sense that God has been bringing us to this moment all our days. That this time the journey we make is one he has ordained for us."

His words fueled a thought within her. "Our families, Simon," she said, laying a hand on his arm. "When our business is finished in Genoa, we must visit our families, our villages."

Simon looked stunned at the thought before a slow smile spread across his face. "And do you think we might make a stop along the way?"

"A stop?"

"At Mont Cenis."

A gasp escaped her throat. "Conon."

He nodded. "I made a promise to come back for him, after all."

Elisabeth's chest warmed. "The Lord would surely have you keep your promise."

A deep voice interrupted. "Am I intruding?"

"Hugo," Elisabeth said, pulling him by the arm toward the bulwark. "How are your quarters?"

"Very comfortable. I think I shall prefer this trip across the Mediterranean to my first."

A hush came over them at his words. Elisabeth felt a familiar ache at the memory of so many lost ones, followed by the soothing awareness that each precious soul rested in the arms of a loving Father.

"Have you decided your plans?" she asked Hugo.

He looked at her with his sapphire eyes. Eyes Kateline once

loved. Shook his head. "Not yet. After so many years of directing my own path, I think it's time to wait for God's leading."

"He's calling you to be his messenger in Europe."

Hugo's brows shot upward. "What makes you think that?"

"He got you on a ship to Italy, didn't he?"

His face colored. "But I'm no preacher."

"A messenger doesn't have to speak before the masses. Just deliver God's good news to one person after another. Surely you can do such a simple thing."

Hugo's jaw tensed, and he spoke with a choked voice. "I have too much blood on my hands."

Elisabeth took his hands in hers and turned them over, palms up. "Look," she said. "They've been washed clean."

Her words wafted away on the breeze. They spoke no more, but gazed out across the silver-blue water.

Elisabeth stood there—one arm looped through Simon's, the other through Hugo's—her heart gliding along with the ship as it sliced through the sea. An invisible wind, powerful and sweet like the breath of God himself, lifted fine tendrils of her hair and billowed the sails.

Dear Readers,

An Uncommon Crusade is a work of fiction based on a mix of fact and legend.

Accounts vary widely, but according to tradition, two branches of a Children's Crusade developed almost simultaneously in 1212. The first began in France when Jesus visited a twelve-year-old shepherd boy, Stephan of Cloyes, and bade him take a letter to King Phillip of France in Saint-Denis, urging the king to liberate Jerusalem from Muslim tyranny. King Phillip declined, but Stephan's 30,000 followers—many of whom were children—roamed France until reaching Marseilles where a number of them were transported across the Mediterranean by two unscrupulous merchants and subsequently lost at sea or sold into slavery in Egypt.

The second movement, inspired by Stephan and led by the charismatic twelve-year-old, Nicholas of Cologne, ended on the Genoa coast when the sea failed to part. Several of the 7,000 followers—children and adults, both members of the nobility and those far less reputable—went on to Pisa and sailed away, never to be heard from again. Nicholas, however, headed to Rome and gained an audience with the pope, only to be told to come back when he'd done a bit of growing up. Some say he returned home eighteen years later, bringing with him tales of glory in Egypt. His father, on the other hand, was hanged by his neighbors for allowing Nicholas to tempt their children into joining the movement.

Scholars believe, rather, that roving bands of poor peasants—including few children, perhaps—gathered throughout France and Germany in the year 1212. Many, under the leadership of Nicholas, perished while crossing the Alps in an effort to reach the shores of Genoa and from there, they hoped, Jerusalem. Some may have gone on to Rome or to Marseilles. None arrived in the Holy Lands. Stephan's followers disbanded upon King Phillip's orders and most of them returned home.

As for the Fifth Crusade, all of the major historical players in this story, such as John of Brienne, Cardinal Pelagius, and Sultan Al-Kamil, are real. So, too, are the significant historical events in Hugo's journey—the delay at Split, the supply raid to Bet She'an, the failed attack on Mount Tabor, the building of the castle at 'Atlit, the lengthy and tragic siege of Damietta, the nighttime discovery of an abandoned tower by four sentries, and the disastrous defeat experienced by the Christian armies on the way to Cairo.

Undoubtedly, I've made historical errors in the telling of this tale. Most inaccuracies are unintentional. A few, however, are quite deliberate for the cause of the story itself. It's fiction, after all.

~ Caron Guillo

LaVergne, TN USA
08 January 2011
211674LV00003B/1/P